s the Stream

Also by Connie Monk

Season Of Change
Fortune's Daughter
Jessica
Hannah's Wharf
Rachel's Way
Reach For The Dream
Tomorrow's Memories
A Field Of Bright Laughter
Flame Of Courage
The Apple Orchards
Beyond Downing Wood
The Running Tide
Family Reunions
On The Wings Of The Storm
Water's Edge
Different Lives
The Sands Of Time
Something Old, Something New
From This Day Forward
Echo of Truth
Mistress of Manningtor

Fast Flows the Stream

Connie Monk

First published in Great Britain in 2003 by
Judy Piatkus (Publishers) Ltd of
5 Windmill Street, London W1T 2JA
email: info@piatkus.co.uk

The moral right of the author has been asserted

A catalogue record for this book is available from the British Library

ISBN 0 7499 0667 7

Set in Times by
Phoenix Photosetting, Chatham, Kent
Printed and bound in Great Britain by
Mackays of Chatham plc, Chatham, Kent

Time is but the stream I go a-fishing in

(H.S. Thoreau 1817–1862)

Summer 1939

Chapter One

'Oh come on, smile, boys, smile.' There was a lilt of laughter in Tessa Kilbride's teasing voice as she switched off the wireless. 'Never trouble trouble till trouble troubles *you*, that's the rule to live by. It'll all blow over. Look at all the fuss there was about Austria, then it turned out that the bulk of the people wanted Friend Hitler there. Aren't I right, Sally?' She turned for support to the other woman of the foursome.

'About not troubling trouble, yes, I'm sure you are. But as for the rest . . .' Not so easily could Sally Kennedy put the seething pot of Europe out of her mind. She'd lived on the Continent too many years.

Her more serious answer was heard but not listened to. On such a morning it was all too tempting to be persuaded by Tessa's child-like trust, her warm smile and eagerness for the day ahead.

This was the first time Sally and Nick Kennedy had joined the Kilbrides on holiday. Until this year she'd always made the arrangements following the same pattern, tugged by the need to sense for herself changes she dreaded finding in the atmosphere yet felt drawn to out of loyalty to her past. Taking the car, they would cross by ferry to the Continent then spend four weeks touring, visiting towns full of memories, trying to instil into their young son some of her own feeling of belonging. Had the choice been hers alone, that's what she would have done this year too, despite the unrest. Originally Nick had been prepared to follow her lead, although, since the Kilbrides had bought The Limit, his resistance had strengthened. It was his final 'I don't work forty-eight weeks a year to spend the remaining four driving from one city of culture to another. I thought you enjoyed being with Tess

1

and Sebastian. Anyway, it's time we thought of Jethro. He deserves fun on his holiday.' Agreeing to the change of plan, Sally had hidden her hurt that through the years, while she'd believed the holiday had meant as much to him as it had to her, his resentment must have been building. A fair-minded streak in her helped her to fall into the new plan with a good grace. Yet deep in her heart was regret for that trip through France and Luxembourg, to Germany, where she would have gauged the atmosphere of Berlin in that summer of 1939, spent time with her father and seen for herself whether the news bulletins that sent a chill down her spine were an exaggeration of the truth. She wanted to experience for herself – and yet she was afraid of the truth her inner self knew she would find. Places she had known all her life – but where were they heading now? Austria ... Czechoslovakia ... How much did Hitler's fragile promise mean? Was Europe hurtling on a downhill slope towards disaster? What were the feelings of the people, how great were the fears of those whose race or faith didn't fit Hitler's dream for his country? Travelling with her father, Eliot Burridge, an international concert pianist, so much of her early life had been spent abroad. Many of their friends were Jewish; some had already been driven out of Germany by the atmosphere of mistrust and hatred, looking for a future either in Britain or on the far side of the Atlantic. But perhaps they were ultra-sensitive, perhaps the dangers were enlarged by the newspaper and the wireless, reporters vying with each other to gain attention.

Even now her expression gave no hint of her thoughts as the conversation went on around her.

'You're right,' Nick Kennedy said to Tessa, standing up from the breakfast table and stacking the plates, something he would never have done at home. 'We're on holiday, the sun's shining; and just look at it, the sky goes on for ever. To sit here listening to that mournful Johnny and his gloom is nothing short of a sin. Just say thank God we're English. Now then, this morning? What's it to be? Beach? Sailing? Fishing? Out to lunch? I say, Sal, this is a hell of a lot better than the culture search we anticipated in Europe.'

She didn't argue. How could she expect him to feel as she did? By chance her glance met Sebastian Kilbride's, Sebastian with his intuitive perception. Perhaps it was that understanding that made him the actor he was. Four people all so different, yet from the onset they had slotted into place like pieces of a well-cut jigsaw. The same could be said for their children, Jethro Kennedy and, eighteen months younger, Zena Kilbride. At sixteen, Jethro was a well-built lad with all the promise that before long, when the awkwardness of adolescence was behind him, he would be as handsome as his father. In years Zena was his junior but she saw herself as his equal. On that July morning they'd already packed their sandwiches and a bottle of cider, and planned to cycle the eight coastal miles to their favourite isolated bay. Sheltered by a craggy and not very high cliff more than a mile from the nearest road, the shore was reached by an overgrown footpath they'd explored a few days previously. Coming to the cliff top, they'd left their bicycles and clambered down to their solitary paradise. On this day they calculated that the tide would be right out by the time they arrived, they planned to collect driftwood and make a fire on the sand. The frying pan they'd taken from the cupboard and the sausages they intended to buy on the way were an unnecessary addition to the mammoth pile of sandwiches Tessa had made for them.

'The boat, that's my idea for today.' Surely there was a purr of contentment in Nick's voice as he gazed out of the window at the waves breaking on the shore.

Were Sebastian's thoughts on the day ahead or on what had gone before? 'Can't believe our luck, you know.' He spoke more to himself than to the others.

'Ours may be luck,' Sally laughed, taking the cloth to dry the dishes, 'But yours, dear Seb, is no more than your just desserts.' And of course she was right. They'd not known Sebastian Kilbride in the days before Fate had taken a hand in his career, Fate in the form of Alexander Morraine the film producer. Had Alexander been less kindly disposed towards his sister who, like Sebastian, had been a member of the touring and third-rate repertory company playing near his home in Surrey, he certainly wouldn't have spent his Saturday evening in the small and none too comfortable theatre. That evening had changed the course of Sebastian's life and Tessa's too. For until then she had moved with him from town to town as the players were booked for a few weeks in one town, then a few in another. By nature Tessa was a home maker, but never once had she grumbled about their nomadic boarding-house existence. She had earned a few extra shillings altering costumes and, out of school hours, kept an eye on Zena. Always there had been the worry that the child hadn't the continuity of a base as she moved from school to school with no chance to make friends and no home to bring them to. In fact their young daughter had never shared their concern, for right from the start the smell of greasepaint, the excitement of applause, the nervous tension as the actors waited for their cues, these things were making their indelible mark. Even so, Zena abhorred ignorance, just as nothing would have shamed her more than being found wanting in some social grace; so, when Sebastian's fortunes were suddenly changed, she accepted the expensive boarding school, determined to excel in everything she did and then to go on to drama college. In her dreams she saw herself, adult, glamorous, as beguiling as anything out of Hollywood, a name to be reckoned with in the legitimate theatre.

In appearance there was little of the matinée idol in Sebastian Kilbride. Anyone seeing the two men together as they made their plans for the day would surely have cast them in opposing roles. Nick wore his casual holidaywear with grace, his physique and his almost perfect good looks set him apart; Sebastian dressed, as he had every morning of their stay, in much-loved and much-worn khaki shorts, an open-necked shirt and pumps. His face hadn't the perfect symmetry of Nick's and yet there was something about him that arrested the attention, a sensitivity that belied the rugged set of his chin, a penetrating gaze, a manliness in some way enhanced by a gentleness of spirit. This, and his very real talent, Alexander Morraine had recognised.

Until with his first film Sebastian made his mark, the Kilbrides hadn't known what it was to have two ha'pennies to rub together. With sudden riches, his feet had stayed still firmly planted on the ground; he wouldn't let himself forget that nothing is more fickle than the public. This year's hero could be next year's yesterday's man. That's why he had sought the help of a firm of accountants and his affairs had been put in the hands of Nick Kennedy. Four years had passed since then; his place in the ranks of the famous was firmly established. Living in Worcestershire, he'd been able to fulfil his lifelong ambition to fly and had joined a flying club in neighbouring Gloucestershire. Nick had a talent very different. Inspired by precision and accuracy, he produced miniature paintings of near perfection. Yet from the onset the two men had been

4

at ease with each other. Never before had Nick made a personal friend of a client, but between Sebastian and him it seemed inevitable, something that had soon stretched to include wives and children.

Watching the two of them standing at the window, the moment was one that would stay with Sally. There wasn't a cloud to be seen in the azure sky, not so much as a white fluffy one. This was *today*, nothing could take this away from them. She was determined to follow Tessa's advice: never trouble trouble.

'We need bait,' Sebastian said. 'OK, we'll sail. But we'll catch our supper at the same time. You girls can man the rods if we need extra hands. Not good for you to be too idle. You know what? Four weeks hence at this time Tess and I will have left all this behind us. We're due to sail just about now.'

'And I shall be back in a musty, dusty office, dealing with the largesse of the likes of you, seeing how I can legitimately make the rich richer.'

'Come on then, old chap, let's make the most of today. You girls pack some food, Nick and I will drive to the tackle shop and pick up the bait.'

Sally envied all of them, even Nick with his dusty, musty office. Sebastian was to travel on the *Queen Mary* to New York, Tessa was going with him and would be sharing all the excitement as they went on by air all the way across the United States to Hollywood. Of the four it was only *she* who would be left behind, nothing but part of the background of home for Nick to come back to each evening. Watching Tessa vigorously clean the washing-up bowl and rub a cloth around the taps she marvelled how anyone could remain so untouched by the glamour all round her. What other film idol's wife could be so unchanged? She knew Tessa was almost exactly her own age, her thirty-eighth birthday behind her, yet there was about her a quality unrelated to years. Her face, void of make-up, still had the innocence of youth, the peppering of freckles all the more pronounced by the recent sunshine; her short fairish hair sprang into natural curls; she had the figure of a young lad and endless energy to match it. By contrast, nothing ever seemed to ruffle Sally's immaculate grooming; from the top of her dark page-boy bob to the tips of her elegantly painted toenails she might have stepped from the pages of a glossy magazine. Neither was there anything in her demeanour to hint at the discontent that niggled her.

'We're going to miss you and Seb,' she said, as she put the pile of clean plates away.

'And us you. Don't bother putting those in the cupboard, Sal, we'll only have to get them out again for supper.' Muddle never worried Tessa. Left to her own devices, with no Gladys and Jessie at home to clean and polish, she still would have managed to convey a feeling of warmth and homeliness in her chaotic surroundings; unlike Sally, who disliked and resented domesticity, yet couldn't bear disorder. 'Oh well, be tidy if you must. Now, for food. What shall we throw in the sandwiches?'

That July day, almost the end of their first week, the four of them sailed, or more accurately Sebastian was skipper, Nick was crew and the girls soaked up the sun and occasionally manned the fishing rods. The sound of the wind whipping the sails lifted them from the rumbles of unrest that threatened. Never trouble trouble till trouble troubles you; and how tempting it was to be lulled into a sense of endless security. So the day progressed, a day much like those that followed.

Not every day was filled with sunshine, even if in retrospect those would be the ones best remembered. There were mornings of mist, evenings of storm when the six of them sat around the kitchen (and only) table playing Monopoly, drawn together in their awareness of isolation from the rest of the world as the rain beat against the window. For the first time in her life Sally found herself donning waterproofs instead of her usual showerproof and umbrella – even wellington boots and sou'wester were an essential for the weather that blew in from the west – and striding happily along the coastal path for a pub lunch nearly two miles away.

Sebastian had bought the isolated cottage, tumbledown, lacking in all amenities except mains water, and had had it restored, brought up to date with the addition of a septic tank and bottled gas. They had decided to call it The Limit, perhaps because of its state when first they saw it or perhaps because of its position where land gave way to foreshore. One thing was certain, it was beyond the limit of the sort of civilisation that made up their normal lives.

The month went so quickly. It seemed that the children had reached an ideal age: old enough to find their own amusement, to go where they pleased unescorted and unworried. On holiday their normal half-past nine bedtime was extended; there were some evenings when the two of them were allowed to make a fire on the beach and cook their own supper. But it was 'their own', it didn't encroach on the other four. The idea of driving the five miles to the nearest habitation, finding somewhere to all eat together, didn't occur to any of them any more than it did for the adults to go out leaving their offspring alone after dark. There was a special magic about those evenings at The Limit. Supper cooked by Tessa and Sally – in truth credit was more often due to Tessa – a couple of bottles of wine on the table, the friendly haze of smoke from their cigarettes. It was at the end of their first week when, after Jethro and Zena's extended bedtime had seen them depart up the narrow creaking staircase, the others pushed the furniture back to make a space, wound up the gramophone and danced.

To be able to take a girl around a dance floor was looked on as part of a boy's training; in fact, once a week Jethro, like the rest of his year at school, had regular instruction. To put what he learned into practice beyond steering another boy (or alternatively playing 'the girl' and being steered) around the gym, was a new experience, but an opportunity he didn't mean to miss. For him and Zena it added to the pleasure to know they were believed to be in bed as, pyjama-clad, they waltzed or foxtrotted around his bedroom, along the landing and around hers. Neither knew what was going on in the other's mind, but both were excited by what was going on in their own. Familiar with his own adolescent dreams, Jethro longed for the thrill of holding her against him, being able to feel the warm softness of her body. Yet he was frightened that she might notice what was happening to him, notice and not understand – or almost worse, suppose she noticed and *did* understand – how could he explain it to her? His fears were groundless. Younger she may have been, but there was little of the child in Zena, or so she liked to think. Purposely tempting, she held herself close to him, relishing the discovery of her power to excite him. While he tried to concentrate on putting his feet in the right place in time to the distant music, her natural sense of rhythm allowed her mind to roam free. We're not just children. That's what they suppose downstairs, they think we're kids who want to play. 'When the children are in bed ...' that's what they believe. Wonder what he's thinking. No, I don't wonder, I'm pretty sure he's thinking just the same as I am. She raised her face to his; instinct was her guide as she gently moistened her parted lips with the tip of her pretty tongue. Poor old Jethro, he'd love to kiss me, I know he would.

'They're stopping,' he whispered, a surge of something like relief flooding over him. 'Hop off to bed. We did pretty well, didn't we?'

She nodded with no trace of the road her thoughts had taken. 'Soon be like Fred and Ginger,' she whispered back with a near silent chuckle. 'Maybe they'll dance again tomorrow. Night, night. If it's fine, let's see if we can get all the way to Land's End tomorrow.'

At that moment he would have gone to earth's end for her. Two minutes later they were both safely in their beds. She lay on her back in the summer darkness, her mouth curved into a smile of satisfaction, her hands exploring the contours of her fast developing body with satisfaction. Tonight had been her first insight into the power she had. Dear funny Jethro, he really had got himself in a state and then imagined she didn't know. I wonder if this is what it's like to fall in love. Tomorrow I won't mention how I know it was for us, I'll act just the same as usual. Otherwise he'll be frightened away. Boys are so silly, why can't they just enjoy it all? Bet he's not asleep, I bet he's remembering what it was like to feel me against him, bet he's still thinking of me. In that she was right. If that evening had been a step forward for her, so it had for him. Until that night, whether waking or sleeping, his dreams had been a journey of exploration, glorying in the discovery of his own sexuality; now it subtly changed, the quest was the same but his imagination was based now on a new reality.

All too quickly the weeks passed; good or bad, time carries it all away. Europe may have been losing its grip on sanity, but through those weeks there was no sign of it at The Limit. Tessa's maxim cast its spell.

On their last full day, Sebastian and Nick sailed the boat to its mooring in the harbour a few miles along the coast while Sally and Tessa packed the cases to be strapped to the luggage grids of the cars, which already each had a bicycle tied securely on top. Next morning the gas bottle was disconnected and, in a moment of nameless emotions, each one of them kept hidden, the front door of The Limit was locked. 'Here's to the next time,' they all sang the familiar signature tune of Henry Hall's BBC Dance Band as they piled into their cars.

Even though the two families lived within a mile of each other, the holiday month had already become a bright and carefree memory – like all things, in retrospect more bright and carefree than the reality. Mulberry Cottage was the Kilbrides' first and only home, purchased when Sebastian's debut into films had given him the sort of money they'd only dreamed of, dreams that had had no real expectation. Like so many 'cottages', it was no such thing. It was a seven-bedroomed house, built more than three hundred years ago and brought up to date by the previous owners with no thought of period or taste, simply an eye on convenience. Great open fireplaces had been blocked up, ceilings lowered and exposed timbers covered. 'Sheer vandalism,' Sebastian had said. Yet in a way they had been glad they'd found it in the state they had, for the thrill of owning it was enhanced with every new discovery as each original feature was restored, each old beam exposed. All that was more than four years ago and by the time the Kennedys first saw it, its recent past might never have been. An invitation to lunch and to see the restoration work had been Tessa and Sally's first meeting, Jethro and Zena's too, a few Sunday hours that had laid the foundation of the friendship that followed.

At that time the Kennedys had been living on the outskirts of Cheltenham. It could be said that the situation of Mulberry Cottage unsettled them, or it could be said that, in the way women do, the two young wives made the decision. Of the two, Tessa was the more contented to make a home, although it was she who had two living-in maids, also a man three days a week to take the backache out of keeping the two-acre garden under control. Domesticity and Sally had never been on more than nodding terms and, although she could see Mulberry Cottage as beautiful, she envied no one the task of keeping it that way. When, about six months after their first meeting, Tessa had told her that Owls' Roost was coming up for auction she'd not given her hopes a chance to rise. The name implied it would be a rustic idyll, something incompatible with her idea of the ideal home. As it transpired, the name was out of keeping with the modern house only a few years old and in half an acre of lawned garden. No self-respecting owl would look twice at it and, fortunately for Nick and Sally, most house-hunters looking for somewhere in the country had shared the same opinion. Under the hammer it had gone to Nick, and within two months their Georgian terrace house had been sold and they had come to live within a mile of their friends. Two mornings a week a cleaning lady come to Owls' Roost and worked her way through the list of jobs Sally wrote for her. For despite having no enthusiasm for housework, her standards were high. Day-to-day cooking was a necessity she couldn't avoid, but face her with catering for a dinner party and she rose to the challenge, presenting a table to compete with a professional. Unlike Tessa, she rejoiced in the arrival of frozen vegetables in the shops and most weeks she telephoned a large order of groceries to be delivered.

Through the months and years they'd lived near each other, there had been a subtle change in the friendship between the two women. By that summer of 1939, even without the strength of the bond between Nick and Sebastian, the two of them had become something akin to sisters. So it was that, of them all, it was Sally who had most reason to look towards the autumn with foreboding. If she wanted the freedom the car allowed, she would drive Nick to his musty and dusty office, agreeing to meet him at the railway station in the evening. The alternative would be to be marooned, the only choice a bicycle ride to the village more than a mile away. And what would she find there? A butcher's shop, a grocer, a dress shop where she'd not dream of buying anything other than stockings. Until now Tessa had always been nearby, but in two days time Zena would have gone to stay with her cousins until it was time to go back to boarding school and in three days Sebastian and Tessa would be on their way to Southampton and the *Queen Mary*. The autumn beckoned, void of everything but the ever-increasing threat people seemed too frightened to acknowledge.

'You're very quiet.' Nick gave her a quick glance of concern as he drove. 'Do you want to stop and get a breather?'

'No. I was just thinking. Two days and you'll be back in the office. Everyone will be gone.' Involuntarily she shivered. 'I hate the thought of it, the weeks, the months, just so much empty time.'

'Now tell me I wasn't right. Of course, you can't. Have you ever come home feeling so flat? Of course you haven't. These last four weeks have been something apart. Isn't that so, Jethro? Have you ever enjoyed a holiday as much?'

'It's been great.' Oh, but they didn't know the half of it; even Zena didn't know. 'How long will they be in America, Dad? This aunt Zena is being packed off to, she's got to go there again for Christmas. It's stupid. She'd have a much better time with us, she hardly knows her mother's family.'

'I suggested our having her,' Sally told him, 'but Tessa said this aunt – distant cousin actually – would be hurt if they didn't accept her invitation. She'd think they'd outgrown the family. And there are children of her own age; she'll probably have quite a good time.'

'Just because her people don't want to look too big for their boots Zena has to put up with it. Jolly selfish if you ask me.'

Nick craned his neck to see his son's reflection in the reversing mirror, his eyes alight with laughter.

'Aren't your school mates company enough any more?' he teased.

'Don't be daft,' Jethro growled, sure that his hot feeling of embarrassment must be plain to see. So he lowered his head and pretended to concentrate on the road map. If they could guess where his imagination guided him and the encouragement he gloried in giving to it ... 'This must be the beginning of Bristol. Hey, look, Dad, on up the road there, there's a Walls' man. See him on his trike? Can we pull in and get some ices? Hot as anything in the car.' Pleased with himself, he'd steered them off dangerous ground.

Nick overtook the ice cream salesman on his familiar blue and white tricycle, then pulled in by the kerb, passing Jethro half a crown. 'You get them. Mine's chocolate. Yours, Sal?' So Jethro took the orders, his mind surprisingly easily diverted at the prospect of looking in the truck and deciding what he wanted. Then, ices eaten, luggage checked to make sure the ropes were still secure, they were on their way again. Soon the inside of the car was wreathed in smoke. Nick drove with his cigarette comfortably between his lips, Sally puffed hard on hers then exhaled clouds.

'What's up?' Nick asked with unusual perception. 'You'll miss Tess, of course you will, but after a month away you'll find plenty waiting to be done. I know what you're like if a weed dares to show its head.'

'I hate untidiness. I shan't be idle. But what a waste of life, looking for jobs even before they need doing, combing the garden for weeds, plumping up cushions the second anyone stands up.

11

Fiddling about cooking meals that get eaten in five minutes and nobody notices.' She heard the grizzle in her tone and hated herself for it.

'It's because Tess has more help in the house, is that the trouble?'

'What's Tess got to do with it? It's *my* life I'm concerned with. Nick, all the time Jethro was a kid I accepted I had to be at home. But he doesn't need me nannying him; as if he'd care if I was at work when he came home from school at his age.'

'Work?' Nick's laugh told her even more than his words. 'We've had a month with the Kilbrides, you've seen what wealth can do for a family —'

'Wealth? Whenever has having money altered Seb and Tessa?'

'It's enabled him to buy a holiday home, a boat, travel on the *Queen Mary*.'

'As if any of that counts. They're the same now as they were when we first knew them. Anyway, Tessa is happy in the home, cooking, making things, that's what she likes. She even sews their own curtains, would you believe. I'm no good at that sort of thing. Wouldn't you rather come home in the evenings knowing that I'd actually *done* something with my day?'

'You've a sizeable house — which you always keep immaculately. You've a garden where a weed doesn't stand a chance. And you have absolutely no need to work. I may not have Sebastian's sort of money, but there has never been any need for you to add to our income.'

'Money! Is that all you ever think of?'

'Actually, no it isn't. Hark at the woman, Jethro! You and I'll have to see if we can't make a bit more muddle for her, eh?'

'You're laughing. I'm not.' There was a pout in Sally's voice.

'Then, try to, Sal. You say what you do doesn't count, but believe me it does. If we were on the breadline it would be different, I'd be grateful that you wanted to help. Perhaps it's me who brings home the money, but you have your own part to play keeping things comfortable. And what happens when I have to phone you and say I'm bringing a client home? You never let me down.' Silence. *Sebastian* might have sensed the frustration that made her clamp her teeth firmly, frightened her voice would betray her. 'Anyway, Sal,' she heard the laughter in Nick's teasing voice, 'I can't see you behind a shop counter and I can't think what other sort of work you'd get. You fancy yourself having a career but, my sweet, a career doesn't fall out of empty air. It needs training, qualifications.' Did she grunt her agreement or did he imagine it? 'Your trouble was, you were too fetching for your own good. And when I had my sights on you my charms were too much for you. Any dreams you might have had for a career were blown straight out of the window. Right?' That ought to cheer her up. 'There's another packet of cigarettes in the glove compart-ment, fill my case and light one for me, will you.'

She did and for herself too. After seventeen years of marriage it was seldom he made anything so near resembling a declaration of affection; his words went some way towards mollifying her.

Thankful that what had promised to turn into an argument seemed to have been avoided, Jethro fanned himself with the road map.

'Rotten fug in here from you lot,' he grumbled. 'I'm never going to smoke. It stinks.'

Once home, the rut she knew so well soon drew her back. By the end of a week it was as if they'd never been away. It had taken Jethro less than forty-eight hours to pack up his tent and, encouraged by a note found waiting for him, cycle to join school friends who were camping in the Vale of Evesham where, they promised, they could add to their spending money by helping with the plum harvest. At Owls' Roost Sally won the battle of a month's growth of weeds, she dusted dust-free surfaces, arranged flowers, somehow expecting them to bring life to her oh-so-spick-and-span drawing room, she used up energy cycling the country lanes on the days Nick decided he needed the car, she drove to Worcester and cheered herself up buying a new shade of lipstick and nail varnish; she felt she was living on the rim of a volcano that was about to erupt, and yet the few people she ever spoke to seemed to hang on to a trust that Hitler would keep his word, that he had no intention of reaching his tentacles any further. If only she too could believe, could be as ostrich-like as they. But she couldn't; her days were overhung with a dark threat she had no power to lift even though it took no positive shape. What would the future hold? For Germany and its new territory? For those who didn't fit Hitler's vision for his people? Perhaps for everyone? There was no one she could talk to; even Nick took the attitude

13

that the government was being alarmist in issuing gas masks and organising a scheme to evacuate London's children. If Hitler had to be taught a lesson, so be it, was his creed. Was he brave or was he blind?

If Tessa had still been at home, despite her 'never trouble trouble' dictum, Sally wouldn't have felt herself to be so isolated. Her father was on a recital tour, giving concerts first in Italy and then Germany. All so distant from her peaceful English home; she'd be happier if he were in his flat in Paris. Yet where was the logic in the thought? Surely he'd be as safe in Italy or Germany as he would in France.

The worry was constantly at the front of her mind as she walked back from the village, silently talking to herself. Almost home, taken by surprise, she moved back to stand against the hedge as a taxi approached, returning along the lane that was no more than a track. A visitor at Owls' Roost? It must be, for beyond the one house there was nothing except gates into fields belonging to Merrydown Farm. Her first thought was Jethro. Away at camp with his friends, perhaps he'd been taken ill, not able to ride his bike home. She broke into a run. Then, coming in sight of the house, she saw two people standing outside the gate, looking in her direction along the track, a man and a child.

Dad! He'd come back! No wonder she ran, hurling herself into his arms with the same abandon she had all her life.

'I've been so worried. Thank goodness you're home, Dad.'

She was flooded by a wave of relief that he was safely home in England. Much of her foreboding stemmed from fear for him, knowing he was in Europe, out of her reach. He would understand the horror that haunted her.

'I was to have played in Berlin. The concert was cancelled. Let me look at you. So sane, so unchanged.' He seemed to be talking to himself as he held her at arms' length. Then, bringing his mind back into focus, he reached towards the girl at his side and put an arm around her narrow shoulders to draw her forward. 'Sally, I want you to meet Helga. Helga Leipmann. You remember, I've stayed with my friends the Leipmanns when I've been in Berlin. They are arranging to tie up their affairs and spend a while in England. In the meantime, as I was coming, I suggested Helga should keep me company on the journey. By coming now, she'll be in time to start at an English school at the beginning of term. So much better than joining in later when her parents get here.'

Sally turned to smile at the child, extending a hand in an informal gesture of welcome. Surprisingly, the solemn-faced girl took it in hers with the dignity of a duchess. She was a thin girl, narrow-shouldered, her figure as flat as Sally's ironing board. How must a child that age – eleven? twelve? – feel to find herself in a strange country, an uninvited guest in a strange house, surrounded by people speaking a strange language?

'We have come and you did not have notice.' Her voice was the first surprise. She spoke English with the correctness of a well-taught foreigner.

'That's the best possible way, it's all the more exciting,' Sally assured her, answering her in German with the ease of one who had grown up with the language, just as she had with French and her own native tongue.

'I do not use your language well?' The thin, solemn child's expression suggested that she was more disappointed than put at ease.

'Oh, but you do,' Sally said, this time in English, if that's what the child wanted, 'it's just such a pleasure for me to speak to someone in another language and know that it will be understood. Here, people are so bad with languages other than their own.'

'You say to me that it is good to come to you without warning? When my parents and I have travelled, we have enjoyed looking forward, taking time for preparation. They said I should come now with Herr Burridge, and just my small luggage. They will soon follow.' Then looking to Eliot for support as memories flooded over her, 'That is right?'

'They have to organise shutting up their home. But yes, my dear, before you have time to settle with this cousin of your mother's they will be here in England finding a new home for you all.'

'You are going on to a relative? But first you will stay with us?' In her pleasure at her father's unexpected appearance, Sally wasn't going to lose him straight away.

'A night or two, if we may,' he told her, 'while I make arrangements for Helga.'

Their cases were stacked outside the front door, her father's just as she remembered, covered with stickers acquired from shipping lines as he'd travelled. The sight of the other one, new and by

15

comparison small, touched Sally, making her reach to take the girl's hand as she ushered them indoors.

'A night or two or as long as you like,' she told them.

Through the open door of the drawing room Helga caught sight of the baby grand piano. Moving away from the others, she went to stand in the doorway, taking in the order, the immaculately gleaming surfaces, the silver rose bowl with its display cut that morning from the garden. The first flush of early blooms was over but, in Sally's battle against neglect, she always took off each dead head and was rewarded by a second if less vivid flowering.

'I wish Mama could see me where I am now,' Helga spoke her thoughts, this time in her own language. 'She will be worried, not knowing. I can picture her sitting at your piano.'

'Your mother is a pianist?' Purposely Sally asked it in English.

'She gives lessons, she teaches at the college. No I tell you what used to happen. No longer does she teach people to play music.' A bald statement, 'No longer does she teach people to play music', but to Sally it brought alive the picture behind the words. And one look at her father's expression as his gaze rested on the child told her the horrors of her imagination had been nearer the truth than people here wanted to believe.

'And you? Has she taught you to play?'

Helga nodded, turning her head away.

'Helga plays extraordinarily well,' Eliot said.

Suspecting Helga was dangerously close to losing her battle to hide her misery, Sally changed the subject.

'Which is your case?' she asked, as if the answer weren't patently clear. 'Let's take it upstairs and I'll show you which is to be your room. Presently we'll get some flowers from the garden and you can arrange them for your room and Dad's too. If I'd known you were coming I would have done them myself.'

Again Helga nodded. Then in one swift uncontrolled movement she turned to Eliot and buried her face against him, her thin arms around his waist.

'Before you even pick the flowers I think you might write a quick note to your parents, let them know you are here and – and can we say – you like the look of what you've seen?' His rallying tone did the trick. Again she nodded, but the movement of her head was different. At any rate, for the moment he'd held her terror at bay.

16

'By the time the letter is brought to my home, perhaps they will already be on their journey.'

'We'll get it in the post quickly, anyway,' Sally told her. 'I'll give you paper and envelope, then write it as soon as I've shown you which is your room. While you and Dad unpack your cases I'll cycle to the village post office.'

It was while Helga was sitting at the dining-room table writing home that Sally and her father wandered into the garden.

'Is it as bad as I imagine?' she asked him.

'Perhaps even worse. The sort of hatred one feels can only go one way. Poor Helga,' as if her story encompassed all stories. 'It hasn't happened overnight, of course, you know how many of our friends have smelled danger and gone before it built to this extent. The Leipmanns should have got away months ago. Imagine being woken in the night by the sound of your windows being broken, imagine going out in the morning to find obscene messages daubed on the walls of your house. As Helga told you, Marte Leipmann, her mother, no longer teaches. Even those who would learn from her fear being looked on as befriending enemies of the regime. They are shunned as if they have the plague. Worse. If you suffer from the plague people might keep away but they look on you with sympathy and kindness.'

'People here can't comprehend. I believe the reason nothing you say really surprises me – sickens me, yes, but not surprises – is that right back to the days we used to be there together we always felt the resentment towards them, not individually but the Jewish race. Why?'

'Too clever perhaps, too bound to each other. God knows. And it's deeper rooted even than just towards them. The hatred extends to the disabled – mentally, physically – oh, Sal, but it's good to be back in England. Hang on to all this, never take it for granted, always be grateful.'

She laughed, linking her arm through his.

'Good to be back, you say. Dad, it's more than good, it was like a miracle to come along the lane and find you here. As for taking all this for granted: with Nick, how can I? The times I've heard him say "Thank God we're English".'

'So he sees where it's all heading? Because it is, Sal, situations like the one that's been building through these last few years have only one way to go and that's forward. Nick sees it?'

17

'Nick is either very dim or very brave, I'm never quite sure which.' Her laugh took any criticism from her words. 'Now tell me about this aunt or cousin or whatever she is Helga is going to. How long do you think she'll have to wait for her parents?'

'If all goes well they will pack their valuables and arrange to follow quickly. Perhaps a week or two, I hope no more, for the child's sake. I arrived on their doorstep on Monday evening. They want to get away but they're having trouble realising their investments to bring out of the country.'

'Will they get their money out? Surely to save themselves is what matters.'

'To me – to you too. But Claude is a businessman, he deals in finance. To him, leaving all he's worked for would be defeat. Monday night – well, I told you, smashed windows, daubed paint and none of it for the first time. Tuesday morning they took me aside and asked me if I would bring Helga to England. For themselves there could be no immediate getaway; apart from his investments, they have to arrange transport for their less portable treasures. The Leipmanns are well off, they have a house furnished with priceless antiques. And apart from the value, if they are to make a new start here they need something tangible of their past to build on.'

'Where is Helga to go?'

'I shall speak to Harry Robertson – he's Marte's cousin – tomorrow. He lives just outside Manchester.'

'So he's English? Scottish?'

'Henreich Rubenstein by birth, but naturalised British, name changed by deed poll some years back. His wife is English and I shouldn't be surprised if he's more English than the natives in his attempt to hide his roots. That's the impression I had from Marte.'

Sally felt a pang of unease. Even in the aftermath of the Great War, surely it wasn't healthy to try to hide his roots, to be so determined to cut himself off from his past.

'I imagined Helga must be half English, she speaks so well. And thank goodness she does, it'll make it so much easier for her to fit in.'

'Not a spot of British blood in her veins, but her upbringing reminds me of yours. Continental children learn languages so much better than in this country, and Helga's parents have always encouraged it. Especially English. From a small child she has been multilingual. I remember her as a solemn three-year-old talking to me in sentences that started in German then, via French, ended in English. Now she has learned to differentiate, but listening to her one is aware it isn't her native tongue.'

'That's because it's so pure, no slang, no dialect.'

'Another reason that her ilk are disliked. As I said, they're too clever. She is a dear child.'

'And you're a dear man.' Sally hugged the arm linked to hers. 'Ah, here she is with her letter.'

That evening Nick added his welcome. There was nothing he liked better than visitors in the house. Was he really so blind to the troubles in Germany, Sally wondered, watching him playing Happy Families with Helga, or was he simply trying to bring some sort of normal childhood back to the little girl?

'She's certainly bright,' he said to Sally as they lay in bed, sleep eluding them. 'Her use of words, even if this were her language, there's nothing childlike in the way she talks. How old is she? Do you know? Eleven? Twelve? Skinny little waif, isn't she. Yet her face doesn't fit the rest of her.' In that, he was right. The bone structure of Helga's face was pronounced, angular, unchildlike. Perhaps one day she'd grow to look distinguished, but never beautiful, at least never beautiful in the glamorous fashion of the day.

'She is fourteen, almost as old as Zena.'

'Incredible. She looks years younger – but so damned sober. Gives me the creeps.'

'Life's so unfair.'

'Humph.' Not always did Nick understand the way her mind worked, but this time he did. 'Bugger Hitler.'

Next morning Eliot went to the village to send a long telegram to Harry Robertson. Waiting for the reply, they had no idea how he and his wife received the news that Helga had already arrived ahead of her parents. It was twenty-four hours before the telegraph boy cycled along the lane with his yellow envelope.

'Arrangements made at local council school until parents take responsibility – stop Will give child temporary accommodation – stop Notify time of arrival – stop Robertson.'

'They're rolling out the red carpet.' Eliot said it a little too

19

jovially, conscious how closely Helga watched him.

'Carpet? I do not understand.' Helga may not have understood but the hope in those dark eyes behind her unattractive steel-framed spectacles was painfully clear.

'That's just an English expression,' Sally told her. 'It means that they are ready to welcome you.'

'That's it,' Eliot agreed. 'What's more they have arranged your school.'

'I will pack my clothes into my case,' she told them. 'Please may I have a piece of paper on which to write to tell my parents?' It seemed she was ready to get on to the next stage. 'It is good, is it not? It is nearer to when they will be here too.'

It was only while she was upstairs packing that Eliot passed Sally the telegram.

Chapter Two

Sally dreaded the dull monotony of the shortening days of autumn, the awareness that she was being swept aimlessly on the tide like jetsam carried on the wash made from passing vessels. Not for a moment was she able to forget the threat that hung over Europe; yet it was as if her two concerns were unconnected, occupying separate compartments. Imagining the horrors that talking to her father had brought even more vividly alive, she was ashamed of her own comfort and peace in the countryside of beautiful Worcestershire, ashamed of her discontent with a life that so many would see as sublime.

Having delivered Helga to her unknown relatives, Eliot made London his base. His intention was to contact his agent and to discuss plans for engagements in Britain. That was in the fourth week of August – surely by then even the most stubborn ostrich must have raised its head and looked disaster in the face. By that fateful first Sunday of September the die was cast, the Nazis had marched into Poland, the coldly gentle voice of Neville Chamberlain announced to the nation that 'we are at war with Germany'.

That Sunday evening Nick shut himself in what they teasingly called his 'studio', trying to give all his concentration to his latest work, a miniature of The Limit, aided by a photograph. A black and white photograph could be no more than a guide to perspective; what would bring it to life would be the colours he carried vividly in his memory. From downstairs came the sound of the piano. Like him, Sally had her own path to solace. For both of them it came as a relief to hear the back door slam. Only one person could destroy the silence with such thoroughness!

'I'm home! Mum ... Dad ... I'm back.' Jethro's shout brought them both into the hall at the same time. 'We heard the Prime Minister. Smithers had brought his portable wireless with him. We thought we ought to get home. Don't know exactly why.' Yet perhaps something in Sally's forceful hug and the vigour of the thump on his back from his father told him why: this day was one none of them would forget, a milestone in history; it was a time for families to be together. For Sally and Nick there was relief in encouraging him to talk about the boys' camping exploits, to watch as he counted out the money he'd earned picking plums, to hear him clumping about overhead in his bedroom. This was normality. She even welcomed the pile of disgusting post-camp washing she knew he'd been bundling into the linen basket. That evening, with a hungry son ready to devour anything he could lay his hands on, there was even pleasure in preparing the meal.

'Hark, isn't that a car in the lane?' His mouth watering with anticipation, Jethro had been watching her take a joint of pork out of the oven, when he raised his head as if to hear better. 'Not expecting anyone?' Then when she shook her head, as mystified as he was, for no through traffic came down their lane, 'It's got to be Grandpa.' In one of his brief telephone calls home to assure them he was all right he'd heard about Eliot's return to England.

'I'm glad we haven't eaten. Lovely, all of us here together,' Sally answered, for who else would come unannounced that evening of all evenings? Her father too must have felt the need for families to be together. From the kitchen, where she was piling dishes on to a tray for Jethro to carry to the dining table, they listened as the car turned into the short drive, then heard Nick's step in the hall.

Silently they waited, listening for the first sound of the familiar voice, looking at each other in shared pleasure. Eliot had always been special to Jethro, perhaps because he was his only grand-parent or perhaps because he wasn't always there, so visits were special events.

'Good God!' Their expressions changed when they heard Nick's surprised greeting. 'What went wrong? I say, but it's great to see you. Especially now.'

'That's just it. Now.' It was Sebastian's voice. 'It was like being on another planet.' Then, as Sally emerged from the kitchen,

22

closely followed by Jethro and his tray, 'Sal! Will it stretch? May we stay to supper?'

The tray was planted on the hall table, hugs were exchanged.

'I was camping. I came home too,' Jethro said. How better to tell them their reason for returning was understood?

'But when did you leave the States? It must have been days ago.' It was still only hours since that message from the Prime Minister.

'We came back the same way as we went out. On the *Queen Mary*. But damn it, Nick, *we* knew, *you* knew, certainly Sal had no illusions. We were on a helter skelter with no way of getting off. Yet, out there –'

'Like Seb just said,' Tessa interjected, ignoring the fact that Seb had 'just said' nothing, she'd jumped in before he'd had an opportunity, 'they might be on another planet. Such exotic luxury, such insular self-indulgence. Perhaps we're unjust; they probably don't see it like that. After all, in all fairness, for them it *is* far away. But it was as if we'd stepped off the world.'

Nick frowned, worried for his friend. 'But your contract? Can you just walk away?'

'I didn't sign. I told them I couldn't. The bait was one film, the reality was a contract with the studio for four years.'

'Even if everything had been fine at home, that's not the life we want.' Tessa's opinion matched his. 'It just *wasn't us*. This is *our* place.'

It was while they were eating supper, a meal which Sally had stretched by opening three tins of tomato soup and cheering them up with basil, that Tessa laid the whole expedition to rest.

'The boat was fun – just the once. But being away pointed out to us the things that matter. Everything we want and care about is here. Never trouble trouble, isn't that what I always said? But it was too late for that. You can't just put things out of your mind. It was so – so – *unreal*. So we turned round and came home where we belong.'

Sally's spirits lifted, she who had been weighed down by the horror to be unleashed on the Continent. It was only much later, as she opened first the newly hung heavy blackout curtain, then raised the blind and threw wide the casement window in the bedroom, that the dark night brought home to her how far that day had brought them.

23

'First night of war,' she spoke as much to herself as to Nick, who was already in bed. 'How many? How long? Nick, they talked about the glitz, the isolationism, but how different are any of us? You know the first thought in my mind when I said "How long?" The same as yours, I expect: Jethro. Sixteen, seventeen, eighteen . . .'

Her eyes were getting used to the dark so she could see his hand held out towards her.

'We'll lick the swine long before that. Great seeing the others, wasn't it. Didn't surprise me, you know. Can you imagine Seb skulking away in a land of plenty when we've got a job to do here?'

She climbed into bed and lay close to him. No longer were her spirits light; the nightmares were once more nudging her mind. A job to do, he said. She thought of Sebastian's love of flying . . . but surely he was too old to have to go to war.

'Nothing can take this from us. Nick, everywhere people must be saying that, people safely this side of the Channel. Little Helga – how will her parents get away now? I just hope they're already on their way, or even arrived.' He didn't answer, simply drew her closer. 'Nick, if everyone has an allotted amount of joy, how can ours go on for ever?'

She heard his soft laugh, she felt the warmth of his nearness, the touch of his caressing hand. Where now was the discontented housewife? She drew him closer, closer, he heard the message in her murmured sigh. That their day ended in sex wasn't unusual, but on that night they needed no erotic adventure, lovemaking was an expression of something beyond the power of any words. Both of them were aware of it, yet, frightened, the other wouldn't understand and would say something to destroy the wonder, so neither attempted to share what they felt. Afterwards Sally reached out silently to an unnamed Deity, her mind a confused jumble of thought: gratitude for being who she was, where she was, gratitude for the miracle they'd shared, pleas to some spirit in the starry night sky, a sky that covered every corner of the globe whatever the hour may be, that nothing would ever change for them, pleas that Jethro would be too young to be caught up in war – and only then, ashamed of her own selfishness, pleas for the people under the heel of the Nazis, for Helga and the many, many Helgas. From there it was only a small step in her mind to recall the picture she'd seen of little children being rehearsed for evacuation from London, gas masks round their necks and their names on labels pinned to their coats, little children who perhaps very soon would be alone and frightened in the homes of strangers. The billeting officer had called at Owls' Roost a week or two ago, but probably because they were so isolated and far from the village school they hadn't been sent any small charges. All these thoughts crowded her mind, one overlapping another; and yet her face wore a look of peaceful contentment. The difference between sexual need and lovemaking had never been more apparent. Even the thought of unrewarding hours of dull domesticity had no power on that night.

The following day the Kilbrides fetched Zena home. There was at least a veneer of normality.

'Have you seen Tess today? Tess or Sebastian?' Nick's first words as he came home one evening about a fortnight later.

'No. I called at the cottage but they weren't there. Gladys said they'd been gone all day. With Zena back at school they'd probably decided to have a day out somewhere. Why?'

'They came in to the office. Sal, he's volunteered. Seb's joining the Air Force.'

Whatever she'd expected, it wasn't this. She turned away, not wanting to see Nick's expression; but there was no escaping the tone of his voice. Envy? Admiration? Excitement? But this was crazy.

'Sebastian can fly a plane,' she heard herself answer. She might just as well have said, 'What use do you think an accountant would be?'

'Yes.' One word, but enough to tell her she'd hit below the belt. Then her thoughts moved on; she tried to put herself in Tessa's place. How must she feel this evening? Never trouble trouble ... but it's trouble that sets the pace. All they needed was here, wasn't that what had made it impossible for them to stay in America?

The news seemed to have added to Jethro's appetite, which was as well, for that evening Sally and Nick did little more than toy with their food, pretending they didn't recognise Jethro's look of envious admiration for Sebastian.

'I'd have thought he'd be too old. I suppose he's younger than you, is he, Dad?'

'Not that you'd notice.'

'Gosh! Yet they still took him? Of course, he knows how to fly, that must have made a difference. I bet the newspapers will get hold of it, he'll be held up as an example. They'll be glad to have him for the boost he'll do for recruitment.'

'And so he is an example. Seb isn't a man to skulk at home.' Nick gave up the pretence and pushed his plate away. Something in his manner and, particularly, in the aggressive way he spoke of those prepared to 'skulk at home' sent a chill down Sally's spine.

'Anyway,' she said, 'it may be ages before he actually goes. I told you what old Colonel Gibbons called it when I met him in the village, he called it a phoney war.' It wasn't exactly what the elderly retired army man had said, but she clutched at any straw to move the conversation, to take that eager look off Jethro's face. She didn't need him to tell her how he felt: *his* was the generation who ought to be fighting the battle – for she knew that in his place she, like he, would be leapfrogging the next two years and seeing herself joining the heroic throng.

The evening promised to drag along on leaden feet. After the meal, Jethro escaped to his room with the excuse of prep to be done and, in silence, Nick carried the tray of dirty dishes to the kitchen. Both he and Sally were aware of all that hadn't been said. They would both miss Sebastian, but for Nick it was something more than missing a friend. Did he feel it as a slight to his own manhood that Sebastian had a skill to offer, something that outweighed the fact that he had no experience of the services and was beyond the age to be called on? In her habitually orderly fashion, so automatically that her mind was free to go where it would, Sally sorted the dirty things, glasses to be dealt with first, then silver and cutlery, then china.

'Did you see that look on young Jethro's face?' Pulling a kitchen chair towards him, Nick sat astride it, his arms folded on the high back.

'He's just a boy.' But he wouldn't always be. How long? With her mind on Jethro she wasn't prepared for Nick's answer.

'Yes, he's just a boy. But Sal – I'm not.'

'Poor old you,' she tried to laugh his remark away, to believe she'd misunderstood his meaning.

'Yes, poor old me. Turn around, Sally, look at me. Do you honestly think I could live with myself if I spent the war where I am now?'

She seemed to lose all power of coherent thought. Was this how Tessa had felt when Sebastian had proclaimed his intention of making himself a hero? She clutched at reason. Sebastian had something to offer; he was a jump ahead of most of the younger men who would rush off to be flyers. Anyway, as Jethro said, he would be held up as an example. But Nick was an accountant, only months off his fortieth birthday. Two men so close and yet in that moment all Sally could see was their differences. Underlying Sebastian's easygoing nature, she knew there lurked a man of great passion and understanding; how else could he get beneath the skin of the characters he portrayed? But Nick loved order, precision; even though she'd never suggested it to him, she'd always looked on his chosen work as dry as dust.

'You mean you want to fly?' It was out of character, just a mad desire not to be left behind.

'Good God, no! There'll be plenty of young gallants queuing up to be trained to fly. Whatever our expertise, that's what we have to offer.'

'So? You're an accountant, your expertise is adding up numbers,' she heard her tone as belittling, she knew no other way, 'making sure your clients don't pay a penny more tax than they have to. I don't see that sort of expertise being in great demand.'

Without a word, he stood up and rammed the chair back where it lived by the kitchen table. She heard him go out of the room; she listened as he climbed the stairs and retreated to his studio. She'd hit below the belt, she knew she had, and she was ashamed. She ought to have told him she couldn't bear him to go, that the dull routine of her days would have no purpose if he weren't here. With her rubber-gloved hands plunged into the washing-up water, she gazed unseeingly at the neatly manicured back garden. All that was *her* doing, the running of the house was *her* doing – none of it done with good grace. But if Nick weren't here what would be the point of any of it? For her it was a moment of truth. She followed him up the stairs, pulling off her rubber gloves as she went and dropping them over the banisters to land with two wet plops on the gleaming parquet floor of the hall.

She expected him to be finding solace in concentrating on the delicate work he was creating, but she was wrong. Just as she'd been staring blankly at the back garden, so he was looking out towards the front, the short drive, the narrow lane.

'Nick.' To her it sounded like a cry for help, but he heard it differently.

'How do you imagine a war can be fought – fought and won – with nothing but front-line troops, flyers, heroes? All right, as you say, I'm not one of those. But it also needs the sort of people you so obviously scorn. Logistics – every battle, every movement, every item of supply or shilling of wages. Not a heroic job, I know that without you throwing it at me –'

'I didn't. Nick – if you're not here nothing counts for anything.' There! She'd said it!

'Nonsense.' But his tone had changed. He came towards her, and when he held her shoulders she leaned against him. 'It all counts, everything here matters, Sal. Perhaps they'll tell me that at rising forty they can do better without me. But if they take me, everything you do here matters. This is our home. Every man who goes to war does it to protect what he leaves behind. When it's all over we shall have the right to the sort of peace we have here.'

For a long moment they were silent, held close by the years that were behind them and by their faith for the years to come.

'It's like coming towards the coast,' she said, her head against his shoulder, 'seeing nothing but stormy water yet knowing you have to reach the land on the other side.'

'Stormy water won't bring us down, Sal. And the sooner we set out, the sooner we get across it. Two years time and Jethro will be old enough. We have to be safely ashore before then.'

That was halfway through September.

If they expected a declaration of war to rock the foundation of their daily routine, in those first weeks they were wrong. Both Sebastian and Nick had volunteered, and when they were deemed physically A1 they both saw their fitness as a matter of pride. Conscious that Jethro and his contemporaries looked on them as yesterday's men, they rejoiced in their clean bill of health. As the days went by, though, it seemed that the country wasn't in urgent need of their aid; each morning they checked the incoming mail – or, in Nick's case, phoned home from the office to see if the postman had brought him the expected buff envelope.

'There's something unreal about the days,' Sally mused, sitting in the autumn sunshine in the garden of Mulberry Cottage. Even the air was still. 'Just imagine, Tess, how it must be for poor stricken Warsaw. We knew it was bound to fall, yet, until now, there has always been *hope*. I'd found where to tune in to Warsaw on the wireless.'

'But even *you* don't speak Polish.'

'Vaguely – badly. We've been to Warsaw many times. But you didn't need to understand the language to feel the dogged spirit; it was in those few bars of Chopin's *Polonaise*; over and over they played it, a message of defiance telling the world that nothing would break them. In those few bars of music was their freedom. Nothing else, just those few notes of their beloved Chopin telling the world "This is Poland, nothing will destroy our spirit." Now, today, it's gone silent. From one side Russia marches on them, from the other Germany. Yet nearly four weeks into the war and here we sit in the peace of the countryside. I'm thankful, yet I'm ashamed. If there is a god of the universe, then how can life be so unjust?' She wasn't sure how much Tessa shared her pity for poor, fallen Poland on that last Friday afternoon of September. But then Tessa hadn't her memories.

'It's as if we're in a different world. I said that to Seb this morning, not particularly about Poland but about the war generally.'

'I'm sure I'd already been to Warsaw, but when I was really young one city was much the same as another I expect. The Colettis – he was my tutor, she was my sort of carer when I was little – and me; wherever Dad was playing we all trooped along. It was before the last war, so I couldn't have been more than ten. I clearly remember the concert in Warsaw. Two soloists: Dad played the Grieg – see, I even remember that. Then a young Polish violinist, everyone was hailing him as a child miracle, prophesying a wonderful future for him: and they were right. It was Simon Szpiegman. I can see him so clearly.' Then, laughing at the memory, 'That must have been the first time I fell in love. Funny how odd things in your childhood stay with you. I've never heard him since, except on the wireless or on gramophone records. I'll never forget that evening. But perhaps that's because I know that over the years he and Dad have become friends.' Then, back from her trip down Memory Lane, the present took over from the past. 'But it's clear in my mind: all those people, all loving the music, all happy – now poor, broken Warsaw. And here we sit in the sunshine. It makes you feel so utterly impotent.'

'We seem to be in limbo, frightened to take anything for granted, unable even to appreciate a glorious autumn day like this,' Tessa answered. 'I see how Seb checks through the post, trying to look casual, but I know very well what he's looking for. I bet Nick's the same. Do you suppose that all these years under their contented exterior they've been subconsciously hiding an urge for adventure?'

'Aren't we all?'

'I'm honestly not. I just want everything to go on like it was, to go on for ever. But nothing can do that. This waiting – I said to Seb, it reminds me of the years he was in rep. and I used to help with the costumes. Those final minutes before the curtain went up, or watching the actors hovering in the wings waiting for their cue. They were excited; each night they were nervous. I could almost feel for them the way their tummies must have been churning.'

'Don't they say that an actor has to be nervous to give a good performance? The men are lucky, Tess. When they get their instructions, off they'll march, cocky as peacocks. But us, what about us?'

'How can we envy them? Sal, I just pray they'll stay some-where safe. All very well trying to make themselves heroes, but ...' Tessa's voice trailed into silence. To speak the horror that haunted her would be like tempting fate. Sure that Sally's inner feelings were the same as her own, she tried to steer the conversation on to more cheerful lines. 'Anyway, we have our own part to play; we have to make sure they know home is unchanged, everything waiting for them. And you still have Jethro to look after, that must be such a help. I wish Zena wasn't away at school. Seb says why don't I bring her home and let her go to town each day on the train like Jethro does. But I can't do that just so that I have someone to fuss over. I heard Gladys and Jessie talking this morning. They didn't mean me to hear but I was on the landing above the yard where they were pegging out the washing and the window was open. I listened. They were talking about what they meant to do; they sounded excited as if being at war has opened the cage and given them a chance to fly. I'll have to look surprised when they give me their notice, but they have both been making enquiries at the labour exchange, trying to get work connected with the war. It's as if there's no other life.'

30

'So Tess, you'll find yourself with plenty to occupy you. This may call itself a cottage but it's anything but – and it's not an easy house to keep in order, I bet.' As Sally said it an image of Owls' Roost came into her mind, with its austere modern architecture, its 'no frills' decor.

'If I'm here by myself it's not even going to oblige me by getting itself in a mess,' Tessa laughed.

'Want to bet?' Sally teased. They both knew that wherever Tessa went she managed to leave a trail of chaos in her wake.

Both of them made an effort to banter, but the unknown tomorrow was already casting a shadow.

'Here by myself ... Sally, I just dread it.' Tessa was suddenly serious.

'You mean you're nervous?'

'No, of course not. I mean, I dread Seb going. When we rushed back from the States, remember what I said? Everything we wanted is here. And so it was, so it still is. But, Sal, if he's not here, then none of it counts for anything.' Just for that moment Tessa let slip the jolly, smiling front she always presented. Undemonstrative Sally reached to take her hand.

'That's what wives everywhere must be saying, Tess. It's the feeling of such utter uselessness I hate. Even your Gladys and Jessie will be doing something to make a mark, something they feel matters – but *us*? We ought to be good for *something*. Whenever I've suggested doing anything other than dust shiny surfaces and all that rubbish, Nick has never let me run away with any illusions about myself. At least you have talents. You worked for ages when you were first married.'

'And before. But it was never what I wanted, that was simply a case of being glad to earn the money. All I wanted was a home of our own.'

'Even if I were employable, Nick would see it as a slight on his ability to support his family. It's arrogant nonsense and I've told him so often enough. But as he says, I've no skill to offer and that's something I can't argue with. Before I met Nick I used to arrange Dad's engagements – after I outgrew the Colettis and there were just the two of us. It gave me a feeling of being part of a team with him. We went everywhere together, all over Europe.'

'And you say you have no talent.'

31

'It doesn't take the brain of Einstein to liaise with orchestras, reserve accommodation in hotels and seats on trains.'

'Yes, but Sal, not necessarily *English* orchestras, *English* hotels. Most of us, even Seb, who can learn lines with no trouble at all, we're so hopeless at foreign languages. And our children aren't any better. Yet you could be accepted on the Continent as a native.' Then, her eyes sparkling with mischief, she chuckled. 'Perhaps you ought to be a spy, a secret agent. Suggest that to Nick.' Her equilibrium was seemingly restored. 'How about Jethro? With all the Continental holidays he's had, that and having you for a mother, I suppose he's streets ahead of the others at school. I've never even thought of it till that moment, but he must be.'

'He ought to be, but he isn't. I've tried. When he was little I used to talk to him in French or German but even then he'd look at me suspiciously and refuse to be drawn. Nick thought it was hilarious.' Then with a quick look at her watch, she got up from the garden bench. 'I must go, Tess. I may have no saleable talent, but at least I have two hungry mouths relying on me to see they're fed.'

Had they but known it, Sebastian's letter was already on its way as they parted company on that late September afternoon. That feeling of waiting in the wings was almost over. Another week and Tessa had waved him goodbye as he leaned from the window of the train. Like a child fearful of the dark, she dreaded the thought of Mulberry Cottage without him. So, instead of going straight home, she went to Owls' Roost. She had lunch with Sally, then together they walked the mile or so between the two houses, Sally pushing her bicycle ready for the return journey. Every time Tessa went home, the emptiness without Seb would be there waiting for her; but being together helped on that first day. Often enough he'd been away on location when he'd been filming, but there had never been the question mark hanging over their future that there was now.

Two weeks later it was Nick's turn to go.

'It may be six weeks or so before I can get home.' Nick spoke to Jethro in a 'man-to-man' voice as they stood on the railway station platform. 'They've got to teach me to be a soldier before they let me loose on the job I might be some use at.'

'A soldier with knobs on!' Jethro beamed his pride in the father who, thanks to experience, expertise and qualifications, was to report to an officer training unit. 'But don't you worry about anything here, Dad. I'll see Mum's all right.'

'Good man.'

Jethro's beaming smile got broader. It was hard to think of home without his father, and he wasn't going to spoil his new pride in responsibility by imagining the gap. The green light in the arm of the signal told them the train was almost there. Just as if he were as grown up as he tried to appear, Jethro felt his hand gripped in his father's in a final farewell. Then, juddering, hissing and snorting in a cloud of steam, the train arrived.

'I'll phone at my first opportunity,' Nick told Sally.

She could feel that through his sadness at leaving them, through his uncertainty about where this next step would take him, there was an underlying feeling of excitement and she was determined not to let him see her as a clinging wife. So her, 'You'd certainly better!' was in a tone to match his own. Jethro was proud of them both, especially as further along the platform a woman was, as he saw it, 'hanging around some poor chap's neck and blubbing'. *His* parents would never behave like that, he thought smugly. The illusion was broken when Nick let down the window of the compartment as far as it would go and leaned out. Just for a moment, as the engine hissed a warning that it was taking breath ready to leap into action and the station master stood poised, flag at the ready and whistle in his mouth, there was an expression on his father's face that made Jethro look away. Better to stare at that stupid blubbering woman by the next carriage. Standing tall, Sally held up her head, Nick's mouth covered hers, the engine snorted its disapproval as it tore the two of them apart and started slowly forward. As it snaked around the bend and out of sight, the arm of the signal fell with a clunk, its duty performed.

If Sally and Tessa had seemed as close as sisters over the last few years, there can be few sisters who shared their innermost thoughts in the way they did in the first months on their own.

'Tess, have you seen the local paper?'

It was just after midday on an icy, cold February Friday when Sally announced her arrival by shouting the question as she let herself in through the garden door.

'It doesn't get delivered until the boy gets out of school,' Tessa answered, running down the stairs in pleasure at the unexpected sound of her visitor's voice. Arriving at this time of day must mean Sal would stay for lunch. Already Tessa's mind had jumped one stage ahead as she decided to open a tin of salmon from her store cupboard and make fishcakes with the remains of yesterday's mashed potatoes. Having someone to cook for was just what she needed to lift herself out of the doldrums – for, even though her ready smile refused to admit to it, the doldrums were never far away.

'Then listen to this: I'm going for an interview this afternoon. A proper job, Tess, something I can actually *do*.'

'From the local paper? Has some business evacuated here, some musicians' agency, I mean? I hadn't heard.'

'You know we wondered about that huge mast we saw last week when we passed Drifford Park? Well, it's there that I'm going. The manor was empty for ages, but apparently work's been going on to adapt the interior. They've made it a listening station, monitoring foreign broadcasts – lots of them will be propaganda, you may bet. They have to be translated. I'm not sure yet what happens then, but I suppose anything important goes to news-papers, radio bulletins, that sort of thing – perhaps even the War Office. I'm only guessing. But they want someone fluent in French and German. As soon as I saw the notice in the paper I telephoned – and they seemed really interested! *Me* – a job!' Then, some of her confidence visibly fading, 'They may say I don't know enough about world affairs, but I don't see why they should. I read the newspaper cover to cover. If they want references, past experience ... travelling with Dad doesn't sound very promising. But, Tess, a job! Imagine doing something worthwhile, feeling yourself part of it all!' Hope had stripped Sally of the ability to keep her innermost feelings under wraps. Her expression was half fear, half irrepressible excitement, and it was *that* as much as her actual words that told Tessa just how much she must have hated being left behind in the fast-changing world.

'Of course they'll want you.' The smile gave no hint of Tessa's sinking disappointment. Sally, her almost constant companion, would be gone from her. 'You've time for some lunch?'

'Food's the last thing I want, I shan't bother with lunch today. Anyway, I want to have plenty of time to get ready, make myself look too good to refuse,' she added, laughing. 'If I don't get it ... oh, but I just *must*. I'm scared to look beyond the next few hours.

It's like tempting Fate to think how it'll be if they take me. And if they don't – you know, Tess, until now I don't think I've ever really known *just* how imprisoned I felt.'

A few minutes later Tessa watched her cycle down the drive to the lane, everything about her an expression of her determination to shrug off the old life and rush towards the new. Even the way she turned the pedals, leaning forward as if that way she would travel faster, deepened Tessa's feeling of loss. There was no need to keep up the charade of pretence; there was no way of hiding from her loneliness. Her pretty, freckled face gave up the battle to smile. She felt utterly alone in the silent house, alone now, alone this afternoon, tonight, tomorrow, day after day. A sob rose in her throat. She didn't even try to fight it as she felt her eyes burn with tears. Not many minutes ago she had rushed down the stairs at the sound of Sally's voice. Now she climbed slowly back up to the accompaniment of her own crying, her footsteps silent on the thick carpet, everywhere silent, everywhere empty. Going into her bedroom she closed the door, then, in a sudden movement, she reopened it as far as she could and went back into the corridor. Going in turn to each of the other six unoccupied rooms, in the same way she flung their doors wide, emphasising the emptiness as she wallowed in her own misery.

Back in her own bedroom, hers and Sebastian's, she dropped to sit on the dressing-table stool. Were her tears self-pity? She told herself they were. If Sal could see me she'd be disgusted, she told herself. Sal would never behave like this. Why don't I get work in a factory, roll bandages or whatever volunteers do at the hospitals? I'll tell you why – and somehow she needed the pain of self-criticism – it's because you're just a *nothing* person. I thought we would go on like we were for ever, me and Seb. Just a silly dream – and he couldn't have shared it or he wouldn't have rushed off as if the country depended on him. That's a hateful thing to say. He went because all this, me, Zena, meant so much to him. He must picture me at home here, keeping everything just as it was ready for when he comes back. Keep the home fires burning till the boys come home, isn't that what they used to sing in the last war? And he will come home, please, please, let him come back. One day all this beastliness will be over, people will stop hating each other. I wish I was like Sally, strong and clever. You only have to look at her to see how capable and competent she is. Not like *me*, just

35

look at me. And turning the knife in her wound of misery, she leaned closer to the mirror where a blotchy-faced woman with eyelids red and swollen, wearing a too-large sweater of Sebastian's, looked back at her. If you could see me now, Seb, you'd be ashamed, she gulped as a sob caught in her throat. Looking for comfort, she left the mirror and went to his wardrobe. With her eyes closed she breathed deeply as she buried her face amongst the suits that hung there, as if she could find something of his spirit. She wriggled her hand up the empty sleeve of an old tweed jacket he'd been too comfortable in to part with.

Without closing the wardrobe door she moved backwards to sit on the edge of the bed, still looking at the row of suits. It was 'his' pillow that she pulled from her badly made bed, hugging it to her, rocking backwards and forwards. Want him so much, she whimpered. Sal says this aching misery is worse because we miss being made love to. But it's more than that: the house is dead, I don't even want to make meals.

Shutting her eyes she lay back on the bed, still holding the pillow tightly against her. Alone and lonely, yet this was something nothing could take from her, something no one could share with her. Her spirit reached out to his. Imagine the warmth of him ... imagine the weight of him ... remember how it always is when we become one, one body, one spirit. Seb, listen to me, help me find you ...

When Jethro arrived home from school he found a note on the table telling him, 'I've gone out but don't expect to be late.' He scowled. Not much fun to get home to an empty house. You'd think with all day on her hands to go wherever she wanted, she could have got back. His scowl deepened when he found the cake tin empty. Reason told him that often enough his mother and Tessa had been late home after an outing to town, but that was before everything had been messed up by this beastly war. Today he was in no mood to listen to reason anymore than he would admit that his self-pity had very little to do with Sally, far more to do with the fact that nothing was like it used to be. Although one or two of his friends had brothers who'd joined up, he was the only one whose father had gone. One short week at Christmas, so much packed into it that they hadn't had any *real* time, just the two of them together. Then, looking and feeling a hero in his brand-new

36

officer's uniform, his Sam Browne gleaming, a single pip on his shoulder, his father had set off to his first 'professional' posting at a camp in Yorkshire. In those first days around New Year, Zena had been home and, if Jethro were honest, he'd not spent much time missing Nick; his mind had been full of other things. On that afternoon in late February his thoughts gave no more space to honesty than they did to reason. Zena had been back at school for weeks; he felt neglected. The sharp pricking sensation on his chin gave notice that before long it would develop into a throbbing spot – a rare thing for Jethro, but somehow in keeping with his present mood. When it suited his mother he was looked on as a child – which he resented; and when it didn't, she gave him no consideration – which he resented even more. Cutting a crust off the loaf, he plunged his knife deep into the butter. If she couldn't be here to feed him then why should he consider the meagre butter ration? Then, taking himself firmly in hand, he withdrew the knife and scraped it over the top of the golden lump, then smeared the butter thinly on his bread. Everyone had to make sacrifices, he told himself.

The sound of tyres on the gravel brought him to the kitchen window in time to see Sally wheeling her bicycle into the shed. Jolly good job I didn't plaster the butter, he congratulated himself, despite himself his spirits reviving at the sight of her.

'Guess what?' She greeted him before she even got inside the door. 'No, you won't guess, you won't even believe it! Jethro, I've been offered a job. And I've taken it – taken it with both hands.'

'Crumbs, whatever will you be doing?' It seemed his opinion of her ability was about as high as Nick's.

So she explained to him about the listening station that had been evacuated to the safety of the countryside.

'Does that mean you'll always be at work when I get home?' All very well for her to look so cocky with herself, it was a rotten outlook for him.

'No. I shall be working shifts. Sometimes I have to be there at seven in the morning; those days I'll leave at three and be home ahead of you. Then there's an eight till four shift, so by the time you've ridden from the station I should still be ahead of you. Those two will be fine. You don't need me here to see you off to school. But, Jethro, I'm glad you're old enough that I don't have to worry about you. There'll be days when I start at teatime and work till about midnight and there's one shift from eleven at night till seven in the morning. I'm so glad you're as old as you are or I'd have to have said I couldn't do it.' Alluding to his near manhood made his congratulations obligatory.

He tried to look pleased; he honestly didn't want to be the one to dim that gleam of triumph in her dark eyes.

'We'll have to work out a new scheme, Mum. Hey, I tell you what! I could go to Tess after school on the days you'll be working. She'd like that. She always likes it when I drop in and offer to chop her wood or bring in the coal, all that sort of thing.'

Sally nodded. 'Splendid idea. Let's ride over and tell her, shall we? She knows I was having my interview so she'll be wondering.'

'You could always give her a ring. She won't expect you to ride over in the dark.'

'What a dull life it would be if we never had any surprises. Anyway it's Friday, you don't have to do your prep this evening.'

Judging by Tessa's reception, she was obviously right about surprises. Having reached rock bottom, having escaped reality in her desperate quest to reach out to Sebastian and, even if her imagination couldn't hold him beyond that one sublime moment, at least she had been raised from the depths. Her tear-stained face had been restored by cold water; her body, much of its tension eased, had found comfort in the warm water of the bath, careful even then to follow government instructions and turn off the tap when she was barely sitting in a puddle. What made her dress in a good skirt and blouse and take trouble with her always pretty face she didn't question. It had something to do with hanging on to the belief that in her moments of despair Sebastian had reached out to her, that he needed her just as she needed him.

The house was locked for the night when the ring came at the front-door bell, followed immediately by Sal calling through the letterbox.

'It's Jethro and me. We want to share our news.'

The memory of her afternoon was pushed away; for the present the devil of despair could find no chink in her armour.

'I'm really pleased for you, Sal.' Pleased or not, her brow wrinkled in concern. 'You'll be out a lot in the evenings. How do you like the idea of coming here after school, Jethro? We could eat together. I rattle around like a pea in a barrel here. I could give you a room to call your own so that you'd have somewhere to do your prep – even sleep here on the nights Sal's on nights.' That devil of despair was slinking away; Tessa's life had found a purpose again.

'Gosh, Tess,' he beamed, clearly as pleased with the plan as she was, 'that would be great. Save you bothering about me, Mum.'

Sally frowned. Save her bothering? What sort of a mother did that make her sound? Yet there was no denying her relief at Tessa's suggestion.

'It would be doing me a favour, Sal,' Tess said. How would she feel if their positions were reversed, if it were Sally offering to relieve her of caring for Zena? She reached to take Sally's hand. 'If it makes it easier, look on it as my war work.' Then with that merry twinkle so much part of her character, 'Why should I be the only one with no glory to my name?'

'Oh ho!' Jethro mocked, 'So now I'm war work.'

'That's it – and having to put up with coming here instead of going home is your war work. But we'll get on swimmingly. And I'll line up all my "man's jobs" in the house for you to do.'

Such sop to his vanity! No wonder he beamed.

The final arrangement was made that on the days Sally wasn't to be at home at the end of the school day, he should go to Mulberry Cottage. On just one condition, she insisted: Tess was to have his ration book. They were all registered with the same grocer and the same butcher in the nearby village – nearby? More than a mile distant – so it would merely mean Tess would be able to add his ounces of butter or cheese, his one and sixpennyworth of meat, his meagre allocation of sugar, to her own. It was an arrangement that suited Sally well; by using the canteen at the listening station, she would be able to stretch her own ration to feed Jethro when he was home. Altogether, the day that had started as unpromisingly as any other ended on a higher note than they'd known for weeks.

Calm and self-assured, that was the impression Sally always gave. Never could she remember her heart racing as it did when her team leader led her for the first time into what she learned was known as the listening room. Excitement? Self-doubt? Her mind was a tangle of emotions. But inborn in her was the need to hold her head high, present a front of confident serenity that was far from the truth. She had no fear of translating the news bulletins nor yet, even after seventeen years of marriage to Nick, of settling into an environment so un-English; yet her mouth felt dry, she was conscious of the effort of each shallow breath. This is *me*, actually *me*, I'm part of all this. Her spirits soared, she was swimming in the mainstream of life, even the unfamiliar nervousness added to the wonder of what was happening. But no one seeing the well-groomed, poised woman would have guessed the workings of her inner self.

At Drifford Park were teams from every European nationality under the one roof, each section with its own area in what had at one time been the music gallery of the manor, now transformed into the listening room. Despite the silence round her as she was led to the German desk, where on that first day she was to work, she was aware that room was the hub, the heartbeat of the station. Isolated from each other, each man was an island, concentrating on the words coming to him, or in one or two cases to *her*, through headphones. Some were sitting with eyes closed, simply listening, concentrating, transported perhaps to those distant shores of home; one or two were making notes. All of them were recording what they heard, the gentle hum of the dictaphone machines barely any sound at all. Despite the stillness, Sally was aware of intense activity. Most translators were attached to the section for their individual language, but then most who worked with the French section were French, most for the Polish were Poles, for the German those who had fled their country during those final fragile years of peace and whose background had been thoroughly vetted by the authorities. Sally was in a different position. English-born of English parents, yet from the age of three she had lived almost entirely on the Continent until she married. Sometimes she would work with the French team, sometimes with the German. Her future had found new promise.

On the first day she mastered the method of recording her allotted bulletin on to the cylinder of a dictaphone, and before her first shift ended she understood the procedure of removing the cylinder from the machine in the listening room and taking it to one of the cubicles off a long corridor where she fitted it to another machine, donned a fresh set of earphones, and proceeded to translate it to a typist. There was nothing in her calm, unemotional tone to suggest that she was uncertain how much was important enough to be needed and how much was dross to be discarded. Of

40

one thing Sally was determined, she would give the impression of knowing exactly what she was doing, she wasn't going to let the typists guess that until now she'd been looked on as unemployable! Before many days passed, without her being aware of it, her knowledge of world affairs had grown far beyond what she read in her cover-to-cover sift through the daily newspaper; she knew what was relevant and should be passed to the editorial section and what was just so much flotsam.

When Nick had a fortnight's leave in May, the chauvinist in him took it for granted that a fortnight for him would mean the same for her. But after only three months at Drifford Park the most she could hope for was three days tacked on to the end of her 'weekend' – the two-day break that as often as not came during the week.

'I don't work nine to five every day,' she placated him. 'Often I'm here until almost teatime. Sometimes I don't go in at all until eleven at night. Of course that means I should be in bed the next morning.'

'The only promising aspect as far as I can see.' His mouth twitched into a near-smile. Then, his thoughts taking a sideways leap and his quick frown warning her he'd found something else to complain about, 'Tough on Jethro, you taking a job with hours like this. Have you ever considered how he must feel? A lad deserves parents at home.'

'Jethro's fine. We're all fine.' Perhaps not the most sensitive thing to say to a husband who had no share in this so fine arrangement. 'Anyway,' she changed the subject, 'Sebastian is hoping to get a seventy-two-hour pass while you're here.'

Clearly that cheered him.

'Good show. Let's hope he can manage it when you're not busybodying at the Park. Be great to all get together again.'

She let the jibe pass. To Nick, the work at Drifford Park was a complete unknown, something he brushed aside as unimportant. Why waste good time and money bothering with rubbish the enemy saw fit to broadcast? Yet, despite what she believed to be his jealousy that she had outside interests, it was because she worked, because her self-esteem was heightened and her old frustrations and resentments gone, that some of the romance of their early years came back into their marriage during those two weeks. And Nick found there was much to be gained by playing the role of a neglected husband. When Sally was at work he would go to Mulberry Cottage, where Tessa loved having him around and, when Sebastian managed to get his 72-hour leave and found it coincided with Sally's midweek 'weekend', the war might as well have been on Mars, so removed were they from it in the peace of the Worcestershire springtime.

The days sped by; soon Sebastian had gone, soon Nick had returned to his station in Yorkshire. For Tessa there was constant dread: Seb was a flyer, so every day brought its own dangers. With Nick safe and more comfortable than he was prepared to admit at his base in Yorkshire, for Sally there were none of those fears; she was free to settle into her new existence with an easy mind.

'Let's make a pact with ourselves,' Tessa said on Sally's first free day after Nick's leave. 'This war won't last for ever, so let's promise ourselves that the first week Nick and Seb are both home for good, we'll go to The Limit. It won't matter what time of year it is – we'll all be together. It'll be like it was.' A pact with whom? With each other? With God, that if they kept their side of the bargain and refused to doubt, then one day they would all be together ... safely landed on that secure land beyond the stormy water. The memory of those words sprang into Sally's mind as, looking fondly at Tessa, she took her hand.

'Done,' she agreed as their fingers clung.

In that early summer of 1940 neither of them imagined that anything other than war could shape their destiny.

Chapter Three

On that last day of the summer term in 1940, despite knowing Sally would be at Drifford Park, Jethro didn't go straight to Mulberry Cottage. With his head down, his satchel laden with textbooks on his back, he wanted to get rid of the last evidence of school. This evening while he was creosoting Tessa's new tool shed, she would be driving to the station to collect Zena. The thought of her eight weeks free of school was great, but more important by far was that by now she would be on the train. Whistling tunelessly, he pedalled along the parched track where the ruts made by the farm tractor were more than ready to throw him. His plan was to dump his books in his bedroom, then change into his khaki shorts and pumps before he set out. He kept his old gardening clothes at Mulberry Cottage, where these days he had a bedroom of his own. Over these last weeks he'd worn khaki shorts as regularly as he had his school uniform, khaki shorts and an old pair of regulation black shoes, just the thing for gardening. Today, though, he would have to be careful not to splash creosote, for Zena's first sight of him was important.

Once in his bedroom, he hurled his school cap on to the chair, dropped the heavy satchel unceremoniously on to the floor, then stripped everything off except his underpants. Today he was in too much of a hurry to hang anything up or even to take his school shirt to the dirty linen basket, but not in too much of a hurry to allow a moment before the wardrobe mirror. All hint of the schoolboy had gone with the uniform – or so he believed. Admiring his 'manly physique' he raised his arms to shoulder height and flexed his muscles, well pleased with what he saw, well pleased with life in general. The arrangement of Sally working

43

suited him admirably even during term time but now, with the thought of summertime freedom ahead, no wonder he smiled.

'Jethro! Jethro, where are you? I saw your bike.' Then there was the sound of the back door slamming.

Grabbing his shorts, he thrust his legs into them, taking one more reassuring glance at the golden brown of his naked chest. Zena!

'I'm upstairs. Come on up, Zena.' At the sound of her running up the stairs he took another quick glance at the manly vision before he flung his bedroom door wide open, coming on to the landing to meet her.

'Were you changing?' Then not waiting for an answer, 'I rode over as fast as I could. I hoped I'd get here before you left.' She didn't say why she hoped it, instead she came to stand close in front of him, her lips slightly parted as she raised her face to his. 'I caught an earlier train. Weeks and weeks of freedom.' So might any one-time childhood friend have spoken. Her smile was eager – for him? For the holiday? Like someone approaching the shallows by the shore, she was testing the water. His expression was the answer she needed. 'You're glad I came?' she whispered in the last second before his mouth covered hers just as she'd intended. 'Don't let's hurry home, let's wait here for a while. I thought the term was never going to end. Now it's as if we've never been apart. Is that how it is for you too, Jethro?' Her mouth was so close to his that he could feel the warmth of her breath as she spoke.

He didn't answer, his mouth was dry, his pulses racing. When she came an inch nearer, shock and excitement surged as her tongue probed gently to trace the outline of his inner lips; through the thin material of her blouse he could feel the warmth of her soft breasts against his naked chest. Only *she* knew how, when she'd discarded the uniform she'd travelled in, with it had gone her bra and school knickers – 'passion-killers', as they were known in the dormitory she'd shared with seven other body-conscious girls. Wearing satin French knickers, no bra at all, like Jethro she had viewed her reflection in anticipation. A dirndl skirt and peasant type blouse, and she'd been ready for the next stage, the stage she had imagined a thousand times. She knew what her nearness was doing to him; for her the rhythmical movement as she stood close against him was the most natural thing in the world. She saw herself as a sophisticated temptress; he wanted nothing more than to be tempted. Wasn't this what he'd thought about for weeks? But what was she doing? Her fingers were fumbling with the buttons of his shorts and in a second they were round his ankles. There was nothing between them except his underpants and already her hand was inside; he felt its firm hold.

'No, no, don't, Zena, my precious, beloved Zena.' Oh the joy of saying those words, to his ears they carried all the poetry that had ever been written, his precious, his beloved. 'If you touch me like that – oh hell, I'll explode.' His tone was a mixture of fear and pride.

Excited by his warning and certain that his 'no' really meant 'yes' she gently eased them towards the bed where he'd thrown his clothes.

'Touch me, Jethro, touch me too. You know you want to, just like I do.' Oh yes, he knew it with every fibre of his being. As if he needed it, she guided his hand.

'No ... yes ... no, we mustn't.'

'We're not doing any harm,' she whispered. 'We're not children, Jethro. Soon you'll be in the Army.' Then she made her first mistake. 'I'm not going back to school.' As soon as she spoke she realised this hadn't been the moment to tell him her plans. He pulled away from her, his moment of near-surrender lost.

'But you haven't even heard whether you've passed your School Certificate. You might have to go back.'

'They say I needn't. I wrote to Dad and he talked to Mum. It's all arranged. I'm never going to spend my life swotting for exams; there's only one thing I want to do.' Then with a teasing look as she pursed her pretty mouth, 'Long-term, I mean, not this very minute.' There! That might get him going again. But it seemed it wasn't going to. 'I'm going to be an actress, Jethro. We've always known that. I shan't call myself Zena Kilbride, I don't want to be given chances because Sebastian Kilbride is my father. What shall I call myself? Zena –'

'Zena Kennedy, that's the name you ought to have. One day you will, Zena. Honestly, I wouldn't stand in your way. I wouldn't be pigheaded like Dad always was when Mum wanted to do something better than faff around here all day.'

'Just an ordinary job like she could do is a bit different! *I'm* going to be famous, really famous. Like Dad is – or like he was until this stupid war messed everything up. Only I don't really want to go into films, I want to be a proper stage actress.'

'You'd be great in the films, Zena, you're so beautiful.'

She lay back on the bed and stretched her arms behind her head, her mouth turning up at the corners into a smile of contentment and her eyes wide open and staring unseeingly at the ceiling. There was something feline in the way she stretched, even in the far-away expression on her lovely face as she visualised the bright lights outside the theatre, heard the roars of applause. Misunderstanding her expression, Jethro found his courage and gently pulled her blouse from the waistband of her skirt, then moved his hand on her warm flesh, cupping her breast.

'We'd better get going,' she said lightly. 'Mum may call us children, but she's not daft. If I'm too long she'll think she ought to keep a protecting eye on me.'

Rebuffed, Jethro stood up and, with what dignity he could muster, reached for his discarded shorts.

There were great changes in the lovely two-acre garden at Mulberry Cottage. These had stemmed from the message on a hoarding near the railway station in town: 'Dig for Victory', and above the bold printing a picture of an elderly man working on his allotment. As soon as she saw it Tessa had known what she had to do! She'd collected her rations from the grocer, hers and Jethro's too, and pedalled the two miles home arriving breathless and excited to tell Ted Cummins, the young gardener. Until then she had laughingly called 'looking after Jethro' her war work, but no one had realised – perhaps even *she* hadn't fully realised – that there was something like superstition deeply embedded in her spirit. To do nothing but wait while other people 'did their bit' was like tempting Fate. She'd found her mission; why ever hadn't she seen it before? Vegetables, fruit and vegetables, all grown in the ground of their beloved Mulberry Cottage, bottled, turned into preserves (if she could afford the sugar), salted, kept in any way she could and only to be used when Sebastian was at home.

That had been near the end of May, too late to see the spoils of her efforts during that season of 1940. Perhaps by next year he'd be home for good – please God let him soon be home – but if she did *nothing* how could she deserve to have her pleas listened to? So through those days of early summer, while Ted Cummins, the fortunately brawny gardener, worked alongside her and waited for his call-up papers, they dug – and dug – and dug. After school, glad to shelve his homework until the light started to fade, Jethro had been more than willing to take Ted's place. By the end of each day, when Tessa had climbed into her statutory five inches of water in the bath, every muscle ached and she'd been glad. In a way she'd not even tried to explain, aching muscles had been a comfort, a physical expression of her faith in the future.

By the beginning of the school holidays nearly half an acre of lawn had been dug and a new shed built. She must have somewhere to hang the strings of onions which, in her mind's eye, she saw hanging from hooks in the roof. That she had no idea how to make a string of onions was unimportant; only a few months ago her gardening had gone no further than planting out annuals or pulling up the odd weed. Now she scoured the bookshops for gardening books, listened to every radio talk about growing vegetables, made notes in a way that would have been out of character for pre-war Tessa.

'It's great, Mum. You and Jethro must have worked like mad to dig all that,' had been Zena's reaction on first sight of the erstwhile lawn. She was glad to see the tennis court had been left untouched, but even that paled into insignificance compared with the image of Jethro with the manly strength to do all this. For she didn't imagine her mother would have been much help. And normally truthful Tessa left her with her illusions – after all now that Ted had been called up it served no purpose in admitting that the lion's share of the digging had been *his* doing.

'Mum says you're going to creosote the new shed,' Zena said as she watched Jethro cover his manly form with a pristinely clean shirt. 'You don't want to mess up a good shirt.' Zena the temptress had become Zena the practical and, rather than being disappointed, he was strangely relieved. Was that normal? Oughtn't he to be feeling wild with frustration? And what about her? As cool as a cucumber; those last moments might never have been.

'I keep a lot of old stuff at your place. You wouldn't want to be seen out with me looking the sort of scarecrow I am when I get down to things in the garden.' The words gave a boost to his flagging morale.

'Don't be daft,' she laughed. 'When we've had tea I'll put some old clothes on and come and help you. We'll see who can do most before the light starts to go. Mum's dead keen on the garden. Quite crazy, she's always been a home bird.'

'Wartime does funny things to people. Ready then?'

She laughed, 'Me? It's you who had no clothes on.'

'You weren't so different.' He let his tone match hers. Now that they were on their way down the stairs he felt himself in charge of the situation again.

Later, watching her working by his side, he fell even deeper in love with her. Who but he knew the fire in her waiting to be ignited? No one. And no one ever would. She was *his*. All right, he argued silently with himself, not *mine* in that way, not yet. But she will be. She wants to be. Next time I'll be ready, I'll pinch some of those sheath things I found when I was poking around looking to see if Dad had a spare packet of razor blades. Yes, that's what I'll do. Just a couple. One I'll practise with on my own so that when we're together I won't fumble about like some greenhorn. Greenhorn, that's funny!

'Why are you smiling?' Her voice cut across his wandering thoughts.

'I guess because it's so great, you and me both here, weeks ahead of us. Enough to make anyone smile.'

'I may not have that many weeks, Jethro. I've written to the Mayflower Theatre Company. They may not take me, but I bet they will. Just to be sure, I told them about Dad. Just this once – to get my first experience. It's not the sort of company where anyone has their name on a programme or anything.'

'You mean you're going away again?'

'Depends what happens. I saw the Mayflower Players during the term. We were doing *As You Like It* for School Cert. and they came to school and gave a performance. All women,' then with a twinkle that made his Adam's apple stick in his throat, 'so you don't need to worry. Some of them are about my age, some quite old, as old as our parents, I expect. They travel all over the country – you should see the huge vans they have, full of costumes and scenery, it's great. I expect I shall hear soon, but they may not want me to join them straight away because I guess they have their holidays this time of year too. Most of the performances are for schools, you see, schools or else in village halls in places right out in the sticks.'

The evening had been so full of promise; now he felt she was slipping from him. How long would she want to bother with *him* once she was a touring actress? His mind raced, back to those moments in his bedroom, forward to making sure he arrived home long enough before his mother tonight to get what he wanted from his father's store. Any feeling of guilt on that score vanished; it was up to him, he had to make her truly *his* and he had to take responsibility; he had to let her see that he wasn't some stupid kid with no thought for her protection. Zena, his Zena, getting ahead of him, growing up and moving into a world of adults. Well, so would he.

'I told Mum I'd be home tonight,' he lied to Tessa an hour or so later, 'I thought you'd want Zena to yourself on her first night.'

'Silly,' Tessa laughed. 'You're hardly a visitor, Jethro! Still, if she's expecting you, you must be sure you're home when she gets in or she'll worry. Tomorrow I think she's covering twelve till eight, so tell her I'll expect her to supper if she can manage it.'

'She panics about you feeding us so much.'

'Tell her Thursdays I get fish from the market so she won't be having anything rationed.'

He half-listened to the message, his mind on higher things.

By the time the light faded too much for them to work, the shed had had its first coat of creosote, shared with their working clothes, their hands and a smear or two on their faces. Despite his dirty state, he insisted he ought to get straight home; he believed Sally had said something about getting away early.

His thieving mission satisfactorily completed, by the time he heard Sally slam the garage door shut, he'd scrubbed and pumice-stoned himself clean and even tidied his bedroom, as if putting away his pile of books and hanging up his uniform removed evidence of those few glorious moments with Zena. Sally had a ration of petrol; living in the country and doing a job considered necessary, ensured that. Even so, if the weather was good and her shifts in daylight, she enjoyed the exercise of cycling the three miles to Drifford Park.

'Hello,' she greeted Jethro in surprise, 'I half expected you'd be spending the night with Tess. Did Zena get home?'

'Yes. That's why I came home. I reckoned Tess might want her to herself. We've been doing the shed, me and Zena.' Such easy chatter, nothing that hinted at the working of his mind. 'Oh and by the way, Tess said it's fish for supper tomorrow, so she'll expect both of us. OK?' It was surprisingly easy to talk about one thing and think about another. 'She's a lucky so and so,' he went on talking as he lit the gas under the kettle, 'Zena, I mean, not Tess. She's been allowed to leave school, Mum, not even wait to see if she got her School Cert., which she says she probably hasn't. She's going to join some touring theatre company. And there's me, much older than her, and stuck at school for another year.'

'It depends what you want to do with your life, Jethro. And if at this stage you aren't sure, then don't spoil your chances. If you can get your Higher Schools next summer, then you'll have the way open to whatever direction you decide. Honestly, it's worth sticking it out.'

'Humph,' he grunted, desperately trying to think of some burning ambition that would give him a springboard into the adult world. But he seemed incapable of focusing on anything other than the challenge of the next few days.

If he'd expected his rehearsal to go smoothly, he was disappointed. His only thankfulness was that he was 'having a go' by himself. However, after a few attempts he started to get the hang of things. In the night, with images of Zena filling his half-waking mind he reached under his pillow to find the object he'd so carefully rerolled after each bungled attempt. Yes, that was better this time; there was a knack to it. Tonight he was taking a giant stride into that adult world; by the time he resettled for sleep he'd even progressed to believing Nick wouldn't miss what he'd taken; sex was for the young.

His plan was laid. Leaving his creosote-splattered shirt at home, he set out for Mulberry Cottage next morning at about the same time as Sally left home for her midday shift at Drifford Park. After lunch, what could be more natural than that he should suggest putting the second coat on the shed, remember his shirt, then persuade Zena to come too, bring her back with him. Everything went well, something for which he quite unjustly took credit. For in truth, if he hadn't thought of an excuse then Zena certainly would. They all cycled together as far as the end of the lane to Owls' Roost, then Tessa pedalled on towards the village leaving 'the children' to collect Jethro's work clothes. Buoyed up with his newly learned skill, he knew exactly where the afternoon was heading and, although neither of them had spoken about it, so too did Zena. He could read it in her every movement, in the way she took her feet off the pedals and stretched her lovely legs in front of her as she freewheeled down the incline towards the end of the lane where they would part company with Tessa.

'I expect we'll be home before you, Mum,' she said. 'Unless we decide to go for a ride. Perhaps we'll do that, shall we, Jethro? It's better to creosote in the evening.' Such innocence in the suggestion. Then to Jethro, 'Race you up the lane,' and she was gone. No wonder Tessa pedalled on towards the village thinking how nice it was to have 'the children' home, and no wonder Jethro's heart seemed to pound right into his ears as he followed Zena's lead. He wanted to sing and shout with happiness. His head was filled with half-remembered snatches from the great romantic poems he'd taken to reading lately, but most of all he wanted to catch up with her, like a cave man of old, to carry her to his lair. But while she seemed to have found a new vigour, his legs might have been made of jelly.

'Come on, slow coach,' she called when, ahead of him she propped her bicycle against the side wall of Owls' Roost.

'Zena.' He leaned his bike against hers, then stood in front of her, hearing his heavy breathing yet not able to help himself.

'Poor old man,' she whispered, 'do I go too fast for you?'

'No, never. Zena, darling, darling Zena, you know you could never be too fast. You know why we're here?' She *must* know, of course she knows. It's really going to happen. I've got to do it right. I can, I know I can. Last night's rehearsal boosted his confidence and added to the wonder of the moment. Once indoors they went straight to his bedroom and purposefully she closed the door. Strangely, the action took away some of the wild abandon that had filled him a moment before; there was something almost businesslike in the way she stepped out of her dirndl skirt. Instinct almost made him pull back, as a thousand memories from their past crowded his mind – memories of the two families, the friendship, the trust. But right or wrong, he had no power to overcome the rush of longing that filled him. Looking into that familiar mirror, he was proud of the evidence of it, his thoughts leaping ahead to the article he'd carefully hidden just beneath his eiderdown. He'd got to get it right, he mustn't fumble. She was already on the bed, lying spreadeagled with arms and legs stretched. Could she know the tantalising view her French knickers allowed? Somehow he was sure she did. He'd believed

51

lately he'd understood all there was to know about desire; imaginary visions of Zena always part of the wonder of the fantasies he'd gratified in solitude. But nothing had prepared him for this! He was one with the great lovers of all time.

'We mustn't stop, not this time,' she whispered, still a little unsure of whether desire would be stronger in him than conscience.

He was on a roller-coaster to manhood. However many times they made love in the years to come, he told himself, this was the time that mattered most. What they were going to do would make her *his, his* woman, *his* mate. Help me, help me, make me do it right, don't let me bodge it up.

Both more frightened of doing something wrong than they were prepared to admit, instead of rushing, for the next few minutes they gave themselves over to what she mentally called finding out about each other and he thought of as something akin to worshipping a body so wonderful as their hands explored.

'We'll do it now,' she whispered, pulling him so that he was poised above her. The right position had been something that bothered him; this was far removed from his solitary night-time acquaintance with the Zena of his dreams. She wanted to tell him that she knew this would be the easiest way, a girl at school had looked through the keyhole at her married sister, but she thought it better not to break his concentration. Then came his moment; like a conjuror bringing a rabbit from the hat he felt just beneath the eiderdown and produced what she saw as sure proof that he'd meant this to happen every bit as much as she had. Praying with all his heart, he managed to get it on.

'Hark! Someone's come!' In an instant they were both on their feet, Jethro craning his neck, Zena standing on the bed to give her a better view.

'Crumbs! It's Nick.'

'Dad? Get your things on!' The mirror showed him his flacid manhood still encased in its much-rehearsed attire, a sorry sight. But Zena wasn't wasting time looking in the mirror, already she'd got her skirt on and was pushing her feet in her sandals.

'I'll be downstairs making us some tea. Don't argue.' And she was gone.

Outside Nick was paying the taxi driver and looking round him as if to imprint the picture of all he saw on his mind. Sal couldn't be home, he supposed, or by this time she would have come out to meet him. Oh, but there were bicycles, someone must be in.

'Hello? Anyone in?' he called as he unlocked the front door and stepped into the highly polished hall. Nothing ever changed at Owls' Roost; already he could feel the calm of it. 'Anyone home?'

'We're home,' Zena answered, coming out from the kitchen, kettle in hand. 'Jethro didn't tell me you were coming. What a lovely surprise.' So pleased was she with her unruffled welcome that she wished Jethro could have heard her. 'I was just putting the kettle on for some tea while Jethro's upstairs digging out his tatty shirt. We're going to be creosoting the shed for Mum this evening.' Dumping the kettle on the highly polished parquet floor, with the charm that came to her so naturally, she kissed Nick then shouted, 'Jethro, didn't you hear? Nick's here!' By that time re-trousered Jethro was ready and came to the head of the stairs.

'Crumbs, this is super, Dad. How did you wangle it? Mum said it would be October before you got another leave.'

'The Army works in mysterious ways, who are we to question? God, but it's good to be home. I suppose it's too much to hope that Sally's due back soon?'

'Afraid so. She's working till eight, then Tess is expecting us to supper. She's going straight there. Just you wait till they see you! Tess said it's fish for supper so we shan't be eating their rations.'

'Better still, I'll take you all to the Drovers. What's that disgusting-looking garment you're holding?'

Jethro grinned. Oh boy, it was good to have his father home. So good, in fact, that the inconvenience of his unexpected arrival was forgotten.

'It's got in that state by honest toil. Creosote. If we don't finish the job off tonight, there's always tomorrow. And I bet you, Dad, that while Mum's at work, Tess will give you a bit of honest toil too. How long have you got?'

'Seven days.'

'Is that all? Did Mum tell you she's booked down that she'll want a fortnight off in October? So I bet she won't get much time this week.'

'Yes, she told me about it.' October, nearly three months away. Had anyone the right to look so far ahead? Then, with a sudden grin that set the mood for the young ones, 'I suppose there's no chance that she left the car in the garage?'

'She was going to cycle. This time of year she only takes the car if she has to come home in the middle of the night. I don't see what difference that makes, I'd never have thought of Mum as scared of the dark.'

'Nor of anything else,' Nick laughed affectionately. 'If the car's here, I'll drive us over to Tess now. We can tie Sal's bike on the luggage grid to come home tonight. You kids can leave yours here, we'll sort them out tomorrow. If we're going to the Drovers we shall need transport. Give me five minutes to get into civvies.'

When Tessa and her parcel of fish arrived at Mulberry Cottage the three of them were there waiting for her. More hugs, more excitement. All the fishmonger had had on his truck had been mackerel so the thought of eating at the Drovers was appealing. Even mackerel couldn't be wasted. Her mind on tomorrow and her extended family, she put them to cook in vinegar in the oven. That way they'd keep fresh and would do for lunch tomorrow with salad. Nick sat astride the kitchen chair, watching what she did. This was what coming home should be, he thought, feeling disloyal that he should be comparing the unchanging warmth of Mulberry Cottage with the cool serenity of Owls' Roost. Upstairs the youngsters were donning their working clothes. If they weren't going out until after Sally arrived home, they might as well get on with their creosoting.

'Fancy getting leave so suddenly,' Tessa said a few minutes later as she and Nick sat in companionable idleness in the shade of a tall elm at the far end of the garden. 'They ought to have given you better notice. You might have wanted to do something special.'

He didn't answer straight away. It was as if he was weighing her words, undecided on how to reply.

'Yes,' he agreed, 'it was too sudden for me to let Sal know. She must get some time off; she can't waste the week in that place.'

'No special reason for it, is there, Nick?'

'What better reason than I want her to share my leave?'

'I mean no special reason for it being so sudden?'

'Who knows the workings of the military mind. I can't believe they made a decision from out of the blue but that's how it was dropped on me.'

Tessa laughed, taking his hand lightly in hers. 'Let's not look a gift horse ...' she said. 'If only Seb could get away for a few

54

hours.' The laughter had gone; over both of them there seemed to hang a cloud. This time it was *his* fingers that tightened their hold on hers. So far the skies over Worcestershire had been empty of the battles that were occurring over the south-east corner of the country. She listened to every news bulletin, her fingers crossed even though her heart sent up a silent prayer. If there had been a shrine to some unknown deity she would have paid homage to that too if it would have helped keep Seb safe.

'If Sally can get time off and you want to take her away for a day or two, you know Jethro is fine here with Zena and me.'

'Go somewhere, you say,' Nick went on. 'This is the only place I want to be, at home, here, amongst the people who make up my world.'

Her brief glance was full of concern. Such a statement was out of character for undemonstrative, matter-of-fact Nick. What was this beastly war doing to them, to ordinary people who just wanted to go on living ordinary lives? Ordinary? That's not how Sebastian's adoring fans would have wanted to think of him and his family; but Nick wasn't one of those. Wholeheartedly, he shared her sentiment.

'I just want it to be over,' he mumbled through almost closed lips as he lit two cigarettes and passed one to her.

'Me too. That's why I've dug up the garden, why I'm planning where I shall put the fruit bushes and what things I can best grow for keeping. If we get short of things now I don't much care; I'm doing this for *afterwards*. It's my signal to whoever designs our lives that I have faith one day everything will be like it was.'

For a moment Nick envied Sebastian her single-mindedness. Things to be like they were . . . what would Sal say to that? She'd been bored with being a housewife – the war had brought her salvation. Would he change her? Would he turn Sal into a happy homemaker like Tessa? His mouth twitched into something like a smile as he imagined it. Hardly realising he did it, he glanced at his watch checking how much longer before she would be there.

'Nothing will ever be just as it was, Tess. The clock keeps ticking; we all experience emotions that weren't part of our peaceful pre-war existence. I like to think of a future when we shall all be back where we belong, but more aware. We took so much for granted. That's something we shall never do again.'

*

55

Sally's arrival rekindled all the excitement of his unexpected leave. Rabbit pie was all the Drovers had to offer, but the meal took on the atmosphere of celebration. Tessa had become adept at hiding her heart, and gave no hint of her ever-present anxiety; Sally saw Nick's unexpected seven-day leave as a gift; Jethro and Zena remembered their oh-so-near moment of glory, knew that it would have to be put on hold for the next week, just the week and no longer.

It was much later; the day was over. Lying close to Nick, Sally felt herself drifting towards sleep, wrapped in a deep contentment. Smiling in the darkness, the thought touched her mind that perhaps separation was turning her into a romantic. There had been a time when she had thought Nick's pleasure in sex had been as much habit as his going to work or cleaning the car. Of course there had been the occasional times when it had lifted them to higher planes. But tonight she had been aware of something different. And now, surely he was still awake? That in itself was unusual.

'Sal,' he whispered.

'Umph?' came her sleepy reply.

'Sal. Haven't you guessed why I'm here? I think Tess did. But I didn't tell her, not till you knew.'

'Umph?' What was he saying? Knew? Knew what? Not what she was thinking – please not what she was thinking. But any hope was short-lived.

'It's embarkation leave. And you didn't suspect?'

She felt incapable of coherent thought. As if to help her take in what he was saying, she sat bolt upright, looking out of the open window into the moonless night. What he had said didn't so much banish that feeling she'd known a few minutes ago, that sense of oneness with him; rather it explained it.

'They should have told you earlier, given us time to – to –'

'To what? Can you arrange your mind so that you can accept something so unknown? For myself I feel – I was going to say "thankful", but that wouldn't be the complete truth. Back last month when that poor broken Army – or what poor devils were left of it – were brought back across the Channel, can you imagine what it felt like to be strutting about in uniform in Yorkshire? I'll tell you, Sal. I felt like a character in some comic opera. I didn't join the Army for that.' She didn't answer. Her mind was crowded with things to say but no words came. 'How long? I remember you saying that the first night of the war. We were thinking about Jethro. There's no turning back the clock. Sixteen then, seventeen now, soon he'll want to join in.'

'He wants to already. He doesn't want to go back to school, Nick.' What a moment to start discussing Jethro's future, yet she clutched at it just as she would have at anything rather than the desolation and uncertainty, all the future offered. 'Zena isn't going back and she's younger. Talk to him, Nick, don't go away with him not knowing how you feel about what he wants to do.'

'Of course. But us, Sal. You will be all right? You will manage?' It wasn't what he meant and she knew it.

'If you mean will I love you just as if you were here, will everything be waiting for you when you come back, you know the answer. Of course I will.'

'Lie down, darling. Let me just hold you. A week, just one precious week.'

'Like standing on a precipice and knowing you must jump, Nick. When's it all going to end? Even now, even being torn apart, we mustn't lose sight of how lucky we are. I tell myself that every day. I think of Helga – remember poor little Helga? There's never been a word of what's happened to her parents – I think of those poor souls who have lost everything, those living in the middle of the fighting. In France there must be thousands left homeless after the fighting that pushed our boys to the coast. And now it's our turn. I ought not to be angry, but I am. I feel knotted up with anger. Aren't there enough men younger than you who could go? That, or regular soldiers? You could have been at home; nothing need have changed for us.'

'Is that what you would have wanted?'

'Of course it is. It's what every woman would want. Like Tess always says, everything was so *right*, so perfect.'

He laughed softly, drawing her even closer. 'Can this be the Sal who longed to do something useful with her life?' To help her more than himself he teased her.

'That's different. To do what you know you can do well is satisfying, I'm not arguing with that.'

'And that, my precious Sal, is why I can't share your sort of bitterness that I'm being sent to serve overseas. Darling, I'm hardly going to be in the front line. I've always told you, I'm not in a regiment of heroes. But I shall be doing something I know I do efficiently. In the morning we must think about the boy. Have we the right to insist he kicks his heels at school for another year just because we're frightened to open the cage door and let him fly? Jethro is never going to be an academic, and next year if this show isn't over he'll be called up whether we want him to go or not. When it's all over I imagine he'll become articled like I was; he's always given the impression that that's what he intends.'

'When it's all over,' she echoed his words, trying unsuccessfully to keep fear out of her voice.

'It will be, darling. Have faith.' Then with a laugh that held little humour, 'What is it they commend? Trust the Lord and keep your powder dry. Something like that. Whatever happens, Sal, promise me one thing.' Whatever happens, *whatever* happens, what did he mean? What sort of warning did the words carry? Even while she hid from the images that tormented her from the recesses of her mind, she knew that one day when he'd gone there would be no escaping. 'News won't always be good, there will be good times and bad, but promise me that you will *never* lose faith.'

'In you? Never. You know that.'

'I didn't mean in me. I meant in what we're fighting for, for the ultimate good, for a lasting and fair peace.' He fell silent, she sensed he was embarrassed by his uncharacteristically serious outburst.

'In you and in that too,' she promised.

'We'll clobber the swine. Only a fool picks a fight with a bulldog.'

Sally's night was short. She was on the early shift the next day, from eight in the morning until four. Normally she would have left home just after seven and cycled, but on that day she allowed herself the luxury of the car. In the circumstances of Nick's leave she was confident she could arrange cover and bring forward at least a few days of her October holiday. Her request was agreed, the members of her team all willing to work extra hours if necessary. So many of the monitoring staff at Drifford Park had left their native lands, where dictatorships had tarnished any semblance of that fair and honest world Nick believed must be the outcome of the present fight. Most of them had come away while they had the freedom to make a new beginning. Of course there were others with good linguistic skills and broad political under-

58

standing but no personal experience of changes in their society. Somewhere amongst this mix-match Sally had found her niche and had made friends. Although English was usually spoken in front of English members of the staff, those from the editorial section or the typing pool would lapse into their own tongues between themselves and Sally was proud to be included, whether amongst the Germans, the French or even the Italians. The sounds and the general atmosphere conjured up memories of her years with her father; they took her back to her roots.

Driving away at the end of the day, her leave arranged for the period until Nick had gone, she looked in the reversing mirror at the old manor house and realised, perhaps as she never had before, how important it had become in her life. Suppose when Nick had come home with his news yesterday, she had still been dusting dust-free surfaces, hunting for weeds, cutting the grass before it had time to grow, waiting for the leaves to fall so that she could sweep them up? What would his going have meant to her then? Without Nick she would have had no life – wasn't that what she'd always said? But now she had. Today she wasn't strong enough to contemplate what it would be like knowing there would be no hope of a phone call in the evening, no hope of his getting home. But at least she had a purpose; what she did was part of the scheme of things. Yet when Nick went away, something of herself would go with him. Nothing would be the same, nothing would be complete, nothing . . . her view of the road ahead was misted by unshed tears.

Just as she had the previous day, she drove straight to Mulberry Cottage, knowing that's where Nick and Jethro would be. She found Nick mowing the lawn, while Jethro was clipping the edges of the vegetable plot. For one brief moment she resented what she saw. If he wanted to cut grass, why couldn't he have got the mower out at home? Both houses had lost the help they used to employ in the garden. Then she thought of Tessa and her project of 'growing for the future' and she stamped hard on what she recognised as jealousy.

'Here, Mum,' Jethro shouted when he saw her. 'Here, come and listen to this! Come and hear what Dad says.'

She did as he said, but even before they told her, she knew. Nick had given his permission for Jethro to leave school. Tessa's appearance saved her having to show the delight the boy clearly expected.

'It seems our children are grown up,' Tessa said as she came towards them, and, from the way her kindly gaze held her own, Sally knew it was said out of support and understanding. 'You and I will have to prop each other up, Sal.'

'We're good at that,' Sally rose to the occasion. 'If it's what you want, Jethro, then as Nick and I agreed last night, there's no point in holding you back from volunteering when by next summer you'd be conscripted anyway. This way you will get some choice in what you want to do.' She was proud of her tone, glad that she hadn't failed her young son, who stood there so eager for life. She recognised his eager pride and, just for a moment, she was back at Drifford Park on that first day, walking into the now so familiar listening room and knowing that at last she was swimming in the stream of life. It was that understanding that gave her the courage to hug Jethro in the most natural way, even to say, 'Well done. But what else could we expect from your father's son?'

'You haven't heard the half of it,' Tessa told her. 'The woman who runs that Mayflower Theatre Company – although the one thing they certainly haven't got is a theatre – telephoned today. Zena's going to see them. Apparently they're giving a perform- ance of *The Chocolate Soldier* in some remote Shropshire village. Miss Hewison – she's the boss lady – is meeting her train in Shrewsbury tomorrow.'

'They didn't waste any time. But Zena has seen them when they played at her school. Is this to test her out?'

'I guess so. She'll be there a few days at any rate. Miss Hewison sounded very forthright; I don't think she'll give any favours on Sebastian's account. Zena has spent most of the day titivating, packing, changing her mind and repacking. I don't think she'll sleep a wink tonight.'

Turning his back on them, Jethro went back to edging the border.

Next day he went with Tessa to see Zena off.

'See you by the weekend,' he shouted as the train took its first jerking movement, carrying her away. No wonder as they'd stood on the platform waiting, heads had turned to look at her, men and women alike attracted by more than her good looks: by something in the way she walked, in the way she held her head, in her eager- ness. He felt himself bursting with pride – in her for being as she was, for himself as he remembered the words she'd whispered as they'd watched Tess reverse the car out of the garage.

60

'It won't make any difference – not to us, I mean. I'll keep thinking of you.'

They expected her to be home by the end of the week; she didn't even say a final goodbye to Nick before she left. All that was changed by a telephone call to Tessa from Sarah Hewison, the guiding light of the Mayflower Theatre Company.

'That daughter of yours has real promise,' her voice boomed into Tessa's ear. 'I've told her I'm prepared to take her, she is keen as mustard to begin and it can't be too soon as far as I'm concerned. You've no objections to her staying on? No, of course you haven't. She wouldn't be with us now if you had. If you parcel up her things, I'll see her trunk is collected from the station.'

'If she has talent, she inherits it from her father.'

'Ah yes, perhaps. Screen and stage, different as chalk and cheese. This girl of yours will have something to offer that's worth offering, of that I'm certain. And her looks are a bonus – not everything, looks can never be everything, but she'll find the world a kinder place with an appearance like that. You can find no objection to her staying?'

'Miss Hewison, it's what she has always wanted. But I'm glad you phoned me. I can't wait to tell Sebastian you have such hopes for her.'

'No need to have spoken to you, I dare say. Zena isn't the sort to let others make her decisions, I can tell that. But I'm old-fashioned. You're her mother.' If the over-loud purposeful tone was meant to reassure Tessa, for some reason it failed. She felt Zena was lost to her. Even the virgin soil of the waiting vegetable plot echoed the emptiness she hid behind her ever-ready smile.

'That was Miss Hewison, about Zena.' She infused her voice with pride. 'It seems she thinks Seb and I have produced something rather special. She's not coming back, they seem keen for her to get involved straight way. She'll have so much to learn,' the smile never faltered, 'costumes, make-up, all the backstage stuff, apart from having to get used to learning lines. Gosh, it takes me back'

'Well done, her. Won't Sebastian be cock-a-hoop.' Sally accepted Tessa's unsullied pleasure without question. Only Nick, not usually the most sensitive of men, saw behind the smile.

'Good job we weren't ten minutes earlier,' he told Tessa, 'you might have missed the call. We've cycled over to collect you. We thought we'd all get a pub lunch at the Highwayman? We'll toast the youngsters, eh? Jethro has gone off to talk about his future at the Recruitment Centre, Zena is on her way to stardom. That leaves just the three of us. Get your bonnet on or powder your nose or whatever you women do.'

Tessa's expression never faltered as she nodded her agreement. 'Lovely,' she agreed. 'That leaves just the three of us,' his words echoed. Where was Seb? What was happening in the skies over Kent? Keep him safe, keep him safe … Only as she went back in the house to do 'whatever you women do' in preparation for what Nick was determined should be a celebration, did she let the mask drop.

Four days later Nick had gone. It was Jethro's turn to watch for the postman each morning. Only just old enough to be accepted for service, Sally hung on to the hope that he would be kept waiting; surely they had enough young men being conscripted to keep the medical examiners busy without taking a boy only just out of the classroom. The powers-that-be didn't share her opinion and within weeks he was being issued with the rough khaki uniform of an army private.

During those weeks, although he always listened avidly when Tessa reported Zena's progress, he said very little about her. Yet Sally wasn't blind to the writing pad he kept in the drawer of his bedside table and the neat pile of envelopes in Zena's writing; she watched as his sheet of stamps grew smaller. But she asked no question and was told nothing. On the mornings when the post was delivered before she left for Drifford Park, he made no secret of how keenly he watched for it. But then, so had Nick in those far-off days when their world still hung on to normality.

It had been the end of September when he left home. Now a weary Sebastian came home on leave, the Battle of Britain fought and won. Over the months of summer he had lived on a knife edge; he believed he would never clear his mind of the physical fear that had gripped him each time the sound of the klaxon had broken the waiting silence of the airfield. Pilots rushed to take their planes up, they were counted out, the lucky ones were counted back; as the gaps were filled promotion came fast to those who were left. Three light-blue rings on his sleeve denoted his new rank of Squadron Leader. But no promotion lessened the way his gut knotted, his palms sweated, at each scramble. Now at

Mulberry Cottage he found peace that seemed to be of another world. Tessa used the garden as a banner of faith in the future; for him it was a hold on reality. The virgin soil needed a second turn before the winter frosts – and even if it hadn't, he needed the healing it provided. Just to tread the fork deep into the soil, to use every bit of energy in turning it, to smell the earth, all this would surely help the horror of yesterday to be overtaken by hope that he must never lose sight of. Fourteen glorious days, the scent of autumn and bonfires, fruit trees planted; fourteen nights when there was nothing but the wonder of the love he shared with Tessa. Only in the small hours did he have no power to control the horror that haunted his dreams.

But it was over; Churchill had told the nation that never had so much been owed by so many to so few. And Sebastian was one of those few, one of the lucky ones who still breathed the fragrance of the autumn air, who still clung to faith in the future. Soon he was gone, routine was all that was left as the autumn storms lashed, and the second Christmas of the war drew nearer. In October, when the Germans sunk the *Empress of Britain*, a ship carrying children who were being evacuated to Canada, Sally's immediate fear was for Nick. Where was he? There had been no word from him. Somewhere on the sea, being taken ... where? Only then did her compassion stretch wider. Tears and Sally were strangers to each other, but that evening, home from Drifford Park and alone, her mind was filled with images of Jethro when he'd been a child. All those children ... and their parents ... how could they bear it to imagine what the last moments had been as the great ship slipped beneath the waves ... the screams ... the cries of 'Mum – Dad' and no one to hear them, no one to help them. She heard the sound of her own crying, for them, for herself, for Jethro, her own boy who thought himself a man, for Nick who was somewhere and she knew not where. The shrill bell of the telephone cut through her misery. Instinctively she squared her chin, rubbing the palms of her hands across her eyes. 'No, no,' she screamed silently, 'nothing bad, please I beg, nothing bad.'

'Sally.' She recognised her father's voice and was flooded with relief. 'I was afraid you'd not be at home. Everything all right?'

'Fine, Dad. And you? Where are you?'

'I'm at Manchester station. I've been here for a lunchtime recital. Sally, I need you to help me. There's no one else I can ask.'

Chapter Four

She had a sense of déjà vu as she approached Owls' Roost. The two figures were waiting just as they had been that other time. All so much the same – and yet how far the world had moved on since that August day not much more than fourteen months before. Under normal circumstances she would have ridden her bicycle to Drifford Park, keeping her meagre allowance of petrol until the bad weather, but today was no ordinary day.

'I got away the moment I could,' she greeted them as she climbed out of the car. 'I put the key under the big stone; that's what Jethro and I always did, but I forgot to tell you.' Always she'd hurled herself into her father's waiting arms, but on this occasion his barely perceptible shake of the head stopped her. With his hand on Helga's shoulder he silently indicated to Sally that *hers* was the important greeting. Not everyone would have understood his message, but Sally knew immediately.

'Helga, welcome back. You're a gift from heaven; you've no idea how I hate having the house to myself.' She was the least demonstrative person, but in true Continental manner she kissed her young guest, first on the right cheek, then on the left. 'Remember last time, how worried you were that I hadn't been expecting you. Well, this time I was. And so pleased, too.'

Perhaps she was talking too much, perhaps she had made a bad move in reminding Helga of that other time and the assumption that her parents would soon follow her.

'Is it all right? Mr Burridge said –'

'I told you, it's more than all right. I honestly am pleased.' Then she turned to her father and, this time, felt herself taken in that familiar bearlike hug.

Knowing Helga was about the same age as Zena, it was impossible not to make a mental comparison. Had two girls ever been so different? Helga had grown quickly and suddenly; already she was as tall as Sally, but still painfully scrawny. Long, bony hands, long narrow feet; altogether she looked unattractively angular. This was nowhere more evident than in her thin face: high cheekbones, long nose down which her steel-framed unflattering glasses slipped uncomfortably, her jaw line strong and square. Her face seemed to say that half starved though she still looked, she wasn't a person to be discounted.

'It was a wretched journey, wasn't it, Helga. So crowded, people filling the corridor, pushing up against the window of our compartment. We travelled first class, but it made no difference. As soon as the ticket collector had been round they started to squeeze in so that we were like sardines, hadn't room to move.'

'For me it was a wonderful journey. And now ...' Helga's huge dark eyes finished the sentence for her and told Sally a good deal about the sort of life she had endured with the relatives who had temporarily taken her under sufferance.

'Is this all your luggage? Are your things following?'

Helga shook her head. 'This is all I have.' Then, remembering, she dug into her well-worn handbag, 'Except for this. Two things I have here. This book for rations and my identity card.'

'Both very necessary,' Sally said lightly. 'Let's go in. Do you remember where your room is Helga? Upstairs and –'

'I remember it. I have thought about it often.'

'Then take your things – and this time I managed to find a few late flowers in the garden before I went to work this morning – remember, last time there weren't any.'

'It is like I always hoped, none of it forgotten, not by me and not by you. I will take my case and yours too, Mr Burridge, if you like.'

No refugee could have looked more in need of love than Helga, but her tread was positive as she went up the stairs.

'It's all I could do,' Eliot said, once she was safely out of earshot, as he followed Sally into the immaculately tidy sitting room. 'Yesterday when I finished playing I went into the dressing room hoping to be in time for the evening train back to London. And there she was.' He closed his eyes as if recalling the scene. 'The same small suitcase, did you notice? Just one case to carry all her worldly goods. She'd come to me; she had no one else. Such a buttoned-up child; every hurt, every cruel blow Fate has inflicted, the damage it has done to her, is far deeper than any physical beating. I feel her very soul is bruised. And yet she says nothing.'

'You've been keeping an eye on her? I know you have. You've told me you've called at the house. Did you feel it was so dreadful?'

'Indeed, I feared it. Too young, she's learned to hide her feelings. I was never sure and yet I couldn't overcome the suspicion that all wasn't well with her. As for the Robertsons, the least said the better. But with Helga, I was never allowed a glimpse of what was behind her polite good manners. Not until yesterday. Imagine how she must have suffered, Sally my dear, in a country that's not her own.'

'It's like Nick says – *bugger this war.*'

Eliot looked at her affectionately, an expression so out of character for her somehow bringing them closer.

'Amen to that,' he said. 'But I was telling you ... she came to me – it would have torn your heart. "I read the notice that you were here," she told me. "I cannot go back." If I'd refused to bring her with me she would have run away. With Helga "I cannot go back" meant exactly that.'

'So, what happened? Why didn't you come straight here last night? You knew I would have made her welcome.' As she spoke she was pouring him a glass of his favourite brand of brandy from an almost empty bottle. Neither she nor Nick drank it; it was known as Dad's brandy, always in the cabinet especially for him, but the bottle was almost empty and there would be little or no hope of replacing it.

'Bless you, I can use that. Your health, my dear, yours, Nick's, young Jethro's – and Helga's too. What happened, you say. I booked us into an hotel, ordered a meal to be sent up to her room, then went to visit those abominable people.'

'Were they difficult about you bringing her? After all, they hardly know you – and me, not at all.'

'My dear, if I'd been a white-slave trafficker they would have tied her up with ribbon and handed her over. They said they'd taken responsibility of her through her school days, more than carried out their duty to a scarcely known relative, and now she ought to be capable of earning a living. I tell you, from the eager way that woman rushed to the kitchen to fetch the child's ration book it was clear she couldn't get rid of her quickly enough.'

'She ought never to have gone there. She would have been better in boarding school like Zena.'

'I honestly believe they begrudged the cost of her food; they'd hardly have paid school fees. If they were poor I could understand it, but they are manifestly prosperous – that's apparent from their tasteless opulence.' He took a long sip of brandy, and holding the fiery liquid in his mouth as if to take comfort from it, closed his eyes. Watching him, Sally felt drawn as if by a magnet. For so long the two of them had known no other family but each other; through her childhood he alone had been her rock, the pivot on which her world turned. Swallowing, opening his eyes and sitting straighter, he smiled at her, his action seeming to draw a line under what was best forgotten. 'However,' he said, 'it's all over now and thank God for it. Now to the future. I must think of something ... remember how you used to look after my bookings, arrange our travelling? Good days, Sally.'

'Lovely days, Dad. We were a good team, that's what I used to think.' Then, laughing, 'What arrogance! A team. I did precious little. But didn't we have fun!'

'Golden memories, eh? And don't belittle your share. I was always confident that the arrangements would run smoothly. Tell me about this place where you work. Is it going well?'

'I love it, Dad. Oh, I don't love some of the reports I listen to on the bulletins from the Continent. How much truth is there in what they put out? How much is propaganda? And the same with what we listen to on the wireless here. Morale-boosting plays such a big part. Yes, I love it there. All the years we lived on the Continent, mostly Paris I know, but Berlin too, Salzburg – remember those weeks in Salzburg? – Warsaw, I suppose that however you spend your youth, your formative years, that's where your roots are. Except for holidays over our more recent years, once we could afford it, I've not been back. Yet none of my memories fade. At Drifford Park I feel at ease with myself – it's the voices partly, Dad. When people learn a foreign language they know the words, serious, polite, conventional things, but they don't laugh – or perhaps cry – with the natives. I'm saying it badly.'

'You're saying it beautifully, Sally my dear,' he answered her in German. Then, in French, he added, 'You are speaking to one who

68

understands just what you mean.' The magnet pulled her close, she leaned over the back of his chair and rubbed her chin against his grey hair as he talked. 'How is it we've let the world get into this state? So many friends – are we supposed now to see them as enemies? It's not easy. Yet, there's evil at work. There's no doubt that poor child's parents have been interned. Can we trust the way they are being treated? Owls' Roost, it's a world away. To me this has always spelled peace, order, happiness.'

'We have to keep faith, Dad.' In her words she seemed to hear the echo of Nick's voice.

'I wish you could get news of Nick, or at least know where they've sent him.'

'I was thinking of him at that minute too. It's what he said – about never losing faith in what we're doing.'

Silence as he took another long sip.

'Play for me, Dad.'

Upstairs, leaning out of the window and breathing deeply as if she wanted to fill her whole being with the earthy, decaying smell of the autumn dusk, Helga heard the sound of the piano. Eliot had called her a child, but the workings of her mind were far from those of a child. They are my friends. Yet I'm nobody to him, I keep telling myself that, and yet I feel as if he belongs to me. Sally's father. I think she's my friend too. They aren't of my faith, not of my race – I'm not of theirs. Are they kind to me because they feel responsible that in Germany *my* people are so hated by people of *their* faith? Is it just kindness? Am I mistaken in letting myself feel that Mr Burridge is partly *mine*? Beethoven's Moonlight Sonata – he knows I love it. Is he trying to tell me he's playing for me as well as her? Quietly shutting the window, she started down the stairs but before she reached the bottom she sat down to listen. It wasn't until the last notes died, that she came to stand hesitantly in the doorway.

'Now it's your turn, Helga. I've had good reports of your progress. So what will it be? Have a look through Sally's music and find something to play for us.'

'Good reports?' Sally picked up what he said. 'Did you have lessons at school, Helga?'

'No. I went to a fine teacher.' Then, to Eliot, 'It has been my music that has – has been my life. I cannot find enough words to tell you – to thank you.'

69

'You don't have to tell me, Helga. It would have been the same for me.'

'Yes, but to say thank you is so little.'

'Then, let me hear you play.'

With a meal to prepare, Sally left them. That Eliot had been paying for the piano lessons was simply confirmation – as if she needed it! – of his nature. Nothing he had ever done had made even the slightest dent in her view of his perfection. From the drawing room came the sound of the piano; Helga played with talent and understanding in advance of her years. With her well-kept hands protected with rubber gloves, Sally peeled potatoes and listened, sharing some of Eliot's satisfaction in the girl's ability. Then, after a pause, while they'd hunted through her music, came the familiar strains of a duet she had always thought of as belonging just to her and her father, the first thing they had ever played together and so particularly their own. It was only then that she felt a twinge of jealousy. She called to mind Helga's circumstances, telling herself she was being mean and small-minded. But the fact remained, no one should play duets with her father except *her*.

Eliot stayed three days, long enough to be able to leave Helga with an easy mind. During that time Sally went each day to Drifford Park, but Tessa, warm-hearted and sensitive, welcomed Helga and him to Mulberry Cottage. With no chance of Sebastian getting home again so soon after leave, with Zena gone and even no 'war work' in the shape of Jethro, Tessa was thankful for any lame duck to look after.

'You have a good friend in Tessa Kilbride,' Eliot said as Sally sat on the edge of his bed, watching him pack his case in just the same orderly way that she would have packed her own, everything folded perfectly, nothing thrown in at the last minute. She was taking him to the station on her way to Drifford Park for the three o'clock shift.

'She's like family,' she said fondly, thinking of Tessa, 'they all are. Even the children are as close as brother and sister. I'm glad she's around while I'm working; we don't have to worry about Helga. Tess is the easiest person in the world to talk to; if anyone can break that barrier of polite reserve, then it'll be *her*.'

'If you can find out from the child what she wants to do; perhaps she has dreams of training for something. Then you know I'll give her all the backing she needs. She might talk to you. I feel guilty dropping her on you. But she can't be set adrift; she's had enough to bear.'

'Don't worry about her, Dad. I'll see if I can get a hint, but she's more likely to talk to Tess. She has that magic touch, you know. Everyone loves Tess.'

'I can see why. You saw how keen Helga was to get there this morning in time for those fruit trees to be delivered. Little Tessa can do with some help planting them – and even if she couldn't I'm sure she would have welcomed the child.'

'That's Tess for you,' Sally laughed. 'I told Helga she could take my bike today, but when she went off I saw it was Jethro's she was riding.'

'Ah yes, a bicycle. I've left a signed cheque on the dressing table, Sal. Take her to the shop and buy a new one.'

'Jethro won't be using his for a while.' Spoken with a cheer she was far from feeling.

'She has little enough that's her own. Transport is independence. Buy her the best you can find, Sally.'

So they settled into some sort of a routine. By the time Jethro came home on his first seven days' leave, his initial training behind him and a posting to an ack-ack battery ahead, between Helga and Tessa there had developed an easy working relationship. Through the weeks he'd been away he'd liked to picture Tessa's pleasure in having him back, someone to do what she'd always called 'man's jobs' in the garden. But it seemed his place had been filled – that scrawny kid his grandfather had rescued must be a lot stronger than she looked. Wood was chopped and stacked so neatly that he knew Tessa hadn't done it, the autumn tree planting was done, bonfires burned and cleared away, even the compost wasn't thrown into a heap like he expected, but was piled into a wooden frame. His place had been usurped and, what stung even more than that, the work had been done with a degree of efficiency he'd never managed. 'That ruddy Hun,' he said silently, 'Jew or no, she's still a ruddy Hun. Only wants a pair of jackboots!' But he said nothing; he was far too fond of Tessa to rock the boat. Anyway, this was Zena's home; out of

71

loyalty to Zena if nothing else, he wasn't going to upset things here.

For all the impression he gained of efficiency and knowledge, Tessa and Helga were a perfect example of the halt leading the lame in their gardening expertise. The great difference was that Tessa was guided by enthusiasm and faith, Helga by religiously following instructions she noted from books she found in the library in town.

It was on one of those trips to town in December that, as she rode past the park, she noticed a group of about thirty small children with a group of navy-blue mackintoshed women in charge. She didn't stop to question what made her hop off her gleaming new bicycle and lift it over the low wall of the park where the railings had been taken, like iron gates and railings up and down the country, to be turned into guns. Propping her prized possession carefully against an almost leafless tree, she walked purposefully towards the group. That was at about eleven o'clock in the morning.

For so long Helga had been a pawn on the board, moved by other players, having no means of shaping her own destiny. What she did that day could hardly be said to be a step on the ladder of ambition in a career sense, but for her the pointer was clear. All these small children being looked after by people who must go under the blanket heading of 'authority' tugged at a hungry yearning that lay dormant in her.

By the time she at last pedalled up the drive of Mulberry Cottage she was more than half an hour late for their normal lunch break.

'I was worried. I thought you might have had a puncture or something. Nothing wrong?' Tessa greeted her.

'I apologise, Tessa.' Helga's over-polite way even after so long set her apart. 'I saw these people ... then they told me where to go to make my application ... it is something I had never imagined, but I know I shall be doing what is right.'

And that's how Helga started to earn her living. The council-run crèche was situated in a one-time warehouse, redecorated in bright colours and equipped with a variety of toys, some new and some outgrown and discarded by the children of well-wishers. Before seven each morning someone had to be there to receive the early arrivals, left when their mothers went to work at the factory.

From tiny babies to those ready for school, they were taken in. Soon feeding bottles and nappies became as much part of Helga's days as turning herself into a horse as she crawled the floor to be ridden by the toddlers, who learned to queue for a turn. She found a new purpose, seeing beyond the tragedy of her own life. The crèche had be manned until the last child was collected at the end of the late day shift. Sometimes she worked early and arrived home at about five o'clock, sometimes she went in at mid-morning and stayed until the door was locked at the end of the day. Combine that with Sally's hours, and the two came and went at Owls' Roost according to the dictates of their rotas.

At the end of Helga's first week of work, Sally came home midway through the evening to find her waiting, the expression on her face hard to read.

'Sally.' Even though her voice was unfamiliarly unsure of itself, Sally knew better than to notice. Instead she took the cellophane off a packet of cigarettes she had managed to buy when she'd stopped at the newsagent's for the evening paper. 'Sally, it is hard to say this, so please let me speak without interrupting what I say.'

'Of course,' Sally concentrated on lighting her cigarette, her mind jumping in all directions as she tried to guess what was on Helga's mind.

'Today I was paid my first wage. No, do not say anything. There is no way even a large sum of money could repay you for letting me live here –'

'What nonsense you talk! You know I'm glad to have your company, there's nothing more –'

'Please, this is not easy to say. I have been given eighteen shillings and six pence for my work. It is important to me – please do not thwart me – it is important that I give half what I earn to you to go into the large expense of running a home.'

'No, Helga. It's not necessary. I told you –'

'For you it is not necessary, but for me it matters. Nine shillings and three pence is like nothing in the cost I make to the home, I know that. And in sharing my wages I know I cannot attempt – I would not even try – to pay for your kindness. That would belittle the importance of your giving me a home. But it is something deeper than paying for food, giving you something towards having my sheets and towels washed by the laundry. If I can pay even a – what is the word? – a paltry sum, then I win a sense of fairness.'

'Would you have paid your mother from your wage packet if you'd been in Germany still?' She sensed they were on dangerous ground, but her question was important.

'I believe she would have allowed me to. Mother has a free and independent spirit; she would have known that for me it is important. For more than a year I was given charity with mother's disagreeable cousin. I am grateful that they gave their charity, but it was hard to take. I have had enough of it. I must feel I am – how can I say this to you? – that I am a working cog in the wheel, not simply like a tyre to be moved here, moved there, stopped, started, but never being part of – of – of the mechanics.'

Sally understood exactly what she meant: it rang a bell in her memory as she recalled how she'd longed to feel herself swimming in the stream of life. It was like looking back at a different world, a world of monotonous certainty, a world where she'd been able to take for granted that her daily life and Nick's were forever entwined.

'I understand better than you realise, Helga. So I will take your money – but not as much as half your wages. Seven shillings and sixpence; that's my final word. That covers your expenses. That's certainly as big a percentage of your wages as I put into the house from mine. And Helga, thank you. Not just for the money, but for knowing the difference between charity and friendship. And there's another way of seeing this, too. Because you come from Berlin, because when I was young I spent so much time there, had friends, some Jewish, some not, but all of them people who loved music, because having you here helps me hold all that closer, you can understand why I'm glad we're together. Holding on to yesterday seems to help light the way to tomorrow. Can you understand that?' Helga nodded. 'Cigarette?'

'Thank you, no. It is a habit I do not have, so what is the point in letting it form when there are those for whom tobacco is important?'

'That's more or less what Jethro says, except that he always adds the rider "anyway, they make a person stink".' Sally laughed, inhaling deeply. 'And you're right, both of you. It's crazy; cigarettes are like gold dust, yet I've never smoked as much in my life as I do at Drifford Park. We're in a constant haze of tobacco smoke. Don't they call it Sod's Law that whatever is hard to come by, everyone craves? Nothing by the second post, I suppose?' No, of course there wasn't or Helga would have said; but Sally had to ask, as if the question brought Nick closer.

When finally Nick's first letter arrived and Sally learned that he was in North Africa her main feeling was relief; the sea voyage was over, he was on dry land. And repeatedly she reminded herself of his assurance: he wasn't part of a regiment of heroes.

Throughout the following winter and spring the country was held in the grip of the threat of invasion. Along the south and east coasts concrete tank traps were built on the beaches; the nation awaited the sound of church bells, silent for so long, bells that would spread a warning as soon as news came of an enemy landing; each evening those too old, too young or engaged on essential war work would meet in their Home Guard centres; they would drill, clean their weapons, listen to lectures on hand-to-hand combat or what to do if they captured a parachutist and, above all, they would share a camaraderie seldom known in civilian life. Then in June came news that gave the country time to draw a second breath: Hitler had marched into Soviet Russia.

Zena was living Life with a capital 'L'. The Mayflower Theatre Company never stayed long in any one place: a day for travelling, a night in makeshift beds usually in the village hall where they would be playing or, alternatively, in the recreation room of some factory; the next day would be the performance with a good many hours setting up their props and sorting their costumes first and repacking their lorries after; another night on the same floor as the first, then on to repeat the whole thing somewhere else. Completely uninhibited, Zena was a natural performer. Add to that the advantages brought by her appearance and the audiences loved her. It was a heady experience to hear the applause. If she'd had any doubt as to the direction her acting would take, even in the first few months the feeling of communication between her and the audience would have decided her. She pitied her father; Sebastian Kilbride, idol of so many movie-goers, how could he have given up even a touring repertory company for an impersonal film set? She dreamed of a future when she was famous, mistress of the legitimate stage. Whether Jethro was part of that dream she didn't ask herself, but he was certainly sharing the road that led to it. Whenever they had a chance to be together they grasped it, but chances were rare and brief.

It was in a village in Bedfordshire that she found him waiting for her in the unlit street as, the scenery dismantled and packed in the touring company's lorries, her make-up off, she came out of the village hall staggering under the weight of a wicker basket of costumes.

'Zena,' he called in a stage whisper, 'I've got a forty-eight hours. I'm staying at the pub in the village. Let me carry that for you.'

'The back of the lorry's open. Just round here.' She passed it over. 'That's the last,' she said as she made a space for his load. Then he felt her arms around him, warm and welcoming. No wonder he forgot the discomfort of his two-hour rail journey, standing packed in the corridor hazy with cigarette smoke. He'd never outgrown his abhorrence of smoking and couldn't understand how, despite hearing the constant complaint that cigarettes were scarce, that same haze hung in the air of every cinema, every restaurant, every public place. The atmosphere and the rocking motion of the train had sickened him. But now it was all forgotten, the night air was pure, Zena was in his arms.

'We're moving on in the morning. That's the last of the packing up. They're getting the beds unrolled on the floor in there. It's ten o'clock already.' The sentences hung between them, each one emphasising the urgency. 'Just twelve hours, that's all we have before I'll be gone.' His pulses quickened. Twelve hours ... what was she saying? By now they could only vaguely see each other, but even in pitch darkness they would have understood each other's thoughts.

'You mean ...? Yes, oh yes, twelve whole hours. I've got a room at the pub.'

'I'll tell Sarah Hewison – she's the boss lady – I'll tell her a friend from home is here.' Then with as near a nervous giggle as Zena was capable, 'She'll think you're a girl, so you'd better keep well out of sight. I don't think she knows there are two sexes in the world. Wait for me here, don't move away.' He didn't move away. He'd wait for her until the end of time. Or so he believed.

It was all so easy. Sarah Hewison's permission was given with a hearty, 'An old friend? Not seen her since school, I suppose. Enjoy yourself. Don't sit up half the night chattering; we have a busy day tomorrow. Back here at half-past nine, not a second later.' Then, Zena forgotten, 'Mildred, don't cut the bread too thick for that toast. That's the only loaf we have.' For the

76

Mayflower Theatre Company, stage drama and that of life were interwoven. They prepared their own meals, all of it either under a grill or in a frying pan. But food was no more than a necessity of living, especially for Sarah Hewison and her equally forthright co-producer, Mildred Chown. They were probably twice the age of most of the players, not a trace of femininity about either of them, although their kindness never faltered. Naive as most of the girls were, none of them – not even Zena – probed beneath the surface of their relationship. They simply accepted them at face-value; 'funny old dears' was one of the terms reserved for them, but said with unquestioning affection.

Once away from the village hall, Zena and Jethro stopped walking and turned to each other.

'A whole night.' She didn't attempt to hide the excitement in her voice. 'No Nick to suddenly arrive, no one to interrupt us this time.' With her face rubbing against the rough cloth of his private soldier's uniform she sniffed. 'Smells funny. I like it.'

'Disinfectant of some kind, I imagine. We live pretty rough, you know.' What pride in his voice: he was a man in a man's world. If they'd been at home he would have been conscious of his eighteen years; here, age meant nothing. He was a man; she was his woman. 'Tonight, Zena – I booked a double room.'

'Took me for granted, did you?' she teased.

'Never. I just hoped, oh God, how I hoped. Listen,' he felt in his pocket and brought something out, but she couldn't see what it was, 'they may be funny at the pub. I want you to wear this. I've carried it in my pocket each time we've met, each time I've hoped, but there's never been a chance – either I've had to be back at base or you've been moving on. Let me put it on.' She felt her left hand taken in his and a ring slipped on to her third finger.

'What is it?' Was he giving her an engagement ring? But when he did that she wanted to choose it.

'We ought to make vows,' he told her. 'It's just a plain gold band. I got it at Woolworths; it's only rolled gold. But I told the man at the pub that I was going to meet a train, hoping my wife had managed to get away.'

She giggled. 'Bet he didn't believe you!' And, if he didn't, that only added to the thrill of what they were going to do.

'You are sure? *I* am. You're the only girl I could ever love, you know that. But once we've – we've – well, you know what it'll

77

mean to you. Everyone says a girl must be a virgin when she marries, but Zena, with this war it might be ages before we can think of that.'

Marriage! War or no war, she wasn't going to rush into marriage. She was sure she loved Jethro; it wasn't that that put her off the idea of marriage; but look at her parents, look at Sally and Nick, their lives were so dead boring – or had been until the war had put a stop to what must have been so monotonously dull. No, that wasn't for *her*. First she was going to make a name for herself. She could almost see the headlines in the paper: Beautiful *Zena* – Zena what? She would have to think of a good name – *marries her lifelong love*. Really, Jethro was very handsome; they'd make a splendid couple. But not yet, not for ages.

'Zena?' he prompted when she didn't answer.

'Marriage? But we belong, Jethro, we don't need some silly vicar to tell us it's all right for us to – to be in bed together. Just think, all night. Don't chatter half the night, that's what Miss Hewison said.' Again she laughed, holding him closer and easing his hand from her waist to her breast, hinting at what was so nearly theirs.

As they neared the pub he was suddenly thankful they'd waited – or more accurately been thwarted – previously. He saw the boy he'd been then as just a callow youth practising with what he'd stolen from his father's drawer, frightened he'd fail in what he was going to do. He was still as inexperienced, but since then he'd had many months in the Army; listening and watching, he'd learned a lot from the men in his hut; he was ready to prove himself. With the confidence of a seasoned Casanova he had gone to the chemist and bought his own supplies.

When Jethro and Zena came into the bar of the Cherry Tree Inn and asked the landlord for his key, they felt every eye must be on them. Impossible that Zena could have walked through a room full of men and passed unnoticed, but on that evening the customers had other things on their minds as they sipped their beer, trying to make it last because they'd been warned the barrel was bordering on empty and then the 'Closed' sign would have to go on the door until the brewery was able to supply more. Other things on their minds even than the shortage of ale: they'd all listened to the nine o'clock news; the gallantry of the people of Leningrad as they held out against the invader brought home to them just how different things might have been.

'Like Nell was saying back at teatime,' one man said, swilling his beer around his tankard and drawing on an empty pipe, 'we ought to go down on our knees and thank whoever it is up there looking after us. Saturday night and here we are nice and peaceful, a lot of mates together – those poor sods.'

'Make no mistake, if they'd landed on our shores they'd have found what we're made of. Face to face with some bugger attacking your home, why you'd lose your inhibitions about the rights and wrongs of killing, damned if you wouldn't.'

'Glad you got away all right, Mrs Kennedy.' Passing the key across the bar to Jethro, the landlord gave the soldier's pretty young wife an appreciative look. 'How about a nightcap before you go up? Not got much to tempt a lady with, but there's a drop of port.'

'No, I don't think so. But thank you.' He found her manner and her smile just as beguiling as she intended. Then they went up the creaking stairs that led off from the bar.

'All right for some.' The landlord gave a wink at his customers. 'She's a cracker and no mistake.'

Upstairs Jethro unlocked the door of their room. 'Ought to carry you over the threshold. Put your arms around my neck.'

'You didn't tell them this was our honeymoon, silly. Only that your wife was coming.'

Inside the room, just for a moment after he'd closed and locked the door, they seemed lost for words. Of the two, she was the first to recover. They had one short night; she wasn't going to waste a moment of it. And if she led the way, Jethro soon caught up with her, his confidence soaring. Tonight she was Zena, the girl he'd loved since he'd wasted hours dreaming of her when he should have been doing his prep; but it would never be like that again. She would be *his*. With my body I thee worship, he said silently. What joined them tonight would be theirs for as long as they lived.

So the months went by, with Jethro and Zena meeting whenever he could get a 48-hour pass that would give him enough time to reach wherever she was playing.

History was written in the December of that year when the Japanese attacked Pearl Harbour, bombing American ships and

79

taking American lives, the act that finally brought the United States into the war. In February Singapore fell to the Japanese and by the end of May they were established in Burma. Back at home, when the wireless sets were turned on for news bulletins, even the most optimistic couldn't find a ray of light. And Sally, monitoring the reports put out by German stations, hearing the hope and confidence in the tone as each new conquest was reported, had an ever harder than usual battle to hide her inner misery. How long? When she'd asked it on that September night in 1939, she had hung on to trust that it would be over by the time Jethro was old enough to fight; and the idea that Nick might volunteer hadn't come into the picture.

By that summer of 1942 dogged determination had replaced optimism. But dogged determination is as grey as leaden skies; people were frightened to imagine a future of carefree peace and even more frightened to imagine anything else. Better to take each day, live it, work hard, wear monotony like an armour against disappointment. It was in June, a Saturday when Sally had left work at five o'clock and ridden straight to Mulberry Cottage. Helga waved a greeting but went on harvesting the early peas. But not Tessa. She put down the bowl she was filling and came to meet Sally.

'Any news?' she asked.

Sally shook her head. 'Still nothing.'

It was more than three weeks since she had heard from Nick and there was no way of hiding from the setbacks in North Africa. Rommel and his troops were advancing on British-held Tobruk. British-held? For how long? The question jumped into Sally's mind before she could stop it, followed immediately by superstition she told herself was insane. She must hang on to faith; she must never doubt. But how hard it was when hour after hour of each day she listened to the triumph in the voice of the German newsreader.

'Saturday's a bad day for post.' Tessa gave her hand a quick and affectionate squeeze. It wasn't the moment to mention that she'd heard this morning from Zena and, apparently, Jethro was managing a 48-hour pass to get up to Lincolnshire to see her. How proud she must be, up there on the stage (a makeshift stage, no doubt, she admitted) knowing that he was watching her. Such trust had Tessa in 'the children' that her images of their weekends were very different from the truth.

'Nothing from Nick, but I did get a note from Jethro,' Sally told her. 'Tess, does it worry you how he travels miles to spend a few hours with Zena? They've never had anyone but each other.'

'You mean in a romantic way?' Tessa was genuinely surprised. 'Rubbish, Sal, they're like brother and sister.'

'Then they're an odd couple. How many brothers can you think of who'd be prepared to chase across the country for an hour or two with his sister? They're not children.'

'I'd not considered they might be falling for each other. They've known each other so long, Sal. But wouldn't it be just perfect!' How pretty she was, her face freckled from the hours spent in the garden. 'Now you've put the thought in my mind, I shall look for signs of it all the time. I just hope you're right. When all this beastliness is over and Nick and Seb come home for good, wouldn't it round everything off just perfectly if they wanted to marry.' For a second she looked less sure. 'Zena has always been so single-minded about wanting to act. But still, so was Seb and look at *us*! Go and say hello to Helga while I make some tea. Unless you're starving we needn't eat until later; I'd like to get all the peas picked that are ready. Tomorrow I'm going to bottle them, not eat them now. They're for afterwards when the chaps are home. I'll give some to you to keep too.'

Hang on to faith, Sally heard the echo of Nick's voice. If only she could hang on to it like Tessa did. Was it easier for her, knowing where Sebastian was? How could it be when *his* war could never be fought at a safe distance: he was in the front line of that regiment of heroes.

'You get on with the picking, I'll make the tea and bring it outside. Even workers are allowed a tea-break.' Sally went indoors and lit the gas under the kettle, then, while she waited to hear it whistle, wandered into the sitting room.

She loved order. Fortunately, Helga had a methodical mind too, and her bedroom was never untidy; if she washed the dishes she always dried them and put them away; if she brought the washing in from the garden she always folded it. They lived very amicably together but, just as Sally had prophesied, it wasn't she who was made the girl's confidante. Most of Helga's free time she spent here at Mulberry Cottage, something that Sally could well understand. What was it about Tessa, dear, warm-hearted Tessa, that turned chaos into cosiness?

81

Sally took in the scene in the sitting room, cushions left with the impression of the last time Tessa sat there, a book left open, the front sheet of the newspaper on the settee and the rest unevenly half folded on the coffee table. Imagine this at home, she thought: just one cushion out of its rightful place and it would *shout* at me. I couldn't live like this; it would drive me insane. Yet here it is *right*. Look at Helga out there in the garden, have you ever seen her laughing and relaxed at home like she is here? But that was something Sally could understand, something she accepted with no jealousy. Like all the others, she too was drawn to Tessa like a moth to the flame.

On the German news bulletin to the German people, Sally heard that Tobruk had been taken by Rommel. Even allowing for the power of propaganda, surely there must be truth in it. The number of British prisoners was expected to be about thirty thousand, the words drummed in her ears. To take such an army of prisoners, then what of the numbers who must have been killed? Don't let yourself start to imagine. Wait, just wait until the BBC broadcast the truth, she told herself. But where was the truth, the complete and honest truth? Wasn't propaganda the belt and braces of morale? When the news finally came, announced in the expressionless perfect diction of 'the voice of the nation', there was nowhere to hide from it: losses were high and some twenty-five thousand men taken prisoner. What of those who'd been killed? She'd promised to hang on to faith; how easy to promise, to believe that in saying the words she would find the courage to live up to them. Not a front line soldier ... not one of the regiment of heroes ... think of the chaos there must be out there, she told herself; no wonder mail isn't coming through. When I hear there will be a backlog of letters. She had to believe, and although she pretended she succeeded, no one, not even Tessa, knew how far she came from succeeding.

A week or so later, coming away from Drifford House at four o'clock, she cycled on into town to her hairdresser. Always so well groomed and smart, if those last years had seen any change in Sally's appearance it was that she dressed with even greater care, never failing to paint her fingernails – and toenails too, even though they didn't show – in a shade that perfectly toned with whatever she was wearing. Her eyebrows were shaped, her clear complexion enhanced by make-up applied with the expertise of years. To look her best was her own personal banner. So that afternoon she gave herself up to being pampered. By the time the beautician finished with her, her dark hair shone like silk; her twenty minutes covered with a face pack had left her skin smooth and clear, ready for the creams and potions that followed. Then, her make-up complete, she cycled the three miles home, hoping that Helga would be there ahead of her and might even have got out the lawnmower and started to give the grass its weekly trim. Keeping her thoughts firmly on the tasks to be done, she refused to let that constant 'will a letter have come?' rise to the top of her mind.

Turning in at the gate, her first disappointment was that there was no grass-cutting going on, but even that thought didn't last. For the sight of Tessa was completely unexpected.

'Tess! Lovely surprise. You didn't ...' The words died. Sebastian! That was her first thought. She'd never seen Tessa look like this. When a face is so tanned, how was it she knew that Tessa's skin was pallid? Perhaps it had to do with the way her freckles stood out, across her nose, even on her cheeks. I've never noticed them on her cheeks before, Sally thought, surprised at herself yet clutching at anything rather than face what gave Tess that haunted look.

'Sal ... this came.' In Tessa's hand was the envelope that had been their ever-present, unspoken fear.

'Not Seb?'

'Helga took it in and phoned Drifford House, but you'd gone. Then she phoned me.'

Just for a second the two women looked at each other, holding nothing back. But, even from Tessa, Sally was quick to hide the terror that flooded over her, aching in her arms and legs, turning her mouth to sandpaper.

'I'll put my bike away,' she said, her tone giving nothing away. In the few seconds it took her to wheel her bike into the open shed, then carefully close the door, she fought and won her battle. Only the less than steady hand she held out for the telegram betrayed her outward calm.

'Missing,' she whispered, 'that's what they say. You read it, Tess. Missing. Lost: they don't know what's happened to him.'

'Oh, Sal.' Tessa's blue eyes swam with tears. 'Oh Sal, we've got to go on believing, trusting. If we don't, it's like failing him.'

'Yes, of course,' Sally answered. She was never an emotional woman, yet the coolness in her tone scared Tessa.

'It'll be all right, Sal. Missing means there's hope. We've got to hang on to *that*. We've got to.'

And again that same cool, 'Yes, of course. Where's Helga? I thought she might be cutting the lawn.' Words, just words. Sally didn't even wait for a reply. 'Come in, let's see if we can find something to drink. Or are you expecting Sebastian to ring you?' Yes, he'll be phoning her. Every evening she listens for his call. In Sally's mind was the image of her own telephone; she almost heard the bell, she almost heard Nick's voice ... almost ... as the image came, so she fought it down. 'You can spare just five minutes,' she heard her voice as pleading. Hang on to hope, hang on to faith. Leading the way indoors, there was nothing welcoming about the familiar atmosphere of the house, only a chill of emptiness.

'Nothing much here,' she said, opening the drinks cabinet. 'An inch of gin, no tonic water, oh here's some sherry. That'll have to do. Where's Helga? Is that all right for you?'

Tessa looked at her helplessly. If only she'd cry, or at least show some sort of emotion, even anger.

'Can you take tomorrow off? Come over to me for the day. You mustn't go in to work; they'll understand. Let me telephone.'

'Of course I shall go to work.' Work was sanity.

That was at the end of June. In the weeks and months that followed she hid behind a protective wall of ice, one that Tessa, who had been so close to her, couldn't even begin to melt. Sebastian's sensitive understanding came frighteningly close to penetrating it. With him she felt vulnerable. She knew it was cowardice that made her unable to accept grief, and she knew too that as long as she refused to grieve, healing couldn't even begin. But it was easier not to let herself think at all, to live each day as it came, to concentrate on working long hours, to beat the battle of the weeds, to wear a smile on her face even though her eyes seldom got the message, and not to let herself watch for the postman. It surprised her how well she managed to play the role she made for herself. When Jethro came home on compassionate leave, when he forgot he was a man and a soldier, and she saw his face crumple as he cried, she comforted him as she might have done when he was a child, saying the right things while her heart was too numb to let her do more than act out her part.

Orderly and fastidious, she clung to routine. On her days off she no longer resented dusting dust-free surfaces, indeed she went through the motions hardly knowing what she did. It was as if her life was firmly stuck in the mindless monotony of routine. Then came a damp Saturday morning in late October when her days off coincided with the weekend. As she and Helga ate their weekly rasher of bacon and one egg she made sure her face wore a look of appreciation. There was nothing in the grey day to hint that the wheels of her world were about to be pulled out of that rut which she'd built for protection.

Chapter Five

'What is it? Sally, what is wrong?' Helga had never questioned Sally's reserve; it was something she could understand. But not this! Of its own volition her mind flew to Jethro. Being stationed with his ack-ack battery on the Kent coast was no guarantee of safety. 'Is it Jethro?' No! Not Jethro! Please not Jethro! Hardly aware of what she did she dropped to her knees by the side of the chair where Sally sat, rocking backwards and forwards, her face contorted, silent tears rolling unheeded down her cheeks. 'What's happened to him?'

Sally shook her head. Holding her jaw stiff, she tried to speak.

'Nick ... from Nick. He was taken prisoner.' Silence once broken, her crying became loud, the noise so out of character that Helga felt frightened and inadequate. 'So thankful – ashamed – I tried to believe – but I couldn't – I knew I was failing him – frightened to hope – but he's safe. Helga, he's safe!'

She felt Helga's strong, thin arms holding her and she, always so determined to keep her independence and control her emotions, willingly leaned her face against the girl's shoulder.

'Yes, he's safe. Now he's away from the fighting, Sally. He'll hate being a prisoner, but he'll be safe and, one day, he'll come home.'

'Don't know what to say. So thankful, so grateful.' Sally pulled away to sit upright. 'I'm behaving dreadfully,' she snorted. 'Just feel like an elastic band that's been stretched and stretched until it snaps. Can't stop crying.' She made an effort; in Helga's understanding she saw behind the façade of polite control the girl always showed the world. 'Don't have to explain to you, you must know. But you've never make an exhibition of yourself like I am. Ashamed.'

87

'Oh, I've cried, Sally. I remember how I used to hide under my bedcovers and cry. I've cried, I've prayed.'

'Don't think I'm any good at praying. He told me to keep faith – and I didn't. I tried to, but I thought he was dead. Nick dead. Couldn't say it – not then. Now I can say it because it's not true.' Through the confusion of her own thankfulness she looked at Helga and was aware as never before how the child who'd arrived on her doorstep in the last days before the war had become a woman. In years she was barely eighteen, but carefree youth had passed her by. 'One day it'll all end, Helga; one day they'll all come home: your parents, Nick, all those who can't see beyond high wire fencing.' More than anything helping her regain control was something she'd never been as aware of as she was at that moment: the loneliness and fear that must have been Helga's companions as she'd watched and waited for letters that never came. Although she had no sure knowledge of the treatment of those of Jewish faith once war had come, Helga had experienced enough before Eliot had brought her to England to have no doubt that her parents would have been interned and no doubt, either, that their treatment would be far worse than that meted out to an officer in the British Army.

For Helga's sake as much as her own, Sally made a great effort at control, to find some shred of comfort they could share. 'Perhaps for them life will be like it is for the Italians we see going off in their trucks from the camp to work on the fields. Perhaps they get taken out each day to work somewhere. That's what we have to believe. We have to have tunnel vision, look just to getting the war over and sanity back again.'

Helga took her hand and held it to her lips. Both of them so alike in their need to keep a grip on their emotions, they were conscious that this was a special moment, one that even though they might never refer to it yet would mark a change in their relationship.

'I wish we could get a message to Jethro,' Helga said. 'It hit him so hard, didn't it.' Sally was aware of the concern in her worried expression, but with so much else on her mind it hardly registered. Anyway, it was gone so quickly as Helga looked round as if to clutch at a new avenue for their thoughts. 'Have we enough coffee for me to make another pot?'

'Yes, I managed to buy a pound of beans yesterday. You put the kettle on, I'll start grinding some.' Action set them back on course; it drew a line under thankfulness and unbearable anxiety alike. Even Sally, who had found faith so elusive, felt a new drive. That Saturday they both cycled to Mulberry Cottage to take the news. From the feeling of elation in the house, they might almost have been celebrating the end of the war.

But of course they weren't, even though on that dull day in the autumn of 1942 they caught a glimpse of light from the end of the long, dark tunnel.

'Sal, do you know what we did four years ago today?' Tessa asked the question as they filled their baskets with yet another year's crop of garden peas. It was a July afternoon in 1943; Sally was spending a day of her midweek 'weekend' at Mulberry Cottage.

'Don't tell me . . . yes, of course I know. The Limit. I remember feeling a martyr that I was foregoing my usual holiday. But Tess, I'm so glad I did. Was it really as magic as we remember, do you suppose? Or was it because it saw the curtain come down on all we'd so willingly taken for granted that it stands out like a ray of unending sunshine?'

'Both, I suspect. Seb says why don't we go down for your fortnight off, you and Helga and me. But I can't do that. If you and Helga want the key you can go – Nick is safe, even though he can't be there with you. And thank God now Seb is instructing. But I'm not going, not until he's home for good and we can all go. That's what I said at the beginning and to break my word would be like tempting Fate.' It was a rare thing for her to come so close to admitting the constant anxiety she'd lived with. 'It's funny, isn't it, Seb hasn't suggested he and I should ever go down when he's home on leave. Not that I would; like I said, I'm waiting till we're all together. We've neither of us ever said as much to each other, but he must feel the same.' There was a smile in her voice, so sure that if there was no logic in her superstition, at least it was shared by him. 'It has to be the four of us. Do you think we're barmy?'

'No. Anyway, if Helga and I went it would spoil all the memories. We'll hang on, Tess. Perhaps by next year we'll all go.'

But by the next year nothing had changed. At least it hadn't changed for those left at home. Rations were a little shorter, make-do-and-mend an ever more accepted part of life, dig-for-victory evident in most back gardens; but there was little in the daily lives of those who waited in the wings to boost morale. In June, when the Allied forces landed in France, Britain was gripped by a great wave of hope. But the fighting was intense, every inch of the way a hard-fought fight. Did the Second Front brighten the light that flickered at the end of the tunnel? Perhaps it would have for Sally, except for one thing, one soul-searing thing: Jethro was part of that fighting force in France. Now there was the daily hope that Ethel Biggs, the post lady, would bring a letter franked 'Field Post Office' and the daily fear that the telegraph boy would cycle up the drive carrying the dreaded buff envelope. No hope now of cheery phone calls telling his mother that he was fine and that she didn't mind, did she, but when he got his next forty-eight hours he wanted to see Zena instead of coming home. Even those phone calls had become part of the routine, something to be accepted. There was no doubt that Jethro was in love and who better than with Zena? Yet, deep in Sally's heart, and for no reason that she could name, was a feeling of disquiet. Did Zena honestly feel the same for him, or would he play second fiddle to the ambition that drove her? Now that he was overseas, would she be content to wait for him? With looks like hers she couldn't walk down the road without heads turning; did she care for him enough not to be swayed by flattery?

One thing remained unchanged. Mulberry Cottage was still the magnet that drew Sally just as it did Helga. That's where Sally was on a bright September Thursday, the first of her two weekly days off. This time it was the runner bean crop that was being brought in, beans so fine they must surely have been fit for the local horticultural show had it not been 'put on ice' for the duration. Sometimes they chattered, sometimes they picked in companionable silence.

'You've turned into quite a gardener, Tess,' Sally said as she reached for a twelve-inch beauty high up the plant. 'In some ways these five years have been good for us, haven't they. We've found a resilience – not just us, all the wives left at home – a resilience we didn't know we had. Remember the things we used to leave for the men to do – mending fuses, putting a new plug on the iron, checking the car tyres and filling the tank,' then, laughing, 'what a lot of namby-pambies we must have been.'

Tessa looked at her with admiration, but didn't answer. She found no satisfaction in doing what she'd looked on as the men's jobs. Not that she wasn't every bit as capable as the next woman, but she didn't share Sally's sense of achievement. Instead, in taking care of things she would have left to Seb, it seemed to her as if she was trying to take his place, managing without him. Admitting, even to herself, a sentiment that Sally indeed would have seen as 'namby-pamby' shamed her. What sort of a woman was she that with Seb away she wasn't living at all, she was just existing? Was it like that for other women, for Sally? No, Sally did things with her life. Her work at Drifford Park broadened her horizons; world affairs, current news, progress of the war, not just where it involved forces from her own country but in every field of action, all these things interested her and widened her knowledge; often on her day off she would take the train to London, meet her father and sometimes his acquaintances from the world of music, an environment she'd grown up in; they'd go to a concert or he'd take her out for a meal; she went regularly to the beautician, cared about how she dressed, simply because that was the sort of person she was. Compare all that with *me*, Tessa silently criticised herself. I could have kept in touch with people in the film-making world, old friends from the rep. company even; perhaps that's what I ought to have done. After all that's Seb's world; he might have liked to think I kept in touch with them all while he was away. But what do I do? Just look at me, I'm scruffy as anything. When I use any clothing coupons it's so that I have something pretty to wear when Seb can get time at home; all I do in the garden is for him, for when he has leave and for after this beastly war is over. Perhaps when that happens, once the excitement of being out of the Air Force fades, he'll find me a bore. Because that's what I am. I can't talk about anything clever. I'm nothing – I'm just *me*.

'Hark, I hear a car,' Sally broke into her reverie. 'Who would come calling?'

'With a car? No one. It's a taxi, Sal.' Her eyes were bright with hope. And when she saw who the visitor was, even though her immediate hope had been that Sebastian might emerge from the taxi, still her face broke into a wide smile of welcome. 'It's Zena!'

The driver was paid and amidst a clamour of excitement the baskets of beans were left and they all went into the house.

'I've left the Mayflower, Mum. It was good experience,' then, with a laugh, 'but stay too long and I might end up like Sarah Hewison and Mildred Chown.'

'Miss Hewison seemed very caring when I spoke to her on the telephone,' Tessa said in her defence.

'Funny old biddies, honestly. Perhaps that's what happens if you live too long in an all-female world. They shared everything – even a bedroom. Made my skin creep.'

'I don't see why it should. You shared a dormitory with enough girls and you never felt there was anything unwholesome about it. They were a lot older than you others; naturally they clung to each other.'

'Anyway, I'm out of it now. I went to the Clifton Players for an audition and, Mum, when I applied I lied about my name. I told them I was Zena Rhodes – a nice ring to it, don't you think? I didn't want to be taken on because of Dad. They seemed dead keen to take me, so after I'd signed along the dotted line I told them my real name. I had to because of my identity card and ration book. But I shall be called Rhodes on the programme. They seemed to think more of me because I'm determined to get there just on my own ability.'

'And so they should,' Sally said.

'I wrote to Jethro while I was on the train to tell him about it. We have a whole season playing in just one town. Be like it used to be ages ago when Dad was in rep., Mum. Remember how we lived in those tacky boarding houses? That won't be for long, though. The Mayflower was the first rung on the ladder, this is the second. Just watch me. I'll be climbing up faster than you can catch me.' How lovely she was, her dark-blue eyes shining with excitement, her discreet make-up enhancing the gifts nature had bestowed.

Tessa had been making tea while she listened; now she took a tin from the cupboard and brought out a cake she had made from a fat-free recipe she'd cut out of the newspaper – in the hope that Seb might manage a few hours at home.

'Listen, you two,' Zena went on, 'There was something else I told Jethro in my letter. I said yes. He wanted us to get engaged when he was on leave before he went overseas, but I wanted to get on that next rung first. Don't know why really, because we knew we couldn't have a wedding while he was abroad, and anyway we wanted to wait till after the war so that Nick's here too.' Then with a look that was neither teasing nor defiant and yet a combination of both, 'It's only a bit of paper anyway, we're as good as married already. You must have guessed that, otherwise why would he have spent so much of his time off with me. Anyway, whether you guessed or not, now you can stop wondering. You know what I mean: we've been sleeping together. For ages – for two years, whenever we could. I know what you think, Mum, but what we've been doing was *right*. I don't regret a single second of it.'

The actress in her was ready for a scene, as ready as any Juliet to proclaim her undying love for Romeo. Falling silent, Zena watched the glance that passed between Sally and Tessa but couldn't interpret it. 'Like brother and sister' Tessa had thought of them. 'No brother and sister chase across the country to spend a few hours together' had been Sally's opinion.

Tessa, married to Sebastian for more than twenty years, surrounded by love, taking 'the children's' chastity as much for granted as she did her own fidelity, might have been stuck in a time warp. Not so Sally. People displaced from the security of their familiar surroundings snatched at happiness where they could. Was that what had happened with Jethro and Zena? For three years he'd lived amongst men, single men looking for enjoyment, married men separated from their wives; and Zena who'd gone from a girls' boarding school to the Mayflower Company: girls, probably all of them virgins and, as mentors, a couple of lesbians.

'It's easier for you,' Tessa told Sally, 'it can't be the same for a boy's mother as a girl's. I know what we wanted more than anything was that one day they'd want to get married – but I wish they'd waited. Damn this war.' If only Seb were here. Their little girl, and for two years she'd been going to bed with Jethro. Tessa was out of her depth. Of course she had to agree to the engagement; of course it was what she'd wanted more than anything – but not like this.

'It's not for us to plan their lives, Tess,' Sally said. 'You mustn't say yes, Zena, unless you are absolutely certain. Marriage is a much bigger commitment than meeting for occasional days and nights of freedom. With him abroad everything is on hold anyway.'

'It's because he's abroad it's so important. I couldn't bear it if I told him I didn't want even an engagement until afterwards, and then –' The unfinished sentence hung in the air. The agony of her expression ought to have set Sally's mind at rest, but it did the reverse. Drama had always been meat and drink to Zena. 'That's why I came home, to tell you how things stand between Jethro and me. My trunk has already gone on to Reading and it's all fixed that I stay in the same boarding house as three other members of the cast. I'll be there for the rest of their season, then we move on to Folkestone. Isn't it a pity Jethro's gone to France; it would have been so convenient for us, both down there on that corner of the coast.'

'Of course you'll say yes to him, darling,' Tessa told her daughter, 'From what you've told us you've already made your minds up.'

Sally looked at her friend with a mixture of affection and exasperation. Always loved and protected, Tessa knew nothing of any other code of living.

That day the arrangement had been that when Helga saw the last child collected from the crèche she would cycle straight to Mulberry Cottage. Sally wished the girl would make friends, that sometimes in the evening after work she would say that instead of coming home or going to Tessa she'd arranged to go to the cinema with another girl – or young man. But it didn't happen. What was it that set her apart from her workmates? Her English was perfect – more perfect than theirs, and with none of the local dialect shared by the others. Did her name make her German roots obvious. Did they treat her with suspicion? Or was it her never-failing correctness that put a barrier between them? Whatever the reason, in the three years she'd worked at the crèche she'd remained an outsider. How much did she mind? It wasn't something Sally could ask.

When Helga arrived, only for a fleeting second did her face show a sign of emotion as she saw Zena.

'I didn't know you were expected. I would not have come. Having you home makes it a special time for your mother.'

'She's been having her special time all day; of course you should have come,' Zena answered. 'We've been waiting till you got here before we popped the cork. We're opening a bottle from Dad's hoard of champagne – saved from before the war to be drunk when it's all over. But today we have something special to celebrate.'

'Yes?' It couldn't be that Nick was coming home. But Jethro, perhaps he was being sent back from France. Helga couldn't let herself look directly at any of them, fearful that hope was emblazoned on her expression for all to see.

'Jethro,' Zena said the name slowly, just the one word, watching Helga closely.

So it must be true! It was about Jethro! Champagne must mean he was coming home. 'But when's he coming?' The question was spontaneous; a little logical thought and Helga would have seen the impossibility.

'He and I are engaged to be married.' The centre of attention, Zena flung her arms wide as if to embrace the world and all in it. 'Aren't you going to wish me happiness, all that sort of thing?'

'Of course I do, Zena. I wish you and Jethro lives that know no sadness.'

'That's jolly kind.' Zena liked the expression, lives that know no sadness. 'You must get his address from Sally and write to congratulate him.'

And that evening that's exactly what Helga did. 'I wish for you every joy that life can give,' she wrote. 'Zena looked so happy to have given you her promise, and it is not necessary for me to tell you that she also looked beautiful. I do sincerely trust that you will soon be home in your own country, living in the peace you deserve.' Soon, did she say? That would be when the war was over, when people tried to pick up the pieces of what was left. Owls' Roost had been her home ever since she left school, but she must never let herself forget that she had no real place there.

With no finger of light allowed to escape the heavy blackout curtains, Sally returned to the dark house late one November evening surprised to hear the sound of men's voices in the drawing room. More than one voice – but it was her father's she recognised.

'Dad!' Interrupting what sounded like animated conversation she burst into the room. 'Lovely surprise. And –' Whoever the stranger was, clearly the welcome she gave her father was extended to include him.

'Look hard, Sally. Don't you recognise him? But why should you, you were just a child.'

'Simon Szpiegman,' she spoke softly, her hand extended to the middle-aged man who more than thirty years ago had been the first to tug at her childish heartstrings, her hero-worship of him indelibly printed on her memory. A slim youth and tall too, or so she'd thought from her mere ten-year-old stance, so she was surprised to find that he was of no more than average height. She remembered his curly dark hair, a face with strong bone structure, even though she saw him as having the soul of a poet. Now his hair was prematurely grey, not white but iron grey, still as strong and curly. He was a successful man, a violinist of international repute in those years before the war, yet there was something about his face that gave the illusion of hunger? More than any of that, though, it was his eyes that surprised her; from her seat in the auditorium she'd not been close enough then to know whether they had been as bright, as alive, as they were now. That was the immediate impression that jumbled with the memory of the childishly romantic dreams she'd woven around the young fiddler who was being given such acclaim. Vividly she recalled the wonder of her secret adulation, feelings as removed from the woman she'd become by that winter of 1944 as her unexpected visitor was from the prodigy who'd acknowledged the thunderous applause with a combination of dignity and humility. She'd lost her heart as she'd watched and listened, and his manner of accepting the rowdy appreciation from the audience had given her a sense of almost personal pride. Yet for all the changes wrought by the years, she spoke his name with certainty. 'I heard you play in Warsaw, just before the First War.'

'I remember the recital. It was the first time I met my friend Eliot. But I believe I did not meet you.' Although he appeared not to have to hunt for the words he wanted to use, yet he spoke with a pronounced accent. 'I have come uninvited to your home Mrs – Mrs? Your father did not tell me the name of your husband.'

'My name is Sally Kennedy. Just Sally. Uninvited visitors are my favourite. Isn't that so, Helga?' Sharing their memory, she turned with a smile to the girl who, this evening, seemed to have blossomed.

'As Simon says,' Eliot still had his arm around his daughter, 'we have arrived unannounced. I even found the right stone that hid the door key.'

Sally had worked a long day; the ride home had been along dark roads where the feeble light from her bicycle lamp had scarcely penetrated the fog that filled her lungs and dampened her spirits. Yet now all that was forgotten. The fire was burning brightly, yet she threw another log on it. Piling fuel on the fire, she wanted the evening to last. And so it did, lasting until well beyond midnight. Eliot and Simon made music, at first playing with all the seriousness of professionals. But as the evening went on, a mood of gaiety took hold of them. Not everything they played was familiar to her, but between them was an ease that told her they often found pleasure together in this way. All four of them threw themselves into it heart and soul. This was a new Helga, uninhibited and happy as, in her native tongue, she sang folk songs of her childhood in a rich and perfectly in-tune contralto. They were golden hours, like an oasis in the desert of the dingy world that had become so normal they were hardly aware of the daily drabness.

By midnight they were all hungry and Helga, enjoying herself more than she had for years, went to 'dig for some food'. She produced toasted sandwiches made with no more than a scraping of margarine covered liberally with Marmite and the remains of the cheese ration grated to make it go further. In their present mood anything would have tasted good, and Helga watched with satisfaction as her pile of sandwiches disappeared, helped along by wine Eliot had bribed his local publican to let him buy. Sally knew these were golden hours that would be as firmly embossed on her mind as that Warsaw recital of her childhood.

As they ate she drew Simon to talk of his family.

'For myself, it is often necessary to be in London,' he told her, 'and Estelle refuses to leave.'

'But you can understand that. If it were the other way round, if *she* needed to be there, you wouldn't find somewhere safer for yourself.'

'Ah, but that is different. She is not in good health: she should live where life is slower, in pure air, away from the soot and what is called smog of a great city. She should not be where there is constant threat of terror. Terror for all of us – but how much greater for one who lives in a world so dimmed.'

'Dimmed? She stays even though she finds it dull?'

'I mean nothing could be done to save her fading sight. It is in her family, her mother, her grandfather. In her case initial progress was slow, but we knew the prognosis even when we married. It was the reason she ended her dancing career while she was at the height of her success. I try to persuade her to move to a place of safety, but she makes excuses that she finds her way with more confidence in surroundings that are familiar; I have no doubt that is true. Through all the air raids, then the flying bombs, she has remained firm.' He smiled at the image in his mind. 'I believe she accepts it as a personal triumph that we have never so much as lost our windows. Perhaps she is one of those fortunate ones who have a private faith. But now there are the rockets with destruction that is tenfold to that of the flying bombs. There is something – something ghoulish in a weapon of evil destruction that descends unmanned to take human life. I have begged her to let me find a safe haven for her, I have told her we have a responsibility to Gizella, our daughter, but she says our duty is to trust. To take the child away from her teacher would mar her future.'

'But there are plenty of good schools in the country. More than in London these days, I expect.'

'Estelle's one dream is that Gizella too will be a great dancer, I believe that in her mind she sees the child's career and her own as one. Gizella's sight is perfect; it seems she has escaped that rogue gene. It is not possible to find a trainer of the same standing in the provinces. She is nearly thirteen now, and I understand great things are expected of her. Ballet is not of my understanding; I merely listen to Estelle. It is her world not mine. If when you lived with your father you were a follower of ballet you may recall her name – Estelle Komanski. But all that came to an end before we married. I suspect that you, like me, know more of music than of the way to dance, yes?'

She laughed. 'My knowledge of any of it is a poor thing compared with yours – or with my father's.' Never had she been so aware of the difference between the routine of her days and theirs. How many years since she had talked to anyone whose life was steeped in music – excluding her father? They talked about the recital tour that had given Eliot and him the opportunity for this overnight visit, about the roots he was learning to put down in this country that was giving him shelter, about Drifford Park and Sally's escape to freedom from domestic imprisonment (not that she described it in that way, but she was uncomfortably aware that he followed her thoughts), about their friendship with the Kilbrides, about Nick and her feeling bordering on relief that he was a prisoner and safely out of the fight, about Jethro ... but here she hesitated, frightened to admit to her constant fear, even more frightened to discount it.

'It will all fall into place, Sally. Calm waters will close over the turbulence of these last years.'

'I remember Nick and I said something like that when war was new, before we'd all got dragged down by dogged routine. It seems like a lifetime ago. Like setting out to cross a stormy sea, we said, no sight of land ahead only the knowledge that if we rowed hard enough, long enough, one day we would reach the shore. And now?'

'Surely we have an occasional glimpse of that distant shore. When the sun rises over the horizon the waters will be calmed. We have to believe dawn is not far away.'

By that time Helga, with Eliot following, carrying the dirty plates, had said goodnight. From the kitchen came the sound of crockery; she, like Sally, never left anything until the morning. Their going hardly made a dent on the conversation of the two by the dying fire.

'You know your father is not giving concert performances as he did? You must not be alarmed when he gives his excuse as advancing years. It is what he would have us believe.'

'You think it's more than that, too, Simon? You see him more often than I do. I want the truth, please don't pretend. Is it that he fears there's something wrong with him?'

'I think he is what you English call "sound as a bell" and, as for his playing – well, you heard for yourself this evening. Have you ever heard Chopin's *Revolutionary* played as we did tonight?' His aquiline features broke into a smile. 'Chopin is my countryman, do not forget. Every pianist plays his music, but few are in tune with his soul. Eliot is one of those few.'

'But if his health is good, what other reason can he have? The concert platform has been his life. Dad isn't old.' In a world where so much had changed, she defied argument.

'I have a theory. I said to you just now that he is in tune with Chopin's soul; with Chopin's, with others too. Hear him play Delius, hear him play Beethoven, Bach, music from an age before the world was torn apart by the tragedy of today. Eliot has lived on the Continent for many years but, like you, deep in his soul he remains English. I do not understand – no, that is not the truth. I do not have the skill to put into words what I know he suffers as he brings alive the beauty of music created in countries he has known and loved. He is going to continue to give lunchtime recitals, selecting his programme, and I know my beloved Chopin will be high on his list. In London, and perhaps in provincial towns too, but I have no knowledge; those lunchtime recitals, given voluntarily, are oases of peace to hundreds of working people. But to sit at a keyboard, to allow himself to experience the joy of being backed by a great orchestra and fill the hall with sounds to give entertainment, sounds that were rooted in happier times in places he has loved, where now men – men on both sides of the fight – are tearing out the heart, that he finds is more than he can bear. I fear I have not found the words to help you understand.'

'Has he told you this? He's never hinted at it to me, he's simply said he is too old for the strain.'

Simon shook his head helplessly. 'His words to me too. But he had no need to tell me these things. I have made music with him for many years – until recently seldom on a platform, but simply for the joy of what we did. Now we sometimes play together in those lunchtime recitals. To me there is no need for him to explain; I can feel it with my spirit.'

'But you? How is it, if you understand and are in sympathy with –' she was at a loss to understand, 'yet you are happy to fill concert halls? And I know you do. I listened to you on the wireless the other evening; I heard the applause.'

'Can you not see, Sally, it is quite different for me. I am a Pole. Do you not remember those last days before my country was ground under the Nazi heel, do you not recall Warsaw's dying message to the nation, those few notes of our great Chopin? But of course you do not. You would hear only from your BBC.'

'Yes, Simon, I remember. I used to manage to get Warsaw on the wireless. I shall always remember: those few defiant bars – and the moment when there was nothing ... the silence.' Helplessly she shrugged. There were no words.

He nodded. 'You do not surprise me, Sally. I should have known. And so you must see why it is that I, a Pole, have to make music. It is *for* my country. I play their music, but I play also the music of composers from countries who are now our enemies. It is surely a reminder that war is but a transitory thing – music was there before it began, and will be there when it is over.'

'And Dad can't see it like that?'

'I'm sure he does. But as I explained so badly, he does not have to play as a man waving a banner for his country. He is an Englishman. The banner is there for all to see. If he had been younger perhaps he would join the fight like your husband Nick has, but he was not. So, unpaid, he will give recitals; he will travel sometimes with me and together we will play. Does that not tell you I am right in what I believe? When we make music together our message is as one.'

Years ago she had thought he had the face of a poet. Now, seeing his earnest expression as he tried to explain the inexplicable, a thought caught her off guard: that there is a narrow veil between genius and romanticism. As the thought hit her, so her guard was back in place. Her feet were firmly on the ground, where she meant to keep them – that was the way she lived. She wasn't prepared to follow the track their conversation was leading them.

But it seemed his own mind hadn't moved on – perhaps with feet not so firmly on the ground he couldn't so easily spring from one subject to the next.

'To know that I fled while I still had freedom, took the road to safety ... it is not an easy thing to live with. There are times, times in the dead of night, when I think of my people, of what sort of lives they must be enduring if they have life in them to endure. Your country has given me succour, even fêted me. *My* life and *theirs*, where is the justice? Is there some wise Deity – your God, my God, anyone's God in the jungle of beliefs men cling to, who ultimately metes out our just dessert? Is there, Sally? Is there anything except the hell men inflict on each other?'

'I'm probably the last one you should ask. I envy those who can cling to the dogma of their religion, any religion, and can feel certain. Are there such people? Surely for everyone there must be moments of hopelessness when you feel like a boat tossed by the tumultuous waves of that stormy sea. Not just wartime, but anytime.'

There was something peacefully companionable in the way he flicked open his cigarette case and offered it to her, took one himself, lit first hers and then his own. Without his being aware of it, their conversation had indeed moved on. They smoked in relaxed silence. They'd burned the last log, the fire little more than

101

a pile of hot ash. Soon they too must climb the stairs; this evening of music and soul-searching would pass into memory, have no more reality than the long-ago recital in Warsaw.

If the night hadn't distanced them from those magic hours, the atmosphere of morning certainly would. Sally and Helga were always up early, one or the other of them out of the house and cycling to work through the still dark, early morning hours of British summer time which had been extended through the months of winter. Helga's duties never varied beyond a few hours, but on that particular day Sally wasn't on duty at Drifford Park until teatime.

With Helga gone she turned on the wireless for the breakfast-time news. It was as the perfect diction of the voice of the BBC wished them good morning that male voices on the stairs prompted her to fill the coffee percolator and put it on the stove. Their greetings were overshadowed by the newsreader telling them that Strasbourg had fallen to the Allies, something that surely gave them a glimpse of that distant shore they strove to reach. Almost immediately, in the same precise tone, it spoke of yesterday's rockets.

The news over, Simon asked, 'May I use your telephone before we move on, Sally? I like to check each morning when I am away.'

'Help yourself. Not much for breakfast, I fear. Would you like porridge before your toast?'

'My roots have not grown deep enough to attach themselves to the British love of breakfast. Just coffee is what I am used to. I will make my call while it is percolating.'

Watching the toast, being careful to take Eliot's off the grill when by her standards it had no more than a slight tan, she could hear Simon talking quietly on the telephone.

'He ought to insist on moving Estelle to the country,' Eliot said. 'I've known her all their married life. She'd already given up dancing. But she can't let go. It's as if in Gizella she lives again. Not fair to the child; not fair to Simon either. But then, life hasn't been fair to her.' Then as Simon came back into the room, 'What sort of a night did they get? No fireworks?'

'Apparently not. They were waiting for the taxi to take them to Gizella's class.'

'Dancing or school work?' Sally asked, trying to sound interested but not too curious.

'Both. Where she attends each day, part of the time is given to essential learning.'

To question why he had said the taxi would be taking *them* would have crossed the border into curiosity. If Estelle's sight was so nearly lost that she clung to her familiar surroundings, why did she insist on accompanying a child of Gizella's age to school? As if right on cue, the back door opened and in burst Tessa, pink-cheeked from her ride in the cold air and even prettier than Eliot remembered.

'Oh, sorry! I didn't know you were here, Eliot. And you have a visitor. Sal, I'm sorry, I knew you weren't going to the Park until teatime, that's why I came.'

'Tessa, my dear,' Eliot stood up. 'What a refreshing sight you make on a cold morning. This is a friend of mine, Simon Szpiegman; we've been given beds.'

Her normal smile becoming even broader as she held out to hand to Simon, who, also on his feet, took it and bowed his head in a way she thought delightfully un-English.

'I didn't know Sally actually *knew* you,' she said. 'I've heard about you – you were the child prodigy in Warsaw, surely. I assumed that for her you'd remained forever young.'

He let that pass, turning the meaning slightly and tactfully, and knowing, even though he purposely didn't look at her, that Sally was embarrassed by her friend's gaffe. 'Eliot and I have been friends for many years,' he told her. 'To make music together is, for us both, a pleasure.'

'Fancy that! Not fancy that you enjoy playing together, I don't mean that. I mean fancy them knowing you all this time. Have you met Nick too? And Jethro? They never said.'

'Regretfully, no. But I am sure the day will come.'

'And jolly soon too, let's hope. Sal, may I pour myself some coffee? Thanks. Why I came in was to say Seb phoned: he's coming home tonight for seven days. Just think! Seven whole days! And just look at me! I wondered if you'd ring that place where they do your hair and ask them to fit me in. They're more likely to find a slot if you ask, and I thought I'd give my hair a treat – or a shock. And a manicure too, Sal, my hands are a disgrace.' Then to Eliot and Simon, she chattered happily on, 'Usually I kill two birds with one stone: wash my hair when I come in from gardening; that does my nails at the same time. But this morning I looked in the mirror and decided: Seb deserves better.'

'Sebastian is a lucky man, my dear. Beautified or not, you look enchanting.'

Unused to such compliments and always aware that she was hopelessly outshone by Sally, Tessa actually blushed. In truth, the colour in her cheeks changed no more than fractionally, just enough to heighten their admiration of such a pretty woman still with the unspoilt naturalness of the very young.

'You'll do that, Sal?' she tried to hide her confusion, feeling quite wrongly that her face and neck must look as hot as they felt.

'Right away. Excuse me, will you. If I call early they might be able to fit her in. And Tess, lovely news about Sebastian.'

The call bore fruit. Within five minutes Tessa was pedalling down the drive and on her way to town and the battle for un-characteristic glamour.

'A dear girl,' Eliot said.

'Tess is a darling. Nothing ever spoils her, nor Sebastian either. All the fame and celebrity he's had showered on him and the two of them are the most normal people I've ever known. Their daughter is engaged to Jethro, Simon, so we're more than friends, we're almost family.'

By mid-morning a taxi had collected Eliot and Simon, but they had said they might break their return journey in ten days' time. Sally half-hoped they would, but something warned her that nothing was ever the same the second time. In that she was right, for when on the return trip Eliot took the key from under the stone and let them into the house he read a note left prominently in the hall: *So sorry that I have had to work – staff illness. This is the car key, Dad, so drive to Tess, she is preparing a meal for all of us. Chicken, no less; gift of Driftwood Farm. Helga going straight there. See you at Mulberry Cottage. S.* To her it seemed perfectly normal and acceptable, it was all part of the more-than-sisterly relationship between Tessa and her.

Amidst the warm hospitality of Tessa's home, Eliot felt ever more drawn towards the pretty, scatterbrained woman; it never ceased to surprise him that two people as thoroughly opposed in character and approach to life as she and Sally could understand each other so well and be so deeply attached. As for Simon, he, like everyone else, fell straight under the spell of Tessa's lived-in and loved home, full of chaotic charm.

Of them all, the one on whom the evening made the most lasting impression was Helga. In Tessa's easygoing and yet caring way of housekeeping, Helga had found a well-fitting niche. Not that there was anything haphazard in her well-organised mind; her methods were much more in line with Sally's, but she had grown used to spending much of her free time at Mulberry Cottage where Tessa gave her complete freedom to do as much or as little as she pleased. Eliot held a very special place in her heart, not only because she had memories of him as a welcome visitor in her own home in Berlin but also because she had a sense of their belonging to each other; it had been he who had brought her to England, he who bridged her past to her future. Seeing him relaxed and content at Mulberry Cottage gave her the illusion that one day her past and her present would be *one*, her parents woven into the pattern of her days.

For Sally there was a vague, unspecified feeling of disappointment in the evening. They stayed so late that, by the time her bicycle and Helga's had been tied to the luggage grid and they had driven home, it was well beyond midnight and tomorrow she had to be at the Park for the early shift. So for her that was the end of the visit.

Next morning the visitors caught the train back to London, and routine closed over those who were left behind, seeming to blinker them, to give them the tunnel vision that let them see nothing beyond day-to-day acceptance. In the canteen at Drifford Park Sally often heard the young typists talking, recounting their previous evening's escapades, the fun they'd had at the Olympia Dance Hall, the new influx of American flyers at the base; for them life was full of hope and expectation. Not that Sally envied them their chase for life (with the capital 'L' so important to Zena), but what she heard emphasised the monotony of her existence, the emptiness of her home. Only at the monitoring station did she find any real purpose, there where the words coming to her over the ether gave her a hold on the shaping of events and an illusion that she was part of the ever-turning wheel of progress.

Another Christmas came and went. Sebastian managed to get leave, but he and Tessa didn't stay at Mulberry Cottage. Instead they took the train north to Zena's current venue, to take pride in her performance and to admire the emerald ring that Jethro had bought in an antique jeweller's in France and sent to her. Sally, Helga and Eliot spent the festival alone at Owls' Roost. Three of them in the house, just as often in the past there had been only three: Nick, Jethro and her. Many people were quite alone, Sally told herself, ashamed at the feeling of emptiness. Nick had been gone for more than five years, Jethro for three. So why was the void so much greater at Christmas? It took all her resolve to instil a feeling of festivity into the three days Eliot was with them – and it took all his, and Helga's, to match it. None of them was prepared to be the one to say what each of them felt: 'I shall be glad when it's over, when another year starts.' Surely before long there must be some hint of the dawn Simon had talked of; surely soon a thread of colour would lighten the sky. They made music together; they even forced themselves to sing a few carols, carols as familiar in Helga's country as their own, even to a girl not of Christian faith. Sometimes they sang in English, but when their words were German, it was for more than Helga's sake.

Coming home late one evening in January, the sound of the piano greeted her as she opened the front door. Immediately she knew who it was. Chopin's *Revolutionary Etude* ... the soul of Chopin ... the soul of Poland ... Simon's country.

She went straight to the drawing room, but Eliot didn't stop playing, he simply looked at her. It flashed through her mind that he had made age his reason for not accepting concert perform-ances; today, even though his playing was as brilliant as she'd known all her life, she was aware of his mortality. Without a word she walked across the room and stood behind him, her hands on his shoulders. When he reached the end she bent forward and moved her face against the side of his head. Something was wrong. Today when he'd found the key under the stone and let himself in it hadn't been with the certain expectation of giving her a pleasant surprise. Even before he spoke she knew he had come to her for help, for comfort and solace.

Chapter Six

'Blind. Defenceless. But nothing he said even dented her determination to stay in London. She refused to be driven away from her goal. But then, that was Estelle. And now *this*. It will knock the foundations from under him.'

'It was for Gizella she stayed.'

'So that the child would dance.' Never had Sally heard such bitterness in Eliot's voice. 'We must trust, she would say. We must not let ourselves be driven down by fear. I've heard it, she would say it with such defiance. I sometimes thought she was plagued by senseless guilt that they had fled their own country, taken refuge where their race and faith would be accepted. She felt that in escaping the evil that was already prevalent under the Nazi regime, they had betrayed the faith that meant so much to her. She'd travelled in many countries, as a dancer and later with Simon; she'd seen many cultures, but Estelle remained Orthodox.' His hands idly and soundlessly caressed the keyboard while his mind went on a journey of its own. When he spoke again he sounded weary, defeated. 'And all the time this was waiting for her.'

None of the houses in the short terrace had escaped, but it had been the Szpiegmans' which had had the direct hit. It couldn't be said it had been the target, for a rocket has no target other than random destruction. Despite the air-raid siren they'd been familiar with for so long, as the rocket tracked its way ever closer, Gizella had gone to pick the snowdrops she'd noticed at the bottom of their unkempt town garden. Providence must have saved her from her mother's fate, but she hadn't been unscathed; the blast had swept her off her feet and thrown her against the brick wall, flying rubble had hit her. In the house Estelle had been alone.

'Estelle didn't know the meaning of fear,' Eliot went on. 'Or, if she did, she knew even better how to hide it.'

'Poor Simon,' Sally whispered. 'He certainly knew fear for her. Do you think he had a premonition? He talked about the rockets: ghoulish tools of destruction, that's how he saw them.'

'Don't we all? A quiet life away from the raids, that's what he wanted for them. I suppose Estelle needed to live again in her child, have another chance. Now she's gone – and whatever Gizella does with her life after this, it certainly won't be as a dancer. I've spoken to people from the neighbourhood and thank God she was unconscious: she didn't see the pile of dust and rubble and know – think of it, Sally, under all that, helpless and blind.'

'Where was Simon? Is he there now for Gizella? When did it happen? How did you know?'

'Yesterday late in the afternoon. I was on my way to see them – I often did if I was anywhere near, especially if Simon was away. She associated me with happier times. I suspect that failing sight had been a great barrier to her learning the language; she'd never been able to move about freely, shop on her own, the things that familiarise a person with normal ways in strange places. So if I was in town and he was away I tried to spend some time with her. The house is gone beyond all recognition. The child was brought out with other victims. Thank God they found her in what used to be the bottom of the garden. But Estelle ...' Then pulling his thoughts back to her question. 'Simon, you say. He'd been playing in Edinburgh. By the time I'd managed to find out how Gizella was, it was late, beyond midnight. I telephoned the hotel where I knew he was staying. The hardest thing I've ever been called on to do, Sally. "Your house a direct hit, reduced to rubble, rubble and the earthly remains of your once so beautiful wife. Your daughter with her life intact but her leg a mess." '

'Poor Simon.' She spoke from her heart.

'Young enough to be my own son. Perhaps that's what drew me to him. I met him when he was just a boy – in Warsaw, you remember. But it was just after you'd married Nick; your going left such a void, I dare say that was how I came to be so fond of him when we met again just about that time.'

'Was he already married?' It wasn't so much that she was interested in the answer as that, for both of them, this evening was too charged with emotion for him to want to talk about his own loneliness after her marriage.

'No. Strangely, I was with him when he first saw her. We went to the ballet to see *Gizelle*. The impact was – was enormous – on him, on me, I dare say on everyone in the packed auditorium. She was magnificent. Not just her dancing, but her beauty. Quite exquisite. I remember watching her, mesmerised by her every movement. What thoughts were going on in his young head I can only guess. A week or two later he told me he had met her. No need to tell me that he'd lost his heart.'

'It's so unfair, Dad. Poor Simon – and Gizella . . .'

'Estelle was some years older than him, you know. Looks like hers endure, but she must have been more than ten years his senior. Falling in love is a natural part of youth, but I've never known anyone fall deeper than he did. Loved? Perhaps it's nearer the truth to say he idolised her. They'd only known each other a matter of weeks when he told me she had agreed to marry him, to give up her career and concentrate on his. She was honest, she never pretended anything less than the truth about her decision. A leading ballerina needs her sight and the specialists had confirmed her suspicions: she was suffering from the same disease as her mother, and before that her grandfather. To look at her there was no sign; her wonderful eyes were clear. But not for long. Then the deterioration was rapid. They'd been married about a year when Gizella was born. I believe from the moment she held that child she resolved to instil in her a love of dancing. She seemed to will the talent that had been hers to pass to her daughter.'

'And Simon? Ten years older than him, losing her sight – was he happy? Did he know when he married her?'

'Oh yes, he knew exactly. The first wild passion of youth may be a transient thing but for him there was the will to care for her, protect her. If he held her on a pedestal he was prepared to worship at its base. And, yes, I believe he was happy. No one ever knows what makes someone else's marriage a success; but theirs was a success, make no mistake. She was always at the forefront of his mind. You saw when he was here – his first thought in the morning had to be to phone her. Yes, with so much against them, yet I believe their marriage was good.'

'He's come back from Scotland now?'

'Ah yes, I was telling you. He promised to get the first train south. I made enquiries at the station and was there to meet him. What can you say to a man who's lost his wife, whose daughter is lying in hospital and whose home is a pile of rubble? No wonder he seemed dazed.'

'Did you go with him to the hospital, Dad?'

He shook his head. 'If that child had been *you*, I'd have wanted no one with *me*. If that child had been *you*, when you came round and heard what that poor girl has to hear, we'd have wanted no outsider with us. Is that not so?' Seated in front of the piano, he felt the pressure of her hands on his shoulders.

It was only then that she noticed the violin case on the settee.

'Simon's fiddle?'

'I took it from him for safe keeping. I don't know what his movements will be over the next days; at least I can look after his Stradivarius. He'll phone me here, tell me the news of Gizella. All right if I impose myself on you for a few days?'

'Silly, as if you have to ask.'

'In fact, I didn't ask.' Making an effort, he turned to her with something like his normal smile. 'I just came, like a rabbit to its hole. This place spells peace, safety, all the things we seem to have lost our grip on.'

Sensitive to other people's needs, Helga had stayed in her room to give them time together. Now she came into the drawing room.

'You've heard, Helga?'

Helga nodded. 'I have been thinking, trying to imagine. We did not know Mrs Szpiegman, but we can shut our eyes and try to be in the only world she knew. Mr Burridge says Gizella's leg is badly hurt; she will not be a dancer. On top of all she has already suffered, Mrs Szpiegman would have had that to bear as well. Was it not the one thing that drove her, the thing that made her stay where it was so unsafe? Suppose she had not been in the house when the rocket hit it, how could she have borne the knowledge that it was because she would not leave the city that Gizella was damaged? Do you not think that, for her at least, there was mercy in her so sudden end of life?'

Carefree youth, eagerness for excitement and the capital 'L' of Life; not for the first time Sally was aware how thoroughly these things had passed Helga by.

*

110

When, after four days there had been no word from Simon, Eliot phoned the hospital where Gizella had been taken. Hearing only his end of the conversation, Sally was puzzled.

'Sally, a piece of paper – anything I can write on – I have a pen ...' She heard the urgency in his request and, true to form, knew exactly where to find the notepad without wasting time hunting. Could Gizella have been transferred to another hospital?

'I'm most grateful to you for your help,' she heard Eliot say. 'One thing more, if you would be so kind. Tell Gizella I shall come to see her tomorrow. You made a note of my name so that she will know? Eliot Burridge, that's right. Thank you so much.' Then to Sally as he replaced the receiver, 'One more call, then I'll tell you what has developed.' Then barely audibly, 'Please God ... please God!' She watched as he dialled for the operator then gave the number he wanted. Remembering his almost paternal affection for his much younger friend, her conscience prompted her to move back into the drawing room, at least to let them talk in private. Then what she heard stopped her in her track. 'Can you put me through to the George Meredith Ward.' Dropping to sit on the bottom stair, she listened as Eliot enquired after Mr Simon Szpiegman whom, he understood, had been brought in on Wednesday morning, two days go. Having explained who he was, and persuaded whoever was on the other end of the line that Simon had no relatives in the country and he was probably his closest friend, he expected the way would be clear for a full report. Not so; it seemed he'd hit the buffers in the shape of a junior nurse who was obeying instructions, giving news only to next of kin. Sally tried to guess what was being said and, from Eliot's expression, guessed his irritation. 'On Monday his house was destroyed, his wife was killed, his daughter injured. Perhaps you'd be good enough to put my call through to someone with authority.' It was a rare thing indeed for him to sound so arrogant – something so alien to his character – and certainly the first time she had heard him use his name as a means to benefit his cause. 'Say that it is Eliot Burridge enquiring after Simon Szpiegman. If your superior has the slightest knowledge of the music world then he will appreciate my anxiety for my friend.' His voice was unnaturally tight, and Sally saw how the clenched fist of his free hand shook. Involuntarily she crossed the hall to his side, covering it with her own.

111

'Are they getting someone, Dad?' she whispered.

'Bureaucratic nonsense. Ah, I hear footsteps.' So she waited, watching his expression, unable to understand how it was that Simon was a patient when he'd not been at home when the house was hit, silently willing the news to be good – but how could it be good when his wife was dead, his daughter injured and his home gone?

At last Eliot replaced the receiver, having left the same message for Simon as he had for Gizella: tomorrow he would visit him.

'Is there any of that brandy in the bottle, Sally?'

She nodded. 'Was he suddenly taken ill?'

'It was first light the next morning. How he managed to get through to the building God knows; I suppose the poor devils who'd been working on the terrace had got out anyone still alive, probably gone somewhere more pressing. The dead must wait on the living. He was trying to shift rubble, trying to find her. Imagine knowing she was lying there under all that. Broken timbers, bricks, dust, concrete. An experienced team know what can safely be moved and what mustn't be disturbed; he didn't. God knows what happened, but he brought a hanging beam down on himself.' Eliot took a swig of fiery brandy, swallowed it and took another more slowly. 'He has undergone surgery. His shoulder and his upper arm are broken; perhaps more worryingly there is some sort of damage to his elbow. Thank God it didn't fall on his head.'

Unspoken between them lay what could be the enormity of the injury: a concert violinist needed two good arms, two strong arms.

'I shall get to London on the first train I can tomorrow. You know, Sally, I'd rushed here like a desert traveller to an oasis. I found myself longing for the peace of this place.' Then, seeming to brace himself and making sure his smile was back in place, 'But relaxation is out of the question, unimportant. There I was, deciding it was time I made a final decision and gave myself a chance to enjoy retirement. At my age that's natural and healthy. But that poor boy' (for hadn't he said earlier he was old enough to be Simon's father) 'is he to have retirement forced on him? Pray God it won't come to that. The waste … and, for him, the utter emptiness of his future.'

'He won't be playing for a while, Dad, but he's going to get well. We mustn't even let ourselves doubt.' If war does one thing, it breeds a superstitious refusal to contemplate the worst.

112

Next day she used her precious petrol allowance taking Eliot to town for the early train.

Just as it always did, like waters closing over a drowning man, the monotony of their unchanging lives closed over them, casting a blanket of acceptance over good days and bad alike. Amongst the young carers at the crèche, with the exception of Helga, who remained always on the edge of the easy companionship shared by the others, concern over an outbreak of measles had more reality than daily news bulletins. Not so at Drifford Park, where the cosmopolitan staff shared the present even though their roots were in distant lands, their memories hidden deep within them. The Russian team were the first to hear the news that Soviet troops had entered the Polish concentration camp at Auschwitz. Sally brought the news to Tessa even before it was told to the nation in the dulcet tones of the BBC.

'Three thousand, that's all there were there. And they were like skeletons with hardly the strength to stand. Open graves, rotting bodies. Tess, there must have been thousands killed, starved, deported – to what? God knows how they got rid of them.'

'Does Helga know? Oh, but these were Poles, weren't they. Perhaps it will have been different for those interned in Germany.'

Sally shook her head. 'Different perhaps, but not better. They belonged to the same race. Good people; we knew so many when I was with Dad. Jew, Protestant, Catholic, what is it that happens to people that blinds them to everything but the bigotry of supposing those of different creeds are wrong-thinking? If there is a creed – a creed in any faith – then surely goodness, justice, love, care for other people, aren't those things written into the rules?'

They looked at each other in silence, disgusted, angry, torn with pity and utterly impotent to change anything.

'Sal, there will be other camps, and the war hasn't done with any of us yet. But, at long last things are going our way, ours and Russia's. Every day we hear of the raids. It can't last long. That's not tempting Fate, that's just sound common sense. We must be coming within sight of the winning post. Think how it was in the beginning – no idea of how long they'd be away, frightened even to imagine in case Fate heard us and decided to get its own back. Now there's *no one* who doesn't realise the end can't be far away.

Seb is safe, Nick will soon be on his way home. Sal, we are so lucky.' Yet even now neither mentioned Jethro; Fate might still be listening, ready to pounce.

Sally nodded; she ought to be able to look beyond the horrors and see the sun coming up over the horizon. If, like Tessa, she had been at home, then perhaps she would. But at Drifford Park, even while she longed for the German surrender, she was always aware that tragedy and triumph go hand in hand. News was fed into the listening room almost as it happened, long before the edited version of events was shared with the nation. A thousand American bombers raid Berlin ... the other side of the world American bombers kill more than a hundred and twenty thousand civilians in a raid on crowded Tokyo ... in Europe the death toll from the British raid on Dresden is even higher; beautiful Dresden, a city Sally and her father had loved ... Buchenwald concentration camp liberated and more evidence of the evil of hatred ... Dauchau concentration camp liberated, the unspeakable being spoken in the bulletins Sally monitored. The atmosphere in the listening room was a cocktail of emotions: there were those who had seen their own countries under the Nazi heel, for them each day brought just retribution; there were those for whom every bulletin carried its own personal anguish. Sally listened, translated, her mind a confusion of thankfulness and pain. The Germans fighting in Italy surrender ... Mussolini is executed ... Hitler commits suicide ... Goebbels, that master of German propaganda, shoots his own family, his wife and lovely children, and then takes his own life ... like a non-stoppable stream the words pour into Drifford Park. British prisoners of war are liberated and their repatriation begins even before Churchill's final and longed-for announcement to a war-weary nation: the war in Europe is over.

It was the 8th of May, the day to be known as VE Day, a day for services of thanksgiving, for the waving of flags, for dancing on village greens and city streets alike. It was a day Eliot couldn't let pass without sharing a few minutes of it with Sally. In this day of reckoning, looking back, looking forward, his thoughts were on Estelle.

'She had lived through the blitz, nothing moved her from her intent. Yet, within weeks of the end, she was struck down.'

'How are they, Dad? Is Simon's physiotherapy going well?'

'Early days yet,' was as far as he would go. 'Sal, any day now Nick will be back. My God, but isn't that a wonderful thing to be able to say. Any day now ...'

'It's like waking from a dream and finding it's still there. All the drab, unchanging years ... we got more used to them than we realised. Now Nick's almost home again. He'll have to have medical checks when he gets to England – today, tomorrow – then he'll be given leave. I'm frightened to let myself believe it's really going to happen. And then Jethro. Imagine not having that constant dread. What are you doing today, Dad? London must be a bubbling cauldron of celebration.'

'I can't equate dancing in the streets with thankfulness. Thankfulness tinged with sadness, with anger even. And in that I know I'm not alone. Simon and Gizella are coming to me for a meal, if they can find a taxi to bring them. Probably cost a king's ransom to get transport this evening. Like a bottle of champagne that has been uncorked, the exuberance, the almost hysterical – un-English I almost said – joyfulness fills the whole atmosphere. But what of all those thousands in every country who will never come home? Or are left at the end of it with no home to go to? You, my dear? How are you spending your day? Waiting by the telephone in case you hear that Nick is this side of the Channel?'

'I'm at work at three o'clock. Victory or no, the world keeps on turning, bulletins keep pouring in. If Nick is as near as being able to phone and can't get a reply here, he'll call Tess.'

'Ah yes,' and from the way he said it Sally knew he was smiling at the thought of Tessa. 'Sally, we were talking about Simon and Gizella. It's time for a fresh beginning for them; there's nothing now to keep them in London. He has decisions to make, for himself and for her too. May I suggest to him that we have a hire car bring us to you? Only a brief visit; if Nick phones we'll disappear before he arrives, I promise. The thought of escaping London for a day or two struck me just now when you said he wouldn't be given leave until he'd undergone medical checks. It would be lovely to see you – and good for Simon, too.'

'Of course you can come. I'd love it. So would Helga. When? Tomorrow?'

'That's it, we'll come tomorrow. I don't need to ask Simon; I know how he'll feel. Book a table for a meal in the evening; we won't eat your rations.'

So arrangements were made, arrangements that turned out to involve not only Owls' Roost but the more spacious Mulberry Cottage as well. After Eliot had rung off, stressing that the table booking must be for six to include Tessa, Sally put through a call to Mulberry Cottage. For everyone the day was a holiday – or almost everyone, for Drifford Park was one of the few places where work continued as normal – and Helga had gone to spend her day off helping spruce up the garden as it blossomed into an era of peace. No one, not even Tessa, who could break down most barriers, was allowed to know the innermost workings of Helga's mind and certainly no one seeing the determined way she pedalled along the country lane where the air was heavy with the scent of springtime would guess at the aching misery in her soul. As long as the war had lasted, even though logic had forced her to accept, still deep in her heart had been a dream that wouldn't fade. One day she would hear from her parents; one day she would find out why they'd not been able to follow her or even to write to her; one day some sort of miracle would make the whole thing fall into place and she would see them again. But now there was no room even for an unlikely dream. She would never know ... only the horror of the reports that had come out of one concentration camp after another.

'I didn't have a chance to ask, Tess, but I know you'll say it's OK,' Sally said when Tessa answered the phone. 'Can you offer a bedroom tomorrow night? Dad's bringing Simon and Gizella down. With only four rooms I have an overflow. Take your pick which one you choose to have.'

'Of course any of them can come. I love company, you know that. But Sal, your father will want to be with you; Simon ought not to be pushed out; that leaves Gizella. I'd love to have her, but she mustn't feel herself an outcast either. Tell you what! Helga's outside cutting the grass, giving it its victory trim; I'll suggest to her that she and Gizella both come here. The two young ones. She will understand: you never have to spell things out to Helga. They'll be good for each other. They have a lot in common, don't they; the war has really hit them hard.'

And that's how it was that the next day, while Sally and Helga were at work, Eliot and Simon found the key under the stone and let themselves in. The hire car that had driven them from London – Eliot suspected at black market prices considering the fare

116

charged and the repeated reminders of how hard it was to get enough petrol to make a living – had made a detour to Mulberry Cottage where Tessa had been waiting to welcome them with her never-failing warmth. If Simon had been uneasy when he'd heard of Sally's call telling her father that Gizella and Helga were to be 'boarded out', any doubts were assuaged. He had no doubts at all that the girl would have a much happier visit in the lived-in chaos that surrounded Tessa than she would at Owls' Roost.

Coming home soon after four o'clock, Sally found Eliot and Simon sitting in the garden in the spring sunshine.

'Dad! Simon!' she called as she dismounted and leaned her bicycle against the wall of the house. Instinct made her turn her back on them, even for a couple of seconds; he mustn't guess at the shock she felt. Could grief have changed him so in the months since she'd seen him? He looked gaunt, the origin of his race pronounced in his aquiline nose and the craggy bone structure of his face. In less time than it took for the changes to register she had herself in hand and was approaching them with her arms wide in welcome.

'What time did you get here? Have you found yourselves something to eat and drink? Have you phoned Tess to see Gizella's OK?' A stream of questions with no time for any answers. It was seldom Sally felt so out of control in a situation.

'We stopped for a meal on the way from London,' Eliot told her, returning her bear-like hug. 'As for phoning Tessa, we'll do that later. We saw the welcome; we know there's no need to worry. Helga's not there yet, of course. A clever idea; the two girls will be good for each other.'

Turning to Simon, Sally extended both hands and they kissed on both cheeks in the accepted way. She felt so full of sympathy for him, yet to try and find expression for it seemed to her to be an intrusion on something too personal for kindly words from an outsider. Could he read her heart? His gaze held hers; she believed he could.

'Simon. I have thought about you, about everything ...'

'I know. Thank you, Sally.'

A strange way of conveying sympathy, or of receiving it, between two comparative strangers, yet in the unspoken message there was complete understanding. Uninvited, there sprang into her memory what he'd said about her father and his playing of

Chopin's music, that he was in tune with the composer's soul. In those few words of greeting she felt certain – and was sure so did *he* – that their souls were in tune. Eliot watched them, an uncertain frown briefly touching his brow. He didn't look for the logic in his sudden feeling of unease; it was safer to turn his thoughts to that phone call to Mulberry Cottage.

'Eliot will have told you of my decision to move out of London,' Simon told her later when he followed her into the kitchen, where she was changing the water in a vase from the drawing room and rearranging the lilac she had cut the previous day.

'Yes. He said you were contemplating house-hunting. How will Gizella feel about that?'

'She will be as glad as I shall to leave London behind. Our home there is gone, we have no yesterday to hang on to. We must get out of London, Sally. I have said it for so long, but always then it was for a different reason. Now – well, now it is too late for that.'

'So why do you want to leave now? Surely once you are well enough to play again it will be more convenient for you to have a base there? From there you can travel anywhere; from the country you will find it more difficult.'

'I cannot be, as you say in your language, an ostrich. The truth is there to be acknowledged or the future cannot start to find a shape. For me, Sally my friend, this is the end of one era; I have to make of it the beginning of another. If Estelle had done as I wanted things would have been very different, for her, for Gizella and perhaps today for me too.' There was no emotion in his voice, he was simply stating a fact and knowing it to be true.

Remembering all her father had told her, she was puzzled by his calm voice; if she were honest, she was disappointed. Surely a true artist could never be so void of feeling. 'You must be so *angry*. All that she had gone through, nothing denting her faith, and for it to end like that.'

Pulling the kitchen chair towards him he sat astride it just as Nick so often had, his 'good' arm on its wooden back, his other with his hand supported between the closed buttons of his jacket.

'You didn't know Estelle. I wish you had. Some people might say she believed in Fate; but I knew her better than that. She had faith, she put her trust in something greater than herself. Her one

118

desire was that Gizella should have a career as she herself had had. I told you it was for that end that she was not prepared to leave London. If she were here now, disappointed, saddened, I do not exaggerate when I tell you I believe she would have been broken by the inevitable changes in our lives; but I do not doubt she would have found the courage to accept what she would have seen as the road she had to walk. Our paths have taken a turning we had not anticipated; for her the very thing I had lived in fear of has happened. Of us all, Estelle is the one who would have found the faith to accept, not to have that anger you speak of.'

'How could she not be angry? For you? For Gizella?'

'It is something I find hard to express, perhaps because I cannot find the sort of blind faith she had. Blind. Did that have something to do with it? For so long my world has been filled with so much more than hers – at least it *was*. Now I cannot look ahead with certainty to the course my career will take.' Ah now, she thought, here is a crack in his armour of reserve. 'If I had Estelle's faith, then I would wait and trust. For me there is nothing to which I can cling.' In his precise phraseology his accent became even more pronounced.

'And Gizella,' Sally said, her mind on Estelle, whom she believed had been the pivot their world had turned on.

'To be a professional dancer will be out of the question for her. Sally, I am ashamed, ashamed of my own weak acceptance. I *knew* the child's heart was never in what she did. She had a rare gift, something in the genes inherited from her mother, but she had no love of dancing. She worked hard at it, just as she would have at music, at mathematics, at any form of learning. Gizella has great strength. But me? I could not bring myself to fight her battle even though I knew dancing would bring her no joy. How could I, had Estelle not enough to bear?'

'And now Gizella doesn't need to pretend, is that what you're saying?'

As if she hadn't spoken, he went on, 'There should be joy. For me there was. I do honestly believe that from when first I drew my bow over the strings of a half-sized violin, Sally, there has been unspeakable joy.' Then, his expression lighting into a smile, 'Joy is there to tempt, to encourage, but it does not lessen the hours, the many, many hours of practising that no child accepts with thoughts of nothing but the joy of it. There were times when I

119

heard other boys at play; I even recall a day when I escaped from my bedroom where, at the age of about six, I was battling with my solitary two-hour practice session after school. I climbed from the window and slid down the drainpipe.'

'Were you found out?' she asked, wanting to keep the light of laughter in his dark eyes.

'I believe I was, but it's not that that I mostly recall. My most vivid memory is going to bed that evening, seeing my fiddle where I had propped it on the dressing table, holding it under my chin ... I have not the words, Sally, perhaps not even in my own language and certainly not in yours to tell you what that moment did for me. Before I climbed into my bed I did my practice, oh not the usual two hours, but long enough to know the incident was closed. For me there would not be football, there would not be games of hide and seek in the woods, there would not be the camaraderie shared by the boys of the village. For me there was a clear path ahead; at the end of it was a wonder I only half-understood but I knew one day it would be mine.' The smile had gone. 'And now? Can I find the courage to face what the medical men tell me is at the end of this road?'

Ramming the last sprig of lilac into the vase in a most un-Sallylike way, she knelt by his side.

'They may be wrong, Simon. You can prove them wrong.'

He was silent. Instinct had made her drop to her knees, but now she felt self-conscious, uncertain how to deal with a show of emotion that had found her unprepared. His smile had gone. Had his shoulders slumped or was her imagination playing tricks?

'I cannot,' he said at last. 'No, Sally my friend, I cannot. My shoulder will become restored and my arm too, but elbows are more complicated.'

'It's your *left* arm, Simon, not your bowing arm.'

'That I realise. I shall play my violin, it will bring me solace. But Sally, I shall never stand with a great orchestra, become part of the wonder of the sound. It is hard to explain to you: this is a thing that unless you have experienced you can never fully understand. Perhaps those within the orchestra know something of the wonder, or a singer who is one of a great chorus of voices. But even for those, it is not, it *cannot* be, the same as playing a solo instrument in a great concerto. With the other players, ahead of them, answering them, calling them, leading them on, part of them and yet raised to a level that is – is – oh, why can I not find the word? – is *sublime*.'

Instinct had her in its hold again, but this time she had herself in check. The easiest thing, the most natural thing, would have been to lay her head on his knee as he sat astride the wooden chair. Instead, Sally the practical kept the upper hand.

'Dad must be going through much the same,' she reminded him. 'Why don't you talk to him, Simon. Perhaps you can help each other.'

She hadn't expected her words to soften his haggard face into the semblance of a smile.

'I have no need to talk to Eliot. The understanding is there for both of us. For both of us this is a time for – for –' It was unusual for Simon to have today's struggle to find the word he wanted; twice he had floundered, a sure sign that he was less in control than he tried to appear.

'A time for reassessment,' she finished the sentence for him. 'Have you tried to imagine how Estelle would have guided you?' For surely, that must be his salvation.

He looked at Sally in puzzlement. 'Estelle? Her whole purpose was Gizella's future. Now that too is changed. My heart is full of thankfulness that Estelle has been spared this reassessment, as you call it. Take away her guiding force and she would have had no wish to survive.'

'Simon, that can't be true. She had great strength, you just said so. Dad has told me about her, about her power of overcoming. In her *you* would have found the strength you will need.'

'I must look for that within myself, Sally. And so too must Gizella. I told you, I was never happy that her life was to be moulded so that she would be a great ballerina. But now I do not know what there is for her. I am anxious, I look within myself for the power to guide her and I am lacking.'

'First she must learn to relax, to have some fun.'

'Ah!' And the smile was back, this time not a fleeting expression but a smile backed with determination, of that she was certain. 'Is that not the answer for all of us? Should we who are left not go down on our knees – as you are now, Sally my dear friend – and thank the God of our fathers that at least Europe is in a state to draw breath and to move ahead into a world that must, *must* be a better place.'

121

'Amen to that, Simon. And may we have learned something from the horrors and devastation, from the divisions that men let grow between them, from the hatred that comes from lack of understanding.'

'You are an unusual woman, Sally. Is yours the way other women see the world as they wait for their husbands to return, or those who grieve that for them there will be no homecoming?'

'It would be if they worked at Drifford Park.'

The visit lasted three memorable days, and it was impossible to know who enjoyed them most. Certainly Tessa was a leading contender, for while Sally worked, the two men made a daily visit to Mulberry Cottage. Refusing to borrow the car, insisting that what meagre ration of petrol she was allowed owing to her 'essential' work and lack of public transport should be kept for when Nick was home, they walked the two miles or more. After the dust and noise of London, the country walk worked its own therapy; add to that Tessa's never-failing relaxed hospitality and their memories of the short stay were indelible. As for Gizella, who had loved her mother above all else, no wonder she was frightened even secretly to admit to her relief in her changed way of life. At her age the warning that in years to come arthritis might result from the injury, such a thing was so removed from life as she'd known it that it had no power to worry her; as for the slight turning of her ankle when she walked, that was a small price to pay for the gift of freedom to carve her future in a way of her own choosing. Yet, even as the thought formed in her mind she stamped on it. Because her one object had been to please her mother; to try and make up to her for what she had lost, Gizella had worked hard to be all that Estelle wanted. Suppose now that death had taken her from them, Estelle could know the thoughts of the people she'd loved. So Gizella didn't let herself imagine the future, instead she lived in the present and, at Mulberry Cottage, she was happy.

On the evening of the second day of their stay, while Eliot played the piano, Simon and Sally sat on the terrace outside the open window of the drawing room, idly smoking, listening and relaxing. The peace was shattered by the shrill bell of the telephone.

Perhaps it was Tessa, Sally told herself; perhaps it was the shift manager at Drifford Park altering her times for the next day;

122

perhaps – perhaps –. By the time she reached the hall her mouth was dry, her heart was pounding.

'Ploxton 201,' she breathed. Let it be him, please let it be him, no I mustn't ask, I mustn't hope, it'll be Tess or Gizella . . .

'Sally! I got in an hour ago. Sally, I'm home.' All the things she'd imagined herself saying and now, at the sound of his familiar voice, she seemed to have lost all coherent thought. 'Sally? Are you there? Is everything all right?'

'I can't believe it's really happening. Nick, oh yes, everything's wonderful. You're home – well, almost. How soon can you come?'

'I only arrived this evening. There will be medical checks, then God knows what other red tape before they set me free. Thursday today; I can't see it being this side of the weekend, the speed officialdom usually works. That'll give you time to get out the red carpet.'

'The red carpet has been ready for – oh Nick, for so long.'

'Better vacuum it then,' he laughed. He sounded just the same. In her lowest moments she had imagined him coming home dispirited, a pale shadow of himself. But his voice was strong, his laugh as spontaneous. Her disbelief evaporated; this was reality.

'I can't hog the phone too long but tell me – the others, Jethro – God, Sal, I went away and left a boy, now he's a man, engaged to be married. Tess? Sebastian? The gorgeous Zena?'

'Everyone is fine.' She wished he'd asked about her father, and was surprised at herself that she couldn't cheerfully say, 'And Dad too. He's here with me now.' But she couldn't. Instead she told him, 'Helga is staying with Tess for a day or two.'

'I'd forgotten she was still there. Funny kid, a real maiden aunt if ever I saw one.'

'She's grown up since you went away. We get on very well – two of a kind in lots of ways.'

'You, my sweet, never reminded me of a maiden aunt. Here, Sal, I'd better ring off, there are other people waiting. I'll ring you again as soon as I know when I'm being given my freedom so that you can meet me at the station. And Sal – oh hell, this isn't the place to say the things I want to say.'

'Say them when you get here. And Nick – just, Nick, isn't it wonderful.'

'It will be. Goodnight, darling.'

*

123

The next day Eliot and Simon returned to London, but it took little persuasion on Tessa's part for Gizella to agree to stay on for a while. So it was that the next afternoon with Sally on one of her midweek days off, they were all at Owls' Roost when a taxi chugged up the bumpy lane. After the weekend, Nick had said, and I'll ring you when I know ... yet as the sound of the engine came nearer Sally knew it was him. By the time the taxi turned in at the gate she had the front door open. Her legs felt as though they had turned to jelly. Was that why she didn't rush out to meet him as he got out of the taxi, or was it that she needed to look at him unseen, to know that he was just as he'd sounded: strong, vigorous, well?

In the first seconds the last of her fears melted. Later she would see that in fact he was thinner, but as he paid the driver and made some laughing comment to him she couldn't hear, joy flooded through her. Then, with no thought that the taxi driver was still negotiating turning his vehicle in the forecourt, she rushed out in a most un-Sallylike way and hurled herself into Nick's arms.

'You said it would be days!'

'They got their skates on,' he laughed, hugging her, then holding her at arm's length. 'Let's look at you, see what the ravages of time have done. Why, damn it, woman, you look just as lovely as I remember.'

'And you. I've been imagining a poor wraith, and here you are, just yourself.' Her voice croaked, she couldn't hold her mouth steady any more than she could stop the sudden tears welling up and spilling over.

'Hey, that's no way to welcome a hero.'

'Sorry ... silly ... not a crying person ...'

'A few tears make me feel appreciated,' he teased, turning to the house with his arm around her. 'I say, isn't that Tess looking out of the window? That's great. I was going to suggest we went over so that I could check in. Who's the kid with her?'

Briefly Sally explained, but in his pleasure at being home, with the extra bonus of Tess being there to add to the welcome, he probably didn't listen to what she said. Full of excitement, he suggested taking them all out to dinner, but Tessa said she and Gizella had to go home or Helga would wonder where they were.

'Never mind, we'll go tomorrow,' his good-humoured smile took in all three of them, the room, the familiar polishy smell of

124

the house, the world in general. 'It must have been Mrs Bond's morning,' he sniffed. 'I bet I'm right.'

'You cheated,' Sally laughed. 'You remember she always comes on Friday.'

'God, but it's good. It's as if I've never been away. When's Sebastian due home, Tess?'

'For good? I don't know, but I hope they'll release him soon. After all, you two have been there since the beginning. But he often gets the weekends home, and I'm keeping my fingers crossed that he'll turn up this evening. Another reason for our being home. We'll get going and leave you two to get reacquainted. See you over the weekend. What will you do about working tomorrow, Sal?'

'I shall go in, but I've got it fixed that as soon as I let them know then I can have leave. So by Sunday I'll be free. I'm on three to eleven tomorrow.'

That was when the first cloud crossed Nick's horizon. But after the others had gone neither he nor Sally wanted to touch the subject of her working. Nothing must spoil their first precious hours together. And nothing did. In the early part of the three years he'd been away his life had been swift moving; there had been action, danger, fear; but after that had come the inactivity of the confinement of prison life. Certainly he had never experienced bad treatment; one of the guards had even managed to get him some paints. The hardest part had been the lack of reliable news, having no idea how the war was progressing, living on hopes and dreams with no knowledge of whether they would ever become reality. Always those hopes and dreams had been of home, of the orderly married life he and Sally had shared, of sexual fantasies that became more prominent in his mind as months turned into years. As for Sally, in the drab routine, becoming attuned to anxiety and shortages, she had known a hunger as great as his. Her fantasies had been woven into her life, combining memory and hope, but more fortunate than him with his bunk bed in a hut with nineteen other men, she had had the privacy of her own space, and could give her imagination full rein. That night, though, for both of them fantasy became reality. In the past their lovemaking had often been the natural enjoyment of sex; occasionally it had reached a higher plane, had exceeded the gratification of their physical need and been an expression of love. But on that night,

125

together after three lonely years, in the moment when he entered her she knew a profound joy almost beyond bearing, even though she knew, too, that it would be impossible for him to hold back and satisfy her. And when all too soon his climax came she gripped him close, her whole being alive with thankfulness.

The euphoria was gone by the next day when they faced the prospect of her working her eight-hour shift. Ahead of them was a fortnight's leave, but from the look on his face as she got ready to set out for Drifford Park that was no compensation for being neglected on his first day home. She knew very well that he wouldn't stay at Owls' Roost; she was sure that by the time she took her place in the listening room he would already be at Mulberry Cottage. Which, of course, he was.

She expected that when she got home at almost midnight he would still be out, for he'd promised to take Tessa and the girls out to dinner. Probably Sebastian would have been with them – and thinking of the party she found it hard to concentrate on the news bulletins. However, she found he was home ahead of her.

'Have a good time?'

'Yes, fine. You know Tess, she's always good company. That girl staying with her, Gizella, she's going to be a beauty. Your poor ugly duckling, young Helga, I don't think there's much hope she'll ever turn into a swan. Anyway, it was fine. Sebastian isn't home this weekend. But listen to this, Sal, he's got leave starting on Monday. So guess what? He's going straight down to Cornwall. The four of us are going to The Limit. What to you think of that?' Anyone would think he'd performed a wonderful feat of magic.

'That's what we planned, Tess and me. We said as soon as you were both home that's what we'd do. Where are the girls staying, here or at Tess's?'

'There, I think. Funny creatures, they seem keen to look after Tess's vegetable patch and those chickens. Now the war's over I expect she'll get some order back in the garden again.'

'The war isn't over. Here it may be, but not in the East.'

'Over as far as Sebastian and I are concerned. And Jethro too. Hope they send the boy home soon.'

Next day, Sally, Nick and Tessa caught the train westward, finishing the journey in a rickety taxi that dropped them in the

126

village so that they could buy stores and walk the mile or so on to The Limit. The fact that they'd gone by train somehow added to the excitement: this was different, this was an 'event'. Sebastian's journey was shorter; he was stationed in Devon about midway between home and The Limit, so he would be joining them later by car. They had already left home when he telephoned with the good news that he was getting away early and would be there almost as soon as they were.

They did their shopping and set out along the cliff-top path to take the short cut back to The Limit. Their luggage was in haversacks for easy carrying – particularly easy as far as Tess and Sally were concerned, for Nick had one on each shoulder while they carried only half-full baskets of essential food. Linking arms, they strode along, singing as they went 'Red Sails in the Sunset', 'I am H.A.P.P.Y.', 'If You Were the Only Girl in the World', the first thing that came into their heads; all that mattered was that *this* was the holiday that 'showed the world' nothing had changed for them; they'd crossed that stormy sea and landed on their safe haven.

'There's a bicycle against the fence. Who would that be?' Sally was the first to notice it.

The unexpected sight broke the spell. They stopped singing, and released their hold on each other.

'Afternoon, ma'am.' The blue uniformed figure of the village constable turned from where he'd been hammering on the front door. 'Would one of you be Mrs Kilbride?'

Chapter Seven

'That taxi ought to be here.' Nick walked to the open front door for the fifth time in two minutes, listening for the sound of its approach.

'We haven't given the policeman long for his ride back to the village.' Sally tried to sound more confident than she felt. Sebastian in an accident, taken by ambulance to hospital ... how bad an accident? It hadn't been that the kindly constable was unwilling to tell them what they wouldn't have wanted to hear; it was simply that those had been all the details he had.

'If only we'd had the telephone installed,' Tessa said, the colour drained from her face so that her freckles looked as though they'd been spattered across her nose and cheeks with a child's paint brush.

'He'll soon be here.' Sally took her cold hand in her own. 'If when we get to the station we have to wait for a train there's sure to be a kiosk where you can ring the hospital.'

'If there's anything of a wait for a train, we'll find someone to drive us – a car with more guts than the rattle trap we picked up to bring us from the station.' Nick said, making another trip to the open door and under his breath muttering something that sounded like 'Come on, come on for Christ's sake.'

'When we get there I bet we'll find him sitting in the Casualty Department waiting for us to fetch him.' Sally made another effort, only silently adding, 'Please, please, don't let it be serious. You've looked after him all through the war, you couldn't be so cruel as to let him be badly hurt, not now. This was the time Tess and I had planned, our own personal celebration. What's Seb ever done to deserve trouble?' Then, struck by another thought that surely ought to give them something to cling to, she said, 'If Sebastian hadn't told them, they couldn't possibly have known they'd find you here, Tess. So it can't be serious.'

Tessa nodded, but whether she'd been listening, listening and really hearing, it was impossible to tell, for her blank expression didn't change.

'Come on, girls,' Nick called, 'sounds like a traction engine: it must be our chap.'

Coming from the station, Nick had sat in the front seat with the driver; this time the three of them crowded into the back with Nick in the middle, one hand holding Sally's and the other Tessa's.

'We're on our way, Tess,' he tried to boost her confidence and his own at the same time. 'By the time he's been checked over we'll be there for him.'

Again she nodded, but there was a hopelessness in the movement as if her spirit was far away from them. As of course it was. The trouble was, she didn't know where it was: sitting in a Casualty Department? Being carried on a stretcher to a ward? Was he conscious, did he know he wasn't alone, that while she tried to act normally with Sally and Nick, her heart was – oh, if only she could see where. With Seb, every second she was with Seb, but where? This very minute, what were they doing to him? Would the police have been notified and sent to find her if it had been just a minor crash where the injured could walk away? Perhaps that was the way it was always done; she knew even a minor calamity had to be reported to the police; perhaps anyone involved had to be checked at hospital. Perhaps when they reached the hospital they'd be told he had been released and he would already be on his way to The Limit.

At least luck hadn't completely turned its back on them. At the station Nick went to enquire the time of the next train and came back with three tickets.

'Due in five minutes. It'll be quicker than trying to get a car. All right, Tess?'

For the first time her mind was pulled back from its own wayward journeying.

'Yes. Yes, of course I'm fine, Nick.' She had to be, that's what Seb would want. If she turned up looking anything like she felt she would be letting him down. What a moment to remember her larder at the cottage, its shelves filled with jams and marmalades, bottled fruit and vegetables. All of it had been prepared for a time so nearly here where he'd be home; this was the 'after the war' she'd scrimped and saved for.

An hour and a half later they were sitting like birds on a perch, side by side on a wooden bench along the tiled wall of a hospital corridor. The air was heavy with the smell of disinfectant, the only sign of life an occasional nurse – not always the same nurse – hurrying past them with a swish of starched uniform, rubber soles almost silent on the highly polished floor. Never a glance in their direction; they might have been as much a part of the furniture as their uncomfortable seating.

It was late afternoon on a Monday, not a time for visitors. Saturday and Sunday afternoons no doubt there would have been other people, but Mondays there was nothing but the routine of the hospital. Even between themselves it seemed impossible to speak; the very stillness silenced them, surely their words would magnify and echo in the empty corridor; and what was there to say? The nurse in Casualty had directed them here, told them to wait, and when the doctors had made their assessment someone would come for Mrs Kilbride. As for Sally and Nick, in the eyes of authority they didn't exist. How long does it take a doctor to assess broken limbs? But had he broken any limbs? The nurse said she was unable to tell them the extent of his injury; they must wait until after he'd been seen by senior medical staff.

Just as one or two nurses had stridden past them, so a navy-blue uniformed woman came into view, the material of her uniform less starched and the frill of her cap denoting that she was a ward sister.

'Sister.' Sally leaned forward as the woman approached. 'Can you give us any idea when Mrs Kilbride will be able to see her husband?'

'I'm afraid it won't be yet. Can I get someone to bring you a cup of tea perhaps? I'm afraid you have a long wait ahead of you.' With one accord they refused her kindness, partly due to the over-powering smell of combined disinfectant and polish and partly because to drink hospital tea was the last thing they wanted when with every passing moment they became more sure that some-thing was very wrong.

'While we're waiting I'll go and find the police station, see if someone can tell me what happened,' Nick told them. 'If you're seen quicker than they expect, wait here for me.'

The seconds dragged into minutes, another hour went by. Then, just as they heard Nick's tread at the far end of the long corridor, from the other direction a shiny-faced young nurse appeared with the message that Dr Chambers would see Mrs Kilbride now.

'Not just me. I want our friends.'

The girl looked uncertain but wasn't a match for the three of them, so with a quick, 'This way, I'll show you where,' she scuttled ahead of them in her soft-soled shoes. Following her, they sounded like a regiment of soldiers. It seemed that this evening – for by now it was well into the evening – all the fight had left Tessa; like a child she walked between the other two holding their hands, even though she probably wasn't aware how she clung to them.

'Mrs Kilbride.' The no-longer-young doctor held out his hand in the direction of all three of them, uncertain which of the two women was the wife.

'That's me,' Tessa claimed. She was Mrs Kilbride, Seb's wife, sharing whatever had overtaken him. The thought helped; she raised her chin a fraction and, releasing her hand from Nick's, held it out to the doctor. 'What's happened to him, doctor? I don't know anything; how hurt is he?'

'I'm afraid he is extensively burned.'

'Burned! Oh no!' The words were scarcely audible as the breath seemed to be expelled from her; visibly she sagged. In a second Nick's arm was round her.

'My dear, I am so very sorry,' kindly Dr Chambers said. 'I'm told he was a flying man. To come right through – and now this.' She hardly seemed aware that Nick lowered her into the chair he pulled forward as the doctor continued, 'There's a hospital in Kent where there have been great advances in treatment of cases of this kind. I dare say you've heard of it and the remarkable things that are done in the burns unit there.'

'No, no, not there!' As clearly as if he were speaking, she could hear Sebastian's voice telling her of comrades who'd been shot out of the sky, who'd been taken there for plastic surgery. They'd both known there were worse things: many men were blinded, many lost limbs and spent the rest of their lives immobile; but Sebastian's nightmare had always been fire and what followed. 'I want to see him, I must see him.'

'No, that I cannot allow at this stage. And he is heavily sedated; there must be nothing to disturb him. I have already made arrangements for his immediate transfer to Kent, I want him taken there as quickly as possible. At this stage it would not be wise for you to travel with him in the ambulance. Trust me, my dear. He is not in a state to be aware at the moment, and that's how the medics will see he remains during the journey.' Then, turning to Nick, 'You are family, I imagine?'

'We are friends, closer than family. We shall look after Mrs Kilbride and tomorrow we shan't let her travel to Kent alone if they say she can see Sebastian.'

'Kilbride ... Sebastian Kilbride ... *the* Sebastian Kilbride?'

'*The.*' For the first time Nick smiled.

'I remember seeing his films before the war ...' Dr Chambers might have been talking to himself as he let his memory drift back. Nick took a quick glance at Tessa and was thankful she'd not listened to the quietly spoken exchange between him and the doctor so the implication was lost on her. To have known Sebastian's name and not to have recognised him. Across Tessa's bent head his glance met Sally's.

'Come to us for tonight, Tess,' Sally said as the train chuffed its way homewards. None of them gave a thought to The Limit or to the rucksacks of luggage and baskets of shopping they had abandoned there. 'Tomorrow we'll telephone the hospital, then if they say you can see him we'll all go together on the train.'

'To you?' Tessa repeated, just two words that seemed to have no meaning for her.

'You don't need to worry about the cottage, Helga is looking after everything. Soon enough to contact Zena tomorrow when we know more.' As if what they knew already, added to what Nick had found out at the police station, wasn't more than enough.

It had happened on a hairpin bend on a steep hill; only an examination of the burned-out wreck might give an indication of whether the steering had gone or whether the fault had been Sebastian's. He had been driving down the hill. If he'd had a guardian angel watching him, then that must have been who'd timed it that a lorry should be climbing towards the bend at just the moment when the car went out of control and disappeared off the road, somersaulting down a ravine to come to rest wedged on its roof against a tree.

133

According to the story Nick had heard at the police station, the lorry driver had shown great courage. He'd abandoned his own vehicle on the bend and rushed down the ravine just as, with a sound like an explosion, the car had been engulfed in flames. The door on the driver's side had been against the tree, but he had managed to wrench open the one on the passenger side. Again that guardian angel had taken a hand, for why else would Sebastian's briefcase have managed to become wedged at the side of the seat so that when the door was flung open it was dislodged and fell to the ground at the lorry driver's feet? Smoke, flames, already Sebastian's clothes were burning as if he were a guy atop the annual bonfire. Seconds or minutes, to the rescuer time had lost all meaning until he, at great risk to himself and searing agony from the licking flames, managed to wriggle Sebstian from behind the steering wheel and drag him towards the door of the upside-down vehicle. The result could have been so different: if the vehicle approaching up the hill towards the bend had been driven by a woman, or even by a man of less than Herculean strength, Sebastian couldn't have been brought out alive. It wasn't until he'd been rolled over and over on the ground in an attempt to put out the flames, that his rescuer became aware of his own injuries, and of the searing agony of his own burned hands; until then he'd been driven by nothing except the need to save a life. By that time the flames and the column of black smoke could be seen from the road. Nick was careful how much of this he described; in his mind he could see Sebastian, his clothes burned on to his body, his skin cooked, his hair gone; he seemed to smell burning flesh. Someone else had driven to telephone the police and the ambulance. The police had moved the lorry, the driver had been taken with Sebastian in the ambulance. Right to the end his presence of mind hadn't failed him; he had made sure the charred briefcase was handed in at the hospital, where amongst his papers had been found the route of his journey and a map of the Cornish lanes leading to The Limit. Nick was glad he had the man's name and address in his pocket; at least contacting him would be something he could do for Sebastian.

A new routine took shape. Sebastian would be in hospital for some time; that was spelled out to them when the three of them went together to the burns unit Dr Chambers had spoken so highly of.

'I can't go home and leave him here,' Tessa said. Like a snappy terrier waiting to pounce, she looked at Sally and Nick, daring them to argue. 'I won't!'

'So, Tess, we'll see if we can find somewhere nearby to stay.' Nick's voice was calm and reassuring. 'There's nothing to hurry home for – Helga will look after your chickens – we'll all stay here while I'm on leave. I'll find somewhere, leave it to me.'

Gladly she did.

'They wouldn't let me even see him,' she said to Sally for the third time while they waited on another equally uncomfortable wooden bench where Nick left them when, sounding more confident than he felt, he set out to find somewhere to rent, a hotel with vacancies, even lodgings in someone's house.

'It'll be all right, Tess. That's what we have to keep telling ourselves. He's in a mess' (There! She'd said it! It was no use pussy-footing around Tessa, frightened to look the truth in the face) 'but this is the best hospital in the country. It'll be weeks, months perhaps, before he looks like himself –'

'He was so frightened of burning.' Even trying to speak with her jaw held stiff and the words having no expression, Tess couldn't keep the croak out of her voice. 'It's not fair, Sal.'

'I know.'

'I wish he'd been a fisherman or a farmer or something, the sort of job where no one took any notice of your face. Seb's never been conceited, and I know there must be men who are better looking – not to me, oh Sal why couldn't it have happened to *me* not him – but if he's scarred – well, it'll take everything away from him. Like if it happened to Clark Gable or Errol Flynn. But this is Seb.'

'We don't know yet, Tess, not for sure. Sebastian has enormous courage. They'll make him better, this won't keep him down.'

'It's me, I'm the trouble. I ought to keep faith. But Sal, I'm frightened to let myself believe – and I'm frightened to try to imagine a future.'

'That's the way we've lived for years, Tess. It's become habit.'

They were still sitting where he'd left them when Nick returned. His smile was intended to reassure Tessa, and perhaps it did. Knowing him better, Sally was prepared to hear something less than they'd hoped.

'A Mrs Griffin in a house not five minutes' walk away. Not much of a place to look at, a tall terrace house. But clean, and she seemed a nice old biddy. I told her what we wanted and she said we can have bed and breakfast and as long as we tell her in the mornings she'll make an evening meal for us. You brought the ration books, Sal? She's a bit fussed about getting her hands on those.'

'Naturally,' Sally answered, composed, efficient, her manner aimed at bringing some sort of normality to the situation. More used to civilian restrictions than Nick, she had made sure before they left home that she had charge of Tessa's book as well as her own and the form granting allowances for Nick's leave. 'While you and Tess wait here, tell me the address and I'll go and give them to Mrs Griffin.' She trusted her own judgement more than she did his and wanted to see what he was letting them in for.

He had warned them that the house on Queen's Street promised to be nothing better than somewhere to lay their heads, and before she parted with their ration books she was determined to vet the place for herself.

'You'll be Mrs Kilbride, did the gentleman say?' Tall, gaunt-looking Mrs Griffin greeted her. 'I'm glad you've come to have a look for yourself. All very well the men thinking they know what's what, but to my way of thinking it takes a woman.'

'That was my husband. Our friend is Mrs Kilbride; it's her husband who is in the hospital.'

'Ah. The gentleman told me something of the trouble. If there's a miracle to be performed, that's the place to have it in hand, from what I hear. Some of them we see walking about, oh dear, oh dear, it fair breaks your heart. So you'll be, let me see, what did he call himself – Nick Somebody?'

'Nick Kennedy – and I'm Sally. He has leave until the end of next week; we want to be with Tess over the next few days.' And then what? Would Tessa come home and leave Sebastian?

Sally was surprised to find herself talking so freely. Their land-lady was of indeterminate age, anything from fifty-five and wearing badly to seventy-five and unbowed; there was something of the Victorian era about her as if, despite all that she must have seen in this south-eastern corner of the country over recent years, she still clung to the lifestyle of her childhood and refused to give an inch to changing times. Sally could see it in the furnishing of what Edith Griffin referred to as the parlour. Immediately she was ushered into it she was aware that it was the 'holy of holies': a black-leaded grate that never held a fire even though the brass fender gleamed from regular polishing; the backs of the none too comfortable-looking armchairs protected with crocheted antimacassars; a long lace runner along the top of the piano on which were photographs, one of a young man in naval uniform, another of a nurse (nephew and niece perhaps? grandchildren?), others dated by their fading sepia; a round table in front of the window covered with a dark-red chenille cloth and crowded with treasures Mrs Griffin prized: various small ornaments, a brightly polished, silver-plated sugar bowl and cream jug considered too good for use, one or two faded photographs. Anything less like the interior of Owls' Roost would have been hard to imagine and yet Sally found herself in tune with her new acquaintance. The bedrooms were clean and adequate, the bathroom with its chipped enamel bath and gas geyser less encouraging; but her general impression was that Nick had done well to find Edith Griffin. Confidently, she handed over their ration books.

That evening, while she and Nick waited anxiously, Tessa was taken to see Sebastian.

'I wonder how long they'll let her stay' ... 'He'll be so relieved to see her' ... 'Perhaps tomorrow we'll be allowed a few minutes.' Neither really listened to what the other said, words, just words, and all the time they watched the door at the end of the corridor where Tessa would reappear. At last it opened. Accompanied by a sister, she came into view. The sister was talking to her, talking seriously. With one movement Nick and Sally got to their feet, as if seeing them would give Tessa the courage she clearly lacked. Was it usual for hospital staff to put an affectionate hand on a visitor's arm? What was Tessa hearing?

'You're with Mrs Kilbride?' Did Sally imagine there was something like relief in the kindly sister's tone? 'I'm glad she has some family with her.'

There was no point in explaining their relationship; they were closer to Tessa than any of her family. Barring Zena, of course, a reminder nudged silently. Now that Tessa had seen Sebastian it was time to contact Zena and tell her what had happened.

'Yes, we're all together. We're staying nearby.'

'I was under the impression the patient was from some distance away.' The gentle compassion they'd seen when she'd talked so seriously to Tessa subtly changed. They were aware of her kindly efficiency but, now that Tessa could be handed into their care, of something that held her aloof. Here in the hospital she was Sister; her patients were all important. But at the end of her shift the woman who emerged had an existence outside. If this evening they sat at a table next to hers in a local restaurant it was likely they wouldn't recognise her, nor she them. Now she turned a dismissive smile on the three of them, neither waiting for nor expecting an explanation as to where Sebastian came from or where they were staying. Murmuring something to the effect that she was glad Mrs Kilbride wasn't alone, she left them even as she spoke. Her next mission was already at the forefront of her mind as she hurried back along the corridor and disappeared.

'How was he, Tess?' Sally had to repeat the question before Tessa seemed to realise she'd spoken. 'How was he?'

Tessa shut her eyes, then shook her head as if she were trying to dislodge something she couldn't bear.

'Is he a rotten mess?' This time it was Nick, his arm around her shoulder as they guided her along the maze of corridors following the 'Exit' arrows. As she walked, Tessa said nothing and across the top of her bent head Nick and Sally looked at each other helplessly. It was only when the came out into the fresh air, air heavy with the scent of summer, that Tessa stopped walking. Her face was a mask of utter misery, misery too deep for the relief of tears.

'Tell us, Tess,' Nick said softly. 'Seb can't want you to hug it to yourself. Just talk, say whatever comes into your mind.'

'How can he bear it? I don't mean the pain. All of it, what it's done to him.'

'Sebastian will overcome the pain, Tess.' As Sally spoke she imagined Sebastian, sensitive, understanding, unspoilt despite all his fame and success.

'I'm not thinking about the pain,' Tessa rasped. 'He looked at me – I might have been anybody, *anybody*. His eyes seemed dead. He knew it was me, but – he wouldn't let me in.'

'Give him time.' Nick's hold on her arm tightened. 'Pain, shock, God knows what it must be doing to him.'

'How bad is he, Tess? His face, I mean?' Surely for Sebastian the whole course of his future must hinge on that.

Tessa closed her eyes as if that would erase what she'd seen. 'Can't believe – not Seb – not fair.' Just disjointed words, but they told the others more than enough.

*

138

On the Sunday Zena came.

'Don't come with me to the hospital, Mum. I want to see Dad on my own.'

'As you like. I expect he'd prefer it too,' Tessa said in the flat tone that seemed to have settled on her permanently.

They waited outside in the hospital grounds. How Tessa felt about Zena's reaction to the sight of her father they couldn't guess, but both Nick and Sally watched anxiously for her to reappear. When she came out her eyes were visible evidence of her tears.

'Doesn't look like Dad,' she croaked. 'And he's in awful pain. I burned my hand on the oven the other day; it hurt like hell. But *Dad*, he must have been cooked,' she snorted, with none of her usual elegance.

'Shut up,' Tessa snapped. 'I hope you didn't behave like that in front of him!'

'Well, you hope wrong, then. I did. I cried and I didn't even try not to. All those chaps in the ward, all of them so dreadful. I talked to one, an airman who was pleased as Punch with what they'd done for him. He was going home soon, back to his old job in an insurance office, he told me. To hear him you'd have thought he was the same as any other man – but his face was all pulled down one side, his eye wouldn't open properly and the skin didn't look like skin. He thought he was cheering me up, telling me how many operations he'd had and what wonderful things they do. But he looked *ghastly* if you put him with ordinary people.'

'It'll take courage, Zena,' Sally said. 'But one thing none of them lack – certainly Sebastian doesn't lack – is courage.'

'Don't you hear what I'm saying?' In desperation Zena looked from one to the other. 'Even a boy like that, with his old job and all his friends waiting for him, even he will need courage. But Dad – what will he do? There's no going back to his old job, not for Dad. I tell you one thing,' and she spoke with such purpose they all waited expectantly, 'I'm going to use my *proper* name, Kilbride. I wasn't going to. I always said I would get there under my own steam. In rep. my name didn't matter; I was just one of the company. But seeing Dad today, I told him I'm going to carry the banner of Kilbride. For *him*. We didn't run away from the truth: Dad will never be able to act again; it won't matter how much they manage to patch him up. When I told him about the name, I think he was relieved. Oh, not relieved that I wasn't going to find some glamorous stage name for myself, but relieved to have us both face up to the truth. Just for a moment I found a chink in his armour.' She shivered, despite the warm day.

'How's the career going, Zena?' Nick tried to steer her on to a new track. 'I haven't seen you since you started treading the boards. And let's see what sort of a ring Jethro has given you.'

Her mind was sidetracked as he'd intended. It was only as they were walking with her to the station that she told them she was being auditioned for an important supporting role in a new West End production.

'And if the press gets hold of the fact I'm Dad's daughter, then I'll be proud. It's funny, isn't it. I always said I had to get there on my own. But now I want him to feel part of it. I've got to do well for his sake as well as for mine.'

Her visit had brought no comfort to Tessa. If, as Zena said, for a moment she had found a chink in Sebastian's armour, there was no such chink in Tessa's. As if they were seeing off a stranger, she raised her hand in polite dismissal as the train steamed out of the station.

So the days of Nick's leave went by. A fortnight ago Sally had been at home, listening for the shrill bell of the telephone and the first sound of his voice. How long ago and faraway it seemed. And there was one emotion that gave her no pride: resentment. This was Nick's longed-for homecoming and they were spending it giving support to Tessa, Tessa who accepted their presence with no sign of interest and who went through her days showing neither hope nor grief. Was this what shock did to a person? Never would she have Sally's impeccable dress sense, but each morning she appeared at the breakfast table looking, by her standards, remarkably well groomed. If they tried to draw her into conversation she complied, answering as necessary but never offering anything that would need the effort of thought. Their days were spent 'taking care of Tessa', a full-time job that left nothing over for finding each other after three years of separation.

Usually they ate at a local inn where the upstairs room grandly called itself a 'Tudor Restaurant', but on the Wednesday evening of their second week they had arranged with Mrs Griffin that they'd eat at home. In the seldom-used dining room smelling of furniture polish they had had a supper of shepherd's pie that owed more to the well-mashed potatoes cooked to an appetising golden brown than to the meagre layer of minced lamb.

'That was surprisingly good,' Nick said. 'Not many days of leave left. Only two more whole days, then I shall be gone. I'll see if there's a train late in the day Saturday. That'll give me a few hours at home on Sunday before I don my khaki and get on my way – for the last time. But you girls will stay on here, of course. Helga will happily go on caring for your farmyard, Tess.'

'*I* certainly can't stay on,' Sally heard her answer as sharp but she was too cross to care. How dare he discount *her* responsibilities. She had a job to go to, one that mattered. She was a cog in the wheel of newsgathering, yet he saw the work she did as unimportant, a way to keep herself amused until he came home. 'These two weeks are the bulk of my annual leave.'

'The war's over.' She heard his laughing reply as patronising. 'At least in Europe it is, and it won't be long now before the Japs throw in the towel. In a week or two I'll be finally released and you'd be giving up then anyway. So drop them a line, Sal, and explain. Naturally you'll stay with Tess.'

'Tess knows I shan't stay. Tess,' Sally turned to her friend, '*you* know I have to get back to the Park. Mrs Griffin will look after you.'

Was Tessa thinking? Keeping her glance lowered, it was impossible for them to read her mind. For a few seconds she said nothing.

'Tess ...?' Sally prompted.

'We'll all go home on Saturday,' Tess announced, in a voice that implied that whether or not they agreed didn't interest her.

'You mean you'll just come down at weekends for visiting hours? It's a long way, Tess. And they've been very good; often they've let you see him at other times.' Nick looked at her with concern, trying not to show his irritation towards Sally and what he considered to be her pigheaded selfishness.

'Seb suggested it. He doesn't talk much, hardly says anything.' She squared her chin in an effort to hold her voice steady. 'But he said he wanted me to go home. He has a lot of treatment ahead. Wants to think of me at home.'

Nick frowned. Was Sebastian being honest? And, if so, couldn't he understand how hurt poor Tessa must be?

141

'I think that's very wise,' Sally said. 'He has so much to put up with, and knowing you are watching, worrying, hoping to see him getting more cheerful – when, let's face it, he *can't* be, not at this stage – all that must put an extra strain on him.'

'You may think so,' Nick said. 'I don't. Even if you can't see him every day, he needs to know you're here, Tess. I'm sure he does. All right, Sal says that seeing you worried is an extra burden for him, but there are burdens and burdens. He needs to know you want to be with him.'

'Is that what you think?' Like a child, Tessa turned to him.

'I'm sure. Mrs Griffin is a kindly old biddy; she'll feed you in the evenings if you don't want to eat out by yourself. Sal and I can come down at the weekends, if she really insists she has to get back to work out her notice.'

Tessa nodded, or rather her head moved in a nodding action, her face void of expression.

'In that case I'll stay. I don't mind being by myself.'

They were both conscious that being on her own might well be easier; there would be no need to make the effort of conversation. Sally wished she could have talked to Sebastian, understanding and sensitive Sebastian. But throughout the fortnight they had been kept away from him; the sister had told them that he was not up to receiving visitors and in any case had asked her not to allow anyone to his bedside. That 'anyone' included his wife and daughter hadn't been considered. Supposing the positions were reversed? Sally stretched her imagination, supposing it were Nick who'd been hurt; surely by this time she would have found the courage to pull herself out of the numbing despair that seemed to envelop Tessa. There were moments when she felt like shaking her friend, trying physically to break the fog of misery that wrapped itself around her.

'Don't you come to the station with us,' Nick said on the Saturday. 'We'd rather think of you here where Mrs Griffin can take care of you.'

Tessa smiled emptily. 'I'll come if you like. I don't mind.' That was one of those moments when Sally's sympathy came near breaking point. Into her mind came the image of Simon, his beloved wife buried in the rubble of their home, his own career snatched from him. Was his grief any the less because he was determined to grapple with an uncertain future and carve a new

142

path? Tessa hadn't lost Sebastian, not the real man. There was no doubt of the depth of her love for him, and of his for her. So surely she could help him build a worthwhile life. No doubt she would, once he came home, once they started to find their way forward.

'It's got to be up to you, Tess,' she said, following her own thoughts.

'I said, I don't mind. I'll stay with Mrs Griffin if Nick thinks I should.'

'Not that. It doesn't matter whether you come to see us off or not. We aren't the important ones, *you* aren't the important one. It's Sebastian. And it has to be up to you, Tess. You've got to help him find his way. How do you think he'd behave if it had been *you* in the accident instead of him? He'd buck his ideas up and see he helped you through.' She surprised even herself with her outburst. Nick looked at her in speechless horror. But the one thing she had done was send a shaft through the dull misery that cocooned Tessa. Those eyes that had been empty of all expression now looked on Sally with anguish and in an instant were bloodshot with burning tears.

'Want to help him, Sal. You know I do. Can't.' Her pale, freckled, but always pretty face crumpled. In an instant Nick moved round the table to stand behind her, the pressure of his hands firm on her shoulders.

'It'll get easier, Tess. God, I've never felt so helpless. If only we could *do* something for him. But he knows, Tess, of course he knows how you feel.'

'Does he?' she sobbed. 'I don't know if he does, don't know how he feels about anything. If only he'd tell me – anything – if he'd break down – if he'd rave against what's happened. But it's as if he's dead inside.'

'It's shock, it must be. Shock and pain. I know we can't even begin to help, but Tess, you know we're always there for you. And Sally didn't mean to sound critical.'

'I know. I'm sorry, I'm behaving badly. Can't stop crying. Like when you uncork a bottle of champagne badly, you can't stop it all bubbling out.'

Outside the door Mrs Griffin had her hand on the handle, sure that by now they'd be ready for their plates to be cleared and the rice pudding brought in. Instead, she retreated. Poor little Mrs Kilbride, such a gentle, pretty little woman. Oh, but it was a cruel world, the things that could happen and tear a person's life to shreds. A blessing she had a good friend like Sally Kennedy; there are those who are sweet and loving and those who are strong and dependable. She'd always prided herself on being one of those herself; when things had knocked her down she'd made sure she bounced straight back up before anyone saw her lying there. And so would Sally Kennedy. Yet when tragedy struck, it was poor little Mrs Kilbride who got hit. Shaking her head in sadness at the cruelty of Fate, she carried her rice pudding back to be kept warm until they'd had a few minutes to recover.

To her surprise, a minute or two later Sally knocked at the kitchen door.

'I've brought everything I could carry, Mrs Griffin,' she said, holding their stacked plates and vegetable dishes.

'I was waiting a minute or two. I thought I'd give the poor soul time to get herself together again before I interrupted.'

'That was kind.' Sally dumped her load on the draining board. 'Mrs Griffin, Nick and I have to leave on Saturday. He is due back at camp by Sunday night and I'm at work next week.'

'A rum sort of leave,' Mrs Griffin said as she piled plates and rice pudding on to the tray. 'She's lucky to have friends to support her like you have.'

'We're more like family than just friends. When my son gets demobbed we really will be family too; he and their daughter are engaged to be married.'

'They say a trouble shared is a trouble halved. Well, she has all of you to share it, but when it comes down to rock bottom not all the friendship, no, and not all the love that she'll give to that poor husband of hers, can change the course of things. Please God the strength will come from somewhere to overcome their troubles. Now then, my dear, are you all right carrying that? Then, I won't disturb you. When you've done just leave it all on the table, I'll keep an ear open for when the coast's clear to come and get the dirties. And one more thing – when you've gone back you mustn't worry about her – no, that's a silly thing to say, for of course you'll worry. What I mean is, I shall keep a good eye on her. I'll try and persuade her to come back here for her supper of an evening, better than being alone. Too old to be much company for the poor girl, but I'm a good listener if she wants one.'

144

'I know. And thank you, Mrs Griffin. She's so quiet, so lifeless. If you could have seen her before, you'd not think it the same person. Everyone always loves Tess, her home is full of warmth and welcome. Yet now ...' The two women looked at each other in silent understanding.

On Saturday, while Tessa was at the hospital, Sally and Nick boarded the train home.

Sally was ashamed of an emotion she couldn't control. Her consolation came from Drifford Park, the knowledge that she had a role to play and was part of a useful team. But it was something she had to fight for.

Throughout the three years Nick had been away, the light at the end of her tunnel of vision had been 'the day he is home for good'. That day came only two weeks after they'd left Tessa in Kent. Yet where now was the elation? Nick was home, Jethro was safe and the war in Europe was over. Was it just the thought of Sebastian that cast a cloud? Certainly it did, a cloud that overshadowed everything. But if it were only that, what she felt would have been compassion, affection unsullied by this feeling she was loath to put a name to.

'I've been in to see them at the office,' Nick told her two days after he'd hung up his uniform for the last time.

'You don't intend to rush back without a break, surely?' Her mind was half on what he said and half on the programme she'd translated describing the desolation of the thousands of those who were bracketed under the banner of 'Displaced Persons', refugees whose homes had been destroyed, their lives broken. What difference if they were German, French, Polish, Italian, what difference which side they had fought on. These were people, families, civilians; for the most part all they had wanted was the sort of daily life that a few years ago they had taken for granted. Sally looked at her comfortable drawing room, the bowl of roses seeming to symbolise the contrast between *her* world and *theirs*; she looked at Nick sitting at ease scanning the newspaper and with the crossword puzzle almost completed. No wonder when she answered him he only had half her attention.

'Take time off, you say? What's the point? Sal, give up that damn fool job you mess about at. Our war's over. Christ! Isn't it bad enough what's happened to Sebastian? Nothing can ever be like it used to be at the cottage. But at least *we* can give them some semblance of normality in their lives. If you don't think I deserve any consideration, can't you have a care for Tess?'

'Of course I do. And you're talking rubbish. As if it makes a jot of difference to them whether or not I go to work. They have to find their own way –'

'Christ!'

'I wish you'd stop Christing!'

He ignored her interruption. 'Sometimes I can't believe the things you say. They are our friends. Or doesn't that count with you anymore? Are you so puffed up with your own importance that you can't remember how it always was?'

'Who's living in cloud-cuckoo land, you or me? How it was, you say. I was never content with doing nothing, or have you forgotten? I looked after the house because I like order; I can't stand muddled houses or muddled thinking either. When Jethro was little I never complained, I had a purpose as long as he needed me.'

'Oh, I remember all right. You could never be a home maker if you lived a hundred years. You always keep it antiseptically hygienic, a speck of dust wouldn't dare cross your threshold, but that doesn't make a *home*.' If he'd said it teasingly she would have laughed it away. But he didn't.

'If I was such a bad housewife I wonder you want to repeat it.' Her tone was sarcastic. For a moment they held each other's gaze, both seeing the hurt, both aware of a sudden fear of where they were heading.

'Of course I want to repeat it, Sal.' Throwing the paper aside he stood up, moving towards her. She must have moved too, for in an instant she was in his arms. 'Don't let's quarrel. We've got to pick up the threads. Your life has been different, and God knows mine has. But all that's over, we're back where we started.' She raised her face to his, her lips parted as his mouth covered hers. 'You know what we want?'

Yes, she knew. But she needed to hear him say it. 'Tell me,' she whispered, 'What do you want? Now this minute, what do you want?'

'I want to take you to bed,' he spoke through clenched teeth as if he were talking more to himself than to her. 'I want to fill your body and fill your mind.'

146

'I want it too.' How often while he'd been away she'd been consumed by this longing. When at last he'd come on his final leave desire had been overtaken almost immediately by anxiety – combined with a melodious bed in a room divided from poor Tess by nothing more than a wall; even back at Owls' Roost the shadow had hung over them, that and in his case the knowledge that he had to share her with work that fulfilled her in a way being a wife never had. So what was different now? She wanted to lose herself in a frenzy of erotic wonder. It was as if their near-quarrel had released whatever had held them back through the first days since he'd been demobbed. A cloud because of Sebastian, that's what she'd thought; a cloud because she was too taken up with that life he couldn't share, Nick thought. In those moments the cloud was miraculously lifted; they were free. There was no finesse in the way they hurried up the stairs.

On that early evening in June there was no rushing headlong to their goal; they travelled on a journey of eroticism beyond anything they'd experienced except in their dreams during the hungry years of separation. At last, exhausted and exhilarated, it was over; only the wonder lingered.

'Sal ... wonderful ...' he panted, 'sometimes thought I'd go barmy ... barmy with wanting it ... you've no idea, Sal, what it was like ... the nights were the worst ... the same for us all ... must have been ... wasn't cut out to live like a monk ... frustrated as hell ... you don't know what it does to a bloke, months, years.'

Silently, she lay close to him. She wished he'd not said what he had – 'wanting *it*' not 'wanting *you*'. Yet of course it was true, and had it been any different for her? But his words echoed: 'You've no idea what it was like', 'You don't know what it does to a bloke.' Oh but she did know. But these last moments – half-hour? Hour? Time had been lost – had belonged to the two of them. She didn't want to hear about his nights of loneliness, or hers either. The here and now blotted all that out.

Drawing her closer, he gave every appearance of drifting into sleep. Instead he surprised her by saying. 'That beats going to that Tower of Babel where you work. Give it up, Sal. Tell them tomorrow.'

'Don't, Nick. Don't spoil everything.'

He didn't answer and she knew the wonder was lost.

Next day she had to be on duty at midday, so she wouldn't be home much before nine in the evening.

'There's no point in me hanging around kicking my heels here,' Nick told her as she carried the breakfast dishes to the sink. 'There's a train a bit before noon; I thought I'd go down and see Sebastian.' A most unlikely suggestion unless Sebastian had made greater progress than Tessa ever hinted when she phoned.

'Whatever time will you get home? You'd have been better to wait until tomorrow and make an early start.'

'Our friend Mrs Griffin will give me a bed. I wonder you haven't found time to go down again since we left Tess – you know there'd be a bed for you.'

'Purposely I didn't,' she answered. 'I know it's shock – for her as well as him – but, Nick, they have to find their way forward by themselves. Imagine what he's suffering. It haunts you.'

'Comes at you when you least expect it,' he murmured. 'Where's the justice?'

'Life is short on justice. If you listened to the things I hear –' One look at his face told her she had slipped on to rocky ground. 'Give Tess my love, tell her if she wants me to I'll try and get over when I have a day off. But don't push it, Nick, you know how I feel. Most important, give my love to Sebastian *if* he's ready for you to see him.' Previously, according to Tessa, whenever she'd suggested Nick or Sally coming he'd just kept repeating, 'No, no, no ... no one.'

'Box office idol or no, there has never been an ounce of vanity in Sebastian,' Sally said. 'It must be just a matter of time. Before he faces anyone else he has to get used to facing himself.'

So Nick set off, his bag packed for a few days. Those few days turned into a week, crept towards a fortnight. Then came the day when Sally came home and instead of the usual emptiness of the house, she was assailed by the appetising smell of cooking.

'Helga?' she called as she came through the outer lobby. 'Lovely surprise. Are you home for the night?' Then, as she opened the door into the kitchen, 'Tess! You've come back with Nick! Are they transferring Sebastian? But how wonderful.'

'Yes,' Tessa answered. There was even something of her normal warmth in her smile. 'Yes, it's wonderful to be back, I mean. But they won't let Seb come, not for ages, I should think. Trouble was, Sal, I don't think I was doing him any good being there. The sister as good as told me so. And he never talked to me, just kept his eyes closed. They say he'll buck up once all the operations are over; they're going to do a lot of work on him when he's ready.'

'But they *are* satisfied with him?' Sally felt uneasy, yet she couldn't be sure why.

'He'll be better when he doesn't have to worry about me sitting there,' she repeated. 'The burns unit is full of men on their own; it probably made him worse having me always hanging round. Anyway, I've imposed too long on Helga. When we've had supper Nick said he'd drive me home.'

That was a Sunday. The following day Nick returned to work. Surely now that he was back in the musty office that had been his life for so long and Tessa where she belonged at Mulberry Cottage, they would find some sort of normality. Yet Sally was conscious of an unexplained foreboding.

Chapter Eight

For years Zena had dreamed of the day when she would audition for a role in the West End. Yet when the dream became reality she felt as though she stood outside herself; she read the lines while her mind was aching with love and misery; it was impossible even briefly to forget the sight of Sebastian.

Nothing could have prepared her. His hair, eyebrows, even eyelashes all shrivelled in the blaze and gone; as for his charred, withered flesh, it haunted her; the ache in her heart was more than grief, it was physical pain. She'd vowed then that she would succeed not just for herself, but for *him*, for a life that could never be the same again. And perhaps he was working through her as she read the lines, perhaps the misery that consumed her gave her greater depth of understanding – or, of course, perhaps it was simply that her outstanding talent cast her competitors into the shade. By any other name Zena Kilbride stood out, a girl of unusual beauty and with perception and understanding in advance of her years.

If the producer wasn't swayed by her pedigree, the same couldn't be said of the newspapers. Every paper carried the story that the daughter of Sebastian Kilbride was being cast in her first West End role. The accident had attracted attention of course, but in a country still celebrating victory it had soon become yesterday's news. There's nothing more newsworthy than a beautiful woman and so as Zena went into rehearsal, even though she had no more than an important supporting role, it was she who interested the reporters. Side by side on the front page of the national newspapers were two pictures: one of Sebastian, who before the war had held a very special place in the hearts of the film-going public and, next to that, a picture of Zena. Underneath, the story was enough to tug at heartstrings and more than enough to ensure Zena a place in the public interest. Even in a supporting role, her presence would have a following.

During rehearsals she managed to get to the hospital as often as she could. Ought she to be glad her mother wasn't there? She didn't look the question in the face. Between her father and her there had always been the added bond of her choice of a career, but now what drew her was something more than that. He hardly spoke to her, sometimes he hardly opened his eyes, yet she was sure he drew some sort of strength from knowing she was there. She made herself look at him, really look, seeing him with her heart as well as her eyes.

'Dad.' Lightly she touched his hand, conscious that he flinched but uncertain whether it was because his burned flesh was so painful or whether he was frightened to relax the invisible barrier he put between himself and everything outside the regime of the hospital. 'Dad, rehearsals are over. We open on Tuesday. Dad, say a prayer for me – for *us*, you and me both. It won't be just me there on the stage, it'll be you too. Please, Dad, be with me, let me feel that you're giving me support.'

'You know I do,' he mumbled through lips that even after all these weeks would open no further. Was the surgery he'd already undergone supposed to have given him back a face?

'Sister says they're going to pretty you up some more later in the week.'

'Why bother?'

'Don't know, really.' She made herself laugh lightly. 'Maybe everyone isn't as clever as me, though. Maybe some of them can't see beneath the surface.'

'Can't bear it, kid.'

'You are the least appearance-conscious person I know. I was always so proud, when Nick used to go about looking up-to-the-minute smart, there was my dad slopping about in his old bags, not giving a damn what the world made of him. That's what made you my hero. It's so twittish to be conceited.'

'It's not that. I'm ashamed. Frightened. Alive, should be grateful.' Then with a scarcely human sob that seemed to come from the depth of his being, 'Zena, oh damn it, oh damn it ...'

152

She'd never seen her father cry before; she was torn with pity and didn't know how to deal with it. Bending over him, with her head almost on his pillow, she spoke softly, distinctly, praying for the right words. 'We all love you, Dad, what you look like can't alter that. Even if you looked like an ogre – and you don't –'

Approaching in her rubber-soled shoes, the sister's shadow fell across the bed.

'I think it might be better if you said goodbye, Miss Kilbride. Wait for me in the corridor if you will, I'm just going to give him a little jab. That'll help him to sleep.'

Feeling utterly alone, Zena left him. She did as she was asked and waited for the sister, putting her play-acting skill to the test as she listened to the voice of authority. 'He'll sleep for a few hours now,' the sister said, her voice kind but firm, seeming to say that her word was law. 'You mustn't worry. He's really coming along very nicely. Just give him time. I'm afraid you've had a long journey for just those few minutes, but he's not fit for anything more, not yet.'

'I didn't mind the journey. It's so hard for him, Sister.'

'I know it is, it's hard for all of them. Some so young ... but they help each other, you know. We do all we can for their injuries. As for the rest, they help each other to accept.'

Zena felt he was a very long way from even starting to accept. But the sister had been here for years; all through the war they'd dealt with horrendous burns. What she said must be right; that was the thing to hang on to.

That was in August, three days before the curtain went up on Zena's West End debut.

'A good thing chickens can't tell the time.' Tessa's voice sounded as if there was a laugh trying to escape; she knew it did, making sure it did. 'They usually have their meal at teatime but none of them argued when I gave it to them for elevenses.'

And, all determined to do their part and 'keep Tessa from brooding', the others laughed. They were travelling to London, Sally, Nick, Tessa and Helga. For Zena's first night Tessa had booked a box, no less. At her invitation Eliot was meeting them at the theatre.

'I do wish Jethro could have got his leave through in time,' Sally said. 'Just think how proud he would have been.' It was over a week since they'd had his letter saying that he was expecting a pass for fourteen days' leave. No chance that he'd get demobilisation for some time; perhaps a year or more as he hadn't joined until the war was half over, but that was something they could all accept.

All through the war Tessa and Sally – and Helga too for that matter – had supported each other. The cloud of fear had hung over them, not for themselves in their peaceful mid-English countryside, but for those they loved. Now the cloud had been replaced by something so much harder: the thought of Sebastian made ordinary pleasure impossible; it made Tessa consciously force her face to smile; it made Nick and Sally consider every word before they spoke it. As for Helga, for her the cloud of fear had rolled away, taking with it her last vestige of hope. For her, though, there was nothing strange in hiding her secret heart; she had done it since she'd travelled to England with her one small suitcase.

The one thing none of them wanted was a lull in the conversation, so they all played their part. And so the journey passed, bringing them to Paddington and to the queue for a taxi.

'She won't be looking out for us; we'll go straight to our seats,' Tessa told them. Perhaps she hadn't used the same words, but she had told them the same thing quite four times. 'You take charge of the tickets, Nick. Will she be frightened, do you think?'

'Aren't good actors always frightened?' Sally answered. 'That's what Sebastian says.' There! She'd said his name. She couldn't bear the way everyone was frightened to talk about him. Sebastian *says*, not Sebastian *used to say*. She cast a quick glance at Tessa and seemed to imagine that the smile stiffened as if she was afraid to let it go. We mustn't be so frightened of upsetting her that we don't speak about him; we have to make him still part of what we do, only talking about him can bring him close. Always there were four of us, still there are four of us and even if he can't be here we've got to feel he's part of the evening. 'Bet you a pound to a penny his thoughts are here this evening,' she said as they climbed into the taxi. She felt Nick glower at her, but she ignored it and took Tessa's hand in hers. Her only answer was a slight nod of her head, that set smile vanished and her expression inscrutable.

'Soon be there,' Nick said unnecessarily, for they all knew very well just how far they had to go. Tessa's fingers gripped Sally's. It

154

was a long time since they'd been to a West End theatre. Indeed, the bustle of London was so removed from what their lives had been in the last years that there was a feeling of unreality about the bright lights, the throng of people in the streets. Some were walking purposefully; others, like them, visitors from the country gazing around them in wonder, wanting to absorb the activity all around them so that they'd be able to recall it when the evening was no more than a memory. Even Sally, who had met her father in London sometimes during the years of the war, hadn't been there since the lights had gone back on. So different from their normal habitat, no wonder they were caught up in the atmosphere as the taxi carried them towards the theatre.

In the foyer the buzz of excitement was almost tangible.

'My dear,' Eliot greeted them, his words addressed to Tessa, 'I feel very privileged to be asked to join you.' He kissed her on each cheek, then turned to return Sally's hug before holding out his hand to Nick. 'Not too late to welcome you home,' he said. His intention had been to give Nick a few days at home after demobilisation, then come to Owls' Roost to see him. The intention had come to naught when Sally had explained that he'd gone back to be near Sebastian. And quite right too; Eliot had approved. 'You're looking remarkably well. How's civilian life? As if you'd never been away?'

'Hardly the same.' Nick's laughing rejoinder was aimed at disguising his impression of how much older Eliot looked. But of course he did, he'd not seen him since the last fragile days of peace. 'Before I went away I had a wife at home to cosset me.' Only Sally felt the sting hiding behind his smile. She slipped her arm through her father's.

'We're living it up tonight, Dad. A box, no less.'

'And quite right too. It's not every night a fledgling flies. And how's Sebastian?' Again he spoke to Tessa. 'My dear, here or a million miles away, this is where his heart will be this evening.'

'... what Sal was just saying,' Tessa murmured. She felt Nick's firm grip on her arm and held her head a little higher. Tonight she wouldn't think of that hospital ward, she wouldn't let herself be haunted by the emptiness in Seb's eyes. A million miles away, Eliot had said, but that's how he seemed when she sat by his bedside. If only his eyes would give her a message, something, anything. She'd get used to how he looked; to her it wouldn't have mattered so long as the real Seb, his mind and spirit, was the same. If he could never act again, was that so dreadful? They could afford to live – and that was the point, to *live*. It was as if he'd forgotten how, as if he didn't want to remember. All through the war she'd just prayed and prayed that he would come home safely. Think of all those others who hadn't. But Seb was alive; they had a future together. Didn't he care?

'This way,' she heard Nick's quiet voice, felt his hand steering her towards the stairs. This way ... what other way was there? This was what life had dished out to them. Together she and Seb must pick up the pieces ... she'd help him ... if only he'd let her near; if only he wouldn't look at her as if she were a stranger, a stranger who meant nothing to him. Behind her she could hear Sally and her father talking with the comfortable companionship that had gone from her own life. Make things better for us, I don't know how. So lonely, lonely for Seb, the proper Seb, the whole Seb. Don't care what he looks like. Just make him himself again, mend his soul. That's the trouble, his soul is as scarred as his poor darling face.

'Here we are.' Again it was Nick, as he ushered her into the box. 'Oh, someone – Christ! It can't be!'

'Hi, Dad, it's me all right.'

Forgetting this son of his was a grown man, Nick let go of Tessa's arm and gripped him; the only outlet to the sudden emotion at seeing him was to thump his back. 'Christ! But – here Sal, see who's here.'

Jethro had developed into a man as handsome as his father. Yet at that age Nick had been very different, for there had been a natural elegance about him that Jethro lacked. Perhaps three years of wartime soldiering had toughened him. Despite the physical resemblance, seeing them together, rather than seeing the likeness Sally was aware of the differences. Nick must have been about the age Jethro was now when she'd first met him and fallen in love with him.

Greetings over and surprise overtaken by sheer joy at their all being together – for Tessa made a conscious and believable effort to match her mood to the occasion – they sorted out their seating: Nick, Jethro, Sally, Eliot, Helga and then Tessa. Jethro hardly bothered to follow the plot of the play, watching Zena as if the sight of her hypnotised him. She was *his*; all this was peripheral to

156

the part of her life that mattered, the part they shared. Tessa's interest was as narrow as his own; she wanted to absorb every moment, every movement Zena made and every word she spoke so that she could relay the wonder of the evening to Seb. She wouldn't return home with the others tomorrow, instead she'd go by herself to the hospital. Tomorrow she would find a way of getting through to him, share all this with him, remind him of their years in sleazy boarding houses; she'd laugh with him about the good times and together they'd find their strength to face what Fate had thrown at them. There in the dimly lit theatre she let herself believe the miracle.

It was during the second and shorter interval that Nick said to Jethro, 'I hope the hotel isn't full. As soon as the curtain comes down I'll go and telephone to get a room for you.' He spoke with natural casualness, a fond parent taking charge of the situation. His remark hardly needed an answer but, hearing what was said as he came back from the cloakroom, Eliot told them, 'If the hotel's full, don't worry. You can come back to the flat with me, Jethro.' The other three waited, aware of the moment and of each other, aware of Nick who'd been out of the picture when Jethro and Zena had hurtled into their first experience of love. Just for an instant Tessa and Sally looked at each other, while Helga, her hands clasped tightly and inelegantly behind the back of her chair, watched only Jethro.

'No need,' Jethro beamed, more than well pleased with the situation, 'but thanks all the same, Grandad. I shall be going back with Zena.'

'The party, yes of course you'll want to go with her to the first-night party.' Nick completely missed the message.

'Of course he'll stay with Zena.' Sally made sure her laugh was light and natural. 'Be your age, Nick.'

'What the devil do you mean?'

'Dad.' Jethro looked directly at his father. 'You don't have to worry about Zena and me. We've been together for ages. I know I've been away for the last bit, but that couldn't make any difference. We're not kids, Dad.'

'You mean ... damn it all, Jethro, when you went overseas you were just a boy.'

'Old enough to fight for my country – is that being a boy? Anyway, I don't want any lectures. As soon as I get demobbed we're getting hitched. Anyway,' he blustered, his repetition of the word a sure sign that he was less comfortable than he pretended, and that not being a kid didn't necessarily mean he was ready to withstand his father's anger, 'I'm already staying there. I went straight there when I got here yesterday morning.'

'Yesterday?' It was Sally's turn for surprise. 'You didn't ring?'

'Sorry, Mum. We got a bit carried away and the time slipped by. Then, knowing you were coming today, I thought it would be a lark to hide in the box and surprise you. But, Mum, about coming home for my leave: it's not that I don't want to, but I want to be with Zena and anyway what's the point of killing time on my own while you and Dad are at work?'

'Of course you want to be with Zena. Come at the weekend, Sunday, Monday. She won't be at the theatre then.'

'We're going to the hospital. I've got fourteen days; suppose we come the following weekend?'

'Lovely.' Oh how hard it was to give him his freedom and let him fly, not to let it show that suddenly playing second fiddle in the orchestra of your offspring's life is a hard pill to swallow. Clearly one too hard for Nick.

'You stayed with her last night, you say? Did you give a thought to what other people in the flats would be saying? Where's your respect? This damned war seems to have destroyed all you young people's principles. The world's changed, the old values seem to count for nothing.'

'Lights are going down. It's going to start. I say, Tess, isn't she great!'

From her seat at the end of the line, Tessa nodded. Of course she was great, she was wonderful. Too dark now for anyone to see her eyes swim with tears.

Next day Nick, Sally and Helga took the train home. There was none of the excitement of the outward journey. Nick's anger was ill concealed; Sally understood well enough that Jethro preferred to stay in London with Zena. If she'd had any imagination she would never have expected him to spend his leave any other way, but she couldn't ignore the disappointment that overspilled into resentment against Nick that he could behave like a Victorian patriarch. And Helga? Her thoughts were her own, but that had long been Helga's way.

*

158

It was the end of October when Sebastian came home. It was better not to ask Nick how he managed to come by the petrol coupons that allowed him to drive Tessa to fetch him, both of them buoyed up with hope: once he was back at Mulberry Cottage, surrounded by familiar things and people who loved him, he would start to pick up the shattered pieces of his life. Tessa was thankful she had tilled so much of the garden; out there working the soil he would learn to find himself. What neither of them had imagined was how seeing him outside the confines of the burns unit would emphasise the difference between 'before' and 'after'. In those far-off idyllic days before the war the four of them had gone to a country fair where he had bought a wide-brimmed leather hat. At the time it had been something of a joke, but he'd formed an attachment to it and had refused to throw it away. On that autumn day, misty and dull before its time, Tessa had brought it in his case of clothes. With his coat collar turned up, the brim of his no-longer-a-joke hat pulled down, he sat alone in the back of the car.

'Will you go in the front with Nick?' Tessa had asked him. 'Or would you rather you and me both had the back?'

'You go with Nick. I'm better on my own, I'll probably sleep.' His voice, the voice that had captivated the hearts and minds of so many before war had torn their world apart, was dull and expressionless.

Whether he slept or not they couldn't be sure. Once or twice Nick spoke to him but had no reply; every now and again Tessa turned and peered at him. He sat with his back very straight, his head bent forward, his eyes closed. Once, when she whispered, 'Seb?' she believed he flinched, but if sleep was only a pretence he hadn't been an actor all those years for nothing.

'Nick,' he said as the car stopped outside the door of Mulberry Cottage, 'it was good of you to fetch me. Didn't fancy travelling on the train.'

'On the train. Come off it, mate, we've been geared up to today for ages.' Rarely did Nick bluster; he hadn't been prepared to feel so thrown off balance at the sight of Sebastian back on home ground. He put his arm around his friend's shoulder. 'Been a hell of a time since we were here together. How many years?'

Sebastian shook his head, frightened to trust his voice, glad that Tessa had gone on ahead to open the front door and turn on the lights.

159

'Poor Tess,' Nick said, his hold on Sebastian's shoulder still firm, 'this is quite a day for her – the light at the end of her tunnel ... She's really been through the mill, you know. It's been a hell of a thing for her to have to stand on the outside and not be able to help. It's going to be all right, old chap, you've got to believe.' Then, with more hope than tact, 'Now the next thing we all have to look forward to is the wedding, eh? Just as soon as Jethro gets home.'

'Nick, I'm so bloody scared,' Sebastian kept his head turned away.

'Today, of course you are. But give it a bit of time, you've got Tess to help you build a new routine. Come on, old chap, chin up. What about picking up where we were, eh? What about facing the elements and striding on the sands down at The Limit?'

'What am I going to do,' Sebastian breathed, just as if Nick hadn't spoken. 'Better at home, you all say it. Christ, oh Christ ...'

'Come on, boys,' Tess a called from the open doorway. 'Sally won't be home till late, Nick, stay and talk to Seb while I get some food.' Then, moving behind Sebastian under the pretext of switching on the standing lamp, she said, 'Have supper with us,' and willing Nick to look directly at her she silently mouthed the word '*please*'.

'Sounds a good scheme. All right with you, Sebastian?'

'Great.' Sebastian forced a smile, a smile that only exaggerated the unnaturally tight skin that pulled down the right side of his mouth and made it impossible for him to open his right eye. The left side was scarred, the skin crinkled like worn crêpe paper. Neither his smile nor his effort at pretending enthusiasm as he said that one word 'Great' fooled either of them. But they played along with the charade. Time must be his healer and always they must be there for him.

Through supper Nick and Tessa made sure conversation wasn't given time to lag; they told themselves this was the way to relax him. Whether or not it did, it was impossible to tell for his face couldn't convey expression. Sebastian Kilbride, whose picture was stuck to many a daydreaming girl's bedroom wall: his eyebrows hadn't grown back, nor yet his eyelashes, but the purple and crinkled skin on his head was showing signs of fluffy down. His hands and forearms were the same hue, the skin shrivelled.

160

'What do you think, Seb? She's sure to want it here.'

'What? Sorry, I was thinking about something else. What did you say?'

'Zena – the reception. Jethro apparently expects to be home before Easter. If he's home by then, the end of the play's run would be the best time.'

'She must have it where she likes, of course she must. No need to think about it yet. No need . . . no . . .' He put down his knife and fork and pushed his half-eaten food away.

'No, whenever they decide, or wherever either, it'll be some time away yet. It's been quite a day.' Nick changed the subject. 'Now you've got your regular help back you won't want me to give you a hand with the dishes, Tess. I'll clear off and leave you in peace. Sal is on early shift tomorrow, so what about coming over to us in the evening?'

'Not tomorrow,' Sebastian said before Tessa had a chance to answer. 'Have a quiet day tomorrow. Or bring Sal over here. Helga's still with you?'

'Seems she's a fixture. She and Sal get on very well as far as I can see; not that you know what goes on in Helga's mind.'

'Helga's a dear,' Tessa put in.

Nick winked at Sebastian. 'Our ugly duckling? Your good lady sees the best in us all.'

'She's no such thing. She's turning out to be quite a swan. There's more to a woman than a bosom like Betty Grable's; that and a good pair of legs is about as far as some of you chaps ever look.' Just for that moment Tessa had forgotten Sebastian. Too late she wished she could recall her words. She wanted Nick gone, she wanted to touch Seb, to hold him, to say a thousand things to him that the long ward of the burns unit had prevented.

'I stand accused,' Nick laughed. 'Anyway, I'm off. Sal will give you a ring. Don't work the old chap too hard; remember he's had months of idleness so break him in gently. Cheers, Seb. Oh and thanks for my supper.'

In silence they heard his car drive away then Tessa stacked the tray to carry it to the kitchen.

'I'll do that,' Sebastian took it from her. 'You wash, I'll dry.'

Her eyes swam with tears.

'Seb, you're home.' She felt her face crumple. 'How many times I've heard you say that – you wash, I'll dry. It's going to be

161

all right, we'll make it all right.' Never more than at that moment had she wanted to feel his arms round her, yet they stood apart, the tray between them. He made no attempt to put it down, simply stood looking down at the dirty crockery on it, looking anywhere rather than at her.

Dear God, help me, he pleaded silently. Why can't I hold her, comfort her, tell her she's my whole world? She is – You know she is. Why can't I? Because I'm not *me*, not *anything*, just a bloody shell. Why couldn't You have let me be shot down, blown out of the sky to die a hero? That would have left her with unscarred memories. Now we've got nothing. Can't look back, daren't look back. And forward? Help me, help *her*.

'Sorry,' Tessa gulped, wiping her eyes with the backs of her hand like a child.

'Lead on, let's get this done.'

'Just that it's been quite a day, Seb.' She opened the door of the dining room and followed him to the kitchen. At least in washing up they would be occupied. His hands looked as if they must be painful; she wanted to ask him but she couldn't. Perhaps there was no feeling in them at all. If only they could talk, if only he would tell her how he felt and what he was thinking. Yet it was like looking at a ventriloquist's dummy waiting for words to be put in its mouth – except that ventriloquists' dummies had faces that endeared them to their audience, faces full of fun and mischief. Stop it! Don't let yourself think it! Looks don't matter, Seb, not between you and me.

'That's done,' she managed to infuse her tone with a note of satisfaction. 'Now let's call it a day. Sal won't ring tonight and I know Zena won't; she said she'd call you in the morning. So let's go to bed.' Then everything will be right again.

'I think I'll have a bath,' he said.

'Is that an invitation?' Surely he'd respond to the teasing look she gave him, the flirtatious lilt of laughter in her voice. Her heart was racing with sudden joy as she thought of the times they'd bathed together.

'If you want it hot you'd better go first. I can't take the water more than lukewarm.'

'I'll settle for lukewarm.' She put her hands on his shoulders, raising her face to his. With a sudden movement he crushed her against him, pushing her face against his shoulder.

162

'Tess, it's no use. I wish to Christ I'd been killed like thousands of others. I can't face it, Tess, don't know what to do.' He was shaken by sobs.

'Darling Seb, we can face anything if we do it together. Looking different doesn't matter, not to me. As for the rest of the world – I don't give a toss and neither do you.'

'I can't explain.' His crying grew louder; he had no power to control it, no power even to try. She pushed him gently into the hard, high-backed chair then knelt in front of him on the tiled floor.

'Seb, Seb darling.' Her arms were around his waist, yet still he was out of her reach. In those first seconds as she'd felt his shoulders shake and knew he was crying she was thankful: now, at last, the barrier would be down. 'Talk to me,' she begged. 'Tell me everything you feel, in your body, in your heart. We've always shared. I can't bear it if we don't.'

'Feel?' he repeated, the tormented sobbing giving way to an occasional grunt, the sort of sound that comes from someone old and weary. 'I feel nothing. Pain?' He shrugged, holding his hands to his tear-drenched face. 'Just numb. Inside, outside, numb, dead.'

'Wait till you've been home a few days,' Tessa told him, laying her face against his knees – not admitting that she did it to hide the fear he might see in her eyes. 'Tomorrow we'll work in the garden. How will that be for therapy?'

'Let's go up, shall we?' he said, urging her to her feet so that he could stand up. He had no feeling, he believed, but if that were true how was it her love had brought him to such depths?

Tessa wasn't going to give up easily. She ran a lukewarm bath for him and by the time he'd undressed and lowered himself into the water she appeared wearing nothing but a smile.

'Seeing that you've been poorly, I'll have the tap end,' she said, stepping into the water. 'Don't tell me I've got thin; I know. Oh, I hate these taps. Open your legs, I'm going to turn round.' Pushing his knees apart she sat in front of him, leaning against him just as she had hundreds of times. She even raised his hands – hands like wrinkled leather – and drew them to her breast. He didn't pull away, so how was it she knew he was as distant from her as he had been through all these months? She felt rejected, unloved. She'd been so sure that once they were together, there in the home they loved, they would find each other.

163

'Don't sit here too long,' he told her. 'I'm not much good at temperatures, but you mustn't get cold. We'll both get out.'

Obediently she did as he said, wrapping herself in a bath towel and passing one to him. His whole body was red, scorched; not burned as his head and hands had been, but sufficiently so that the marks would stay with him for years if not for ever. Once in the bedroom he took various packets of tablets from his toilet bag.

'What are they for?' she asked.

'Various. Sedatives, pain killers, sleeping pills. Shake me and I rattle.'

'You won't need sleeping pills tonight, Seb,' she promised.

'Don't, Tess! I know what you're saying. Damn it, I'm no good even for that. May be all these bloody pills.'

'Of course that's what it is.' She held out her hand. 'And of course I want us to make love, but that's because we both want to.' How sure she sounded, hiding from him the misery she felt. Then, with a laugh that was aimed at telling him she understood, 'But with a cocktail of tablets like that, I'm not surprised you're not your rampant self. Come to bed, Seb, let's just hold each other, hold each other and say a huge Thank You to whoever plans our lives. So many people have no future, or face the years ahead without the person they loved. That's been what haunted us for years.'

He got into bed and put out the light. Feeling the warmth of her naked body so close, surely, even if he couldn't make love to her, he ought to be aroused out of his apathy. He felt nothing. Kissing her lightly, he turned his back.

They both played the same game: breathing evenly, being careful not to wriggle about and hint that they were awake. Downstairs the clock struck midnight ... one o'clock ... two o'clock.

'Seb ...?' she breathed. No reply. His spirit was numb, but instinct didn't let him fall into that trap. Giving a deep and believable snort, he still 'slept'. Finally, of course, nature overcame both of them. In the morning, she said to him, 'I bet you slept well, back in your own bed.'

'Went out like a light,' he lied.

'Me too.'

His first full day home started with a lie, a lie that was to weave itself into the new relationship they had to build.

*

164

'I can't see why you have to invite strangers,' Nick accused Sally, a fortnight before Christmas.

'Since when has Dad been a stranger? And don't forget, Nick, he's very special to Helga.'

'Best thing would have been if Helga had gone to London and stayed with him. This year we ought to put Tess and Sebastian first. *He* won't visit if we have people here, you know that. Neither will he invite them to the cottage. Anyway, this other fellow, Simon Something or Other –'

'Don't make yourself out to be so damned ignorant. Of course you know his name. And just because he's not English that doesn't make him some sort of freak! He may be a stranger to you, Nick, but during the war he used to come here sometimes with Dad, and his daughter, too. Seb isn't the only one to have troubles; we've been so fortunate ourselves that it's easy to see his as the only tragedy. Simon lost his wife when their home was bombed; his daughter was training to be a dancer but she'll never dance –' she didn't intend telling him of Gizella's relief now she was at boarding school and being treated the same as every other pupil of her age '– and Simon, one of the finest international violinists with his concert career shattered. Does he make a martyr of himself? Of course he doesn't.'

He gave up the pretence of reading the newspaper. Some people might have cast it aside, an obvious expression of their irritation; but not Nick. She saw the set of his mouth, the quick movement as with characteristic precision he folded it and laid it on the coffee table.

'If you've already invited these people, there's nothing I can say, is there. I'd have thought you might have put yourself in Tess's position. What sort of a Christmas will it be for her? A day like any other. I'm going over to see Sebastian for an hour. Are you coming?'

It was Saturday morning, for once Sally's days off coinciding with the weekend. From where she was busy raking up leaves and making a bonfire, Helga watched them go. Nick still referred to her as Sally's ugly duckling, but in truth she had developed into a young woman who, although she'd never be beautiful, had a look of distinction. Above average tall, she was still thin but there was nothing waif-like in her appearance, nor yet anything gracefully elegant; on Helga, thinness hinted at strength, agility. She wore

165

her straight, dark hair plaited and pinned round her head; her steel-framed spectacles had been replaced long ago under Sally's guidance and with an eye to fashion; her complexion was clear and free of make-up; her shoulders were broad; if her long bony wrists and hands hinted that no job would be beyond her, her strong facial features confirmed the impression. Whether or not she was happy was her own secret, but come what may nothing ruffled her calm acceptance.

Now as Sally called out to her that they were going to Mulberry Cottage she waved an acknowledgement of the message then turned back to her raking. This was the sort of work she enjoyed, a way to use her energy while it left her mind free to wander. Where was her life heading? Throughout the war Sally had given her a home, even made her feel that she belonged at Owls' Roost. But all that was changed. Oh, not changed as far as she and Sally were concerned, but the situation was different. The Army was being demobilised, evacuees both young and old had gone home, leaving the district to welcome back its own. She was twenty-one years old; scholastically, her education had been disjointed, leaving her with nothing to show for it. The nursery had been her salvation, giving her an opportunity to do something useful and try to win her independence; that the wage had been abysmally low hadn't worried her any more than it had that the girls she worked with had left her on the outside of their magic circle. They'd seen her as different; she'd known herself to be different. On a winter morning like this, alone in the silent garden, she came nearer to happiness than she ever could as one of a chattering group of her contemporaries. Yet there was no way of escaping the truth: she had come to a crossroad in her life and was ashamed that she could find no beacon directing her the way forward.

The slam of a car door alerted her. It couldn't be! Yes, yes, it was. He was home. Jethro, not khaki-clad, but wearing a grey suit and trilby hat, the garb they were to come to know as his 'demob gear'.

Still holding the rake, she stood like a statue watching him as, without looking her way, he paid the taxi driver then walked towards the side door of the house. Suddenly she sprang to life, threw down the rake, and ran after him with more speed than grace.

'You're out of the Army!' she called, unnecessarily.

'Yep!' he grinned sheepishly, aware of the none-too-good fit of his issue of civilian clothes. 'You see before you an ex-serviceman. How's Helga?'

'I am very well, thank you. And I see that you are too. When your parents know that you are here they will be overjoyed.'

His grin grew even broader. What a funny, prim creature she was. It couldn't simply be that she wasn't at home with the language; she'd lived here years enough for even the thickest to have learned to talk the same as everyone else.

'You say they're out. Be a good kid then, make me a cup of coffee, will you. When will they be back? Not out to lunch, are they?'

'They have gone to Mulberry Cottage. They said nothing of the time to expect them home. Lunch is what Nick calls a moveable feast. But if you are hungry I will move it forward; you can eat something – something on toast, perhaps? – with your coffee if you choose.'

'Well done. Do that, Helga. I'm going up to change out of my civilian uniform. Won't be five minutes.'

As she sliced the bread and waited for the grill to heat, her racing heart was set on putting before him a meal worthy of the occasion, but there was little she could do with the remaining piece of their cheese ration (sold by the village grocer under the label 'Tasty', the choice being that or 'mild' and neither giving any indication of their source) and the last remaining egg.

'Looks good,' Jethro told her obligingly when she put it before him. 'I'll just eat this, then I'll ride over to see the others. Thanks for stopping work to get it for me.' Which surely meant 'Don't hang about while I eat it.' She went back to her bonfire.

Five minutes later, his dirty crockery left in the sink, he pedalled off down the drive, giving her a cheery wave of farewell. The sun still shone, yet surely it had lost some of its brightness. She *must* look ahead, she *must* think of a way to earn her living. The crèche was closing at the end of the year, just three weeks away. If she found a job from the local paper it had to pay her enough that she could afford a bed-sitting room somewhere. But she had no qualifications – add to that, she wasn't English. Working there in the garden, her salvation came from using up more energy than she possessed. So, the leaves smouldering and sending up a spiral of smoke into the still air, she took her rake and

167

began working on the lawn, scratch, scratch, scratch; no weak blade of grass nor square inch of moss stood a chance. Next spring the new growth would be thick and healthy. But where would she be? No, don't think about it, not now, not today.

Nick was wrong about Christmas Day being the same as any other at Mulberry Cottage. Late on Christmas Eve, Zena arrived home, the taxi having dropped Jethro at Owls' Roost on the way. After spending one weekend at home, clearly impatient to be away, he'd spent the intervening two weeks since his demobilisation with her in London.

'I told Zena I'd go to the cottage for Christmas dinner. You don't mind, do you Mum?' he said during breakfast.

'Try and persuade them to come back here with you later, Jethro. Sebastian mustn't be allowed to turn himself into a recluse.'

'Remember the Christmasses we used to have before the war,' Nick said. 'You youngsters were just kids. What a laugh it always was.'

'To remember the days before the war is to remember another world,' Simon said. 'For those of us lucky enough to have the opportunity there *has* to be the spirit to make a fresh start.' He spoke with serious intensity, something Nick found irritating. 'Even for those who are returning to their homes and, like you, Nick, to the work they have always known, time cannot move backwards. For us all it has to be a new road to move along. But for a man like Sebastian Kilbride, how hard it must be to find the light of hope. His work has been snatched from him and nothing put in its place, yet he has to move forward just like the rest of us.'

'There is always a way,' Eliot said. 'We may not see it, but if we keep our eyes open, our eyes and our minds too, there will be a glimpse of something. Has he ever considered directing, I wonder?'

'Before he thinks of anything, Dad,' Sally said, visualising Sebastian, 'he has the most enormous hurdle to overcome. He has to get used to *himself* before he can face a new career.'

'Ach, faces!' Simon scoffed. 'We all seek shelter behind our appearance, all conform, hide what is our real self behind the convention of appearance. But a changed face cannot touch a man's soul. Look deeper and your friend is still there for you.'

168

Nick glared at their visitor, not even trying to hide his irritation. What did some damned stranger know about Sebastian's suffering? All right, the great Simon Szpiegman could no longer fill the concert halls with audiences come to hear him playing some concerto or other with an orchestra but, damn it all, there didn't appear to be anything wrong with the man. Couldn't hold a fiddle for long enough to perform a whole work, wasn't that the tomfool rubbish Sal had said? What the hell did that matter? Easy enough for him to talk so glibly about finding a new path; he wasn't reminded of what had happened to him every time he looked in a mirror.

'Lend me the car for an hour, will you, Nick?' Aware of an uncomfortable tension, Eliot purposely made the request to his son-in-law and not to Sally. 'I'll drive Jethro over to the cottage. I've a little parcel for Tessa and I'd like to see them all.'

'Of course you can have the car. See how it goes; if you can get to see Sebastian this morning that'll break the ice for him; you *may* be able to persuade them to come over here later.' His emphasis on the word 'may' said as clearly as any words that if Sebastian refused to come it was because they had other visitors. 'Unlikely that they will. Poor Tess, what a Christmas for her. Arrange anything you can: I could keep Seb company if she and the youngsters wanted to come out, but I doubt if she'd leave him.'

In that he was right. So mid-afternoon he went by himself to Mulberry Cottage, dressed in the same Santa Claus Christmas outfit that he used to wear when the children were young and a sack of presents to carry into the cottage on his back. Helga took Gizella for a walk, which left Sally, Eliot and Simon at home.

'It is I who am guilty,' Simon said, as always in his agitation his accent more than usually pronounced. 'It is because I stay here in your house that your friend will not come. Is that not so?'

'I don't know, Simon. Yes, I suppose it is. But you and Gizella, and Dad of course – Sebastian wouldn't even see him, remember – are here because I invited you, because I wanted you. If Sebastian had tried to please Tess and come, then after the first few minutes we would hardly have noticed the difference.'

'That is not the truth. Always you will notice, always you will be saddened when you see how the fire has eaten into him. Always he will feel that people avert their gaze. But that is but his flesh.

169

Why cannot he make himself see, whatever life deals out – and I am thinking at this moment of the wicked treatment of my own people, my own race, Helga's people, treatment that destroyed their bodies – nothing, *nothing* can touch a man's soul. You know who taught me that? Estelle. The comfort I have found from her certainty through this last year is beyond measure. But there, I talk too much. It is the effect you have on me, Sally, my dear friend.'

Sally could think of nothing to say; her experience had been as nothing compared with his. She laid her hand lightly on his.

'What about some music?' Eliot suggested. In moments heavy with emotion, in moments empty of hope, in moments too joyful to be encompassed with words, it was to music they always fled. As the afternoon ticked away he played the piano, sometimes solo, sometimes accompanying Simon in a single movement from a violin sonata. Ten minutes or so without a break was as long as Simon could hold and control his instrument, but as Sally listened to his playing she knew that nothing had changed: his virtuosity was as it always had been. Would physiotherapy ever give him total recovery? The experts said not. But did they always know everything? Listening to him, watching him, Sally willed his recovery with every ounce of her strength.

'I'm being guided towards a new path,' he said as he put his fiddle back in its case. 'Until now I have not spoken of this, Eliot, even to you. Perhaps it was that I wanted you to hear of it together. There is a school, Merton Court. I am told that here in your country it is looked on as a very fine school. You have heard of it, perhaps?'

'Yes, of course,' Sally said. 'But it's for boys, Simon. Isn't Gizella happy where she is? Can we help you find somewhere else.'

He smiled, his gaze holding hers. 'This school is not for Gizella. Indeed, she is happy as – what do you say? – a sand girl? I am seeking that road I spoke of to Nick, that road that must be my future. Perhaps providence led me to hear that the director of music at this Merton Court has, because of ill health, been forced to retire. A new road for him too – one that makes my own seem smooth. I have talked to the headmaster; I have come very close to accepting the appointment. Close – yet there is before me a hurdle I find difficult to overcome. Me, a teacher?'

'How many schoolboys learn to play the fiddle?' Sally, the practical, frowned.

170

'Very few, I expect. The violin is almost incidental to the other music of the school: choir training, piano lessons. What do you think, Eliot?' Then without waiting for Eliot's reply, 'Training the orchestra, directing the annual performance of one of the operettas of your country's Gilbert and Sullivan. It is different from anything I have known, but if amongst those who want to play the violin I can help just one child of promise then should I not be prepared to accept the rest?'

'No!' Sally cut in. 'No, Simon! It's a half-measure: you can't live on a half-measure.'

'As for teaching the piano, I think you are more than capable,' was Eliot's opinion. 'You have the two essential qualities: you play well and you have infinite patience and understanding.'

'But to waste all your own precious talent on classrooms of rowdy boys, most of them boys who would rather be out there on the rugger field. Don't do it, Simon.' Sally had no right to tell him what was right and what was wrong, but she couldn't stand by and see him waste himself. What did he know of the average schoolboy brought up in the communal spartan life of an English boarding school? She thought back to Jethro in those years, his mind on cross-country running, football, athletics, rowing, fishing, until puberty had put other thoughts in his head.

Simon shrugged. 'I did not pretend to you that it is an ambition. I say just that I am not content to do nothing with my life; I cannot let my mind dwell on what is no longer possible. I *must* have a goal. You, you above all people, Sally, I know you understand what I am saying. To find even one boy with talent, with love of the things I love, would that not make the rest tolerable?'

Between Sally and her father there had always been great understanding. Now they looked at each other, saying nothing, both aware that their thoughts were running in harness as across the silent room a message passed between them. Then, with a barely perceptible nod, Eliot listened, watching the daughter he loved so well.

Chapter Nine

'You two look remarkably healthy and pleased with life.' Eliot greeted the returning walkers affectionately as, heavy shoes and overcoats discarded in the cloakroom, they burst into the drawing room, their cheeks glowing. He must have seen Sally at their age rosy-faced from the winter cold a hundred times, but on that Christmas afternoon their energy and good health changed the atmosphere of the room. Perhaps it was something that happened with the passing of time; without one even being aware one grew distant from the natural energy of youth. Even as the idea came to him his smile deepened. Oh no, he hugged to himself the new promise of the future. One must have a goal to work for, wasn't that what Simon had said not an hour ago? Indeed one must. Comfortable old age! Away with it! The future was suddenly challenging – and he'd never been beaten by a challenge yet.

'We went to see Tessa and the others,' Gizella told them. 'Well, not him.'

'Sebastian sleeps in the afternoons. I expect that's why they wouldn't come over here.' Helga could be relied on to protect people's feelings. Sebastian no longer hid from her, which was a far cry from supposing he was comfortable with her any more than he was with anyone – even himself. But she believed there were moments when they understood each other completely. That had nothing to do with her having known him for years, for that had been that sort of superficial knowing which would have left her as removed from him as the people he avoided. It had stemmed from a time during the last days of the war when he'd been home for a weekend. Sally had been working, and as she often did Helga had come to Mulberry Cottage. There, even

173

though she arrived to find he and Tessa had gone out, she had dragged the mower from the shed and started to cut the grass. Walking up and down the lawn (a lawn so much smaller now than before Tessa's 'digging for victory' campaign), her spirits had plunged lower and lower. Each day in the newspaper she read lurid descriptions of what had been found as the concentration camps fell into the hands of the Allies, scenes that haunted her, scenes where she saw her parents, thin, starving, ill-treated, perhaps taken to the newly discovered gas chambers or perhaps left to sink until merciful death released them. Up and down the grass she'd strode; even as her eyes misted and she'd felt the tears at last running unchecked down her cheeks, in true Helga fashion she'd walked a straight line, evident from the light and dark stripes on the grass in her wake. Then she'd heard the car coming up the lane. Her one thought had been to escape and hide, but once believing herself safe from view she'd given up the battle for control; her body had been racked with sobs. That's how Sebastian had found her, drawn by the sound of her crying.

There had been relief in the comfort of his arms around her, his shoulder to lean on, his large handkerchief to mop her face. In silence he'd listened to the outpouring she couldn't contain.

'There's no real comfort I, or anyone else, can give you, Helga. The love you feel, the loss you feel, is something you have to bear alone. But if they could know how you suffer, that would surely grieve them. Remember they loved you enough to send you away with Eliot. Don't you think that was because even then they knew their own chances were bleak?' She supposed she must have said something; afterwards all she remembered was his gentle understanding. 'Whatever they suffered – and there's no way of deluding ourselves – what they would want for you is a peace they weren't to know for themselves.'

Her gaunt face must have been a mask of misery, her angular nose red, her eyes bloodshot. In more than five years of wartime he'd seen plenty of tragedy, but nothing could lessen how moved he'd been by the sight of her. She believed that because of that afternoon and because she had held nothing back from him, now she was able to read his own tangled misery. On that Christmas afternoon she had been drawn to Mulberry Cottage even though she had been less sure about taking Gizella with her. But today was Christmas: she knew Nick had gone to the cottage especially

174

to be with Sebastian; Zena and Jethro were there too; was that the irresistible magnet that drew her? She wouldn't even let herself ask the question. Surely Sebastian couldn't live through the first Christmas Day of peace as if it were no different from any other; today he would have taken a giant step forward. She had been proved wrong.

With the girls home, the other three said no more about what they'd been discussing. Yet they were conscious that the secret held them in an invisible bond; between them there was an electricity, an urgency. Only hours ago Simon had talked of finding a new road; when he'd told them about his intention of accepting the post at Merton Court he'd forced himself into believing it was the way he had to go. Then Sally had thrown his plans into disarray with her certainty of the rightness of what she was saying and with her expression of excitement as she'd enlarged on her theme. As the three of them had talked, the image of himself in a boys' school had faded like a dream on waking. Here was the road he must tread, perhaps not an easy one for the first few miles – or years – but the vision at the end left him in no doubt.

The shrill bell of the telephone cut across Gizella's description of how Tessa had decked the cottage with greenery, and how the smell of the spruce tree greeted you as you went in. Getting up to answer the call, Sally looked at her tall vase of white lilies and knew that the girls must have found them sadly lacking. But what was the use of a house bedecked for festivity? Happiness came from within, and there could be little of it for Tessa, or for Sebastian either.

'She's a brave girl,' Eliot said, listening to the girls' excited description of Mulberry Cottage. 'Her present life must tax even *her* good nature.' Sally nodded her agreement as she crossed to the hall to the telephone.

'Sal.' It was Nick. 'Listen, I have to talk quietly. Tess is upstairs trying to persuade Sebastian to come for half an hour's walk before the sun disappears. Look, Sal, you aren't on your own, so you'll be all right if I stay on here. The kids have shut themselves away – young lovers, I suppose. Today's been difficult – hellishly difficult. I'll tell you later. Expect me when you see me. You understand? You'll be all right.'

'Is Tess OK? Of course you mustn't leave her if it's easier with you there. Give her my love. But, Nick, are you sure they aren't better on their own?'

175

'Absolutely sure. I'll see you when I do.'

'I wish we could talk to Seb, get some feeling that he really *hears* what we say. Why can't he understand that we want him for himself; it doesn't matter a damn to us what he looks like? We could have music –'

'I tried saying all that earlier. Look, I can't talk now.' His voice dropped to barely a whisper. 'Must ring off.'

How was it that Nick's absence cast such a shadow on the evening? Certainly his presence would have added nothing to their sing-song (traditional songs, some in English, some in German, and even an old Polish folk song, played on the piano by Simon and sung as a duet by him and Gizella).

'My mother taught me that when I was small.' With a conscious effort Gizella used the word 'mother', for despite the years she had lived in England and despite her easy use of the language, for her Estelle had remained the Polish mother of her early years. For Gizella she would always remain so.

Getting up from the piano stool, Simon put his arm around her shoulder, a casual action – but not to Gizella. Watching them, Sally wondered how they used to celebrate when they'd been the three of them together. Polish Jews, refugees in a strange country. Yet that old Polish folk song had been part of the festival for them.

The evening moved on. To say it dragged on leaden feet wouldn't be true, but there was none of the timeless happiness there had been in years gone by when the Kilbrides and the Kennedys had shared the festival, had played silly games and generally behaved as if they were all the same age as their children. That's how it should have been this Christmas, each one of them adding their own thankfulness. The war was over, yet they were still all together. So if it was hard for her, Sally thought, how much worse it must be for Simon and Gizella, and worst of all for Helga, who had clung to empty hope for so long.

Every few minutes, always surprised that so little time had passed, Sally checked her watch. What could be happening at the cottage? No chance that they would be playing party games. Charades . . . remember charades and how Sebastian used to throw himself into their amateurish sketches? Perhaps with Zena home to encourage him, they had broken through his wall of defence. Please, please, let that be what's happening. Nick's there to help him; Nick truly loves him like a brother. Poor Tess. How can she bear it? How could I bear it if it were Nick? It isn't looking different that matters – different? No, be honest, what's happened to Sebastian's face makes him look evil. There, I've actually owned up to it. It's not his fault; no one could be less evil than Sebastian. It's as if his face isn't his own; his countenance can never be an outward expression of his thoughts. Some of those young men in the hospital had looked blank, empty of expression, after their faces had been rebuilt. But Sebastian looks evil, his mouth pulled permanently into a sort of sneer, the skin taut, one eye not opening properly. Help him, please, please help him. If there are such things as miracles, then can't You see this is the time for one?

'Wakey, wakey,' Eliot prompted her. 'Your throw.'

So the quiet, unfestive game of Monopoly went on.

The day was over and they were all in bed when she woke to find Nick climbing in by her side in the dark.

'You were late. Is she all right? And Sebastian. Was it awful?'

'Don't know how she stands it. I don't blame him, poor bugger. Honestly, Sal, I've never felt so helpless. It's as if he isn't *there*, doesn't hear anything, isn't part of anything. It's those bloody tablets they give him, I'm sure it is. Tess says so too. Supposed to calm his nerves or help him sleep or some damn thing. She says she looks in the medicine chest and counts them, that's how she knows he takes them even during the day; he must keep himself doped on the damned things. If he didn't he might stay up instead of shutting himself in the bedroom hour after hour every day; his mind might start to work. Even Tess doesn't seem to register with him. I can't believe it could happen to him – to them. When I phoned you he'd been up in his room more than a couple of hours; as, the girls will have said, he went upstairs before they came.'

'Did you manage to persuade him out for a walk?'

'Tess went to get him – that's when I rang you – but she said he was sound asleep. When she spoke to him she couldn't wake him. Oh hell, Sal, what's he playing at? The youngsters were in; we left them to snog in peace if that's the way they wanted to spend their afternoon. Poor Tess, it was the first walk she'd had for God knows how long. We didn't get home until well after dark. But as I was saying, Sal, somehow we've got to help the poor bastard. Tess said he was sound asleep – doped up to the eyeballs, that's what she actually said. But the truth was, he was no more asleep than I was.'

'So why should she say he was?'

'No, you don't understand.' He lay staring at the dark ceiling, in his mind seeing the scene as he and Tess had set off for their country tramp. 'He purposely fooled her. It's the way he escapes. Yet when we set off, not two minutes later I glanced up at their window and he was standing there watching us.'

'Why didn't she go back and try again?'

'Don't you hear what I'm saying? I didn't tell her I saw him; how could I? Your husband is hiding the truth from you – is that what you want me to say to her? No, she didn't glance up and I didn't say I had either. When we got home he was downstairs. Jethro said he'd been there about ten minutes. Zena had been up and got him.'

'I suppose he was just scared of being seen outside.' But he couldn't spend the rest of his life like that!

'I think it's more than that. I think his mind, his spirit, call it what you like, I think that's as withered and dead as the flesh that burned. It's as if he has no interest in anything or anybody, no interest in living.'

'Don't, Nick,' she moved close to him. 'Perhaps now, there together in the dark, they still find a way to come close.'

'No. Not even then.'

She frowned, not wanting to hear what he said. Had Sebastian talked to him, told him things that she didn't know?

'We can't know that. They've had more than twenty good years together – nearly as long as we have. A thing like this can't come between them.'

'It's been a hell of a Christmas for Tess. One day gone, one to go.'

'Not for me.' There was a smile in Sally's voice. 'I'm back to work at four o'clock tomorrow, remember?' His silence spoke louder than any words. 'I told you, you knew I had to go in.'

'I suppose I'd forgotten. Still, I might have guessed.' He turned his back, succeeding in making her feel guilty.

'I'm truly sorry, Nick. But I've had today and I'm off for New Year's Eve, I can't expect every day. The beginning of a new year and new hope. Dad and Simon have enormous plans. Listen, I'll tell you about it.'

'Not tonight. I'm not in the mood for the wonderful Simon Szpiegman and whatever his courageous plan is for his new road.' It was said with such sneering venom that Sally knew he had heard Simon's remarks that morning as criticism of Sebastian.

'Simon, Sebastian, thousands and thousands more – they have no choice but to find that new road. Not like the other hundreds of thousands, those who haven't the chance.'

'Here endeth the second lesson. It's late, go to sleep.'

The first Christmas of peace, yet through those years of war and separation she'd never felt lonelier than she did lying awake, listening to his even breathing, suspecting that he was play-acting as surely as Sebastian had been when he had hidden from Tessa and the outside world. To a small degree Sally felt some of Tessa's helplessness. If Nick could turn his back on her, so she did on him, hurt and irritated. She'd wanted to describe to him the sudden flash of inspiration that had come to her as Simon had talked about his future; she'd wanted to draw him into the aura of excitement. Instead she sought comfort in remembering.

How could Simon have been so blind as not to have seen it for himself? When he'd talked about taking the post at Merton Court he'd said he would find satisfaction if *one* boy had talent. Sally had known he was trying to make himself believe in something that could never be more than second best. Then, like a vision, the answer had sprung into her mind.

'There are dozens of talented children, talented, ambitious, needing the tuition and, even more important, the inspiration you could give them. The Szpiegman School, a school for future musicians, children who will grow up to be professionals. Simon, with you at its head it could draw talent from the whole country – from overseas. It would develop into a music school with an international reputation as well known as your own name.'

His reaction had been immediate. He'd heard her words, he'd seen the challenge in her eyes; and the way forward had been lit by a beacon at the end of the tunnel.

'What about it, Eliot? Tomorrow's violinists, tomorrow's pianists? Are you willing, or how is it you say – are you *game*?'

'Indeed I am,' Eliot had told him, 'and grateful that Sally has had the vision to see it.'

'It is a feeling so strange,' Simon had told Sally, 'it is as if my eyes had been dim, my vision no more than my dear Estelle's, and now suddenly I see with clarity, I see what must have been there in the – the confusion, yes and the unhappiness, of my mind even though I did not know. Sally, my dear friend, my gratitude is greater than my words.'

'It won't be easy, Simon. It won't happen in a week or even a year.' Minutes before, she had been certain; only then had she seen the hurdles. 'At Merton Court you would have been given a salary cheque at the end of each month. At the Szpiegman School you will have enormous expense in setting it up, enormous risk; only gradually will the rewards be seen.'

'No, that is not the truth. From the moment I find a suitable property I shall see the start of what will end in success – great success. Eliot?' He'd turned again to the older man who had been father-figure and friend to him for many years.

'I'm with you all the way, Simon. With your name the school can do nothing but succeed and prosper. You both know that, of my own choice, my days on the concert platform are already well in the past, with the exception of the occasional recital. Teaching though, passing what expertise one has, what love one has for the instrument, to someone whose future is ahead, surely there could be nothing more rewarding. Sally, my dear, you've taken years off me in these last minutes. I'm not ready for my slippers and the fireside.'

'I should think not,' she'd laughed, her own enthusiasm riding as high as theirs.

The memory was still with Sally, her annoyance towards Nick forgotten, a smile touching the corner of her mouth as she fell asleep.

By next morning they woke to a clean slate; whatever emotions had prompted their less than loving end to the previous day were forgotten. While she cooked breakfast he raked the fire for the boiler and fed it with more anthracite, then put a match to the ornamental gas fire in the dining room. With her attention on her cooking, his on scrubbing his hands under the kitchen tap, she told him the news she could contain no longer.

'Easy enough for him –' she could hear the criticism in Nick's voice '– your poor friend who has been stripped of his performing career. Oh yes, he'll find a brave new road easily enough, I can see that. A pain in his shoulder if he fiddles too long hardly merits being called a hurdle. It's not to be compared.'

180

'Then don't make comparisons,' she snapped. 'No one else is. Nick, I don't understand why, to me of all people, you have to adopt such a protective attitude about Sebastian. Do you think I don't care about him? Do you think you're the only one?'

'Me the only one? Christ, no.' He gave the boiler fire an unnecessary and vicious stab with the poker. 'I suppose it's because I feel so damned helpless. You dash about as if life depends on that footling job of yours; I've got a living to earn; everyone's days are organised and full. And that would be fine if their life hadn't been knocked base over apex. Sebastian exists but, God knows, he doesn't live. And where does that leave Tess, what is there for *her*? How often, I wonder, while you chase around like a scalded cat? Do you find time to spend with her? How often do you put yourself in her place and try and make things a bit more bearable for her?'

'As often as I can. *She* knows that. Don't forget, Tess and I had years when you and Sebastian were away: we learned to stand on our own feet. She doesn't need me to spoonfeed her.'

'Sometimes you astound me! Have you no imagination at all? She needs affection.'

'Everyone needs affection. She needs it from him, not from me and not from you. Love has to come from the right person, or it's worth nothing. If it were you, not Sebastian, do you think my life would suddenly be a bowl of roses if *they* spent their lives looking out for *me*? If you were in his place and treated me like Seb does her, no outsider could help.'

'So we let things go on as they are. Is that what you're saying?'

Putting the last two eggs on the serving dish – eggs beyond their meagre ration and by courtesy of Tess's hens – she listened to the overhead footsteps, trying to gauge how near the others were to appearing, all the while turning his words over in her mind.

'I suppose I am, really. I love them both: they're like family as far as we're concerned. Tess knows that.'

'All so bloody unjust.' He looked at her helplessly, his expression taking her back down the years and there was Jethro, small and hurt, his beloved wind-up train in his hands with its spring broken, looking trustingly to her for help. Going to Nick, she put her arms lightly around him, rubbing her face against his.

'Sounds as though they're coming down. Is the table ready?' he asked, seemingly completely restored, perhaps by her action and perhaps because he was Nick and had a rubber ball ability to bounce back. 'Put the warm plates on the tray with the dish. I'll carry that if you bring the coffee and toast.'

So Boxing Day started.

Jethro had gone straight from school to the Army. Now he was engaged to marry his beautiful Zena, and determined to make a career worthy of her. So when she left for London the morning after Boxing Day he went with her. He chose not to see his father's tight-lipped disapproval. Always Nick had been his hero, his role model, and he hated to know that what he intended to do was earning his disapproval. Jethro tried to make himself believe it was because he didn't intend to follow the career planned for him; but he knew the real reason he was disappointing his father was because he intended to move into Zena's flat with her before they were married and before he could earn a living to keep them. But that wouldn't be for long; his youthful confidence bounced back. Like Dick Whittington he would search for his dream, even though as the train huffed and puffed eastward he had no clear picture of where he would start looking nor yet what he hoped to find. He'd grown up imagining that he would follow in Nick's footsteps, become articled to a firm of accountants, take his exams, probably live in the same middle-class comfort he'd grown up with. But that had been before he'd fought his way through France. Etched in his memory were images of the homeless, all that was left of their worldly goods either in the trucks they pushed or piled on to the occasional wagons pulled by horses as broken down as they were themselves. There had been one group he'd seen, a woman and three young children, scrabbling in a field with their bare hands, trying to steal potatoes. There had been an elderly couple leaning on each other for support, dragging their feet – for it couldn't have been called walking, there's purpose in a walk, it has a goal – moving slowly along the road to nowhere. Liberation! Was that what liberation did to people?

'You might be able to get a job for a while at the theatre,' Zena had suggested when they'd planned that he should return to London with her. 'I could talk to the theatre manager, use all my girlish charm on him. That would give you a chance to look around for something better.'

'No.' He had been adamant. 'I have to do this on my own. I mustn't start off with favours, even if they're made generously from some chap who eats out of your hand. Maybe particularly because of that. You're *mine* – I don't want you crawling to anyone, not even to help *me*.'

Her lovely face had broken into a teasing smile, 'Who said anything about crawling?'

'No, I've got to find my own way. I'll soon have a wife to support, remember?' Just saying it, knowing at last it was the truth, had been enough to send every other thought from his head. But as the train neared London his determination grew. Tomorrow he would go out job-seeking. He wouldn't go to the labour exchange and tell some clerk that he was a returning soldier with no experience. No, that would gain him nothing. He would make a direct approach, 'follow his nose' and let himself be drawn to somewhere he wanted to make a future. But that was tomorrow. For today he would let his mind travel no further than the two of them. He'd stayed in her flat before – and here the memory of Nick's disapproval reared its head again – but this was different. This was the beginning of the rest of their lives. They intended to plan the wedding for when the play came off, but at present the theatre was full every night; bookings hadn't even started to drop off. In a way he was glad they had to wait. Already she was being noticed in the stage world; at the moment he was nothing. Of one thing he was determined, when Zena became Mrs Kennedy she would be proud to be seen as his wife. And with the exaggerated image of success – although not the path to finding it – clear in his mind, he gave himself up to living the moment, the hour, the wonder of where his life had brought him.

Next day he wandered through the busy London streets. He stopped and gazed at the thriving department shops of the West End, wondering, imagining what sort of a future he might find there. When he found the right thing he was sure some inner voice would speak to him but so far it was silent. After eating a solitary lunch in a Corner House he left the West End, thinking perhaps he might find the unknown something he was looking for in a less prosperous district.

That's when the inner voice he'd been so confident about shouted at him. His eyes were drawn to a large greengrocery store, open fronted, its fruit and vegetables piled decoratively. In that instant he saw that Frenchwoman with her three children scrabbling for potatoes. Above the shop he saw the name Chas. Palmer & Co. Ltd. and in small writing over the door the address of their head office. That was it! That's where he had to go. It was still only three o'clock, he'd go straight away. He'd ask to speak to the – the what? Manager? Chairman? Director? He had no idea but, just as the shop had appeared when he'd needed inspiration, so the right approach would come to him.

If he'd decided that to ask for the Manager was the right approach he might have found employment at one of the company's branches. But when, speaking with confidence, he asked if the receptionist would request he might be spared a few moments of Mr Palmer's time, it appeared he played the best card in his pack. A self-made man, Charles Palmer appreciated boldness; that was the only way to get on in this world.

'Don't know the name,' he said to the receptionist. 'You say he asked for me personally? Well, send him in. I'll hear what he has to say for himself.'

Whatever imaginary picture Jethro had built of the owner of the large greengrocery chain, it was nothing like the man who turned from the window to look at him as he was shown in and closed the door firmly behind himself. A man of medium height, more than medium build, but neither description painted more than half the picture. Charles Palmer wore his far from new grey suit as though it had been put on in a hurry, one shoulder of the jacket higher than the other, his trousers hoisted by braces inches beyond his waist so that the legs left an inch or two of sock exposed above his workman-type shoes. The knot of his tie had almost disappeared under one side of his collar. As for his hair, was he bald or did he have the barber put the clippers across his head?

'Kennedy, the gal called you,' he greeted Jethro. 'Should I know you? Memory isn't what it used to be I dare say.'

'No, sir, we've never met. But I hope you *will* come to know me.'

'Hah!' Cheeky enough, young fellow. Well, that's the way to get on, best hear him out. 'What's in your mind then, lad?'

'I came to you because – well, because I reckon if you want to get on you have to aim to the top of the tree.'

'Hah!' Charles Palmer barked again. 'So what is it you're after?'

184

'I want a job. Not just a job in one of the shops, one that will never get me anywhere.'

'Well, I'm jiggered.' Charles sat down behind his desk and nodded to a chair for Jethro. 'You'd better do some talking and I'll do the listening. Tell me what makes you think I might be what you're looking for – and more to the point, what makes you think *you* might be what *I'm* looking for.'

So Jethro started at the beginning, how he'd always expected to be articled like his father had been, how the war had thrown all his preconceived ideas awry. He even told him about the battered and homeless refugees and the woman with her three children stealing potatoes.

'When I set out this morning I didn't know where I was going to look for work. Then I saw one of your shops, the food so essential to everyone. I thought of the people who had nothing. Don't really see the connection – except that I don't think I could try and earn a living from anything – anything fancy. Food is vital. There's too much suffering in the world, too many people have to make do with too little. That's why I believe you are what I need. As for me being what you need, that's a different matter. When I left school I went straight into the Army – just before Christmas I was demobbed. I've had no experience. But I'm not stupid and I want to learn.'

A more conventional man than Charles Palmer would undoubtedly either have told him that he had no vacancies or, at best, sent him with a note to one of the branches to ask that he be given work.

Changes were in the air, not least for Helga.

'I'm going to take the train to town,' Helga said at breakfast a week or so later. With the end of the year and the closing of the crèche her job had ended and yesterday's weekly local paper brought no hope. 'I want to go to the labour exchange, but what sort of work I am looking for I don't know. An office – I have no skill; a shop – I really don't want to work in a shop; another nursery isn't likely. I have saved some money, perhaps I ought to go to be taught shorthand and typing then I might be more useful.'

'Is that what you want to do?' Sally asked. 'Perhaps there would be something for you at Drifford Park.' But she said it without much confidence. Helga had been brought up German;

185

when she'd come to England she had been proud of the English she had learned, English that on arrival had been about on a par with her French. But that was more than six years ago. Now the only difference between the way she spoke and the way of the local girls she'd worked with was that her grammar was precise and her words pronounced with no trace of the local dialect. As for her native tongue, that was something she would never forget; but her knowledge of world events was limited and overshadowed by the experiences of her own family. So would she be given work at the Park, or would a refusal do no more than add to her lack of confidence?

'Come in with me,' Nick said affably. 'It'll save you cycling to the station.'

Helga's plain face lit with a smile. Somehow it seemed to her that Nick's invitation was a good omen; it augured well for the day.

They'd been gone no more than a few minutes when the phone rang.

'Sally, I was afraid no one would be home.' Eliot's voice greeted her. 'Simon has just rung me to say that in his morning post he has details of something that sounds remarkably suitable. We went to two houses yesterday, good enough places in themselves, large, with possibilities of conversion. But this one is different. It's on the outskirts of a village called Millbrook, according to my map about twenty miles from you. Do you know it?'

'I may have heard of it. What's it like, Dad, the house I mean?'

'Apparently it was taken over by a boy's school for the duration of the war, the house used for living accommodation and a series of classrooms built in the grounds – quite extensive grounds. It's been empty since the school left. Not a property for the average purchaser.'

'That sounds promising, promising but expensive.'

'No business can be set up without expense. I'm sure we can get financial backing and once it gets established money will start coming in to repay the debts. Unfortunately Simon is tied up for the next few days – hospital appointments, then taking Gizella back to school. He can't get to view it before the weekend, but he has asked me if I could see it in the meantime. What he actually suggested was that I should ask if you could come with me. What about it, eh? When is your day off?'

186

'Tomorrow and the next day. I'd love to come. You say Simon suggested it?' She was surprised at her pleasure.

'If he hadn't, then I would have,' he replied. 'It was you who dreamed up the idea.'

It was arranged that he would make an appointment with the agent for the following day.

'Come here today, Dad, then we can set off early. We'll dump Nick at the station and keep the car. Helga's gone into town with him today; she's looking for a job.' Listening to her, it struck him, not for the first time, how good she had been to take 'the child', as he still thought of Helga, into her home and make her one of the family. While Nick had been away, Nick and Jethro too, the two of them had fitted together very well. But what now? Could Nick be expected to accept her in the same way? He pulled his thoughts back into line as Sally went on, 'I hope she finds something, something that's right for her. She never mixed with the other helpers at the crèche, you know – people can be so *bigoted*. Working there might not have been very ambitious, but at least the children were good for her – they haven't the preconceived ideas of some of the adults. Somehow her confidence seems to have melted now the crèche has finished.'

'She'll make her own decisions, Sally. She may not be gregarious, but Helga is nobody's fool.'

'You're right there. Anyway, Dad, about the place we are to see ...' So she put Helga out of her mind. A few minutes later, having said goodbye to her father, she worked her way through her mental list of the things she had to do before she set off for the Park. Her standards never slipped, the house was always immaculate despite the fact that her help only came one day a week. As for her own appearance, to be well groomed was second nature. She would have been surprised if she'd known the attention she aroused amongst her colleagues. Glamour wasn't part of the turnout of those who worked with her in the listening room, people not only of many nationalities but of varying ages, most of them beyond the first bloom of youth and none without a shadow of memories. No one – and that included Sally – had a vast wardrobe of clothes; they had been a short commodity for too long and even though the war was over there was no sign that clothes coupons were to be abolished. But she had that thing that couldn't be taught: she had flair. So by the time she set out for work just after noon her nail varnish matched her lipstick, the colour enhanced by the exact shade of the scarf she wore knotted at her neck. She'd had her red leather handbag for years, always living by the rule that it paid to buy quality; her red shoes were an extravagance she'd been tempted to because the colour was so right. Just as her translations were accurate and concise, so her appearance was smart but never flamboyant. There were plenty of prettier women on the staff, particularly in the typing pool where the girls were scarcely more than half her age, but there wasn't one who didn't notice Sally Kennedy and envy her air of confident elegance.

Arriving home at about half past six, Nick stood in the hall of the empty house. On the table next to the telephone was an arrangement of hot-house carnations; whether or not they had any scent he had no idea, for all he could smell was the polish on the gleaming parquet floor.

'Christ,' he grumbled almost silently, 'what a bloody home to come back to. What the hell am I in this place? Just another job to be done before she rushes off to that mind-consuming place? Put out my food, oh yes, she'd never fall down on the job. As if she's feeding the dog. God, if we had a dog, at least that would be something to wag its tail and let me know I existed. What's she left to greet me today?'

While he'd been cooped up in that prison camp Sally had had gas fires fitted in both the drawing room and the dining room, the practical way to heat the room when there was anyone at home to need it. When first he'd come home it had been summer, and by the time winter came he'd become past caring. He'd persuaded himself that the gas fires were good looking; clearly she'd bought top of the range or at any rate the nearest to the top that had been available; they even gave the impression of burning coke. Anyway, they fitted the mood of this surgically hygienic house. So, on that evening, he looked into the drawing room and saw she had laid a lace cloth on the small table, even gone to the length of putting a display of greenery with the first four snowdrops from the garden in a minute vase. The matches were on top of his napkin. Sally forgot nothing. From there he went to the kitchen to see what sort of a feast she had prepared. On top of the lid of a casserole dish was a note: *This only needs reheating. Fifteen minutes in Mark 7, everything in the same casserole.* Like taking your car to the garage and telling the attendant 'Five gallons please'. Was that all food was to her, just fuel for the body? He bet his young clerk, Ben Bristow, whose wife had just had their first child, sat down to a proper meal, talked, told her about his day, knew she listened and cared. Oh, she'd left another note; what was this? *Three phone calls. First: Jethro rang to say he has started his job in the buying department of Charles Palmer the green-grocery people, he's writing. Second: Dad phoned to ask me to view a property with him tomorrow (my day off, remember?) so I suggested he should come here for the night first. P.S. Third call just this minute as I was about to leave the house. Tess sounding v. down, hoped I was on v. late shift and could have gone to see her before I went to work. I suggested Helga would go over when she got back (I'm leaving a note for her too) but it might be a good idea if you gave Tess a ring. Tell her I'll try and get over either before or after my trip with Dad tomorrow. Enjoy your supper. Tell Dad I'll get home about 9.30.* He read it twice, screwed it up and hurled it in the direction of the waste bin, not bothering to pick it up when it landed on the floor. Then he went back to the hall, to the telephone.

When, less than half an hour later, Eliot arrived, he found the house in darkness and had to grope under the stone for the key. On the kitchen table he found the lidded casserole, that same note on it written in Sally's hand, and printed at the top the one word: *Eliot.* Only Nick called him by his Christian name. Pleased with their thoughtfulness, he put the dish in the oven; even more pleased to find the welcome had extended to a fireside table in the drawing room, he lit the gas fire and settled down to enjoy his wait. A good meal, a piano to play, anticipation of Sally soon coming home and, adding to his pleasure just as he started his meal, the appearance of Helga who had hurried home as soon as she'd heard he was coming.

'Come and talk to me while I eat.' He smiled. 'Sally tells me you've been job-hunting. What have you in mind to do?'

'That's the trouble, you see, Mr Burridge, I don't know. What would I be any good at? Ought I to try and train for something? I could, you know, I have saved as hard as I could from my wages at the crèche. I wondered if I ought to learn to type; that would make it easier to earn a living.'

189

'If you train for something, it has to be something you really *want* to do. Don't use your hard-saved money on anything that isn't important.'

How worried she looked. At her age she ought to be having fun; surely this was the time when she ought to have been at her prettiest. Her uncertain and confused expression did nothing to help her. Yet her face was full of character. He could imagine her in fifty years' time, one of those women who are the backbone of the country, perhaps the pillar of the Women's Institute or the dependable and unchanging wife of some local squire – brogue shoes, tweeds, hats that might be better suited to a scarecrow, yet with honesty and goodness that earned the respect of all who knew her. Now how was it he could think that was the way her future would go, poor, plain Helga, cut off from her roots? Saved as hard as she could, she'd said. How different her life might have been. Her father had been well to do, her mother a talented teacher ... saved as hard as she could ... in the hope of making a career. As what? He knew enough of the world to realise that whatever she made her choice of training, she would have not only to do well but do better than the rest of her class. If she and one other applied for the same job, the name Helga Leipmann alone would give the other a head start. Add to that that it was more than likely that same other applicant would have more sex appeal, perhaps even be pretty. Hadn't the child had disappointments enough to overcome without having to face more? He couldn't bear to picture her rejection.

'Sally grew into the work she did, you know,' he said conversationally. 'She'll have told you how when I was touring in Europe – as I was far more than I was in this country – even as a child she came with me. We had an Italian couple who travelled with us; he was a splendid teacher for her, who taught her more of life than she would ever have learned if I'd sent her to board at school. And his wife took good care of her right from when she was small. Languages, they are the door to understanding. You speak excellent English – well of course you do, you did when you arrived and you've lived here a long time. German – naturally. Anything else?'

'I used to enjoy French. Sometimes Sally and I talk nothing else, just for fun, you know. Mr Burridge, she has been so kind to me. I'm not a bit good at saying thank you properly; sometimes I want to tell her but to say it would sound – sound not very close. Can you understand what I am saying?'

'Yes, like writing a polite thank-you after a party. I'll tell you something about Sally: she has shared her home with you for these years for one very good reason and that is, she enjoys having you. No, no,' he held up his hand as she was about to speak, 'let me finish. She has told me herself how you and she are two of a kind–'

'But how can we be? She is lovely, she is clever, she is smart – she is all the things I can never be.'

'She makes the best of herself,' Eliot laughed, 'and yes, she is an attractive woman. And so, my dear, will you grow into being.' If only he could believe it, but at least he made sure he sounded convinced. 'But that has nothing to do with what she meant. Two of a kind, you have minds that run on parallel tracks: you are methodical, you are hard working, you hate muddled thinking or muddled living, you hate things done badly and carelessly. Am I not right? So that is why she has always enjoyed having you living here. And from enjoying it, she has come to look on you as family – part friend, part daughter.'

Even as he said it he saw Helga's eyes turn bloodshot from hot tears she blinked away. Not one overspilled and yet their very presence so near the surface was enough to make her long, bony nose turn unattractively pink.

'Now then,' Eliot went on as if there had been no pause, 'I was telling you about the work she used to do. During the Great War we were both back in England, just the two of us by that time. Wherever I went, she came. We were a team.' He laughed, remembering. 'That's what she used to say even when she was a child. And it was true. Before the war ended we returned to France. She grew into keeping my engagement book, she booked our travelling tickets, she made hotel reservations. That was before she met Nick and got swept off her feet. I missed her, not just for herself but for the way she took all the responsibility for organising our lives.'

Helga nodded. 'She has often talked about it.'

'Now then, Helga, my dear, you know about this school Simon is planning. I say Simon, for he is young still, something I can't claim. The Szpiegman School. One of these days it will be heralded the world over as a place for music students of all races.

But I am looking ahead a long time. From little acorns do great oak trees grow.'

'I beg your pardon?'

'Just a saying, my dear. It means that everything has to begin at the beginning, nothing grows out of nothing. In the early days there will be organising, setting up the domestic side of the house – if we take this place Sally and I are going to see tomorrow, then it's not too far away from here; I know she'd always be there for you to fall back on. In fact she will want to feel she is part of what we do.'

'I do not understand. I play the piano just for amusement, I cannot use my savings on piano lessons for I have no hope of being good enough to earn my living. Please don't misunderstand –'

'My dear, if I were going to give you more piano lessons – and I hope there will be the opportunity – I would not charge a fee. Listen, hear me out, and if you think the idea is dreadful then we are good enough friends for you to tell me so.'

But as she listened and he talked of their plans for the school he saw such hope on her face that it hurt him to look at her. He explained to her what her job would be: first she would help arrange the living accommodation, then later, once the students started to arrive and there were domestic staff in place for catering, cleaning, looking after their welfare, gradually her own job would take on another aspect: organising timetables for lessons, practice periods. It was as if heaven had dropped at her feet.

'You think I could be useful to you and Mr Szpiegman? Does he know what you are suggesting, or are you asking me because you know I need work and will not find it easily?' She held his gaze, willing him to be truthful.

'No such thing. Perhaps it's because I know you will do things so much like Sally did that I have no doubts about suggesting it.'

'And does Mr Szpiegman know?' she persisted.

'Yes.' This time he looked directly at her and lied. 'We have discussed our hopes and plans to the last detail.' He followed the lie with an exaggeration, intended to put her at her ease. If Simon didn't know now, he would do later in the evening once Helga was in bed and out of earshot of the telephone. And Eliot had absolutely no doubt that he would applaud the plan. 'If you agree to it, you must see how much better it would be from our point of view. I have just one daughter, one very dear daughter, if you are looking for ties of blood. But to me you are – no, I can't call you a daughter, why you're younger even than Jethro – you are like a granddaughter, just as Simon is the son I never had. When we set up this school it will be all the stronger if we are bonded by ties that are already strong. One thing you will probably need to learn, and that is to use a typewriter. So, Helga, if you are prepared to throw in your lot with ours, then spend your savings on a few months' tuition. I'm not going to offer to pay your fees. And why? Because I know you have a strong streak of independence. What do you say, humph?'

'I can't believe it's real. Are you *sure*?'

Eliot smiled, a smile that answered her better than any words. 'If you feel relieved to see a shape in your future, how do you think I feel? Not ready for retirement, not by a long chalk. But you know, living out of a suitcase, one hotel after another, after all the years I'd done it the shine had gone out of it. I miss the music; any soloist must miss the joy of playing with the backing of an orchestra. That's something Simon and I both know. For I'm yesterday's man; I haven't the stamina for it these days. But this new challenge ... we'll make it something really good, Helga. I've never believed in Fate, not until now.'

'Yes,' she said, crossing the hearth to where he sat by the table, the empty casserole in front of him. Shyly she touched his shoulder. 'I will work so hard to be a good typist; I will learn too about what we need to furnish the rooms for the students. I promise I will try not to let you regret giving me this opportunity.'

He covered her hand with his. 'Take my plates out while I open the piano. We'll have a few minutes' music until someone gets home.'

She did as he said and, listening to her washing up his dishes, was it only in his imagination or could he really hear her happiness in the clatter of the china? Sally was the next to arrive home, just before ten o'clock. In her excitement at hearing the new stage in the plans she hardly noticed how late Nick was. For an hour or so they talked, then Helga went to bed. More talk. Eliot wanted to give her time to settle before he spoke to Simon.

Nick's mood on returning home was considerably more cheerful than it had been when he'd left for Mulberry Cottage.

'Was Tess all right? She sounded really miserable this morning.' Sally asked him while Eliot was making his call.

'When I got there she was quiet; she look quite drained. She said he'd been very difficult today. She'd tried to get him to do some gardening with her but it had been, to use her expression, and not like Tess to talk about him like this, like talking to a brick wall. She called upstairs to tell him I was there but he didn't come down. So I went up to see him. He never used to be moody, did he. I suppose shock – and it must have been a hell of a shock apart from the agony of it – shock can do damage that lasts a long time. Honestly, Sal, it must wear her down. Tonight he was – oh, God knows, it was as if he was on another planet. I talked to him, I reminded him of how we used to play the gramophone and dance. I think he tried to smile; he said something about wanting to hear the music. Said for me to go and put some records on; said unless he went to sleep he might come down and watch Tess and me dancing. Why watch, for Christ's sake? What reason for him not to dance with her himself? How does she stand it? He was already in bed but, damn it, it wasn't even eight o'clock.'

'He didn't attempt to come down and listen? Why doesn't she *make* him?'

'For the same reason that we can't *make* him do anything; he might be made of stone. If only he'd get *angry*, if only he'd *cry* even. I put all the old dance tunes on: great rhythm some of those bands, back in the 30s. She and I danced. I could feel her shaking off her gloom. It's what she needs, something cheerful. I was thinking, coming home, next week the local 'Am Drams' are putting on a Noel Coward play in the village. No good trying to persuade him to come, but at least she might. Anyway, that's not till next week. More important, what did Jethro have to say about this job?'

Gone completely was his resentment towards Sally, and when Eliot joined them his welcome was natural. Nick liked a happy life, he liked people round him; and he was still warmed from the glow that never failed at Mulberry Cottage, a warmth that even Sebastian's behaviour couldn't banish.

It was just as they were on their way up the stairs to bed that the telephone rang. In silence they looked at each other. Midnight ... what could be so important that it couldn't wait until morning?

194

Chapter Ten

'Can't believe it ... can't ... saw him tonight ...' Nick repeated half-finished sentences as the car sped to the end of their lane then along the country road before turning towards Mulberry Cottage.

'Perhaps it's not too late.' But in her heart Sally knew it was; she knew she ought not even to hope it for him. To have fallen so low that he could have done this; what right had any of them to hope that some miracle of medicine would bring him back to a future he couldn't face? Forget the *now*, think of the real Sebastian, the whole Sebastian, the kind, caring, loving, understanding Sebastian. 'We can't wish that on him, Nick, not if we love him. And we do.' Sally had trained herself that tears were a sign of weakness, and weakness was something she scorned. Yet now as she felt their hot sting, she heard her voice break.

'Where's the justice? I'm so *angry*, why couldn't he see what he was doing to her?'

'To Tess? I bet it was partly for Tess he did it. We all knew what being like he was had done to her life. He loved her –'

'We thought he did. But if he had, if he'd put her before himself, how could he do this to her? Don't tell me it was Tess he was thinking of.'

'Shut up. Don't say things like that about him. Of course he loved her. How can we know what he must have been suffering? All any of us ever did was say things like "What a dreadful life for her", "He was difficult today", "Why can't he pull himself together".' Sally gave up the battle and almost gloried in the sound of her own misery. 'Poor Seb, none of us ever got through to what was going on in his heart. When did any of us really, *honestly* try and feel what it must have been like for him? Go ahead and be angry at him if that's the way you feel, but I don't. In my heart I always trusted that his spirit would heal in time like the flesh that had been so burned.'

'He had no right –'

'Like his burns, I said,' she went on, as if he hadn't spoken. 'And I suppose that's what happened. They healed, they botched up his face, but the scars, his poor deformed face, nothing could heal that. And nothing could heal the damage to his spirit, nothing could make him whole.' Her sentences were disjointed, interspersed with gulps and snorts as she cried in a way that was as unnatural to her as everything else about this night.

'Pull yourself together, Sal. We're here to help Tess, not to wallow in our own grief.'

'I'm not wallowing,' she made an effort.

'Do you think I don't care that he's gone? My best friend. I tried to help him, you know I did. It was like a stone wall. Why the hell couldn't he have looked outside himself and seen we all cared – for us nothing had changed?'

Sally rested her hand on his knee. Then, as they covered the last bumpy patch of lane towards the old cottage, she concentrated on trying to restore her face to some semblance of calm. As he'd said, what use could she be to Tess if all she could do was blubber like a child?

Slamming the car doors, they looked towards the house, expecting Tess to be waiting to fling open the door as soon as she heard them. But nothing happened, so they rang the bell. Still nothing ... not a sound. They looked at each other, even in the dark knowing the fear they'd read in the other's expression.

'Oh God,' Nick whispered, something in his tone telling Sally it had to be she who took control.

'Let's see if the back door's open. The lights are still on; she may not have locked up yet,' she said, instilling confidence she was far from feeling into her voice as she led the way along the cobblestone path to the back of the cottage. Between the glow of light from the curtained windows there were patches which by contrast seemed extra dark on this moonless night and with everything pushed from their minds except what Tessa had just told them, neither had thought of bringing a torch. The outer lobby leading to the back door was in complete darkness, but familiarity led her hand to the latch. Then they were in the warm kitchen, blinking in the sudden light.

'Tess,' Sally called, shocking herself by her inability to shout loudly. It was as if the place was held in the hush of death. 'Tess, we're here. Where are you?' Silence.

'Oh God.' Nick again. Sally looked at him, forgetting her own red-eyed and tousled appearance, aware only of his pallor and his haunted expression. 'No, Sal, she can't . . .'

It was as much as Sally could do to be mistress of her own behaviour; at that moment she had no room to spare to protect his feelings. Leading the way, without even looking to see if he was following, she went out into the hallway and towards the stairs.

'Tess . . .' Again she said it as she started up the narrow, three-hundred-year-old flight. It took all her courage, more courage than she knew she possessed, to go forward at a steady pace, not to hesitate as she made for Sebastian's room. What would they find? Sebastian and Tessa . . . how strange that in these last few minutes she'd forgotten the images in her mind weren't of what the last months had done to them, but of the happy couple they'd been. It was that that frightened her most.

She saw the door was half open, proof if proof were needed that Tessa would have heard them arrive. Ahead of Nick, Sally walked into the room, schooling herself to look at the bed, schooling herself for some sort of Romeo and Juliet tableau. That's when the steely hold on her reserve snapped, relief mixed with irritation, irritation with compassion.

'Tess! Tess!' There was nothing hushed in the way she shouted. Tessa was sitting on the edge of the bed, her head bent as if she were engrossed in the note she held in her hand. This time she looked up, a lost child taken in hand by a kindly stranger, and seemingly unaware of Sally's uncharacteristically dishevelled appearance.

'Why?' She sounded lost, helpless. 'Loved me, he says. If he loved me he couldn't have done it.'

Together Sally and Nick read the note, written in Sebastian's familiar hand. There was nothing wild or unbalanced in the way he'd formed his letters, the writing was clear, the lines on the unruled paper straight.

There is no other way, Tess. I can't go on, and I can't bear to watch what I am doing to your life. All I want for you is happiness. Tell Zena how proud I am.

'How *could* he? I tried to help him. All the time had he been planning this?'

'Have you sent for the doctor, Tess?' Sally the practical asked.

'Doctor? Too late for a doctor. Seb's dead. Dead, don't you understand?' Tessa answered as if she were surprised at the question.

'I'll go and ring him,' Sally said. 'He'll have to come, Tess. Nick, take her downstairs, make her have a brandy or something.' She was surprised how as Nick held out his hands towards Tessa, she stood up without protest, letting him lead her out of the room. How long had she sat there before they arrived? Sally knew she ought to follow them down the stairs to make the phone call and, in a minute she would. But first, with only herself and lifeless Sebastian in the room, she stood looking down on him. Even though his eyes were closed, his expression in death was as unpleasant as it had been through all these last months. Coming close, she bent to rest her face against his. 'We'll take care of her, Sebastian, dear, dear Sebastian. Wish I could pray, would that help you if I prayed? Or don't you need help anymore? Are you free from all the misery? Has your soul found itself again? Please, please God, whoever you are, wherever you are, don't let what he's done be for nothing. He must have been so dreadfully unhappy. Not now though. But don't let him be in a void, unhappiness gone, everything gone. Give him peace, the *real* Sebastian. The peace which passeth all understanding, isn't that what they say? He can't find it while Tess is unhappy though, can he? Why did you let any of it happen? Why didn't you help us get through to him so that he found comfort in being with people who loved him?' She pulled her thoughts back and forced herself to look down on the still form. 'I promise you, Sebastian, we'll try and help her through this, we'll try and help her get back in step. Remember how good it used to be, all four of us? Yes of course you do. That's what we'll remember too, not these last months. You know what? If I shut my eyes I can see you so clearly, not the mess you were in after the accident, but before. When you used to laugh, when life was good.' Somehow, that image seemed like a message, as if he were trying to tell her he was free. Gently she kissed his forehead, then went down to phone the doctor.

Cut off from the world of stage and screen, cut off from the press, those were the things that had first attracted Sebastian and Tessa to

198

Mulberry Cottage. Certainly he'd never fallen completely out of the news; even through the years of the war his picture had been in film magazines, even sometimes in the national press. But then the same could have been said of any famous screen personality. Apart from anything else, it did wonders for recruitment. Then had come the accident which had brought him right to the forefront of the news. Since he'd been home Tessa had had various phone calls asking for interviews with him; she'd even intercepted letters with the same request. But she had protected him. Who could it have been now who reported his death? Certainly not her, nor the Kennedys, nor the doctor. Later on, when they came to wonder about it, they might find that the news of his death came from the theatre where Zena was appearing. For, before Jethro left for work on the morning following Sebastian's suicide, Sally rang him to break the news so that he would be the one to tell Zena. Next in the chain was the theatre, where she was pulled out of the cast and her understudy, rejoicing that one person's bad luck was another's opportunity, took her place while she was away. She travelled back to Mulberry Cottage on her own.

After working for Charles Palmer such a short time Jethro only intended to ask for a day's leave to attend the funeral, so he was surprised when he was told the following day Charles Palmer wanted to see him. Had he done something wrong? Inexperienced and still uncomfortably aware that he needed the job more than the job needed him, he answered the call.

'You wanted me, sir?' he asked expecting the worst even though he couldn't imagine what he'd done to be called before the boss.

'This morning's paper,' Charles greeted him. 'You've read it, I take it?' He tapped the front page, which carried a pre-war photograph of Sebastian Kilbride. 'The father of your young sweetheart, that's what I've been told. Is that right, lad?'

'Yes, sir. Zena and I are going to be married when her play comes off. Her parents and mine are – well, I guess we're like family, really.'

'Bad accident he had, so I believe.'

'Dreadful.' Surely Charles Palmer wasn't using him to dig into a celebrity's story?

'When's the funeral, lad?'

'I don't know yet, sir. I was waiting to hear so that I could ask for the day off.'

'Day off be jiggered. You just get your coat on and get off home. Like family, you say. Poor devil. Paper says he was in the burns unit for – forget how long, but long enough to tell me a thing or two. A nephew of mine got shot down in flames. Nasty business. Isn't till you come face to face with it that you know. So you get home, that's where you ought to be, and take care of that pretty little lass of yours. I went along to see the play the other night. You've got a bit of competition there, lad.'

'Who do you mean?' Someone in the cast? No, Jethro didn't believe it. But he asked it anyway.

'Not a chap. No, worse than that, unless I'm much mistaken. Your rival will be fame, ah, fame with a capital "F" for that young lady.'

'She's jolly good, isn't she?' Jethro beamed.

'Ah, she's got what it takes and no mistake. But can anyone be that good at two careers, being a star or whatever rubbish they call these people and being a wife too? Well, don't let it be said Charles Palmer didn't do his bit to give you a chance. She'll need a shoulder to cry on, likely enough. So just you sling your hook and forget about us until she comes back to town when the funeral's over.'

'I can't go yet, sir. There's an autopsy first. The funeral won't be until after that.'

'Who's boss, you or me, lad? I said get off with you.'

Jethro grinned. 'Gosh, that's jolly good of you. I'll start fresh when I get back, is that all right? I mean – wages – I mean I don't expect to be on the payroll at all until I can get down to the job properly.' He felt rather pleased with himself; offering not to count his first week as counting towards his wages seemed to him a very grown-up suggestion.

'What I pay or what I don't pay is up to me. Now don't stand there, I've got work to do even if you haven't. Just you take care of that little wench.'

So by noon, only one day after Zena, he was on his way home.

The autopsy found that Sebastian's death had been caused by an overdose, which surprised no one. A natural death would have lasted the newspapers one day for the announcement, a second for the funeral and perhaps one more going back through his career. An autopsy added extra scope and the inquest which followed

200

attracted more reporters than officials and family combined. Photographers crowded outside the door of the building when they arrived at the coroner's court, their greatest interest in Zena. A few words with the widow would be worthwhile; the band of pre-war cinema-goers who had made an idol of Sebastian Kilbride would buy any newspaper or magazine that followed the story of his final days. But those halycon days when people used to queue outside any cinema where his films were showing were long since gone. Zena was today's world, today's and tomorrow's. She who had always vowed she wanted to rise to the top on her own merit felt pride in the interest of the press, pride for Sebastian's sake and for her own that she was his daughter.

The doctor confirmed the quantity and dates of sleeping pills he had prescribed.

'You administered his medication to him, Mrs Kilbride?' the coroner enquired.

'Sometimes at night I fetched them from the medicine cupboard for him. But when he rested during the day he took them himself.' Tessa's voice was tight, her jaw unaturally stiff. 'I always checked, I always hoped he'd managed without them during the day. But he never did.' It was like living a nightmare, one that she knew would return to haunt her.

'So you were aware of how many he had left?'

'Yes, I was. Only enough for six days. I was going to ask the doctor to let him have some more. But he didn't even use them, those in the medicine cupboard were still there after – after –'

Sally watched her helplessly, her concern entirely on Tessa, so that she was surprised when Nick got to his feet.

'May I make a statement?' He could feel all eyes on him. Clearly this wasn't the usual way for a case to proceed, but he had no regard for that. He couldn't bear to see Tess standing there alone; physically he felt as though he had a lead weight in his chest as he suffered with her.

'And you are?'

'I am Nicholas Kennedy. Sebastian Kilbride was my best friend; we are near neighbours; my son is shortly to marry Zena Kilbride.' A perceptible ripple of interest amongst the reporters as they wrote furiously.

'And you are able to add some useful information to what Mrs Kilbride has told us? You may return to your seat, Mrs Kilbride.

Eh, Mr er ah yes Kennedy, I believe you said –' after a whispered prompt from the clerk '– you may take the stand.'

So Nick told them what he had seen on Christmas Day, how he had realised that Sebastian had only made a pretence of sleeping. The Coroner listened and made notes; the reporters listened and scribbled hard.

'Am I to understand that you were aware that the deceased made a pretence of taking sleeping tablets during the day, during each day? That he took them from the medicine chest and secreted them to some hiding place? Am I to believe that he duped his wife, now sadly his widow, and you became aware of this and did nothing?'

'I did nothing,' Nick confirmed. 'But I had no reason to believe this was his habit; I simply knew that on Christmas afternoon he feigned sleep so that there would be no pressure to make him come walking with us.'

'You may stand down.'

Then the doctor was recalled and questioned as to the state of Sebastian's mind; the state of his mind inevitably stemmed from his disfigurement, to his refusal to leave the house. What should have been straightforward – at least in the opinion of the family it should have been straightforward – became a macabre re-enactment of the past months. Had Sebastian's mind been unbalanced? The suicide note was read, and considered to have been written by a man of sound mind.

Words, words, nothing but words pounding in Tessa's brain. What were they suggesting? In her misery she hardly listened, or rather, she listened, she heard, but her emotions were numb. Then at last it was over. The coroner, sitting in judgement like God Himself, decreed that Sebastian, an actor whose career had been destroyed with his natural appearance, had been unable to face an empty future and had taken his own life. No rider about being of unsound mind; but wasn't it worse to hear that your husband saw his future as empty? What did *he* know about their marriage, about everything they had shared, about trusting and believing that, faced together, there was nothing they couldn't have overcome? But it hadn't been enough. She'd tried, she'd wanted to weep with him, to sink to the pit of despair with him – oh, but surely her own pit of despair had been as deep as his. Yes, but it had been *her own*; that was why she'd not been able to help him.

202

Each of them had suffered, but he'd not let her come close enough to read his innermost thoughts. All the time he'd been at home, each day when she'd believed he'd been dosing himself on pills and escaping into daytime sleep, now they were telling her that he must have been planning to do this to her. Love her, he said. What sort of love was that?

'It's all over,' Sally whispered to her, taking her hand and standing up.

Like a whipped dog, Tessa looked at her. How could it be all over? How could it ever be over? He'd deceived her; he'd not trusted her enough to tell her he couldn't go on. Suppose he had, suppose he'd said, 'Let's go together.' Like a train hitting the buffers, her thoughts came to a full stop.

'We have to face the cameras again,' Nick whispered to her, coming to her other side and putting an arm around her shoulder.

'Not me,' Tessa heard herself answer, her voice no mirror to the tumult of her mind. 'It's Zena the press will want; she's carrying the banner for him now.' And even that hurt. It was as if her part in Seb's life had been incidental. And had it? If it had been as meaningful as she'd always believed, surely he'd still be here. He couldn't have done this thing, couldn't have left her feeling she'd failed him.

And so the days passed: autopsy, inquest, funeral – then nothing.

'Jethro,' Zena said, waking on a Sunday morning a week or two later, 'I've been thinking ...'

'Well done,' he laughed, pulling her closer. There was something very special about Sunday mornings; neither of them had anything to get up for. Presently, but not yet, they would bathe, dress, go out somewhere for lunch; all eyes would be on his lovely Zena.

'Even before all this – Dad I mean – I'd not been happy about the plans. The wedding, I mean. We'd wanted it to be such a perfect day, nothing but happiness. But how can it be, now?'

'It's what your father would have wanted for you. Imagine how he'd feel if he thought he'd cast a shadow on your wedding day.'

'I know. It's not just Dad, though. It's Mum. She's hardly going to want to celebrate, is she? The play comes off at the end of April. But, listen, Jethro, I've had this script sent me; it's an absolutely

203

wonderful part. When we get up I want you to read it, see if you can see me playing it. I can. It goes into rehearsal just before the end of April. I could cope with the timing.'

'But not if you have a wedding to clutter up your time. Is that what you're saying?'

She was genuinely shocked at his tone.

'No, it's not what I'm saying at all. Darling Jethro, of course we're going to be married. We have the whole of our lives to be together. I can't see that it makes much difference if the wedding is now – which is much too soon for it to be anything but a resurrection of all the unhappiness about Dad – or later on. We live together in any case. The only person to be boot-faced about that is Nick. He'd like us to creep off somewhere and tie the knot quietly so that he can see me as an honest woman. But that's not going to be possible, even if we wanted to. And I don't. I want a proper wedding, yes and I want the photographers; I want all the coverage the press will give me. Don't you see, there's nothing people like more than a good romance. And ours is a good romance, darling Jethro.'

'You make me feel I'm being pushed to one side until you can find me a convenient slot.'

She chuckled, teasing his mouth with hers. 'Like now?'

On the edge of the village of Millbrook and originally built for Cuthbert Higworth, a prosperous mill owner as long ago as 1786, Higworth House had been lived in first by him and then by his descendants until the line had died at the passing of Lavinia Higworth in 1931. It had been inherited by a distant relative whose grandmother had been a Higworth until she had married and emigrated to Australia. With no interest in the property, he had put it in the hands of a none-too-go-ahead estate agent – and from the distance of half the world, how was he to know *that*? – and waited for the money. It was once a great house, well staffed, a showpiece of the district, but since the early days of Queen Victoria not a penny had been spent on updating it. So the none-too-go-ahead estate agent had been unable to find a buyer with money to spare for bringing it up to date. He'd tried for the first year and then, its beautiful furniture sold and the proceeds helping to ease its inheritor's disappointment, he had left the details in the back of his filing cabinet. At the beginning of the war he had been approached by the principal of a lesser public school seeking a safe haven. Bartering had begun and it had finally been sold at a knock-down price and work put in hand to make it ready for some two hundred boys of prep school age: bathrooms, toilets, electricity, central heating, essentials of modern living, bearing in mind that a spartan lifestyle was considered character-building.

Nearly seven years on, Highworth House prepared itself to become the Szpiegman School. An army of builders were there again: dormitories that had originally been large individual bedrooms were once more transformed, this time into cubicles, where each music student would have privacy. Each would contain a single bed, a hand basin, a built-in wardrobe, a book-shelf, a desk and two chairs. Still spartan but at least the floors would be carpeted, the bedspreads brightly coloured.

By the gate at the end of the curving drive was the lodge; built of the same Bath stone as the house, it had three small bedrooms, a kitchen, a scullery, which as a priority job had been turned into a bathroom, a small living room and even smaller parlour. Eliot's piano would take up half the floor space in the parlour so, after much discussion as to whether or not it was safe to remove the dividing wall, the builders had compromised and knocked out a section of it, forming it into an archway between the two rooms. When the work in the house was complete the lodge would be no more than a place to escape to, but in the meantime Eliot and Simon used a bedroom each and the third was Helga's in term time, and shared with Gizella during holidays.

For Sally the preparations for the school were a great pull. On her days off she always drove the twenty or so miles. She wanted to be part of it. The pleasure on her father's face when she got out of the car said more than any words. And not just her father's. All the week Helga looked forward to Sally coming, sometimes on her own or occasionally bringing Tessa with her. There was a party atmosphere about those days. If Tessa came she invariably brought food that she'd prepared, perhaps cakes she'd made, perhaps a cold chicken; she had never found the courage to kill one of her own chickens, staying right out of sight and sound of it while Nick wrung its neck and divested it of its feathers.

It was on a day in May when the two of them were driving home from one of those visits that Tessa asked Sally to tell Nick she'd had a letter she didn't understand about probate.

205

'You don't know how glad I am that he is looking after everything for me. I would have hated dealing with the solicitor. Nick's been so good ... don't know what I would have done.'

'Good? I don't think being good comes into it, Tess. Nick wants to help *you*, of course he does, but he does it for Sebastian too.'

Tessa frowned. 'I hate being a chore.' There was a pout in her voice; she didn't attempt to disguise it. 'Do you think Seb knows Nick helps me, and do you think he knows how hard it is to be dependent on someone – even on Nick?'

'He of all people learned that lesson. You know the date, Tess?' Sally took her left hand off the steering wheel and rested it on Tessa's.

'Yes, I remember. A day full of hope, taking everything we had for granted. I'll never let myself do that again, I swear I won't. A year ago we were excited, our bags were packed,' Tessa said. 'All ready for the post-war holiday we'd talked about for so long. If we hadn't done that, if we'd stayed at home instead, none of it would have happened. A year ago today Seb was still – still *himself*, not warped, not bitter, not empty.'

'You know what I feel? Perhaps you do too, I hope so. Tess, when I think of Sebastian now I can hardly remember those last unnatural months. Sometimes I seem to hear him laugh; I hear his voice quite clearly; I see him in my mind just as he *was*, just as he always will be.'

Tess nodded. 'I do too. I wake in the night and just for a moment I forget; I put out my hand expecting he'll be there.'

'So he is, Tess.'

Tessa turned to look at her briefly, seemed about to say more then thought better of it. Only after a few seconds, 'Just a dream, it doesn't last ... so lonely for him. Does he know, does he understand?'

Sally the practical answered honestly, 'We've no way of finding out. I remember an old aunt – great-aunt, I think, an aunt of my mother's, I think she was. Dad and I went to see her when I was a child and she talked to me about my mother even though I couldn't remember her. Aunt Bertha – Betsy – something like that, I don't remember her name. In fact all I recall is her taking me to one side and earnestly telling me that I mustn't think of heaven as being like the pictures in the Bible, all cold marble halls and angels sitting about playing harps; it couldn't be or no one would

206

want to go there. I don't know what she was talking about, but I remember thinking it wouldn't be polite to tell her that I never thought of heaven one way or another. But it was what she said after that that matters, even though at the time I found it very puzzling. She said what we should pin our trust on was love, love we had for the person who'd died and love that person had for us. Love was warm, comforting; trust in it and it never failed. I think she was trying to make me – I must have been about six – make me feel that I had a mother somewhere who was watching over me and loving me. Although I was young, I could feel that Aunt Whatever-her-name-was had an inborn mistrust of foreigners; she was fearful that I would be wrongly indoctrinated because I was mostly living on the Continent and being cared for by a couple who weren't English. That's all I recall about going to see her, that and the fact that we had crumpets and strawberry jam for tea and she wore her hat. I knew she wanted me to connect what she said with my mother and I felt guilty because I couldn't even remember her so I couldn't. Yet it was something I thought about – not then perhaps, for I was too young, but as I grew up. I'm sure it's true, Tess. Think about him, hold him close, the real Seb before his spirit got damaged as surely as his body.' She knew Tessa was crying. When they came to a gateway leading to a field of sheep, she pulled off the road.

'You know what I did, Sal?' Tessa sobbed, beyond trying to control herself. 'I've never told anyone, tried not even to think about it. I've never felt such anger as I did towards him. How could he do it to me? He said he loved me, yet really it was himself he was loving or he would have stayed with me.'

'No, Tess. Don't say that. It's easy for us, yes, even for you. You loved him just the same whatever he looked like. But think how you would have felt if it had been *you*; if *you'd* looked in the mirror as he had to and seen – seen a mask of evil. Could you have believed he still loved you and what he felt wasn't pity?'

'He should have known. I was so angry ... wanted to hurt him, even though he wasn't here to hurt, that's all I could think. All the time at the inquest, the funeral, having those hateful cameras watching. He could have been with me still – but he hadn't wanted to.' Nothing could stop her now: the floodgates were open, her words drowning in her torrent of tears. 'I made a huge bonfire. I carried his things to the garden, all this clothes, everything, then I emptied petrol from the mower on it all and threw it bit by bit on the fire. Sal, it haunts me. Stood there watching the flames eat his things, just like the flames must have devoured his body. It was the day after the funeral. Zena and Jethro had gone back to London, you were at the Park, no one would know. Whatever I'd done no one would have known.' Her voice rose hysterically as she relived that dreadful winter afternoon. 'I was an island, deserted; all I could see was the image of Seb in those last months; not once in all that time had I been able to reach him, and that's how it was as I watched his things burn. I was alone – and he could have still been with me.'

Ignoring her final cry of isolated loneliness, Sally dug in her mind for a way to help. Tess, dear, loving, unchanging Tess, always ready with warmth and caring even while inside her had raged misery she'd not been able to share.

'If you couldn't get near him before, surely you can now, Tess,' she said. 'He'll understand why you did what you did. Don't you think that even then in those first days, if only you'd been able to – to – what? To listen, listen with your heart? Don't you think that even then he was understanding your hurt?'

'Don't know. Just wish I hadn't done it. Wish I still had his things in that hateful empty cupboard.' She was quieter now, sitting hunched, looking utterly defeated. 'When he was flying I used to open his wardrobe, I used to touch his clothes, sniff the material and bring him close. Expect you did that with Nick's while he was a prisoner. Now I can't.'

Sally frowned. No, she'd never sought Nick's presence in the feel of his empty suits, the lingering smell of tobacco in the cloth. 'You don't need inanimate objects. It would be macabre to build a life round things just because they used to be his.' Sally ached with pity for her friend. Suppose it had been Nick, not Sebastian, who had been in that accident; suppose she had been the one to be left. Would she have hoarded everything that had been his? Nothing if not honest, she knew she wouldn't. 'Tess, would it have been any easier if you'd taken his clothes to the Salvation Army? It would have hurt you just as much, perhaps even more, to think of someone else wearing his clothes. But you *had* to do something with them. The only way forward is to let go of the trappings of the past. You know what I think?'

'Something sensible,' Tessa sniffed. 'I envy you, Sal, you're always sensible. But I wasn't. I was sort of crazy, couldn't behave any other way.'

'I know that, silly.' Sally took her hand, such a small hand. 'I think what you did was wiser than you imagine. Have you no mementoes you've saved since you were a child? Knowing you, I bet you have. Even I have, and I'm the least sentimental person. It's certainly superstition not sentiment that makes me hang on to the few bits and pieces I accumulated when I was growing up. Because the truth is, we save things, memories of a happy outing, programmes from some concert or play, even photographs. And what does time do? We half-remember what each one was supposed to represent, and what we can't recall accurately we probably imagine. Even photographs. A picture that seems to hold the spirit of the person, yet we look at it until in time it's as if *that* is what we hold in our memory. So what you did was right, Tess. Now there is nothing to clutter your mind. You have a direct line to all that you and Sebastian shared.'

For a whole minute Tessa sat quite still, her hand still in Sally's although she may not have been aware of it. All her energy had been sapped by her crying and when she finally spoke she sounded drained of all hope.

'Glad I told you. Like exorcising a ghost. Direct line to Seb . . . if only . . . just so lonely, Sal . . . can't find him . . .'

'Yes, you can, Tess,' Sal tightened her hold on Tessa's hand as if she would force into her some of her own strength. 'Like you said, you've laid a ghost. How can he be at peace if he knows you're unhappy. You say if he'd loved you he wouldn't have done what he did, but that's rubbish; that's just you making excuses for your own anger. Sebastian loved you, Sebastian loves you still and he always will – the same as you will always love him. But that doesn't mean – it *mustn't* mean – that you spend your life looking backwards. Why did he take his own life? Partly because he couldn't find the courage to face his own future, but partly so that you would make something of your own. And so you will.'

'I expect so.' But she obviously expected nothing of the sort. 'I'm only any good at being at home, looking after people I love. Zena's gone – of course she has, I'm proud of what she does and I know she and Jethro will make a wonderful life. Expect there will be grandchildren.' Even that prospect did nothing to inspire hope.

209

'We must get home. Come back with me. Either Nick or I will run you home later.'

'No, I won't do that. I'll go home. I want to think about the things you said. And thank you, Sal, you must think me awfully floppy.' Tessa probably didn't expect an answer. But Sally turned the remark over in her mind. Did she think Tessa floppy? No. If she'd behaved like it herself then she would have been appalled, but Tessa was different.

'Floppy? No, I think you've been through a hell of a time and are entitled to have an attack of the flops. But mostly, Tess, I'm grateful that you told me about it all – the bonfire and all that. You know what I think you ought to do? What I'd do, at any rate? I think you ought to sort out your own wardrobe. I bet you have things there you haven't worn for years, things you mustn't hang on to as if that way you keep your memories. Get the meths bottle out and let them go the way of Sebastian's. Then, say, keep the winter things in your own and put the summer ones in Sebastian's. And I bet when you do it he'll come one stage nearer to finding his own peace of mind. He wants you to move forward, Tess. Don't you think that's what he meant when he said he wants you to be happy?'

A comfortable silence settled between the two of them as they covered the last few miles and Sally pulled up at the door of Mulberry Cottage.

'Sal, don't tell anyone will you, not even Nick. Promise.'

'Tell Nick? Of course I wouldn't. We women have to cherish our secrets,' she laughed, determined to end their outing on an up-beat note, and was answered by something akin to a smile on Tessa's tear-stained face.

'And Sal, don't forget my message to Nick about the letter I've had. If he'd like to give me a ring this evening I'll read it out to him and he'll know if it's important.'

'I'll tell him.'

That drew a line under Tessa's outburst; neither of them referred to it. Whether or not Tessa made that second bonfire Sally had no idea, but it seemed to her that as the weeks went by and spring gave way to summer there was a new – or was it a return to the old? – appreciation of life in her friend. She dug no deeper; after all, Tessa had confided in her once and so she would again if this new aura were nothing but a façade. For Sally there was plenty to hold her interest. The work at Higworth House was progressing well. As young men were demobbed there was no shortage of labour. The outbuildings which had been classrooms were soundproofed, just as was the further block that was being built as additional practice rooms. The end result of their vision was taking shape and by the end of summer the national press had carried articles, Simon and Eliot had been interviewed for magazines, press releases had been sent abroad for publication in America, France and Scandinavia.

At Drifford Park there was no hiding from the chaos left by war; Sally was aware that the beginning of peace didn't mean everything was running on smooth lines.

'Are you too soon?' Sally said to Simon as they gazed across the green sward to where the new buildings were taking shape. 'Is the world ready for music?'

He seemed surprised. 'Too soon? Music has never been needed more.'

She felt a great pull of affection towards him, even while her more logical mind saw the hurdles he appeared blind to.

'You're right there,' she agreed, almost wishing she hadn't cast a doubt to cloud his vision. ' "If music be the food of love",' she quoted, overlooking that his knowledge of the language may not encompass the writings of Shakespeare, 'then it has never been needed more. I expect it's because I work where I do, every day listening to reports, talking to people there; divisions within Europe, and Palestine – so much in the melting pot. Administrative divisions may be necessary, but these are ideological. Peace should be more than cessation of war. Isn't this the time we should be trying to understand each other? Yet do we ever come any nearer to it?'

'Understanding cannot be born with the signing of a piece of paper,' he said gently. 'Think of a person who is suffering great pain; then there is an operation to bring a cure. Does that person leap from bed, full of good health? No, it cannot be so. First there has to be a time of recovery – convalescence, is that not what you call that period? Before the people of a war-torn world can learn to understand each other and to forgive, they have to become known one to another. The hurts are too new, peace has to be worked at, only gradually can it be built. And you say is it too soon for music? No, surely that is the healing balm every man needs.'

211

He spoke so earnestly. Hardly realising what she did she slipped her hand into his.

'I know you're right, Simon. And I know the day will come when this place is full of music,' then with a smile that seemed to emphasise the words, 'tomorrow's musicians learning at the hands of today's masters.'

'Yesterday's, would you not say? There are moments – oh, I do not give them the opportunity they are seeking to turn my thoughts back on what I can no longer have – but there are moments when I draw the bow over the strings of my violin, I hear the sweet sound, and I long for an orchestra, I long to be lifted and carried on the glory of it. But I am ashamed to admit such things even to you, my very true friend. It was your vision that pointed me to where I am now; without you I might have been teaching a school of boys who would rather have been kicking a ball.'

'Of course you long for things to be as they were. Musically, I know Dad does too – and for you the past held so much you have lost.'

It was she who had taken hold of his hand, but now his fingers were firm on hers. Yet when he talked she felt it was as if he was thinking aloud, hardly aware of her.

'Losing my blessed Estelle? I believe that in the confusion of my thoughts there is relief. No, the sound of that is hard, unloving. I have chosen the wrong words. I loved Estelle; indeed like other men before me and perhaps after me too I fell in love with her the moment I saw her on the stage. When I first knew her she was the most exquisite woman I had ever seen. I could think of nothing but her. Right at the beginning she told me that her sight was going; she knew there was nothing even the most clever surgeon could do to save her; generations in her family had been affected and yet neither her brother nor sister had inherited it. It was cruel. She knew what was ahead, she knew that not for much longer could she be a dancer. I had just one desire: to protect her, to take care of her. Almost as soon as we married she gave up dancing. For some time there was nothing to make me believe she was getting worse. It wasn't until Gizella was born that I noticed the change: she would knock into things, put out her hand to pick something up and knock it over, trip over a step she hadn't seen. It was natural for both of us that I did more for her and yet we neither of us talked about it. She had

212

great love for Gizella; she insisted she could care for her herself. Her fear was that the child had inherited her rogue gene, but I thank God that she shows no sign of it. My own sight is good, so always I hope.' Sally was surprised when he turned to look at her, for she had honestly believed he'd been speaking his thoughts for himself alone. 'She was so brave; she never complained. Sometimes I would watch her, try and get inside her mind and know what pictures she was seeing, where she found her courage and hope. Or was the hope but a pretence? I could not know her thoughts, her dreams; I could but imagine, for she would never allow them to be shared. Perhaps you consider we had a strange marriage; certainly it was not like your own. Our relationship changed over the years. But you must not misunderstand what I am saying: our affection and loyalty grew stronger. She was my strength in so many ways: I talked to her of my career, I talked to her of the troubles that were building in Europe. She, who had no sight, was my guide. In practical caring, it was I who looked after her, but if you asked me who it was who controlled our family I would tell you it was Estelle.'

'You were away from home so much. Did she travel with you? Strange places must have been difficult for her.' What had he meant when he'd said it hadn't been a marriage like her own?

'In the early years she did, even when Gizella was very young. But it became more difficult. Her sister Lizelle came to live with us in Warsaw; when I was away she took care of things. It was early in 1939 that Estelle told me she wanted us to leave our homeland. It is a hard thing to do, Sally. We wanted to bring Lizelle for we had no doubt that the future looked threatening. Lizelle refused to come with us. I felt the scorn she had for me that I could go. Of course I did it for Estelle and for Gizella, but if I am honest I know I did it for myself too. I am not proud of it. We all knew that Hitler meant to take back the Polish Corridor, we all knew that with one foot in the country he would not be content. As for Russia ... I don't think we had vision enough to know that Russia too would invade.'

'But it's over, Simon. Poland has been liberated.'

'How can you say that? You, Sally, who are not a stupid woman. What Poland has is not liberation, we both know that. There were many brave Poles. I wish I could number myself amongst them. But how easy it is to say that when it is too late.'

213

Sally still gripped his hand. 'I don't listen to the bulletins from Poland, but I read the transcripts often and the country is becoming organised. You know they've brought out a five-year plan; surely that must have given the people hope.'

'Some may feel hope. Some will know that the end of war is not the end of repression. There are right-thinking Poles and wrong-thinking Poles.'

'You can say that of people the world over. There are those who prefer the easy way and, just as bad, there are others who are eaten up with bigotry; but always, in every country, there are also those who look for understanding. Policies, ideologies may be on lines that some will be content to accept but it is *people* who make up a country, people with differing views. None of them feel themselves to be wrong. But surely what is lacking is understanding – and the will to forgive.'

'I know what you say is right, but Sally my friend, it is not easy. I should learn to forgive those who have ravaged my homeland. What of Lizelle, of the others of Estelle's family, of my own cousins? We know nothing, nothing of what happened to them, even if by some miracle any survived. They were not like me; they did not run for safety. Those who were brave enough to stay behind or to get away to join the fight for freedom, can I expect they will forgive me for putting myself, my career, my family before my duty?'

'Yes, Simon you can expect them to. You had to be Estelle's eyes, you had to be the one to protect her and Gizella. And above all you have kept the spirit of your country alive with your music; you have been an ambassador.'

'I hid my cowardice behind my wife's blindness. Sally, I am not proud.'

'Then you should be. Look at Gizella and compare the life she has with what might otherwise have been. Don't you think that is more than compensation? Doesn't it make you thankful you made the decision you did? Anyway, you say yourself, it was what Estelle wanted. She was a brave woman, so it must have been for Gizella that she was prepared to come to a strange country.'

'You are right,' he spoke with new determination, 'and for Gizella I swear I will make a success of the future that has been handed to us.'

214

On the far side of the lawn Eliot and Helga appeared, deep in earnest conversation. A busy squirrel darted into sight and out of it again; behind them a drowsy bee buzzed. Another summer was nearly over.

Afterwards when Sally looked back on those months, sometimes she blamed herself for not seeing, for her unthinking contentment.

Chapter Eleven

It was a Sunday morning the following January. Just as he did every Sunday, Jethro brought their breakfast and the newspaper to bed. The only thing that marred the absolute perfection of his life with Zena was the knowledge that his father disapproved. Oh, not of Zena. What man could disapprove of Zena? What he frowned on was that they seemed content to let life drift by while they were living together unmarried. In his heart Jethro agreed that it would take very little time to 'tie the knot', whether at the registry office or in a church. Whenever his thoughts alighted on Zena's reason for putting it off until there was time for a reception and the fanfare of publicity that would be attracted, he pulled them quickly away. He would see no wrong in her. And in fairness, could he blame her for looking for publicity? The feckless public loved a star. So on the occasions when they spent a Sunday either at Owls' Roost or Mulberry Cottage, he ignored Nick's tight-lipped disapproval. Sally and Tessa had both been to the flat, but like some Victorian patriarch Nick refused to visit, as if by staying away his views would carry more weight.

Zena was being watched with interest, and not simply because she was Sebastian's daughter. Her ambition had always been for the stage; she had looked on that as superior to a film career. There had been times when she'd been to the set with Sebastian and had been appalled at the lack of continuity. How could an actor sink himself into the character he portrayed if the producer decreed all the scenes in a certain place would be shot irrespective of where they fitted into the story? Actors weren't machines to be switched on and off at command. At the time she had secretly scorned her father for his obedience to direction. But that had been *then*, while he'd been at the height of his fame and with a future ahead of him. Now all that was turned on its head, her natural love and admiration for him left no room for criticism. When she was approached with a script and the offer of a contract for a film to be made by an American studio partly in London and partly in Hollywood the number of noughts on the cheque threw her high principles into doubt. And was it perhaps too that deep in her subconscious was a feeling of guilt that in thought she had betrayed Sebastian? Was that why she wanted to follow his path, carry the name forward?

As if she were doing no more than sharing some casual piece of gossip, while she ate her toast and marmalade she told Jethro about the offer.

'When did you hear this? Why didn't you tell me when you came home last night?'

'Oh, a few days ago. Thursday, I think the letter came. I'm not going to rush at it; they'll appreciate me more if I keep them waiting,' she laughed, passing him the empty tray as he got out of bed.

'Is it what you really want?' He wanted to pull her back from where she was heading. In one way, he told himself, he ought to clutch at the idea; the play was nearing the end of its run; it was then that they would be married. Under her guidance the plans were already going ahead: a marquee in the grounds of Mulberry Cottage, a firm of London caterers had been contacted (despite Tessa's objections and assurance that she was perfectly capable of doing the catering herself), Nick was to give her away (although Tessa had a cousin who was ready and willing to play a leading role in such a high-profile ceremony). So if she signed this contract, what difference would it make? Would she rush straight off to some film studio. Would their honeymoon be put on hold? Even so, if it was what she wanted, then Jethro tried to want it for her too. But there was the other side to the argument that went round and round in his mind: if she were to earn that sort of money it made his own pittance worthless. As it was, she was paid far more than he was, but the difference would be multiplied. How would he be looked on by her new friends in what he saw as the glitzy film world? A country yokel she'd brought from home? A good enough companion perhaps while she was on the lower rungs of the ladder but one she would soon rise above. 'I thought you

218

always turned your nose up at screen acting. That's what you used to say even about Sebastian: you used to say he was worth better.'

She shrugged her shoulders. 'So he was. So I am too. But wouldn't I be a fool to give up a chance like this? Think what it would mean to *us* –'

'That's what I am thinking. I'm thinking and I'm scared. What would you want with a chap like me once you got fêted by some handsome film bloke?'

Laughing, she too got out of bed, took the tray from him and put it on the dressing table then wound her arms around his neck. 'Is he looking for compliments, then?' she teased. Then, seeing he was genuinely uncertain, she said seriously, 'Jethro, you and I are partners. Right? Living together like we have and not being married hasn't meant we are any less partners for always,' then, with a chuckle, 'although try telling Nick that! What a silly old puritan he is.'

Silly old puritan or not, his father had always been Jethro's role model; even now he couldn't help feeling guilty, knowing he had fallen short. At any other time he would have sprung to his defence, but now his mind was on themselves. 'You deserve the best anyone can give you, and I want that person to be *me*. Even if I keep my nose clean, learn all I can, the best I can ever do is be in charge of Palmer's buying – and that's years away. A few months ago I would have thought that was a great goal: fixing prices with the growers, deciding where to buy our stocks, all that sort of thing. It sounded like something worthwhile and important. But if I worked all my days I'd never touch anything like the sort of money they are offering you. It's a big pill for a bloke to swallow. I ought not to care; I ought to just try and be glad for you.'

'Not for *me*, for *us*, Jethro. Being in films didn't do anything ghastly to Dad; he never changed a jot. So why do you think it would turn me into some sort of gold-digger? You seem to think I'm stupid enough to be tempted by shiny dross. Listen, listen hard,' she stood in front of him, her hands on his shoulders, her face raised towards his, 'I love you, Jethro. You are the only man I shall ever love.' Then, frightened by a feeling of fervour that was unusual in their relationship, she buried her face against his shoulder.

'And me,' she heard his voice husky with emotion, 'that's why I'm scared. Don't change; promise me even when you're rich and famous you'll still be the same. Even when I'm nothing but a kept man, someone waiting for you to come home to, promise you'll still feel the same.'

'Nothing could ever change for us; how could it? Remember when we were kids, well, that's all we were really even though we wanted to think we were grown up. Before the first time – I used to work so hard to vamp you. Had you any idea of what I was doing? I thought if a girl tried to get a man to bed, then he'd be there like a shot. But *you*, you were stubborn as a mule.' There was a lilt in her voice, laughter was just under the surface. It seemed she was back in charge of the situation. 'I kept trying to tempt you but you're no one's pushover.'

'Tempt me! Couldn't get you out of my head. Was just frightened I'd make a bodge-up of it.'

'There you are, you see,' she chuckled. 'You were scared you'd not raise me to dizzy heights in bed; now you're scared I'll find someone else, some self-opinionated prick of a film star. Well, you were wrong the first time and so you will be the second.'

He turned her face up to his, his mouth covered hers, her lips parted and he felt her tongue teasing. How many years ago was it when he used to lie in bed, wakeful, practising so that when the moment came he wouldn't fumble with the object he'd stolen from his father and, as he put it, make a bodge-up? And all this time she'd loved him; even while he'd been away she'd been faithful to him. What was she doing? Her hand was warm; if she'd tried to tempt him then, the years between had perfected the art.

'So that's decided,' she nuzzled against his neck. 'I'll accept them. I'll tell them at the theatre; we'll be married after I finish with the play just like we're planning. Now that's settled there's no need to spoil Sunday thinking any more about it. What would you like to do?' As if she didn't know the answer!

'You know what I'd like to do; what else could I want when you do that?'

'Good. Me too.' Even as she spoke she unwrapped her negligee and, in one action, slipped that and her nightdress off her shoulders. The seven years since the afternoon when their inexperienced fumblings had been interrupted by Nick had altered her very little; there was nothing of the sensual seductress in Zena; she knew the way she meant them to spend their Sunday morning;

she knew Jethro was as ready as she was for all the fun waiting for them, so what was the point of silly posturing?

'Today off – and in return you are working all night tomorrow?' Nick put the last bite of his breakfast toast and marmalade in his mouth. 'Sounds like bad organisation if they can't even arrange their shifts.'

'Rubbish, this is something we fixed between ourselves. Walther had a last-minute invitation to the theatre tomorrow,' Sally answered. Clearly she had offered with no feeling of martyrdom. 'I'm going over to the school today. But I'll be home in time to meet your train.'

'I wish you didn't waste your free days always rushing off to your father,' Nick grumbled.

'Waste my time? That I certainly don't.' Sally heard it as a criticism, but on that Thursday morning in February, nothing was going to destroy her eagerness for the hours ahead. The sky was a hard winter blue, the air stung with cold; she imagined the lawn at Higworth House white with frost, the smoke from the chimneys rising heavenwards in the still morning. 'Helga is glad to have me there. She's doing incredibly well, you know, Nick, her selection of furniture is ideal. I couldn't have bettered what she's done. But it gives her a boost to have an older woman's confirmation. Today we shall be hanging curtains, us and Mrs Strang, the new house-keeper. I think Dad and Simon had something to do with engaging her, but Dad said they made sure Helga took part in the interviews and they let her know they listened to her opinion. Isn't it great the way he's taken her under his wing?'

'If you say so. How much longer are they going to be before that great place starts to bring them a return for their investment? Not a business head between them. It'll surprise me if the whole thing doesn't flop.'

'Then brace yourself to be surprised. This week the first of their students will be arriving. First-rate students too. They're coming from France, three violinists and two pianists, all of them with recommendations from the music school they've attended. There is enormous interest – I knew there would be. The names Szpiegman and Burridge will be a tremendous draw. I wish you'd come over there, Nick, see for yourself what miracles they've performed – or had performed for them. More coffee?'

'No thanks, no time. And if you're wanting the car you'd better leave these dishes and take me to the station. You needn't worry about meeting me tonight, Tess said she would. It'll save you rushing home and having a meal to prepare. Remember I thought you'd be working late and I'd be faced with a reheated meal to be eaten alone. I want to go over her monthly accounts with her. Even after all this time poor Tess looks for confirmation that what she does is right. I suppose even during the war Sebastian was home regularly enough to go on holding the reins. Not like you. If I dropped dead tomorrow you'd need no help from anyone.'

'Paying bills hardly needs the brain of Einstein.'

But Nick didn't seem to be listening. He went on, laughing as he spoke, 'And she tells me she has one or two what she calls man's jobs lined up. She's decorating Zena's old room, you know. Or didn't you know? God knows when you last found time to go and see for yourself.'

'I often look in after work. And yes, I did know about Zena's old room. You try and fight Tess's battles that aren't even there, Nick. Tess and I are fine. I don't need you to tell me what I should or shouldn't be doing. I tried to persuade her to put an advertisement in the paper – even in the national press if she didn't get any local replies – for residential help in the house. Before the war they had those two girls; now she seems determined to look after that great barn of a place by herself.' While she talked she'd been putting on her coat and getting the car keys off the hook by the back door.

'Whatever Mulberry Cottage is,' Nick replied, fastening his coat and picking up his briefcase, 'it is certainly no barn.'

'No, I chose the word wrongly. What is there about Tess that turns a centuries-old, hard-to-run house, into a haven of comfort?' Then, laughing, 'One thing, it certainly isn't routine. When I went there a couple of days ago it was mid-morning and she still had piles of washing-up waiting, plates, glasses – honestly, she must have been storing it up for days; one person couldn't possibly use so much crockery. She shouted to me to come through to the drawing room and there she was with the floor covered with plans she'd been drawing for the lay-out inside the marquee, those and guest lists.'

'I'll drive,' he said, opening the passenger door for her. 'I expect the mother of the bride has a lot to arrange. Something you'll never have to worry about.'

222

'Not true. I shall when Helga gets married.'

'Your ugly duckling? Time will tell. I say, we must step on it or I shall miss that bloody train.'

After she'd left him at the station she started towards home; as she covered the two miles from the village her thoughts drifted towards Tessa. Just imagine how wretched it was for her there in the house alone, stripping Zena's wall of the paper she and Sebastian had chosen with such trust in the certainty of their future. Then she thought of that accumulation of dirty dishes; how many days had that been piling up? One person alone – especially if that person was Tessa – probably used a single plate and either a glass or a cup and saucer. The ever-ready smile was once again back in place, but deep down, hidden even from her dearest friends, how depressed was she? Sally resolved that as soon as she'd got rid of the evidence of breakfast, before she set out for the school, she'd go to Mulberry Cottage.

'Lovely surprise,' Tessa greeted her half an hour later. 'You just caught me before I finish the last coat of paint. The youngsters have made do with it up to now, but I made up my mind it would be spruced up for the bridal pair's next visit – whenever that might be.'

'Well, it won't be yet, Tess. So come over to Higworth with me instead. We could come back in time to meet Nick together.'

'I thought you were working. I thought today was late shift.'

'It should have been but I changed my days off. Walther Schumach didn't want to do his night shift tomorrow: he's off to town to the theatre, so I did a deal with him. Nick tells me that, thinking I'd be tied up all the evening, he'd arranged to go over some accounts with you. He said you'd promised to meet him and bring him straight back here. What about if instead of that we come back from Dad in time to collect him from the station together? It's quite time he took us out for dinner.'

Tessa looked uncertain. 'I really did want to get the room done, Sal. Let's leave things as Nick arranged. Or, of course, if you want to come home early and meet him yourself, then you do that. Tell him not to bother about me and the accounts: he can go over those with me another evening. And he's promised to help me with the ceiling. But first I want to get the gloss paint on.'

All Sally's persuasions were to no avail: Tessa was determined to get the top coat of paint on the window frame, apart from the ceiling all that remained to be done.

'No, don't put off going through your accounts,' Sally told her, 'Stick to the original plan. You meet Nick and bring him back here. To be truthful, I shall be glad to have the evening with them at the school. Tomorrow is their Big Day: the first of their students arrive from France. And from there on, if the enquiries are anything to go on, they are going to have precious little time for the likes of *me*. Except for Helga; I feel I can give her some sort of support. She really has blossomed, hasn't she.' It wasn't a question, it was simply a statement of a fact they were agreed on.

Her day at Higworth House – at the Szpiegman School, as they had to get used to calling it now – was everything she knew it would be. By that time Eliot, Simon and Helga had moved into the big house. Now that Mrs Strang was in charge of domestic arrangements with a young war widow, Hilda Jennings, to help her indoors, and Jeremy Bryant, a one-time merchant seaman, outside, Helga no longer prepared their meals.

'I dare say I'm no better than a silly old matchmaker,' Eliot said as the two of them watched out of the window and saw Helga striding back up the drive from taking letters to the post box, 'but you know what I always hope? I hope that one of these days we shall get a student a few years ahead of those who are coming tomorrow. It worries me that the girl sees nothing beyond here; she has no friends except you and Tess and us. What's to become of her, Sally?'

Sally laughed, taking his hand in hers. 'Helga is fine as she is. Don't forget she is behind most girls of her age. Most of us grew up confident of our future because it was built on our past. She had to start all over again. It's no use our trying to play God – or Cupid either. The right person will come along one of these days.'

'Humph,' he grunted, which could have meant anything or nothing.

'It's strange though, I'd not thought of her in relation to boyfriends. Yet this morning when Nick and I were talking about Zena and Jethro and about Tess being up to her eyes in arrange-ments, I said then that it would be like that for me when Helga got married. Twice in one day . . . a premonition perhaps that romance is just around the corner for her.'

'I'd like to think so.' Eliot might like to think so but patently he had no such expectation. 'Ah, there's Simon coming in too.' They watched as Simon slowed down and wound down the window of

224

the car. Whatever was being said, the two watching saw Helga make some laughing reply as Simon drove on to the back of the house and the one-time stable block now transformed into garaging for four cars. 'Now if he were a few years younger ...' Eliot mused.

'Dad, you're getting obsessed. I tell you, Helga is *not* looking for romantic adventure. Anyway, Simon's old enough to be her father. Here we are, gossiping like a pair of old washerwomen. Come and make some music.'

'Later on we will,' he said. 'Our home will never be our own in quite the same way after tomorrow. So this evening, unless you have to rush away, we'll all four of us enjoy some music.'

Much later, driving home, the sounds of the evening still echoed in Sally's head. Each time she'd told herself she ought to leave, one or the other had played the opening notes of something that made it impossible to force herself from the atmosphere she loved and face the wintry night. So by the time she parked the car it was after midnight; the house was in darkness. She felt her first pang of guilt and resolved to be quiet, not to disturb Nick. That's why she undressed in the bathroom and, naked and shivering, crept into the unlit bedroom. Even though she tried to make no sound, she was surprised when she drew back the covers on her side of the bed and there was no movement from him. Once nestled under the blankets she wriggled closer to him, turning on her left side and putting out her arm, just as she usually did, partly to bring herself nearer and partly looking for warmth. That's when she realised the reason for the silence: he wasn't there! Often if Tessa was upset, or if he was helping her with some job or other, he might not come home until perhaps half past ten or eleven o'clock. Switching on the bedside light, Sally looked at her watch. It was a quarter to one. Ought she to ring them and see what was wrong? But if she did and he'd already left, then the telephone would wake Tessa with a fright. She'd wait until one o'clock. But to lie in bed listening was impossible, so she got up and put on her thick dressing gown and went downstairs. He'd be home in a minute, of course he would. But all the time at the back of her mind was the memory of Sebastian. Tessa would have brought Nick home, supposing there had been an accident. She ought to ring the police; they could reassure her that they'd heard nothing. No, it must be that they'd started papering the ceiling and hadn't

225

realised how late it was. Any second she'd hear the sound of Tessa's car. Minutes ticked by, the only sound the rising wind starting to howl in the chimney. Normally she would hardly have noticed and would certainly not have heard it as eerie, a harbinger of catastrophe. Perhaps it was the contrast between the serenity, the rightness, of the earlier part of the evening and the way it had ended that gave her such a feeling of doom. Sally, always finding the practical approach to any situation, was a stranger to the sensation of the nameless fear that gripped her as she sat huddled in front of the flickering gas fire. Perhaps none of them were ever quite free of the ghost of Sebastian's accident. Make me hear the car; let it just be that they've been so busy they forgot the time. If I don't hear anything by quarter past one I'll phone the police. That gives them ten minutes. Please let me hear the car; let me know they're all right.

Straining her ears for the first sound of the engine, she seemed to freeze with fear when she heard footsteps coming to the front door. The police! It must be the police with a message. Her mouth was dry, her throat tight, her heart pounding so that she could hardly breathe as she went towards the hall, bracing herself for the sound of the doorbell. Instead, what she heard was the key in the lock and the next second, as coming into the dark house Nick automatically put out his hand for the switch, the hall was flooded with light.

'What happened? Where's Tess?' Seldom did Sally's imagination take her on such a journey of horror as it did as she saw Nick blinking in the sudden glare.

'Where do you think she is? I wouldn't let her bring me, if that's what you mean. I didn't want her driving on her own at this time of night.'

'You're so late ... I was going to call the police ... thought you must have had an accident. You could at least have phoned to tell me you'd be late?' Anxiety was turning to anger. For a second, uninvited, her memory took her back some twenty years; she was in one of the large department stores in Oxford Street, her mind firmly on her choice of a new hat, when Jethro, an over-curious toddler, had gone missing. When finally a kindly assistant had tracked him down, she had been consumed by anger; it had been the only outlet for her relief.

'And if I had? Would you have been here? Most unlikely,' Nick answered coolly.

226

A rare nudge of jealousy fuelled her anger. 'Oh, so you expected *I'd* be capable of driving alone at night.'

'Seeing that you come home from Drifford Park at all hours, I'd be wasting my time if I worried about you being molested. Even changing a wheel wouldn't be beyond your powers.'

'And so I should hope, mine or anyone else's with a modicum of intelligence. Well, anyway, now that you *are* home we might as well go to bed.'

Only when they were lying side by side between the cold sheets, he on his side of the bed and she on hers, did she hold out an olive branch.

'I suppose you started on the ceiling and didn't want to stop?' she said, the anger gone from her voice.

'Umph. Sal . . .'

'Yes. I'm listening,' she wriggled closer.

'Nothing. The night'll be gone. Let's get to sleep.'

On the days when she knew she had to work from midnight until eight the following morning, she found it difficult to rest. Some people could sleep with no trouble at all, but for Sally sleeping in advance was well-nigh impossible.

'This evening you make sure you have a rest before you go off to the Park,' Nick told her, his manner natural and amiable. 'Knowing you were going on duty, Tess promised to meet me and feed me again. That way you won't have to bother about anything except yourself.'

'She's an angel,' Sally smiled, as fully recovered as he seemed to be. The arrangement was nothing unusual: Tessa was always more than willing to smooth the way for her unsocial rota.

If they'd papered the ceiling the previous night that must mean the room was finished; this morning Tessa would be glad of company. As it was Mrs Bond's cleaning day at Owls' Roost, Sally decided to leave a list of what she wanted done and let her get on with it. So making sure the key was in situ under the appointed stone she set off to Mulberry Cottage, certain of her welcome and anticipating Tessa's pleasure at showing her how clever she and Nick had been in their papering exploits.

'Sal!' Tessa opened the door to her knock, looking pale and uneasy.

'I tried the back door but it was locked. I expect you were shattered after last night.'

Tessa shot a brief glance at her then immediately turned away to unnecessarily move the position of a brass statue in the alcove before she closed the front door.

'How do you mean – after last night?' There was an unfamiliar edge to her voice.

'I was worried. But Nick told me what made him late. It's always like that when you get wrapped up in what you're doing; time melts, doesn't it.'

'Nick told you ...? Sal, it was *my* fault. All of it's my fault. I don't know how I would have coped if I hadn't had Nick to help me.'

'But of course Nick was there to help you. For what I'm worth, so am I. Come on, Tess, don't fret about last night. As he said, what would have been the use of phoning me? I didn't get home myself until midnight. Come and show me Zena's room. And the wedding? Have the invitations come from the printer yet?'

'Yes, they came this morning. I'll show them to you. But the room? There's nothing to see since you saw it last time. I did the wood around the window; now there's just the ceiling. Nick's going to do the papering while I hold the steps and do the pasting,' then with a laugh that wasn't quite natural, 'and probably get showered with paste or have strips come unstuck and land on me. But there's enormous satisfaction in actually *doing* the room instead of having decorators.'

The papering not done? But surely Nick had said ...?

'I must have misunderstood him. I thought Nick told me you got it finished last night.'

'Did he say that? No, you must have misunderstood, Sal. Started, but not finished. It's the hardest job of the lot.'

'I expect I wasn't too wide awake by the time he crawled in.' Sally laughed. 'Anyway, let's see the invitations. We could start writing the envelopes if you like; you don't want to do all that lot by yourself.' She looked at the elegant cards. *Mrs Tessa Kilbride requests the pleasure* ... 'If only he were here, Tess.' As soon as she spoke she regretted the words. The wedding had to be a happy occasion, and if Sebastian's spirit was watching then, for his sake as well as Zena and Jethro's, that's what they had to make it.

'If Seb were here he'd be dreading it. You know that's true. When the day came I'd bet my last ha'penny that he'd not even attend. It happened so often, Sal, and over much lesser things than this. He'd feel ill, hide himself upstairs and be asleep – *pretend* to be asleep. No, for his sake we ought to be glad he's not got the choice of failing Zena or facing the guests. Guests, press, a big splash of publicity, for Zena I want it to be like that. But Seb couldn't have stood it.' Sally knew she was right, but she hated to hear it put into words. 'Nick will be absolutely splendid,' Tessa went on. 'Oh Sal,' her voice broke on a sob she couldn't hold back, 'it's all such a bloody, *bloody* mess.'

After all this time was her heartbreak still as raw? Sally took her hands and was surprised when Tessa pulled away.

'Don't, don't be nice to me. So ashamed. Didn't mean to . . .'

'Go wash your face and we'll break the back of the invitations. We'll give it until twelve o'clock; we might even get them all done. Then we'll go to the Drover's for lunch. It's cattle market day so you can be sure they'll have good steak on the menu; they always do when the farmers are in town.'

No more was said about Sebastian; no more was said about the papering of the ceiling. It wasn't until they came back from town, the stamps bought, a steak lunch eaten, that Sally referred to the evening ahead.

'Nick says you're meeting his train and feeding him. You're a saint, Tess. Get him to lend his tongue to some of those stamps; if he's to get the glory of giving the bride away he might as well do something to earn it.'

'Sal, I'm not a saint. I never meant any of it to be like this.'

'We none of us did, Tess. We just have to take what life hands out.' She looked at her dearest friend with a mixture of pity and affection. No matter how they tried to support her, any help could never be more than superficial. Easy for her to say we have to take what life hands out, but if it strips you of love how do you find the strength or even the will? 'I may see you tomorrow, but after night duty I'll probably go out like a light. Don't want to waste the day though. I'm off until Monday afternoon. Weekends are precious.' Now, that wasn't a very clever thing to say either, she silently rebuked herself. Weekday or weekend, where was the difference for Tessa?

But with Tessa dropped off by the gate of the cottage at half past four, it took Sally little time to get her thoughts under control. She'd go home, make a cup of coffee, then, secure in the thought that there was no one to disturb her, would set the alarm for nine o'clock and go to bed. That would give her comfortable time to have a shower, get dressed, 'do' her face, repaint her nails, and still arrive at Drifford Park well before the midnight bulletin. She quite liked working night shifts; there were fewer people on duty for not all stations put out bulletins during the night hours; the canteen was never full and those who were there were drawn together with a feeling of camaraderie. Usually in the morning she was able to get away before her appointed eight o'clock, something she always tried to do; having had the car all night, she had to be in time for Nick to get to the station in the morning.

On that particular morning, though, everything conspired to make her late. By the time she bumped and jolted her too-fast-for-comfort way up the narrow track to Owls' Roost it was already half past eight. Today Nick would miss his train. But why was Tessa's car in the drive? She must have forgotten Sally had been working all night and come with the suggestion they went somewhere. That was the first thought, followed immediately by another that Tessa must have taken Nick to the station. Her brain rejected both as implausible: there must be some other reason, bad news from the children ...

'Sorry I'm late, I drove like the wind,' she called as she came into the hall. Then, when there was no reply, 'Tess, did you take him?' At that same moment the drawing-room door opened and there stood both Nick and Tessa, side by side and facing her in a way that sent a shiver of fear through her. The children ... something was the matter with one of them ... 'What's happened? Is something wrong?'

'You honestly don't know, do you?' Could that be criticism she detected in Nick's tone? But why?

'Don't know what? Is it Jethro? Zena?'

'It's my fault, I told you yesterday it was my fault,' Tessa croaked. 'Oh Sal, can't you see? I didn't mean to let it happen.'

The truth was there before her, stark and obvious. How could she not have suspected?

'You ... you mean, you and Nick ... but when? How?' she heard herself ask, knowing the questions were unimportant. Nick and Tess ... was it something new or had it always been there just beneath the surface? Hadn't they all four of them loved each other? Four corners of a square, evenly balanced; take one corner away and the square becomes a triangle. But the word triangle implies that into the relationship of two people comes a third, a third who means more to one than the other. It had never been like that with Tess. She'd been dearer than a sister ... but all the time ...? If Sebastian were still here none of this would be happening. Shock was a physical thing; it ached in Sally's arms and legs. Thoughts crowded into her head, half-formed, half-understood. Her world was collapsing around her; only instinct made her stand erect, her chin high, her face void of expression. 'So what are you telling me? You love Tess, but we always have, Nick. Just like *I* love Sebastian, *I* still do, *I* always will.' Ah now, she thought smugly as she emphasised the '*I*', that's hitting below the belt – and I'm glad.

'If you weren't so wrapped up in your own affairs,' came Nick's retort, 'that bloody job that seems to make you believe you understand the problems of the world, that and the experiment your father is set on losing all his money with, you might have had time to notice what was happening. We neither of us planned it.'

'Sal, oh Sal, I am so sorry,' Tessa wept, making no attempt to stem her tears, simply turning her head against Nick's shoulder as he put his arm around her.

'Sorry about what?' Sally sneered. 'Sorry you're breaking up our family?'

Nick drew Tessa closer. 'If anyone has destroyed the family, Sally, then look to yourself for the answer. If Sebastian hadn't done what he did, then we – Tess and I – would have had to hide what we feel.'

'How considerate,' Sally mocked. Then with such venom it shocked her to hear herself, 'Have you considered why Sebastian did what he did? Have you thought that he may not have been as blind and self-absorbed as you say I am?'

'For Christ's sake! You know that's not true!' They glared at each other, Nick plainly appalled that she could have sunk to such depths. The first to pick himself up from where she had thrown them, he hit the ball into her court, sensing her moment of weakness. 'You don't expect me to believe your life is going to be upset whether I'm here or not. One less chore for you when you don't have to leave food for me – like feeding some bloody dog – when I get home in the evening.' And how often was that? Usually not more than twice a week. Sally said not a word, but the scorn in her expression spoke clearly. 'When have we ever looked to each other for companionship? Not since you've been wrapped up in the woes of the world you listen to. Did you think that was what I fought for? Then let me tell you: I came home expecting things to be like they used to be.'

'So they were. The things that mattered hadn't changed.'

'Oh Sal, it's my fault,' Tessa wept. 'I ought to have been brave. I ought to have stood on my own feet and not looked to Nick. That's what you would have done. You're always so brave; it was the same all through the war. Don't know what I would have done without you. I'm so sorry, so sorry. I couldn't help letting myself rely on Nick. Even when we were four of us together I ... I ...'

'That's the truth,' Nick took up what she had almost said. 'Four of us together, and if you want the truth I always knew there was some sort of pull between you and Sebastian. As for Tess and me ... now that it's all come out in the open I can look back and know that I've always loved her. Sebastian was the best friend I'd ever had; she was his wife. And that's how it would have stayed if it hadn't been for that bloody accident. But life goes on, Sally. You don't need me, you don't need anyone. If ever a woman was self-sufficient it's you. Just look at this house and what do you see? It has about as much warmth as a dentist's waiting room.'

'You've never said these things before.' How long had he thought this way? What of their memories? Did none of them mean anything to him? Even as the thought hit her she pulled back from it, frightened to think, fear spurring her on. 'If you want to live in piggery that's up to you. I don't – and neither do I want favours. *Poor Sally, I'm so sorry your husband loves me instead of you.*' She spat the words at Tessa, Tessa her dearest friend, Tessa who'd shared her secret thoughts. 'I don't want that either. As you say, I can manage very well on my own if that's the way you want it.' Her voice was hard; she met their gaze squarely. 'I take it that's what you're telling me? When are you slipping into Sebastian's bed, or have you done that already?'

Like a cutting knife, she felt the sting of Nick's hand across her face.

'Don't, Sal,' Tessa cried. 'Please don't. You make it sound horrid; it's not like that. We've battled, honestly we have. We didn't want to hurt you.'

'Did I say I was hurt?' Instinctively she moved another step backwards, distancing herself from them. She wanted them gone.

'You must be hurt. All through the war we used to plan for afterwards; remember how we used to share all our dreams? Now everything's different. Nothing's like we expected,' Tessa wept.

'Nothing indeed. Who is going to tell the children, you or me?'

'It'll be all right, Sal,' Tessa made a supreme effort, mopping her face with the handkerchief she took out of Nick's breast pocket. 'The wedding, I mean. This won't stop us all being friends, planning it together, sharing it like we intended. It mustn't spoil any of that. We have to think of the children.'

'Dear me, no,' again that sneer, again they seemed deaf to it, 'of course it won't make any difference to the children. One big happy family.'

'We will be, please Sal, let's try and make it like that. We can't be happy if we think we've spoilt things for you.' Muddly, warm-hearted Tessa was recovering; she was even catching glimpses of a future full of hope.

'I wish you'd go.' Sally's voice was cold. 'Unlike you I haven't spent the night in bed.'

'We can't leave things in the air like this, Sal,' Nick said, speaking more quietly. Until then he and Tessa had stood blocking the open doorway of the drawing room, Sally just outside in the hall. Now he moved aside, his hold on Tessa not altering as he indicated for Sally to come into the room. 'We have to talk. There are things to be sorted out.'

'I thought we'd said it all. If you expect me to sit down and discuss how we divide our home, then I'm afraid you are to be disappointed. After all these years – tidy-minded, clinically fastidious, all the things you delight in throwing back at me – you should know that's not my way of doing things. I shall go to a solicitor.'

'I've got things in the house, things I need.'

'Of course you have. And I shan't stop you taking them. But not now. Just *go*, can't you.'

They went. She heard Tessa's car start; she couldn't stop herself looking out of the window; she even took masochistic pleasure in seeing it was Nick behind the driving wheel. Nick, who before he pulled away took Tessa's hand to his lips. As the sound of the engine faded she slumped on to the arm of the sofa, the immaculate room seeming to mock her. The elegant vase filled with gracefully bending sprigs of winter forsythia, the only flowers she could find in the garden, arranged with such artistry that they looked artificial in their perfection; the grey phoney coke on the gas fire might glow red in the heat but would fool no one; the furniture gleamed; the fireside chairs were empty, their cushions undented by the weight of a human body. He'd gone ... it was all over ... everything she'd taken for granted ... loyalty, love, sometimes passion that had seemed to her to make them as one ... but how much had any of it mattered to him? Look back to the fun the four of us used to have, to that month at The Limit; even then he'd been watching Tessa, loving Tessa, envying Sebastian – *making do with me*. When he was a prisoner, when he thought of home, was it me he pined for or was it *her*, the one he wanted and couldn't have? Did Sebastian see things that I didn't? He was sensitive; he must have known.

Sliding to her knees, she grabbed one of those pristine cushions and crushed it to her face as if that would shut out the images that taunted her.

'What'll I do?' she sobbed, hating the sound of her own tears and yet glorying in being dragged by them to the depths ... down ... down. 'Nothing was ever any good, isn't that what he meant? I thought it was ... thought we were happy ... poor Jethro, he'll be so hurt.' Only as her storm of crying wore itself out did she look deeper into how all this would affect Jethro. Perhaps he too had seen her as nothing but an efficient machine; perhaps he'd wondered how his father had stood it for so long. He'd always been fond of Tessa – who hadn't? – and married to Zena they'd be one happy family. Nick was already taking the place of her father at the wedding. Jethro's wedding; two days ago she and Tessa had addressed the envelopes for the invitations. Jethro's wedding. Mother of the bride, so much to see to, such a big day. Bridegroom's mother – how could she be there, the spurned wife, seeing the four of them together? But she must see Jethro married. More images: this time she saw herself in the front pew of St

Peter's Church. She'd even decided what she was going to wear; now she couldn't bear to imagine herself in her finery sitting alone in the ancient building. Nick would be on the left side of the aisle; when he'd given the bride away he would join Tessa; only *she* would be on her own. But of course she wouldn't. Dad would be there with her. Dad and Simon and Helga; perhaps Gizella would get the weekend off from school. So she wouldn't be alone. Keep thinking *that*, she told herself, they'd always be there for her. Sitting back on her heels she held the damp cushion away from her face, then put it back in its place on the sofa, even then automatically seeing that its position matched the one at the other end. Her hands were shaking and when she stood up she felt as though she were made of jelly.

'I'm tired, that's all it is,' she said aloud, making her voice strong even though her legs were weak. 'I'm going to bed. Yes, and I'm going to sleep. I won't think about them, I won't even *think*.'

So easy to say.

Jethro held his father's letter in his hand, one page in his right hand and the other in his left. It couldn't be true. Dad couldn't walk out on everything. And what was it he'd written?

You may not be surprised to read what I am telling you, you have always known the closeness between us. I have left home and am living with Tess. Living with her until such time as your mother and I are divorced and Tess and I will be free to marry. You have discovered for yourself that the most important thing in our lives is to be with the right partner, and I wonder just how surprised you will be at what I am telling you. If Sebastian were still alive, Tess and I wouldn't have let ourselves acknowledge what we feel. But he isn't and she is alone. To start with you will probably see me as the black sheep, but I want you to try and look on it in a wholly adult way. Your mother is far too capable to be thrown off course by this – and I have every intention of seeing she is provided for. Naturally you have affection for her and I am not trying to come between the two of you. But you and I have always been close and now that you are grown-up I know I shall have your understanding – and your support. In a few weeks you and Zena will be married and as arranged I shall take the place of her own father. That will be just the beginning for us. I know you have always looked on Tess almost as a mother, just as to her you have been like a son. And so it will continue. Tess will write to Zena, but she finds it more difficult. Zena was so close to Sebastian. I look to you, Jethro, to help her understand that what we are doing is in no way disloyal to his memory; he was and will always remain my dearest friend.

Phone me if you like, but I hope instead you will put pen to paper. I need – and I mean that, I *need* – to look at your words and know that you are man enough to understand.

Give my love to Zena, Your always affectionate Dad.

Standing by his side Zena tried to read what was written. Then, almost as if she believed she had misunderstood, she took the two sheets from him and read the letter through again.

'Don't look like that, Jethro. Like he says, or what he means anyway, we don't choose who we fall in love with. Fancy, at their ages! Wouldn't you have thought they were too old?' Was it laughter that shone in her eyes? 'It could all work out rather nicely. Not the same as if Dad were still here. But I tell you what, I bet if there's a heaven he's glad to know about them. He'd hate to see Mum lonely and miserable.'

'I don't believe what I'm hearing!' Not what he was hearing or what he'd been reading either.

'Jethro darling, we can't dictate people's lives. I can see them being really happy as they get older, and don't you think that's good?'

Snatching the letter from her he screwed it into a ball and hurled it in the direction of the waste-paper basket.

'Don't any of you give a bugger about Mum? About all he's walking out on?'

'Of course I do, and they do too. But Sally's not the sort to want him if she knows he'd rather be with someone else. What is it he says? Capable, wasn't that what he called her? And so she is. She has a good job. She doesn't care about making a home like Mum does. She's never been the sort of wife who sits up and begs for her husband's favours. We'll go and see her – and she'll be at the wedding – everything will work out beautifully.' Poor Jethro, he

236

looked really upset. The trouble was he'd always made such a hero of his father. She glanced at the clock then wound her arms around his neck. She had half an hour before she had to get ready to go to the theatre.

Pushing her off, Jethro went to the window, staring outside and seeing none of it.

Chapter Twelve

Sally's world had fallen apart; the only bridge between yesterday, today and all her tomorrows was her characteristic need to hang on to control. This went deeper than hiding her grief; for her, hanging on to control meant being in charge of her own destiny. If Fate was to play a part, she gave it no credit.

Because of the arrival of the first students at the Szpiegman School the absence of both phone calls and visits from her during the week after Nick's leaving passed unnoticed, or at any rate unmentioned. She needed time and space; before she could talk even to her father she needed to have a firm hold on her future. At Drifford Park she gave no hint of the turmoil in her mind; just as it had been when first she'd gone there, again it was her lifeline. It gave her an insight into lives that had been scarred by war and loss, lives where in those early years of peace people were trying to find their roots again or, more often, trying to form new roots. The battles of war demand courage, and for some the aftermath demands a courage every bit as great. By comparison her own plight paled – until at the end of each working day she returned to Owls' Roost and was assailed by the emptiness, the smell of furniture polish, the echo of her own footsteps as, needing to feel the pain and yet dreading what she would find, each day she went to Nick's 'studio' to see whether he'd collected his artist's material, then checked his wardrobe. Was she driven by hope that, even now, he would come back to her? The thought would be there before she could push it away: but not for long, for she wouldn't give it a chance to settle. She wasn't there to be put down and picked up at his whim, she mustn't be, she wouldn't be. Think of all she had: a satisfactory and interesting career, a

239

comfortable home, a loving and loyal father ... and here her mind would go off at a tangent. Simon, he was her dear friend; one day when the raw hurt had dulled she would be able to talk freely to Simon. And Helga, dear, understanding Helga who had known sadness in a strange country, lonely, miserable, frightened for her parents and, finally, having to face her worst fears. Thinking of those two, Simon and Helga, helped to put the mettle back into her.

It was at the end of the first week that she opened the door of Nick's 'studio' and found the desk empty, the easel gone, all traces of his drawing things and his paints cleared away, not so much as a single miniature left as evidence of the thousands of hours he must have spent there. She knew even before she opened his wardrobe and drawers what she would see.

'Gone. Now he's really gone. Nick doesn't belong here.' She spoke aloud, hearing defeat in her tone. The momentary lapse was quickly overcome. Raising her chin she stared at her reflection, defying pity as in ringing tones she told the woman in the looking glass, 'He won't be coming back. You know why? Because Tess will be happy to let her life revolve around him. Well, I couldn't, I wouldn't.' This time she heard the belligerence – she wouldn't hear the heartbreak it hid. She ought to telephone her father; she ought to telephone Jethro. Not today. Tomorrow. She didn't quite follow the thought that before she spoke to either of them she wanted to practise in her mind exactly what she would say; she mustn't be caught off guard, she must be ready to brush off their sympathy.

And that's when Fate took a hand.

The next morning when she arrived at her desk in the listening room she found an envelope awaiting her.

'For most of us, our roots are not deep in this area, and it seems accommodation is not to be a problem. For you ... well, read it for yourself. Let me say though, without you our team will be the poorer.' Herman Mueller was a one-time teacher of English in a German school and many years her senior, and had been her friend from the first.

Not following his meaning, Sally neatly slit open the envelope and took out a single typed sheet while Herman stood by, watching and waiting to read regret in her expression. She gave nothing away as she read it through first once and then again, her

240

outward concentration disguising fleeting emotions that chased through her mind: relief that when a door had closed on her life a window had opened; sadness for what was lost to her; optimism and determination that this was a chance to make something of her future. Success or failure depended on *her*; she was dependent on no one – again her mind tried to take a sideways step, whispering to her that depending on herself was no more than a confidence-boosting way of admitting that she was alone. But she crushed the thought. He travels fastest who travels alone; was there ever a truer adage? As an added bolster to her determination she rekindled the anger she used to feel through the years she'd been no more than a housekeeper (not a home maker, oh no, that role had always been Tessa's); in her memory she seemed to hear Nick making it plain that in his view she was unemployable and, in any case, her job was to take care of the house. Well, now she was free.

There was no hint of where her thoughts had been as she folded the letter and met Herman's anxious gaze.

'It might have been designed especially for me,' she smiled. 'I hadn't said anything, but my husband and I are separated.' No need to tell him that less than a fortnight ago her world had been intact; don't let him guess how raw the wound still is. 'My son is working in London. As you say, one place or another, I'm a free agent. A move to Berkshire might be just what I need.'

When the listening station had moved to Worcestershire the war had been in its first year. Because its original base had been bombed, it had stayed long after the armistice. In the village there would be regret when news passed that Drifford Park was once more to be empty, for the large and mostly homeless staff had bolstered the coffers of the shopkeepers and, although there was cubicle accommodation for those who needed it in the old manor house, many more rented rooms outside. Add to that local women who found work as typists and manned the 'round the clock' rota, the closing of the station would mean unemployment the district could do without. Even though she was aware of all this, Sally's feeling was a combination of desperation and hope. She had to see it as a challenge; she ought to be thankful – that's as far forward as she let her thoughts go.

It was that evening that she telephoned Higworth House.

'This is the Szpiegman School.' Never off duty, Helga answered the telephone in her small office.

241

'And that is a very efficient-sounding Helga,' Sally laughed.

'I have called you twice but you have been working each time. Even Nick was not at home.'

'Helga, that's one of the reasons I am phoning. Is Dad there? I really ought to tell him first – but I want to talk to you too.'

'He and Simon are playing chamber music with two students. Can I ask that he rings you when they finish, or do you think I ought to interrupt them? I would be happier not to.'

'No, don't. Helga, I said I wanted to talk to you.' A deep breath; stare ahead at a point on the wall and keep the right expression in your voice. Here goes! 'There have been lots of changes here at Owls' Roost. What I am going to tell you probably won't come as a surprise. Nick and I have separated.'

'Sep . . .' the word died before it was born. 'What has happened, Sally? You and Nick never quarrelled. Are you saying you have found someone at the Park? If only Nick had shown an interest.'

'There is no person at Drifford Park, but in a way it is because I care so much about the place, about what I do there. When Nick is free he and Tess are going to marry.'

'No. Oh, but that is *wrong*, wrong for them, wrong for you, wrong for Sebastian. And why don't they see what it will do to Jethro and Zena?'

'They have been almost family for so long, it will be easy for Jethro and Zena.'

'It will *not*! What sort of a person are you saying Jethro is, that he can settle cosily into what you say is almost family already?' Helga seldom showed emotion, but what she had heard had destroyed her natural reserve. 'And Tessa, is she so unable to be without a man in her life that she can do this to everyone?'

'Don't, Helga, dear Helga.' Sally kept her jaw rigid, frightened to do more than whisper for fear her voice would betray her. She'd imagined herself breaking the news, she'd schooled herself into saying what had to be said, but she'd been unprepared for Helga's reaction.

'What do you want me to say?' Clearly Helga hadn't detected how near breaking Sally was. 'Am I supposed to wish them well, to say it doesn't matter that he can cast aside my best friend, that he takes advantage of Tessa's loneliness so that he has a woman to waltz around him, making him feel like a male god? I do not wish them well. They will have a few months believing they have

242

found some sort of second love, then they will have the rest of their lives to look back with regret. And Sebastian, did she not love him enough to live with his memory?'

Helga was very young and untried, that's what Sally told herself.

'You sound crosser than I do.' She forced her voice to be light. 'Yes, it was a shock, we'd all been friends for so long. But looking back, oh I don't know, Helga, perhaps the mistakes were in the past not the present. Dear Sebastian, we mustn't think she wants to forget him. And certainly Nick doesn't.'

Helga snorted her contempt. 'You will think I am too young to understand – I have never even had a sweetheart. But a sweetheart is not a necessary factor in the understanding of loyalty. So am I not right? They cannot find lasting happiness if in the taking of it they bring misery to others.'

Had she been able to see Sally she would have spoken differently, for in saying what she did she destroyed all Sally's pretence.

'They have to be happy, Helga, not just for a few exciting months –'

Another snort interrupted her. 'Middle-aged – are they frightened of getting old? Is that what is wrong with them? I think it is disgusting, yes, Sally, that is what it is. Disgusting to chase romantic love at their age.'

This time Sally's laugh was real and unexpected.

'Oh dear, is that how you see us all?'

'I suppose you hear what I say as proof I do not understand.' Helga came near to apologising.

'No, dear Helga, I know you feel as you do because you and I understand each other; we have been friends a long time. But hear me out. After this there could be no future for Nick and me together. But it mustn't be for nothing. If they are happy, then it must be something that lasts. Jethro will understand. I haven't spoken to him, Nick wanted to be the one to tell him. He must have done that before now, but I haven't heard. So doesn't that disprove what you say? Jethro must be accepting the new situation. I worry a bit about Zena; she thought the world of her father; she may resent Tessa wanting to remarry.'

Another snort.

'I will ask your father to telephone you. He will want to hear it from you not from me.'

'Yes. And now for the good news,' she said, a new strength forced into the telling of her move with the listening station to yet another large and empty manor house in Berkshire.

That night, after talking to Eliot, with the hazy shape of a new future beckoning her, she slept as she hadn't since Nick had left.

Zena was puzzled. Of course it was rotten for Jethro that his parents had separated, but it wasn't as if Nick had gone off the rails with some strange woman. And neither was it as if Sally was the sort of clinging type who let life revolve around her man. Anyway, what gave him the right to behave as if only *he* was affected? *His* parents had separated by choice, not like *hers*. If either of them ought to be miserable, then it was *her*. And she was. She was miserable to the depth of her soul that Dad wasn't here any longer, that he couldn't look with pride on the career she was making; but she didn't intend to be beaten by circumstances she couldn't control, and if Jethro were half a man neither would he. Looking at the situation squarely Zena was sure that, as far as it would affect either Jethro or her, the outlook was none the worse for what had happened; in fact – and here, she wasn't quite able to let the thought take positive shape – it was a lot better than if her mother had been on her own, a situation that would have nudged at her conscience uncomfortably. With Nick looking after everything at Mulberry Cottage, it took away from her any filial responsibility. Yet Jethro was behaving in a way that made it impossible for her even to discuss the wedding with him.

On that same day when Sally had snatched thankfully at the offer of accepting relocation to a new district, Zena could stand his near silent hang-dog expression no longer.

'Let's go home on Sunday, go and see Mum and Nick for ourselves. You may not like what they've done, but what gives you the right to think you can play God just so that nothing rocks your personal boat? They're adult people, and for heaven's sake Jethro, so are we. We don't know what's best for them. If Mum and Nick make each other happy, then we ought to be glad.' She willed him to meet her eyes, ready for an argument even though she could see no reason for it.

'You go if you want. I don't want to talk to them. Don't know how you can be so forgiving.' His face was that of a sulky child.

'Because, like I said, it's not up to us to play God with people's lives. At least you might telephone, talk to Nick. How do you think he feels? You treat him as though he were a leper.'

'I would look on a leper with compassion. Anyway, it's hardly the same. He and Mum always seemed ...' His voice trailed to silence. How had they always seemed? The happiest times he could remember had always been when the two families had been together. Had Dad always had his eye on Tessa? It was beastly, it was disgusting. Think how he climbed on his high horse about me living with Zena before we were married! Different for him, oh yes, he's entitled to get into Sebastian's side of the bed and – he didn't want to think about it. But Mum, she must think about it; she must lie in bed at night imagining the two of them. All right, he conceded they weren't young: at their ages Dad couldn't have rushed off with Tessa for sex. Or was that what it was? Christ, he was nearly fifty years old, middle-aged, beyond falling in love.

'It's a sort of middle-aged madness.' He glowered at Zena as if she were responsible. 'He's frightened there's nothing ahead of him but digging himself deeper into a rut. Bloody old fool.' He said it loudly, taking pleasure in the inward rage he felt for the father who had always been his idol.

'If Sally had made the rut a bit warmer, a bit less antiseptically hygienic, he might not have looked to Mum for affection.'

'Anyway, I don't want to talk to him. Zena, right now I can't talk to any of them, not even Mum. They were all right together; I know they were.' But did he? Had he ever seen beyond what they were prepared to let him – or anyone else – see? Mum must feel empty, unloved, cast aside, of no more value than the things they used to sort out each February for the Boy Scouts' jumble sale. Being *her*, she wouldn't admit to being hurt, she would reject sympathy. No ostrich ever dug his head deeper than Jethro did as he pushed the image away.

'Of course they seemed OK together. If Dad were still here, I expect none of this would have happened. But Nick knows – we all know – Sally is pretty hard-baked; she's not vulnerable like Mum. I bet you haven't even spoken to her on the telephone. You pretend to care so much, but the truth is you are frightened.'

Over the days since Nick's letter she had tried various ways to find a reaction she and Jethro could share, but he held himself away from her. Following the route she had believed infallible,

245

she had bought a tantalising, black, fine chiffon nightdress; she had used his favourite perfume; she had met him from work and led him to an intimate Italian restaurant even though the meal had been spoilt by her having to keep her eye on her watch so that she wouldn't be late arriving at the theatre. Yet through it all he had held himself aloof from her; he'd been courteously friendly, but never once had they touched on the raw bruise that with each day took deeper hold. Not one word that was uncivil, not one word of affection nor yet of anger. Sometimes she'd even suspected he'd looked at her with something akin to pity. She supposed it was because she'd lost her father, and her mother was putting someone else in his place. But it wasn't like that! Was he such a child that he thought because Mum needed Nick, needed someone to love her, that meant Dad was forgotten? Anyway, no one had the right to make someone else's rules.

'We'll go down for the day on Sunday. Perhaps we'll see them all – Sally too if you think that's a good idea, although I'm not sure that it is if we are spending the day at Mulberry Cottage – but seeing Mum and Nick will make you feel happier about them.' She frowned. 'It's not fair that *our* lives get upset – and that's what you're letting happen. We're all grown-up people; it's no good your carrying on like some tragedy queen,' then, with a chuckle that to his mind was extra evidence of how little affected she was, 'tragedy king. Why do we always say queen? If you ask me, women have more guts than men when it comes to the crunch.'

'Very likely,' he answered, in a voice that said he didn't care one way or the other.

'And the weekend? We'll do that, shall we?'

'As you like.'

She turned away. 'If you can't show a bit more interest I don't know that I do like. If you don't want to go, for goodness sake say so. If you do want to go, then show a bit of spirit. What's happened to you? You're a grown man, for God's sake, not some wimp of a child hanging on to his mother's apron strings.'

'Yes. I'm sorry.'

'We'll do that, then. We'll see how the wedding arrangements are going. There will be replies by this time.'

Jethro clenched and unclenched his fists; his mouth felt dry; his heart was beating fast. He loved her; for years she had been the

246

centre of his existence; she always would be, she must be. Nothing other people did must come between them.

'Zena, we've put it off before. Don't you see, we'll have to put it off again. Imagine the field day the press would have.'

But surely that was what they wanted! Zena Kilbride, fast climbing the ladder to the stars, given away by the father of the groom, Nick Kennedy who was the close friend of her famous father Sebastian. The press would have a field day. But was Jethro right? What if the prying reporters realised that Nick was living with her mother? People were so ready to condemn; they had no more compassion or understanding than Jethro. Another image flashed through her active mind: Sally, sitting alone in the church, the deserted wife whose husband had so soon stepped into his dead friend's shoes – or, more likely the thought would be 'his dead friend's bed'. How would that reflect on the Kilbride ménage?

'Perhaps you're right.' She frowned. 'As far as we are concerned it might not make any difference, but people are so quick to lap up anything that hints at smut. The papers would probably suggest that the four of them had been wife-swapping before Dad's accident. It might not matter to *them*, Mum, Nick and Sally, but gossip sticks. Perhaps you're right, we ought to leave things until the divorce is over and Nick and Mum are respectably married.'

He closed his eyes. What was happening to them? To them, to all of them?

At exactly the usual time he left for work, walking to the underground, catching the usual tube train, treading the usual path to the office that was his base, barely conscious of what he did. Today he was scheduled to visit one of their established growers at a farm in Hampshire, and it wasn't until he was on the train heading westward from Waterloo that the numbness gradually left him. The pale winter sunshine made no more than a feeble attempt to clear the frost that covered the desolate fields, yet it lifted his numbed spirit. The situation was unchanged; only by the time he climbed down to the platform, the only passenger to alight at the country station, his soul was his own again, his footsteps firm, something of his joy of life restored. Even then he knew the change in mood was only temporary. He could think clearly, but the fog of misery was hovering ready to envelop him. He breathed deeply of the cold February air, seeming to gather strength with each step. As he'd anticipated, there was no cab at the station to take him to his destination. Last time he'd been here, he'd telephoned and waited for one to arrive. This morning he decided to walk the two country miles; with each step, with each great gulp of 'pure' air (on that particular morning even passing a pig farm did nothing to detract from his sense of well-being), his heart felt lighter. God's in His heaven, all's right with His world. He heard it in the call of the crows from the tall elms, he felt it in the rough frozen ground he trod. Later he would be on the train back to London; perhaps the mist would engulf him again and this new clarity would be lost. It was as if the strands that made up his life had been tightly tangled; now some power outside himself was guiding him, he was un-ravelling the knots. The way forward wasn't clear, but the half-seen vision drew him forward. Tonight he would talk to Zena. He loved Zena; she had been the centre of his world since they'd both been at school. She would understand, she would let him direct her to the road that called him. Where it would lead was still uncertain, but the direction was clear. Until he'd had that letter from his father he'd been as near contented as he believed possible; then – because of the news it had brought him or because of Zena's reaction to it? – he had felt isolated. He'd been aware of why she'd bought that alluring nightdress; he'd hated himself that instead of it exciting him as she intended it had brought alive what he thought of as disgusting: his father's adultery. He'd looked at Zena, his lovely Zena, and found himself wondering if Tessa was going to these lengths to lure her best friend's husband. Before the advent of the letter, their lovemaking would have been thrilling, adventurous, complete. Through these last days he had recoiled from the thought of it.

Tonight he would meet her from the theatre, he would take her out to supper on the way home, he would try and describe to her the revelation. What was the expression? Scales falling from one's eyes, was that it? It sounded pretentious, but he knew it to be true. For a few seconds he stood quite still in the deserted lane, to either side of him the winter fields empty, overhead two or three rooks black against the pale winter sky. 'This is the first day of the rest of my life,' he said aloud. Is Mum saying that too? His thoughts rushed on. How can she? But she will, she's strong and brave. Not like me. I was a wimp, that's what Zena thought. Perhaps there's more of Mum in me than I imagined.

248

Then, hurrying as if to make up for time wasted, he strode on towards Merrydale Farm where it was his job to try to browbeat, coerce or persuade in any way he could Mr Riley, whose fields were given over to supplying Chas. Palmer & Co., to accept a lower price for his wares. Jethro enjoyed his trips to the growers; he'd yet to meet one he hadn't got on well with, but he disliked the business side, the knowledge that a contract with an important wholesaler was an outlet not to be argued with. Chas. Palmer & Co. paid the piper so Chas. Palmer & Co. called the tune (or in this case, set the rate).

The next day was Friday, the first day of Sally's 'weekend'. With no enthusiasm but rather as one-in-the-eye for the mockery of an empty house, she went into the garden to see what she could find to replenish the vases. From around the few trees in what they had ostentatiously called 'the orchard' she gathered snowdrops, with which she filled a small, granite, bowl-shaped vase and put it on the hall table. Next, with the secateurs she cut graceful, flowery branches of forsythia, looking around in the vain hope of finding something to add. At the sound of a car in the lane she stood stock still. Nick? No ... he'd taken his things ... Nick had gone ... unless he'd come with his solicitor ... but he wouldn't do that: he didn't even know she would be at home ... an estate agent perhaps; was he putting the house on the market? And if he was, what difference did it make to her? She was going away. All this would belong to someone else. The thoughts crowded her brain, not singly but one on top of another, in the second or two before the car turned into the open gateway.

'Eliot said it was your day off,' Simon said as he drew to a halt and opened the door, in one simple action. 'May I come to visit you?'

'Since when have I asked if I may come to the school – I just arrive and take my welcome for granted.'

'Indeed and that is correct.' This morning she was more than usually aware of his un-Englishness. 'Have I arrived too late? I see you have already gathered flowers for your always so beautiful arrangement.' As he spoke he reached on to the back seat and produced a large bunch of daffodils.

They were a breath of springtime; no wonder she smiled.

'You have arrived at precisely the right moment, Simon. I have cut forsythia, but the garden has nothing else to offer except bare twigs.' She took his offering, holding them to her face and taking in a great gulp of that pungent, almost earthy, smell that heralded spring.

'We'll go in and I'll arrange them while you make the coffee,' she told him, her smile giving every impression of being natural and relaxed. If he was puzzled by her normality he managed to hide it. Only last night Eliot had told him about that stupid swine walking out on her. He'd driven here half-expecting her to be – to be what? Tearful? No, not Sally. Angry, with Nick, with Tessa, with life? Yes, perhaps. Yet here she was, just as elegant, just as much mistress of herself and the situation in which she'd been thrown as ever he'd seen her. Indoors the house gleamed its highly polished welcome, all evidence removed of what she'd had for breakfast or yet what she intended to have for lunch. It was almost as if no one lived here at all. He ran water into the bottom bowl of the coffee maker, then spooned the ground coffee into the upper one and fitted the two together.

'I have no matches.' He looked at her enquiringly

'Right-hand drawer of the dresser. These are lovely, Simon. The first of the year.'

'They are a promise that winter and its gloom will soon be gone. Spring, new life. Do you not find it a fresh miracle each year? It seems this miracle comes to Jersey before it does to us. But be patient a little, Sally my friend, soon it will be ours too.'

She nodded.

'Dad told you? Yes, of course he did. That's why you've come, why you've brought me flowers.' Misery enveloped her; it ached in her arms and legs, her jaw hurt with the effort of holding it in control.

'Yes, it was what Eliot told me that – that left room for nothing else in my thoughts. For me the night was long. I wanted to talk with you. Do you hear what I am saying and find it intrusive? I hope that is not so, Sally my dear friend. Between you and me there is great understanding. Am I not right?' While he talked he'd lit the small lamp under the bowl of the coffee maker. The moment made an indelible impression on Sally's memory: the combined smell of ground coffee and methylated spirit, the perfect English

250

in that foreign voice, 'Sally my dear friend' threatening to destroy her hard-fought-for composure.

'Of course I'm glad you came,' she forced a laugh into her voice. 'And the daffodils are just perfect with the garden's humble offering of forsythia. Is Dad all right? He's not too upset about what I had to tell him? I've been putting it off for days.'

'Eliot has a difficult role to play: he knows he is powerless to help you, this is something you have to face alone. I am not going to try to strengthen you – what is it you say? To bolster you – by speaking ill of Nick. That is no way to help you find peace with yourself. But how can I not feel that the man is a fool?'

'No, he's not, Simon. I look around at this house, and I know exactly what he meant. Warm, loving, untidy, generous Tess, looking to him for help, trusting him, taking him her troubles, feeling safe with him – and you say he's a fool?' She shrugged, giving every appearance of concentrating on the flowers she was arranging. 'I am not a home maker; I can never be his or any man's "little woman".' This time she raised her head and looked very directly at him; once again she was in charge of the situation, her moment of weakness behind her.

'Indeed you cannot.' Simon laughed as he moved the spirit lamp away from the coffee maker and the dark liquid started down the long funnel, hissing as the last drains reached the bowl. 'Here,' he held his hand to her and drew her towards the steaming, aromatic brew. 'Even in the making of coffee there is a lesson we can learn, do you not see? We started with pure water – pure and untried as once we all were. It boils; like a frenzied spirit as it grows hotter and boils it is forced up to bubble and seethe in the coffee grounds – just as we are all forced to face our own tragedies and hardships. But see it now, friend Sally: no longer clear water, but rich stimulating coffee; no longer a seething mass, but calm, still, invigorating. For you, too, life will be like that. Believe me, Sally, nothing is for nothing.'

What had happened to her resolve to be calm? When she felt the sting of tears she made no effort to fight them. Instead, she turned towards Simon, her face a mask of misery. Gently he drew her towards him, his hand on her straight dark hair as he pressed her head against his shoulder. Her tears were warm on his neck.

'I'm behaving badly . . . don't be kind to me . . .'

251

'You're behaving wisely. I thank my God that I am the one privileged to be with you.'

'Me too,' she snorted, a sound quite out of character.

'Only tears can bring healing. Believe me, Sally. You are I are two of a kind. I fought my grief when I lost Estelle; I fought until I felt myself removed from the world round me; everything I did or said was like acting a part. Do you recall the day I came here with Eliot, how you and I talked? That night, in bed here in this house, I will remember to my last day the relief of giving way to the tears. Not tears of anger, not even of shock by that time – tears for myself, for my terror of a future I could not envisage, and even more than that for Gizella, who had lost a mother who had been her constant companion, but above all for my blessed Estelle, who had borne so much and then lost everything. At this time, Sally, you are in that state; to me you have no need to explain your fear of a future that is without shape. Until you have grieved for what is gone you cannot know that ahead of you there is another spring-time, there is sunshine that will melt away the ice around your heart.'

She raised her tear-smeared face, even then amazed at the relief of being able to expose her hurt and even more amazed at the relief she felt. If anyone else had spoken to her as Simon had, she might have been embarrassed, considered the words artificially emotional. Perhaps it was his un-Englishness, perhaps it was something she understood and shared in the depth of his love for making music, perhaps it was … she questioned no further, instead now that the floodgates had opened there was relief in hearing herself put into words the thoughts that haunted her.

'I can't look back,' she gulped, her dark eyes seeming to plead for his understanding. 'When you lost Estelle you must have found comfort in remembering. Can't even do that. Thought we were happy but now all I can think of are the times we were all four of us together. They were the best. Even then he must have been watching Tess, wanting Tess. Did Sebastian know, is that why he did what he did? The children, even they united as if we all fitted together. But we didn't. I gave him no warmth, that's what he said. The house is cold, not like Tess's, lived in, always in a cheerful muddle. I must be as insensitive as he believes or would have known – I was an accepted part of routine, like his going to work. I bored him. There, I've said it!'

252

'No, Sally. If your friend Sebastian had lived, if everything had gone on in the old unchanging way, none of this would have happened. Don't close your mind to the good times. If you do that, what of Sebastian? If you make yourself believe – yes, *make* yourself, for if you look back with clarity you will know what you now suspect is not the truth – but if you make yourself believe that secretly Nick and Tessa felt for each other as they do now, then what of Sebastian?' He spoke softly, but in his mind he raged against the man who could do this to her. 'There is no way of returning to what is gone. We are none of us masters of our own fate; when we have to follow a new road we have to tread it firmly, we have to make ourselves believe that it will lead us where we see light through the darkness of our unhappiness.'

Without asking him, she pulled the folded handkerchief from his breast pocket and scrubbed her face. Just like Tessa did with Nick's, came the silent mockery.

'Got make-up on your handkerchief,' she said unnecessarily, looking at the discoloured damp patch. 'Another symbol,' holding it towards him she forced a smile, 'something to do with starting to see through the mists, getting rid of illusions. Or is it symbolic of a battered soul that I look such a mess?'

'This cannot be Sally casting her net for a compliment.'

'Not this morning, Simon. Today we want nothing but truth: plain, hard to swallow truth. You're right, that's the only way to move on. And I *will*. I must have a guardian angel somewhere to have given me the opportunity of a new beginning in a different place. While you pour the coffee, I'll put a match to the gas fire in the drawing room then go and redo my face.'

'I would take it as a compliment if you left your face as it is.'

This time her laugh wasn't forced.

'Well, it's you who has to look at it. I'll just do the fire.'

'No. We will drink our coffee here in the warmth of the kitchen. What did you eat for breakfast?'

'Actually, I didn't.' Then, in case that gave the impression that unhappiness had taken away her appetite, 'Working shifts gets you used to eating at odd times.'

'Good. You will be hungry for your lunch. First we will drink this soul-restoring coffee, then while I clear away the cups and leave your kitchen just as you would leave it yourself, you will recreate the face you want to present to Cheltenham. After that I

253

will take you to the finest restaurant in town and we will eat a huge and celebratory lunch.'

'Celebratory? The school is getting off the ground well? But of course it is.'

'Indeed, Eliot and I are heartened. But that is not my reason for celebrating. It is because I am to lunch with a friend I esteem above all others. The daughter of Eliot, I knew she would be my friend even before I met her. But I had no conception . . . Enough. Do you have milk or cream in your larder. Not for me, I prefer it black.'

'Me too. Isn't it the manifestation of the calm strength of our lives? We mustn't cloud the waters with cream.'

'Nor sugar either,' he laughed. 'We ask for no artificial sweetness.' Then, raising his cup, 'I drink to you, Sally, to the firmness of your step on the road laid down for you – and I drink to the hope that there will be times when you allow me to share that road with you.'

'To that and to the Szpiegman School. Tell me, how is Helga getting on?'

So the conversation moved on, the burning feeling in Sally's eyelids lessened, her aching misery lifted even though she knew it was lying across her path like a shadow, waiting its moment.

Simon wanted to take her home with him after lunch. He tried to persuade her to spend her free time at the school. He knew he ought to be glad of her adamant refusal; didn't it show that she wasn't afraid of facing up to being alone? She compromised by promising him that she'd visit on her next 'weekend'.

She knew she could no longer run away from what had to be done. There had been no word from Nick, not even a note when he'd taken his things. But surely even he couldn't imagine that she could go on living at Owls' Roost, seeing as her own everything they'd chosen together for the house? Rather than accepting his lack of action as kindness, it fed her resentment. Did he not expect her to want to build a life of her own? Was he the only one to take as his right a planned future?

He wouldn't be home (home? Even now she couldn't think of Mulberry Cottage as Nick's home) until at least half past six. Until then the time had to be filled. So, working with determination and giving not an inch to sentiment, she started to turn out drawers and cupboards. Everything was in order, and she found a comforting satisfaction in imagining the chaos that Tessa would have to face if ever she left Mulberry Cottage. But she won't leave it, came the answering voice in her mind, she'll stay there growing older and more contented, memories will fade and she and Nick will make up the whole world for each other. 'Stop it,' she said aloud, 'don't be such a stupid, maudlin ass. Just look at all this stuff of Jethro's. He ought to come to sort it.' Did it make it easier to speak out loud? One thing it did, it gave her the resolve to face up to Jethro's silence. Picturing the four of them, Nick, Tess, Jethro and Zena, all one happy family, she knew herself cast out and isolated. Only a few weeks until the wedding. Well, she'd show them! By then she would have moved to Berkshire (and if a voice whispered maliciously that her home would be no more than a cubicle in the staff hostel, she wasn't going to let herself listen); she would arrive at the church dressed to outshine every other woman there; she'd hold her head high; she'd make it plain to Nick and to anyone else who might be interested that she was no one's cast-off housewife. The scene in her head was vivid, so vivid that as she automatically sorted the linen cupboard, making a neat pile to be taken to the Salvation Army to be handed out to the needy, she didn't hear anyone coming into the house through the back door.

'Sal, are you upstairs? The door was unlocked so I let myself in.'

Tessa! For a moment Sally's wall of defence crumbled – Tessa sounding just as she always had, Tessa her dearest friend, Tessa who'd knocked her world awry.

'I'm sorting the linen cupboard.'

Without waiting to be invited, Tessa came up the stairs. 'I bet it didn't need it. Not like mine.' And did Sally imagine it or was there a note of uncertainty in the laugh that accompanied her words? 'Gosh, what a tidy stick you are.'

'I hate mess, Tess. Did Nick ask you to come?'

'No. He doesn't know. Oh Sal, we can't be like this, you and me. All the time the men were away, all the – the nearness. One of us had to make a move, and this lunchtime I made up my mind. I phoned, but you were out. I thought if I came now, I'd be here when you got back from work; we could talk before Nick gets home.'

Home to Mulberry Cottage! Sally shrugged. 'Go on then, talk if you have things to say.'

'Don't be like that. Of course there are things to say. I didn't mean any of it to happen, but I couldn't stop it. Nick couldn't either. We didn't want to hurt you. Honestly, Sal, he fought it. But with Jethro gone, with you always at Drifford Park, can you blame him for wanting something better than the hours you found convenient to give him? If you hadn't been working, if you'd been here for him, if he'd thought for a moment that his going would hurt you, then he wouldn't have needed me.'

'Poor dear soul,' Sally's voice dripped with sarcasm.

'Don't be beastly. Let's try and work it out amicably. I say "let's try", but the truth is, as Nick says, we *have* to for the children's sake. Nick won't expect you to leave Owls' Roost, he told me that. So when the children come surely we can all be together.'

Sally went on methodically checking her linen, her Salvation Army pile growing, never faltering in the way the perfectly squared corners lined up.

'I take it Jethro has spoken to Nick. I know the first thing Nick would have done would be to get in touch with him. And you with Zena, I imagine.'

'That's another reason I came. Yes, Nick wrote to Jethro, and then so did I to Zena. She has phoned me; she has taken it very well. Of course she has, as she says the last thing she wants for me is that I should be miserable and on my own. Sal, you've no idea how – how *heartbreaking* it was with Seb like he was. If ever I was on my own, it was then. Or I would have been except that Nick was my rock. Zena isn't a child; she understands. But although she didn't tell me so outright, I think she is having a hard time with Jethro. That's another reason I came. He's not answered poor Nick's letter. And with the wedding in not many weeks there are millions of things to sort out. Zena says she's coming home at the weekend, so that's one blessing. But when I said "What about Jethro?" she was vague. He must be being difficult about it. If it were Zena behaving like that, I could almost understand. Losing Seb was so hard on her, she could think I'd forgotten him.' Tessa's pretty, almost childlike face, was a picture of anxiety. 'But Jethro? Has he talked to you?'

How Sally wished she could have said yes he had. Instead, concentrating more than was necessary on her task, she shook her head. 'And neither have I contacted him. I knew Nick would. Bad enough for him to know what's happened, without having first one parent and then the other on his tail.' How hard it was to keep this sort of distance between herself and Tessa, so hard she gave up the struggle and gave her long-time friend her honest and full attention.

'Tess, what's happened has happened. We have to accept and move forward. Do you believe Fate plans our course whether we would choose it or not? If Nick hadn't abandoned his marriage – and that's what he did, you needn't look at me like that – I should have given up my interpreting job very soon. Drifford Park is closing, the station is moving away. As it is, I shall go too. In any case I certainly wouldn't have gone on living in this house. So, if Nick hasn't already seen an estate agent, I suggest he gets on with it. There's very little I want here. But the piano is my own and I shall arrange for that to be taken to Dad for the time being. The rest – well, it's up to Nick. I've never been sentimental about possessions. You know, in a funny, nonsensical way, losing the trappings that have made life comfortable makes me feel better. These last years so many people have suffered, while here you and I used to be so *cosy*.'

'How can you say that? Our husbands were both in the war – Jethro too.'

'Yes. I can't explain.' What would be the use of trying? Dad would understand, Helga would understand ... Simon too, and so many people who made up her world at Drifford Park.

'About Jethro, Sal. You say you haven't been in touch with him. That may be what's stopping him accepting what's happened. Will you try and talk to him – or write? Tell him what you told me about Fate pointing the path; let him be sure you're OK, don't let him harbour bad feelings about poor Nick. He and Jethro were so close. It would hurt both of them if that changed and it has to be you who makes him understand. If he knows you're all right, he'll not be frightened of coming with Zena to Mulberry Cottage. I tell you what! You come over too: the children would be so much happier.'

'I'll talk to him. I've been putting off phoning him – I hoped he'd call me. You say he hasn't talked to Nick either. Poor Jethro.'

Tessa's laugh was clearly forced, but she was making an effort to take the brightest possible view. 'Maybe we're just a pair of mother hens. We call them children, but of course that's not how they see themselves. Very likely he's not too bothered about the happenings back here; he and Zena are full of their own affairs. I could tell that when I talked to her.'

'I'll phone anyway. God knows what sort of a story Nick concocted – I don't really care. But I do care that Jethro might be unhappy about the mess we've all made. So you can trust me not to play the hard-done-by wife.'

'You?' And surely this time Tessa's chuckle was spontaneous. 'That's the last way anyone could possibly see you.'

'Thank God at least for that.'

'You know what I wish, Sal? I know it's crazy, illogical, because I could never have fallen in love with anyone except Nick – but that's what I wish. Imagine if some other man had come into my life, nothing would have changed for you and me. A futile thing to say, though. Deep down, underneath loving Seb, I honestly believe this tie between me and Nick was always there.'

How could she talk like that, as if Sal were nothing except her friend, as if what she and Nick had done hadn't torn her life apart?

'Yes, a futile wish. Anyway, I must get on. Tell Nick I move out of here at the end of March and it's up to him what he does about the furniture. I shall get the piano moved before I go; I shall keep enough essential linen to see me settled wherever I decide to move into, a few pictures, but most of the trappings of the years he can get rid of as he likes. Now, Tess, leave me to get on, my time is precious.'

Standing back so that she wouldn't be seen if Tessa looked back at the house, she watched her go. For one wild moment she wanted to call after her, to bring her back, to hang on to the friendship that had been part of their lives for so long. But reason got the upper hand. Didn't coming here as she had prove, if proof had been needed, an insensitive streak that must always have been there? The thought was immediately followed by the image of Sebastian. What sort of a God could have let it all happen? Dear, kind, gentle, understanding Sebastian. And all the time had Tessa been carrying a torch for Nick? No, she didn't believe it; it was just that she was the sort of woman who could never be complete unless she had a man to look after, a man to pander to, a man in her bed. Disgusted with Tessa, disgusted with herself, Sally went back to the linen cupboard.

She asked for the number and waited.

'I'm trying to connect you,' the efficient voice of the operator told her. Then, 'The number is ringing for you.'

258

Sally could hear the ringing tone. She started to count, one, two . . . fourteen, fifteen . . . nineteen, twenty.

'I'm sorry,' came the voice of Miss Efficiency, 'I'm getting no reply to your call.'

Zena would be at the theatre; perhaps Jethro was there too. She'd try again much later when they would both be home.

So a little before midnight she again asked for the number. This time a male operator told her to hold and a minute later, 'I'm connecting you now.'

It was Zena who answered before Sally even had time to speak. 'Jethro!' And the way she said it told Sally all wasn't well. 'Where are you? I waited as long as I could before I went to the theatre, then I thought you'd meet me afterwards. Where are you?'

'It's Sally. I wanted to talk to Jethro. Tess says he hasn't answered Nick's letter.'

'He's been childish about the whole thing. At his age surely he ought to be able to stop fussing about his parents. He even says we've got to postpone the wedding.'

'And you don't know where he is?'

'You hear about middle-aged people disapproving of our generation, but it makes me sick, Sally. Why can't you lot act responsibly? It's not fair, messing everything up for Jethro and me.'

'Lots of things aren't fair, Zena.'

'You mean because Nick walked out on you. Mum gave him a better welcome than you did; she knows how to make a man feel loved. I don't mean to sound critical, but it's no good a woman blaming anyone else if her husband tires of her.' Zena was in no mood to consider her words. 'And it's certainly not fair that you mess other's people's plans up.'

'Why didn't he talk to me?'

'Ask him, not me. Although where in the world he is, God knows. He was in a funny mood this morning – has been ever since he had Nick's letter. He went off to work as usual, but he hasn't been back. And *I'm* expected to carry on, give a good performance, smile for the press. I'm tired; I'm going to bed.'

Sally was tired too, tired of the battle to keep her sights on a future that there in the loneliness of the empty house had no goal of hope.

Chapter Thirteen

Jethro had told her Charles Palmer was an unusual character, but Sally wasn't expecting the owner of a successful London business to sound like the voice she was met with in answer to her telephone call, as if he'd come to London on a charabanc day trip.

'The boy needs his arse tanning, giving his folk the worry he has.'

'No, Mr Palmer, I'm not an anxious parent. I know Jethro is capable of looking after himself. But there is a reason – a family reason – that has given him concern. That's why he hasn't contacted either his father or me.'

'Humph.' From the grunt she suspected he was more astute than he sounded and had jumped to the conclusion that Jethro contacting neither parent implied they weren't together. She must be more careful.

'Is it possible for you to get a message to him, to ask him to ring home. I'd be most grateful. An awful cheek I know, but I would be extremely grateful.'

'Cards on the table now, Mrs Kennedy. Like I said, the lad needs his arse kicked and for more than not keeping in touch with his family. If I knew where to find him I'd do the kicking myself. Young bugger, that's what he is. And I told him so last night when he came to me like he did.'

'Last night?' she prompted. Then the tale came out. Yesterday Jethro had been out talking to one of their regular growers. 'Reckon he was drunk with a drop of country air after the noise and muck of the city. Silly young fool, what does he know about eking a living out of the land? Been sent off yesterday morning to set a new price for the veg we take from one of our regular

261

growers. Near nine o'clock at night it was – I had m' coat on ready to draw a line under the day – when in he storms full of his high ideals, talking to me like I was no better than a crook. Times aren't easy. I didn't build this business on philanthropy – and that's something he'll learn before he's more than a season older. Took to that boy of yours from the day he walked into my office. All he had to do was keep his nose clean and put the business first and there's no telling how high he might have climbed. Told him so last night. But what did he do? Threw it back in my face. Something badly amiss with the silly young fool. I tell you, Mrs K, he ain't the boy he was when he came asking for a job, jiggered if he is. Is it to do with that pretty piece he's marrying? Are fruit and veg not glamorous enough for her sort? Or has she chucked him? Is that what he's running away from? Well, not my business so I'm not asking.'

'They're to be married in six weeks. No, whatever he is doing, Zena will be part of the picture. Why yesterday? Had he been offered something outside London?' She gave up all pretence of not being an anxious parent. Two people couldn't be more different than she and Charles Palmer, yet instinctively she knew she could trust him. Whatever had upset Jethro, she was sure it wasn't this kindly-under-the-prickles man.

'If that's what had got at him, some offer that gives him a better crust than he gets here, then I could understand. Mind you, I'm not saying I wouldn't have been disappointed in him, but with a wife he'll need to earn all he can. But no, he's got some hare-brained notion that he can make all he needs out of a bit of land he was offered to rent. I tell you, Mrs K I did my best to change his mind, but he told me just what I could do with my job. Best you try wherever it is he lives. And tell him from me – not that I ain't told him straight enough already – if he comes crawling back here for a reference I'm buggered if I'll give him one.' A sniff so loud that she had no doubt it was his way of drawing a line under what was gone. Then, his voice somehow less aggressive, 'Thought a deal of that young man, had great hopes for him. Reckon that's what makes me feel so bushed.'

'You took him on trust, Mr Palmer, and I know he appreciated the chance you gave him. You deserved better from him.' She tried to placate the gruffly spoken man, glad the moment had come to bid him thank you and farewell. Putting the receiver back, she stared unseeingly at the silent instrument. Ought she to telephone Nick? Were they responsible for Jethro's uncharacteristic behaviour? Yes, of course they were; the answer was there almost before the question formed.

The day stretched ahead of her, hours of listening for the call that might not come, hours of sorting drawers and cupboards in the dismantling of her home. Do something ... *do something ...* sort out the tangled threads of your mind. No wonder she thought of Eliot, of the school, of the hope and trust he and Simon had in the future they meant to build. Ten minutes after speaking to Charles Palmer she was on her way to Higworth House, drawing some sort of satisfaction from doing what until after Simon's visit yesterday she hadn't had the courage to do. Talking to her father on the phone had been the first step; but she knew that it was Simon who had, at least for the moment, restored some of her shattered confidence. Now there was another reason she needed Eliot's undemanding support: Jethro.

Less than an hour later she turned into the drive. The sight of the sloping lawn, the practice blocks, the house which gave the impression that it had stood unchanged as around it history had unfolded, were balm to her troubled spirit. On that crisp morning in early March, despite the deceptively clear, pale-blue sky, despite the chorus of birdsong seeming determined to proclaim the coming of spring, she wasn't letting herself be fooled. That's when the memory of yesterday and the bubbling water being driven up the spout of the coffee maker came back to her; when Simon had taken away the flame from the lamp, it had hissed as it rushed back to the lower bowl, no longer clear water but dark, aromatic, invigorating coffee. A smile played with the corners of her mouth as she slammed the car door and turned towards the house; she had been crushed by the shock and emptiness of finding herself cast aside but even more than that by her own sense of failure. But that was yesterday, she told herself. Today I'm back in control. And if a not-so-sure voice whispered 'I have to be, I won't be beaten', there was nothing in her bearing to give any hint that she let herself hear it.

'I'm ringing to set your mind at rest,' Eliot told her a fortnight later. 'Jethro knows I'm contacting you –'

'You've heard from him. Where is he? Why doesn't he speak to me himself, Dad?'

'He's not ready; he's turned his life upside-down. Bear with him, Sally. He needs time.'

'Is he all right?' Questions – and accusations too – rushed into her mind. But that one was ahead of the rest.

'Physically he is very well. I've never seen him look better. Don't probe, Sally my dear, I had to give him my word his whereabouts were safe with me. Think of this as convalescence, I believe in a way that's what it is. I told you, what he needs is time.'

'That's not what Charles Palmer said.' Then, making a fine job of mimicry, she said, ' "Needs his arse kicked and if I had the young bugger here I'd do it for him", that was *his* opinion.' It was a relief to laugh even though she saw no humour in the situation, and a greater one to hear the chuckle on the other end of the line.

'And maybe Charles Palmer wasn't so wrong. For any chap to jilt a girl six weeks before a wedding would be bad enough. For Zena's sake we have to be glad she turned the tables and put out the announcement that they had decided they weren't ready for the commitment of marriage. Worked pretty well for her: got her plenty of news space.'

'Yes. But if he realised the mistake, what he did was right. Surely better than to regret when it's too late; marriage is a sacred commitment et cetera.' Eliot heard the underlying bitterness in her voice.

'Umph.' A long silence.

'Tell me one thing, Dad: has he got another job? Is he managing all right? I suppose he'd been saving what money he could. But I don't know. You must have tried to persuade him to get in touch with me – or with Nick. He's not a child; he's lived away from home for years. Is it our divorce that's messed up his life? Is that what's scared him of commitment? He's only had eyes for Zena since he was a schoolboy, we both know that. Four years in the Army did nothing to change him.'

'Probably the trouble. Both of them too inexperienced to know. And I don't believe you or Nick have much to do with his plans. And he *has* plans. Your break-up may have been the catalyst, but don't feel guilty. I've never seen him happier with himself.'

She frowned. None of it was making sense. If Jethro was so happy with himself why was he frightened of seeing *her*? It was understandable enough that he wasn't sure what sort of a reception he'd get at Mulberry Cottage, but surely he could have picked up a telephone and talked to *her*.

Eliot saw it differently. 'He came to the school so that I could see for myself how he is. I know exactly what he is up to – and I commend him for it. How easy it would have been for him to marry Zena (and been the envy of thousands, no doubt), worked his way up the ladder at that greengrocery place, and somehow along the way never quite *found* himself. Personally, I was one of the lucky few. There aren't many of us who earn a living doing what we enjoy more than anything else. That's what he said to me – and I know he's right. And Sally, I thank God he has seen what's right for him. Perhaps he'll never be worth a fortune, but there is far greater worth than the money we accrue in the bank. Haven't we lived through enough to know that peace within yourself – combined with sufficiency, I grant you that – is more important than opulent wealth?'

This time it was her chuckle that travelled the miles. 'Opulent wealth would hardly have been the likely outcome from keeping his nose clean in the fruit and veg trade of Charles Palmer.'

'Nor peace within himself either,' Eliot agreed. 'But opulence and wealth will probably come to Zena Kilbride.'

'I hope so. How proud of her Sebastian would have been.'

'Would have been and *is* my dear. Do you believe that spirit of his isn't with her every step of the way?'

Sally frowned. 'I don't want to believe it, Dad. If he is close to Zena, then this everlasting glory we're supposed to believe is waiting for us must have a dark cloud over it if he keeps his eye on Tessa and Nick.'

'I think not, child. Sebastian's cloud would have been darker knowing that he'd left her alone and miserable.'

Sally didn't answer. She felt distanced from her father, something so rare that it stripped her of the ability to pull some light remark out of the air, something that would turn the conversation back on to safer ground. Was there *no one* who condemned what Nick had done? And what comfort would she have found in hearing the wrong he'd done her being put into words? Before she could stop it, her mind was back to the morning when Simon had brought her her first daffodils of spring; with him she had been aware of sympathy, that's what had broken her resolve not to give

265

way to self-pity. At the first break in her voice Eliot's concern and love would envelop her, and with it would come his pity, something she couldn't bear. So she forced into her voice a lilt that was far from her heart.

'I expect you're right, Dad, and certainly you are when you say how proud he would be of Zena.' She meant that to draw a line under the conversation; clearly he wasn't going to tell her anything more about Jethro. 'How are things going at the school? Is Helga coping?'

'She is more than coping. I'm very fond of the child and I know you are. Child? She'd not like to hear me call her that. Twenty-two years old, yet I still think of her as the frightened little creature I brought away. Remember it, Sally? Not a tear from her; such pathetic trust. Dear God, but what a mess we humans make of things.'

'Not you, Dad. Never you.'

'We all play our part. Hark at me! I call you to give you good tidings of Jethro and end up bemoaning the troubles of the world. Peace they call this, but what does the word mean to you? Surely more than the absence of war. And you know even better than I do of the hardships, the battle to make something of an existence that has been shattered.'

'Because of Nick, you mean?'

'My mind was in Europe. But yes, what difference what life hurls at you, at home or in a background destroyed by a war. The destruction of the security of one's existence, that's the root of most of the tragedies if we dig deep enough – Helga, Simon, and you too – even Tessa, for this wasn't the way she planned her future.'

'You lost my mother; you didn't look around to see whose wife you could tempt away.' She was ashamed of the venom in her answer. 'Sorry, Dad. I know quite well that if his marriage had been enough then Nick would still be here. Anyway, this call isn't about me, it's about Jethro. Promise me one thing, Dad.'

'If I can, without breaking my word to him.'

'You say he's fine and I believe you. But if things go wrong – promise me you'll tell me.'

A long silence before he answered, 'Yes, I give you my word Sally. And I promise you something else: if it's in my power I'll make sure nothing does go wrong for him. One thing I can tell you now: you know he learned to drive while he was in the Army? He's bought himself some sort of little runabout, a van.'

'Spending the money he'd saved to start married life, I suppose.' The thought did nothing to reassure her. Money was hard to save, but easy to spend.

'Now tell me about yourself,' Eliot moved the conversation on.

So she did. She told him of the coming changes in her own life, changes which on that spring day seemed distant but which so soon became reality.

It was almost the end of July, Sally had a spare hour and was spending it with the *Telegraph* crossword puzzle in the garden of Ridgeway, a First World War hospital which had been converted to the needs of the listening station. In the grounds, ugly and none too comfortable cubicle accommodation had been made from the isolation wards, still known by the staff as the Sanatorium. From the Comfort (Comfort? That wasn't as Nick had seen it, an inner voice never failed to remind her) of Owls' Roost, the only space that was her own measured ten by twelve feet, space enough for a single bed, a chair, a bookcase, a small wardrobe and chest of drawers. Her pleasure had never come from domesticity; she'd said so a thousand times, usually to herself but sometimes to Nick in her resentment for being taken for granted. Now she realised that in truth she had drawn pleasure from the spotless precision she'd achieved in the house and garden. Stripped of that, she lost the appetite for the job that had meant so much to her.

Filling in the final blank spaces of the puzzle, she put the paper down on the bench beside her. Her life was full of news items; with two hours free of them even the editorial held no appeal.

'The man on the door told me I'd find you out here.'

Helga! As if someone had turned on a switch, waking the life in her, Sally sprang to her feet. In uncharacteristic fashion the two hugged each other; today there was nothing of the accepted kiss on each cheek. And behind Helga came Gizella, grown tall, looking out of place in her beige linen summer uniform, her slim legs in knee-length white socks and her narrow feet in obligatory strapped sandals. No matter how Gizella was dressed, nothing could detract from her beauty. Looking at her, Sally seemed to hear the echo of Simon's voice telling her of the first time he'd watched Estelle, the most beautiful creature he'd ever seen. Surely

267

he must remember her each time he looked at their daughter. The uninvited thought threatened Sally's sudden joy at seeing her friend.

'Simon couldn't get away, so I've been to collect Gizella from school. It wasn't many miles out of our way to come here. Letters, conversation on the telephone, they are not the same as seeing. Your father – and has he told you what I call him now? – well, in a moment I will – he and Simon want to have a clear view of how you are living, how happy you are.'

'I'm fine,' came the all-too-bright answer. 'You were going to tell me what you call Dad.'

'He said to call him Grandad like Jethro does. But I couldn't do that. He is *Jethro's* grandfather; to do that would be like trying to steal him. So my name for him is *Grand* and no one can argue with that. He is the most grand of people.'

'Indeed he is,' Sally laughed. 'Well, you can tell him that I am OK. Soon I shall look for somewhere better to live; being in a cubicle is rather like being in a prison.'

'That is how I feel at school,' Gizella laughed. 'But if the results of my examinations are good enough, I shall leave and my father is letting me go to an art college. He is happy that I paint. Perhaps he always understood that I didn't want to dance. Do you think, Sally, that my mother would think that I'm betraying her because I'm glad my ankle won't allow me to dance?'

'I think your mother would understand that all those years you trained, it was because you loved her and didn't want to hurt her. Surely that is the most important.'

Gizella beamed. In her pleasure at the answer she forget to curb her tongue. The words tumbled out before she remembered what Helga had told her.

'We've been to see Jethro too. Oh –' She clamped her hand across her mouth, but it was too late.

'You know where he is? Helga, can't you tell me? Dad knows, you two know, I expect Simon does – and I bet Nick too. Why is it *me* who is kept out of everything?'

'Let us sit down – you on the bench, Sally, Gizella and I on the grass. I will try to explain. I am sure he has not spoken to Nick or Tessa – or Zena probably. He came to see Grand in the beginning because he knew he could be trusted to keep a secret and he wanted to be sure you knew there was no cause for worry.'

268

'We messed his life up, Nick and me.'

'Oh but you didn't. Do you not believe, Sally, that it is too easy for us to carry on like a gramophone record with the needle stuck in the groove, each week the same, one after another? It may be easy, but it is not the way to hear the music.'

Sally frowned. How right Helga was. But what had that to do with Jethro? He was hardly a needle stuck in a groove; all the time he'd been in the Army he'd loved Zena and none of that had changed. No, it was because of what she and Nick had done, them and Tessa too; they had broken the rock he'd built on. What faith could he have in any relationship lasting when even anything as unchanging as hers with Nick had disappeared overnight?

'Jethro had chosen his own future; he'd been in love with Zena for years.'

Helga shook her head. 'He had not,' she said calmly. 'He had been in love with the idea of being in love. If what he had felt for her had been real love, he would not have been brave enough to run away. There could have been no happiness for them, and do you not think Jethro deserves what is right and best for him?'

'Well, if you know so much more than I do, tell me: what is right and best for him?'

Helga moved to kneel in front of Sally, looking at her earnestly. 'I do not know how the picture will be when it is completed, but I do know that the background for it is *right*. Sally, I am going to do a dreadful thing. I am going to break my word and tell you what he is doing.'

By nine o'clock the next morning Sally was on her way to the address Helga had written down for her. There seemed no breath of air beneath the leaden sky, and already there was the rumble of distant thunder. Nothing diminished her excitement; within the hour she would see Jethro; all the doubts, all the imagined barriers would be overcome. But excitement stemmed from more than that: it touched something that had lain hidden within her own psyche. Jethro had dragged himself out of that comfortable and familiar groove, wasn't that what Helga had said? 'It's as if he's found himself, he's a whole person.' Reason told Sally that those were the words of a romantic, a romantic who was still searching; and reason had always been Sally's linchpin. Yet as the country miles brought her closer to Jethro she shared his enthusiasm, she

269

envied him the challenge. No, she told herself, she didn't envy him what he was doing, simply that it presented a *challenge*. Wasn't that what she had been seeking when she'd put through her first telephone call to Drifford Park? And now? Don't question, not today. Today belongs to Jethro. She felt as though he had been given back to her, for honesty told her that he had been gone far longer than the months since he'd run out on Zena. Zena? There had been pictures of her in the papers with Craig Marchant, the leading man in her first movie, a long article about her, a gloriously beautiful rising star who'd inherited her father's talent. Nothing to suggest she was suffering from a broken heart. Had Helga been right? Had she and Jethro shared the wonder of sex and believed it was love? Helga? Was it her work at the school that had given her her new confidence, or was it something deeper? Sally turned away from the question. Between Helga and her there had always been an unspoken understanding, and she didn't want to acknowledge the sentiment that gave her young friend such certainty about Jethro.

Perivale Cottage. At the end of a narrow lane a wooden board bore the words in white paint. If she thought the lane to Owls' Roost narrow, this was no more than a track. A gate to the right led on to a field where a herd of cows showed no interest in the passing car; a little further on the left was a yard leading to a barn, and from the evidence and the 'healthy country aroma' she concluded the building was in fact a milking shed. Helga had said Perivale Cottage wasn't much further.

Rounding a bend in the track she saw it, a dwelling typical of its type. It was perhaps a hundred years old, its latched front door set back within a porch with bench seats each side, a single chimney stack from which even on this sultry morning smoke curled lazily into the atmosphere, filling the air with the sweet scent of burning wood. For a second or two Sally sat in the car taking in the scene, losing herself in the peace and silence. Seconds perhaps, but no longer. Everything about this morning seemed to impress itself indelibly on her; whatever Jethro's challenge and adventure, in that moment it was hers too. Flinging open the car door she swung her legs out, aware now not of silence but of a symphony of country sounds. Somewhere there was the distant sound of sheep, in the background a continuous hum of insects – then, from behind the cottage there was a sudden burst of noise and movement as a young terrier rushed towards her barking ferociously even while its short tail wagged out of control. Behind the dog came Jethro, suntanned, larger than life. If he'd had the advantage of a tail, that would have welcomed her even before she heard his loud, 'Mum! Where the hell ... how ...?' But did it matter how she'd found him? With huge strides he came down the narrow path, his bearlike hug the first thing that told her that here was a different Jethro. Found himself, Helga had said. Perhaps that was the truth, or perhaps the change was in her too. Here in front of this ramshackle cottage, for both of them all the inhibitions had melted.

'You don't mind me coming? All this ...' She cast her glance round, hearing things that had gone unnoticed: the clucking sound of hens, nearer at hand than she'd supposed, the baa-ing of sheep.

'Gosh, this is great. When Grandad was here a week or so back he wanted me to let him tell you. But I said not yet. I wanted to finish doing the place up a bit first.' There was such a teasing light in his eye that she could only laugh when he added, 'I know what you are for order. It's all a bit chaotic, but Mum, I'm getting there. And this is *me*, it's *my own thing*. Can you understand how important that is?'

She nodded. 'Tell me about it all. How did you find it? What made you do it the way you did?' Yet he knew she asked out of interest not criticism.

'The day I threw in my hand at the fruit and veg place, and wrote a letter to Zena – that was a rotten cowardly thing to do; that's the bit I'm not proud of – I didn't leave home in the morning knowing that's what would happen. I came out here to see Bob Riley; he's a grower for Palmers. The job sickened me, Mum. Old man Palmer was always good to me, but he was as hard-nosed as any man when it came down to business. Poor Bob Riley was working his butt off, just about keeping his head above water; and my job was to beat him down. I couldn't do it, Mum. That was when I realised I'd never get on in business. I sat on a stile, God knows how long I sat there for, and – I say, this sounds sort of wet, but it's true so I'll say it – it was as if I was being healed. All my anger, all my disillusionment about the things that had happened, you and Dad and Tessa, yes and Sebastian too, somehow it all dropped away. I knew I couldn't go back, it was as if – as if –' He looked at her helplessly, lost for the right words.

271

'As if you'd been a chrysalis and suddenly you found yourself a butterfly.'

He laughed; they both laughed. 'Something like that,' he agreed. 'Was that how you felt when you first went to Drifford Park?'

She didn't want to think about herself, but he deserved an honest answer.

'I believe it was. Like that or like a prisoner suddenly freed. That's a long time ago, Jethro; we've all come a long way.'

'And now? You still feel the same about having a career? This business with Dad and Tessa. Oh hell, I ought not to be asking you.'

'Oh yes you ought.' She stooped to pick up a chewed ball and throw it for the terrier. 'But it's not easy to answer. When I stopped outside here this morning I felt such envy for you. What does that say about my enthusiasm for a career? But if a magician offered me the chance to go back and try again – with Nick I mean – back to being a housewife, back to that groove I found so frustrating and I believe he found utterly comfortable, I couldn't do it. Perhaps that's because I know now that for him too there was always something missing, something harder to find than answering an advertisement for a job.'

'That's not true, Mum. It was great at home in those days. Remember that holiday at The Limit. Crumbs, what a lot of trusting innocents we were. If Zena hadn't gone on the stage, if she'd stayed like the kid she was then, I reckon she would have understood about this place. Not now. And Mum, I know now she and I weren't right for each other. You know the trouble? Sex.'

She frowned. 'But I thought all that was fine for you and Zena. Why ever did you go and live together if –'

'It was great. But Mum, you can't spend all your life in bed.' He looked at her, uncertain whether she would be offended. 'She'd have got bored with me; I'd have been jealous of all the attention she got; it just wouldn't have worked. I think I'd known that for some time but hadn't let myself face it. To start with I'd honestly thought that what we had was all there was. Then I was sent down here to browbeat poor old Bob Riley. It was uncanny, Mum. Before I got to his place I stopped walking and sat on a stile. It was as if all the threads fell into place. I could see our future; I knew I had to do what I did. Sex can't be enough. As kids we used to have

272

a whale of a time, but all that went when we – well, when we were lovers. So I did the dirty: I walked out on her.'

'You did the honest thing: you gave her her freedom. She could have been no more happy with you than you were with her. But – here? Hiding yourself in the country?'

'I told you, everything fell into place. I knew what was going to be right for me. Up to that point I never had. I'd originally expected to follow Dad into accountancy – thank God I didn't. It was seeing those poor devils during the war, Displaced Persons. Isn't that what the newspapers call them? As if Displaced Persons can tell anyone what it's like to scrabble in the fields to try and steal potatoes, to –'

'You don't have to describe it to me, Jethro. The images have haunted me.'

'That's what sent me to ask old man Palmer for a job. Not that it helped those who were in my mind, but food is the most essential thing. I thought it was the nearest I could get to doing something worthwhile. But I was wrong. All I was doing was bleeding the growers so that the firm could make a good profit.'

Sally the practical, Sally the efficient, at that moment understood exactly what had driven Jethro from a world of commerce to find peace and, surely, satisfaction, grappling with the land.

'Where did you get this mongrel? Or do I do it an injustice?' She changed the subject, but he knew from the tone of her voice that she understood.

It was his turn to throw the ball. 'I saw her in town in the pet shop window. Couldn't resist her – and she knew it! Fitted into the palm of my hand pretty well. I wanted to weigh her when I got her home but without scales I couldn't. Held her in one hand and a two-pound bag of sugar in the other and they seemed about the same. That was the first week I was here; the place was a hell of a tip; you'd have had a fit to see where your son and heir was dossing down. Anyway, what her ancestry is I've no idea. I took her to be a terrier of sorts, but the rate she's growing God knows the size she'll be. I call her Licorice: she's a bit of all sorts.' Hearing her name the dog brought the ball to him, gazing hopefully, her tail trembling in anticipation.

'Your job, Mum ... you didn't sound as keen. Is it going OK?'

'Oh yes, it's interesting – heart-rending pretty often too – but it's true what I said about envying you. Perhaps it's your youth, your confidence in the future. Helga says you've found yourself.'

'So it was Helga who told you. Actually I'm glad. And to be fair, I had never told her not to, it was Grandad I'd made promise. She comes here sometimes, Mum, when he lends her the car. You knew she'd been taught to drive? That was his doing too. Yes, she comes here and gives me a hand. How long have you got? I want to show you everything.'

However Sally had envisaged Jethro's future, she'd never foreseen anything like this. In the months he'd been at Perivale Cottage he'd worked hard on its transformation, but the improvements were superficial: mains water had been there, but still there was no drainage; lighting was from oil lamps; the only means of cooking was the archaic range which made the only living room unbearably hot on such a morning.

'It's early days yet, Mum,' adding quickly before she made the offer he knew would have been in her mind, 'it's not that I haven't a few pounds stacked away, but I'm OK as I am now in the house; I've tidied it up no end. My first priority is the ground. Come outside and I'll show you how far my boundary goes.'

As he led her – and with pride she found uncomfortably touching – to point out the two small fields that went with the cottage, her mind took her back to her childhood. Her 'school-work' had been carried out partly in English, but often enough her essays had had to be written in French, German or – and this more rigidly corrected as, from this distance, she was sure – in Italian. It had been in English that she had been given the task of imagining herself eking a living from two hectares and one cow. She smiled at the memory. Hectares in England? No doubt that had been just one of the errors that had slipped through the net. Now here was Jethro, his sights set on making just such a living.

'You're smiling?' He looked at her quizzically. 'You do like it? You do understand don't you, Mum? I've got masses to learn, but Bob Riley – the chap I was sent to see – is only half a mile or so away and he's helping me no end.'

'How much land do you need for your sales to earn your living?'

'First thing, I want to grow enough to keep myself. I've got books telling me how to keep things for the winter – bottling, salting, jams, chutneys. Then there are chicken. Already they are

274

coming on to lay. I'll get a pig; if it were properly cured, I'd have enough ham to feed more than just me. I thought once I get going I'd take a stall to market. What do you think, Mum?'

Such an unfamiliar sensation surged through her: excitement, love, hope, enthusiasm, she couldn't put a name to it. It had nothing to do with career prospects and ambition, everything to do with Jethro's certainty that what he was doing was right. She was usually so undemonstrative, yet she couldn't hold back the hug she gave this surprising son of hers.

'I think you're living in a paradise – I envy you your dreams – just hang on to them; pick yourself up each time you get knocked down and your paradise will last.'

'That's the way I see it,' he agreed 'Helga talked about mushrooms. I'd need some sort of background heating, but that tumbledown shed could be repaired. Another string to my bow, eh?'

They ate a ploughman's lunch together in the Bottle and Glass before she set out on her drive back to go on duty for the late shift. Logic told her that what Jethro was doing would never earn him more than a poor living, but for once logic wasn't given pride of place. Pulling the car off the country road to park in the gateway of an empty field, she longed for the sort of vision that had come to him as he sat on his stile. If only, like a blinding flash, something would point a way ahead. The truth was, relieved as she was to know that her fears for Jethro had had no base, being with him had only made her more aware of the void in her own life. Think of the years I battled and argued for the opportunity to find my independence in work; remember how those wartime bulletins absorbed me whether they covered reports of major battles or the personal tragedies in the lives of ordinary people, ordinary women and children, ordinary civilians aged before their years. And here I am, safe, adequately fed and housed (is a cubicle adequate? For many it would be luxury), I lack for nothing – and yet I lack something fundamental in every life. If Nick hadn't thrown me aside, where would I be now? Out of work, trying to pretend running Owls' Roost was a life, believing our marriage was complete. Instead I have truth. But in my case that's no more than a negative: no marriage, no home, a son who has found himself and needs no more parenting, a job that ... ah, now am I coming nearer to the crux of my emptiness. I need a challenge; everyone should have a challenge.

That blinding flash she longed for didn't come, but the analysis of her situation at least brought her to a decision. She would find a house, somewhere of her own, not because she had a burning need for domesticity but for solitude. Pictures started to build in her mind: she saw a drawing room, the grand piano that had been her joy ... and somehow the image changed and the room was that at Owls' Roost; it was her father at the piano and by his side was Simon. She could almost hear the sweet singing tone of his violin. Simon, her true friend. Another leap of her imagination and she was at the school and that brought her to Helga, who recently had found a new confidence. 'She comes here sometimes, Mum,' Jethro had told her, saying it so naturally that at the time it had been easy not to remember how scathing he used to be about poor Helga. But she wasn't 'poor Helga' these days; she too seemed to have found herself.

Pulling her thoughts back in step, she glanced at her watch. Twenty to four; she was due to take the five o'clock bulletin from Paris. Was the fault in her that what she did was no longer enough? She tried to find an honest answer, wanted the sudden clarity that had come to Jethro; instead she felt she was blanketed in fog.

By a quarter past four she was back in her cramped cubicle accommodation where, with sure Sally determination, she set her mind on the evening ahead of her. She changed into a crisp linen suit, brushed her hair and redid her make-up, then walked across the courtyard from the erstwhile sanatorium to the front entrance of the main house.

'Mrs Kennedy,' the porter hailed her, 'I saw you were on duty at five. That's what I told the gentleman. Far as I know he'll still be waiting. You'll find him in the garden. I did ask his name, but I expect he didn't hear me. Been out there most of the afternoon.'

Nick! If Sally had sought clarity, surely it was there in the inexplicable way she felt such certainty. But she was adept at hiding the workings of her mind. She thanked the porter, her frown aimed at overcoming an emotion that had taken her unawares as she said, 'I can only give him five minutes, so it was hardly worth his waiting.' Not quite true, but it was her habit never to wait until the last second before she arrived for her shift

276

and she wasn't going to let *Nick* of all people throw her off course. 'I'll go and find him.'

She might have guessed! At the sight of her visitor disappointment mixed with anger – at herself, at *him* for robbing her of the hope she'd been frightened to admit to.

Simon stood up from the bench seat and came to meet her.

'Sally, I made a detour on my journey back from attending an appointment. The man at the door told me you were out; he said that you'd been gone all day. That is why I waited. I guessed where you must have gone to be so long. Helga said she had told you where you would find Jethro.' She felt both her hands taken in his. The kiss of greeting, first on one cheek then on the other, had every appearance of formality, and gave her time to stamp firmly on the images that had forced themselves on her. 'Now you have to rush off to work, that too I know. Believing you must be visiting Jethro I waited for your return, but I promise I will not hinder you. I thought you might want to talk–'

'And have no one to talk to? Simon – oh damn work.' Damn more than work. Damn Nick and the power he had to do this to her. 'Yes, I do want to talk but I don't know what I want to say. It was wonderful to see him, so fit and even more importantly, so sure. And yet I want to talk. I want to put into words how I felt. Oh damn the five o'clock bulletin.' Yet she had no thought of not being at her desk, headphones on and the cylinder turning on the dictaphone by a minute to the hour. That was something familiar, it was a shield from an emotion that threatened to rob her of her habitual appearance of calm. She was a sham, that was the only thing she knew with any certainty. This front she showed the world, efficient, never caught off guard, this never-a-hair-out-of-place woman, why couldn't she be honest? But where was honesty? Her marriage had failed; nearer the truth *she* had failed to keep her husband's love. If it was a moment of truth she sought, then perhaps this was it. Her sense of failure overshadowed all else, even her relief for what she'd found at Perivale Cottage.

'How long before you're free?' Simon put his hands on her shoulders as if he sensed her need to escape.

She looked at him directly. The trouble is, she told herself, he touched a raw nerve in knowing I have no one to share my day with. And yet ... why is he holding my shoulders so tightly, why is he compelling me to meet his eyes? Be calm, be firm and friendly. She reminded herself how scathing Nick had been when she'd applauded Simon's determination not to be beaten when he'd learned he couldn't continue his concert career. Nick hadn't the imagination to know what it must have meant, she thought accusingly, needing to whip up her resentment. Simon was her unchanging friend; he had the perception to put himself in her place and affection enough to want to be her support.

'The bulletin takes twenty minutes.' She was pleased with the controlled tone of her answer. 'I listen and record it. Some will be mere froth, some I will need to keep. When it's over I have to send for a typist so that I can transcribe to her anything of note. I shall be more than an hour. Then, during the evening –'

'I'll wait.'

'Simon ...' She meant to tell him not to: she would have little more than an hour free after she'd dealt with the five o'clock bulletin. He ought to go home ... he mustn't look on her as someone to be pitied. She wanted to get away, to find the courage to face the realisation that had come to her so unexpectedly ... to face it and find that it had been a momentary illusion.

'I'll wait out here. Is there anywhere we can go to talk? Your rooms perhaps?'

'I have a sleeping cubicle; visitors aren't allowed.' Then with a laugh that held no real mirth, 'Rather like boarding school. But I'm going to find somewhere else; only today I made my mind up.'

'We'll talk about that too. How long will you have after you have dictated this bulletin?'

'No more than an hour. Then I shall be busy until I've dealt with one at midnight. If you really want to wait, we can have something to eat in the canteen. It's not wonderful; it'll probably be either rabbit or macaroni cheese.'

'I should enjoy that.' Whether he meant the company or the food remained unclear.

The news bulletin consisted more of froth than substance; a spare typist was booked out to her straight away which was unusual: more often than not there was a waiting list. Perhaps all the teatime bulletins had been similarly superficial. Whatever the reason, by six o'clock Simon was carrying their loaded tray to an empty table at the far end of the canteen.

'Somewhere else to live, you say?' he prompted as they started to attack the prophesied macaroni cheese, mashed potatoes and

278

processed peas. The waiting sponge pudding and custard looked no more promising, yet Sally's spirits had taken a huge upward leap.

'I don't see me spending the rest of my life in something no bigger than a prison cell. And I miss my piano. I have a battery radio, but, Simon, it's an insult to the ears.'

He was watching her closely.

'I wish you'd talk to me, Sally my friend. Really talk, not just make conversation. If you recall, it was you who stopped me taking a position that for me would have been –' he held his hands out helplessly, palms upwards '– would have been *wrong*, wrong for me, wrong for the poor children I would try to teach. I am forever grateful, but it is not gratitude that makes me want above all things to be allowed a glimpse of the secrets that lie hidden behind your outward acceptance.'

Her throat felt tight. He had no right to recognise the confusion that was her own secret.

'Everything is going well,' she answered, her voice steady. 'I have been offered a good promotion, leader of the European section.'

'Justly deserved, or it would not have been offered.'

'To be honest, I'm not sure merit has much to do with it,' and this time she met his gaze, her eyes alive with laughter. 'I believe it's because I am English. To offer it to a German, a Frenchman, Pole, Italian, any race you can think of, all the others would have been up on their hind legs in horror. But me, I am a rarity here – born English, brought up something of a nomad, with a seldom-used apartment in London and another in Paris, a travelling life in Europe, an Italian tutor and friends wherever we went. Not many children have such good fortune. And that, I am confident, is why the offer has been made.'

'And you will accept?' He surprised himself by asking, for of course she would accept.

'I don't know. Simon, I don't know. Is it what I truly want for my life? I am nearly forty-six years old –'

'So young,' he smiled, reaching across the canteen table to take her hand in his, 'or so it seems to me, for I have reached half a century.'

'And you are content, happy with where life has brought you?' Was it fair of her to turn the conversation? Her conscience nudged her. 'Happy? No, I shouldn't ask. You have lost Estelle.'

'I do not need to tell you how dear Estelle was to me, she still is; in memory she always will be. But for her I do not grieve. She had no joy in life, she had no freedom of movement, no easy friendships here in a country that was foreign to her. Above all, I could not wish her to know Gizella is not to dance. Life at second hand is a poor thing, but without that she would have had nothing.'

'She would have had your love.'

'Ah yes. But you ask me if I am content. Ahead of me is one thing I want above all else.'

Sally looked at him with affection. 'If you know what it is then, Simon, nothing can prevent you achieving it.'

'You do not ask me what it is.' His grip on her hand tightened.

'That's because I *know*, and I truly believe things will be good for you again. Your arm is getting stronger all the time. Why, remember when I was last at the school. You and Dad played that Schubert sonata – not just the first movement but right the way through. Six months ago you couldn't have done that. Things will get better; we all have to trust – that, and you make sure you never cut down on the exercises you're supposed to do.'

'Indeed, I am sure you are right. But it is not to do with my playing.' He seemed to pause, compelling her to hold his gaze. 'Only *you* have the power to make my life complete. God of my fathers, hark at me! Here in a canteen, whispering to the accompaniment of clattering crockery. Music feeds my soul, Sally, I always believed that was all there was. But now I know it cannot be so, it cannot be enough. My heart is lonely – for you, only for you.'

No one had ever spoken like that to her before. Macaroni cheese held no appeal. She pushed her plate away. If her mind had been confused before, that was nothing compared to this. Her dearest friend . . . no, think deeper, go right back to the beginning. Wasn't he your first love, the idol of your childhood years. And now? Surely any woman would find him physically attractive with his iron-grey hair, his aesthetic good looks, his strong well cared-for hands that brought alive music that touched her spirit. My friend Sally, that's what she was to him; she mustn't hurt him. Was that what she really felt? The silent question pushed to the front of her mind. Was it really that she didn't want to hurt him, or

280

was it that she couldn't bear her answer to spoil what was between them? The image of Nick stood between them.

'I am a fool,' he said, letting go of her hand and reaching in his pocket for his cigarette case. 'Let us forget what I said. The friendship we have is precious above all others. I beg you, do not let my words put a – put a chasm between us.'

She took a cigarette from the case he passed to her and held it to the flame from his lighter. Anything to give her time.

'I don't want to forget it. Simon, you are my dearest friend. I almost think of you as a second self. But – oh hell, this is so hard to say. The divorce is going along the usual slow channels, it's all so fresh. I'm too newly bruised to see beyond it.'

'You are still in love with Nick.' It wasn't a question.

'How can a person change overnight? We had been married twenty-five years. Yes, I hate to think of him with Tessa. Every inch of his body is as familiar to me as my own.' Purposely she sought the masochistic pleasure she found in hearing herself say it.

'Of course.'

'Don't you see? It's not *him*. it's not *you*, it's *me*.' Such a strange sensation came over her as she watched him; she knew her behaviour was out of character yet she had no way – and no wish either – of stopping herself as she told him, 'Simon, I wish I could go to bed with you, I really do wish it. But I know I can't, not with you or anyone else. Nick would always be there, reminding me that I'd failed, that what I was wasn't enough for him. You say I am in love with him still. Yes, I suppose I am. It's so hard to put this into words. I lie in bed at night, aching for love. But, Simon, it's beyond my reach. I try to put it out of my mind, for just remembering is like hearing his voice – with *her*. But me, I'm like an old cast-off coat,' then with a choking would-be laugh, 'a pre-war model.'

'I came here today intending to be your support, to talk about Jethro. Forgive me. And Sally, dear, dear Sally, nothing has changed for us. You are never last year's model. No, that's not the whole truth. You are last year's, this year's, next year's. I asked you to talk to me and I'm grateful that between you and me there is honesty.'

The time had gone so fast. As if by mutual consent they got up from the table and she walked with him to his car. Five minutes later she had restored her 'face' and was making her way to the listening room. Not until half past two did she return to her soulless cubicle, and even then sleep was beyond her reach, the memory of Simon hauntingly close.

It was a week later when she spent her off-duty days making enquiries at estate agents. The first day was fruitless, but on the second she was taken to view two properties. One was a characterless two-bedroomed bungalow in a neglected patch of garden; the other a semi-detached house of the Victorian era. Certainly the rooms of that were large enough to take her piano but there was nowhere to park a car, the front garden was small and the privet hedge depressing.

'Neither are what I want, I'm afraid.' She tried to sound brighter than she felt.

'There's nothing else I can show you,' the none-too-pleased agent said, probably annoyed that he'd wasted so much of his afternoon. Didn't she realise there was a housing shortage? If she were wise she'd take what was on offer and be glad.

'I need a bigger garden, I need a garage, I need large rooms but not necessarily as many as in that last house. If anything else comes in you'll let me know, won't you.'

He didn't say he wouldn't, but something in the set of his shoulders gave her his answer.

Before she went back to her 'room' she decided to call at the main house and see if there was any post for her.

'Seems your visitors like to come calling when you're out, Mrs Kennedy. Twice in just a few days. You'll find him in the garden.'

Her mood lifted at the thought of seeing Simon and this time she felt no wild premonition that Nick had come.

'Sal, I thought you were never coming!'

That familiar voice, confident, sure of her welcome.

'Nick!'

Chapter Fourteen

Nothing about him had changed. As Nick came towards Sally, it was almost as if none of these last months had happened. When he'd tied his necktie and put the matching silk handkerchief in his breast pocket with the casual elegance he'd made an art, had he remembered the day when on a shopping expedition to Cheltenham she'd seen the set and bought it because it was so exactly right for him? Such wild joy gripped her, it robbed her of all coherent thought.

But not for long, for almost in the same instant, sanity returned. He must be here to discuss something regarding the sale of the house. It was weeks since she'd set the slow wheels in motion for divorce; perhaps there was something he wanted them to arrange amicably before a date was set for the case to be heard.

'Sal, where can we talk? And don't say you've got to rush off to that damned job of yours.' Indeed, nothing had changed.

On this occasion Sally wasn't going to admit to the truth of her limited accommodation.

'If it's something private, let's sit in your car – Tessa's car,' she added for good measure. 'In our circumstances I can hardly take you to my rooms.' She emphasised the 's'.

'Yes, it's private, Sal. And when you hear what I have to say you'll see there's no reason to keep me out of your rooms. However, if the lady wants the car, then the car it shall be.' There was something almost jaunty in the confident way he took her arm and turned her towards the front of the building where the familiar car was parked.

'Why didn't Tess come with you? Surely she's as much part of this as we are.'

'Never mind that for the moment. Hop in.' He held the door for her. Hopping in was far removed from the naturally graceful way Sally sat on the seat then swung her legs in one easy movement. Watching her, Nick smiled.

'You don't change, Sal.'

'Did you think I might?'

'Listen – don't say anything – wait till I get in the car.' With no idea what had brought him she was hardly likely to say anything. But she was glad of the few seconds it took him to walk round the back of the car and open the driver's door. In that time she took hold of her racing emotions. Nick, casually friendly and yet with that same arrogance. Once upon a time, hadn't that been one of the things she had fallen in love with? Then, honesty and truth prevailing, came something she had no power to dismiss: this was the dream that had lain unacknowledged through the months since they'd parted.

'Sal, all that bloody fuss you made about being independent,' he started as he climbed in to sit behind the steering wheel, 'you can't expect me to believe that *this* place is what you wanted? Anyway, never mind that. There's a lot I have to say to you. Not sure how to get started, but just don't interrupt. Go back to the beginning. If you hadn't been so pig-headed when I came back from the war you would have packed in your job and we should have gone on like we always had. I was quite capable of earning without you scratching about after an extra few miserable pounds. Did you ever wonder what I'd felt – me and thousands of others – while we'd been away? We expected home to be unchanged. So it could have been. Not only *us* – Jethro too.'

'Don't be stupid. Jethro had been in the Army for years, he was hardly likely to come home to his parents the same person as he'd been when he left school. No one could have lived through those years without being changed.'

'Just hear me. Try and see it from my side. Sebastian meant a hell of a lot to me –'

'And to me.'

'Don't you think it was natural enough for me to want to look after things for Tessa when he wasn't there any longer?'

'Nick, there's no point in going over all this. When did I ever try and stop you helping Tess? Of course I didn't.'

'I doubt if you even noticed where I was.'

284

'Let it go, Nick. I accept that you think it was my fault as much as yours – at this stage there's no point in raking over dead ashes.'

'Dead?' He turned to look at her, his quietly spoken words more meaningful than any that had gone before. 'Are they dead, Sal? For you, are they dead?'

This time he wanted an answer; instead she sat silent, the back of her head towards him as she gazed out as if the view held sudden fascination.

'Anyway,' and she heard his erstwhile confidence replaced by impatience, 'unlike you, I'm not prepared to think just of myself. If you and I had put our marriage before our needs – yours for this damn fool wish to be admired as a successful career woman, me for the need to know I was important in someone's life –'

'That's not fair!'

'Just listen and try and understand the truth of what I'm saying. If we'd both been prepared to give a little, to accept that for Sebastian's sake we *both* had a need to care for Tessa instead of your being intent on making yourself indispensable at Drifford Park, then we could have weathered the storm. Has it ever occurred to you that it was the break-up of our marriage that made Jethro treat Zena so despicably? He'd built his faith in marriage on us. We failed him.'

'Jethro always used you as a role model,' she answered, ashamed of the sneer in her voice and yet drawing strength from it. Why had he come to her like this? What was he wanting of her?

He ignored her taunt.

'What we do must inevitably take its toll on those close to us. You lived with me as my wife, but we both know you had no real interest in anything other than proving your independence. Jethro must have known it too; I'm not surprised he was so keen to get into uniform and away from home. After the war, I was no more than a necessary chore in your well-ordered days – and nights.' Hearing him, she clenched her teeth. She wanted to scream at him that he was wrong! But she couldn't. He mustn't know how night after night in the lonely cubicle that had become her home, her body still craved for him. Through the lonely years of the war there had been comfort in purposely, eagerly, arousing passion that was more than physical, always carrying her in her moment of triumphant joy and relief to the certainty that she had reached out to him. What a moment this was to recall sharing her most intimate

285

secret with Tessa, and immediately following on that memory was another: her aching need for what was lost, the temptation to follow that sure way of satisfying her sex-starved body, and the utter impossibility when at the forefront of her mind was the image of Nick and Tessa, a reminder of her failure. As these thoughts crowded in on her she kept her gaze on the almost empty car park, looking anywhere rather than at Nick, fearing that he might read her thoughts and know the emptiness of her life. She tried to concentrate on what he was saying. 'So was it such a sin that I turned for comfort – for warmth and love – to Tess? Jethro and Zena, everything planned for their wedding, and can you blame the boy that he took fright? He has a right to a stable home behind him; when that went is it any wonder he was frightened of commitment? And that brings me full circle. Thank God, Zena had the wit to use the broken engagement to her own advantage. As she says, image is important. Tess bought a woman's magazine reporting an interview with her, full of probing questions and answers that gave no hint of what the boy had done. She loved Jethro deeply, she told the interviewer, but they were neither of them ready for the solemn vows of matrimony. She talked of her father, the wonderful marriage her parents had had. And of course, so they did, Sal. It was just rotten luck for them – for all of us, I suppose – what happened. Anyway, rather than showing her as a jilted bride, Zena comes out of this extremely well, a model for young people.'

'A short-term policy, surely,' Sally said coldly. 'A few more weeks and the papers will have another field day when Sebastian's adoring widow is cited in a divorce case.'

'Sal, we mustn't let that happen. It's a slur on Sebastian.'

'You think that's how Sebastian will be seeing it? I thought you believed he'd be glad to have you step into his shoes – pyjamas – whatever.'

'For Christ's sake, Sal, we haven't sunk to slinging that sort of mud at each other.' She was conscious of his suppressed anger; she was ashamed that she could have taken the easy way of trying to hurt him – hurt all of them. Still not looking at him, she was taken by surprise when he reached to take her hand.

'It's not too late, Sal. Twenty-five years can't be wiped out in a few short months. Tess knows that as surely as I do – and so do you. Stop the divorce. I'll take Owls' Roost off the market. Come home, Sal and let's make a fresh start.'

Wasn't this what she'd longed for, what she'd dreamed that one day he would say? For a long moment she didn't answer, just turned in her seat so that she faced him. Conscious of her scrutiny, a slow smile played at the corners of his mouth. All his natural assurance settled back in place. At last she would give up this hare-brained idea of being a career woman; even if she wasn't prepared to admit it she must have learned a lesson. Running a home would be a rest cure after days ruled by the clock. She and Tessa – darling Tessa – would pick up the threads of friendship. There would never be four of them as there had at one time, but somehow they would find a way of accepting that love could be based on a triangle as much as it could on a square. They'd always been a team, and that's how they would remain.

'No divorce, Mrs Kennedy,' he told her softly. And how long was it since he'd looked at her in that affectionate, even flirtatious way? Yes, she'd dreamed of this. Now that it was happening she felt empty of all emotion. Looking at him, seeing his handsome casual elegance, she felt no joyous rush of thankfulness at his words. 'Say something, Sal. Think of Jethro – and Zena. Once they know what we've decided, that will bring them back together again. Don't you think we've done damage enough without having all our affairs laid open for the public? You know what the press is like if it gets a sniff of scandal about anyone famous. Think of Sebastian. Naming his widow, Zena's mother, as co-respondent will make great gossip.'

Sally sat watching him; her ears carried every word to her brain but her heart was untouched, she seemed to stand outside herself, looking, listening. When she'd bought him that bow-tie his neck had been slimmer, came the inconsequential thought; Tessa's love for cooking was beginning to show. Only when he reached to put his hands on her shoulders as if he would draw her towards him, did she stiffen and pull away.

'Sal?' he prompted. 'We had good times, so we will again. Let's go together to see your solicitor. Sal, say something.'

The drive from the Szpiegman School to Perivale Cottage might take no more than an hour and a half on a good day, but on the morning of the same day of Nick's visit to Sally, Helga found herself held up by one tractor after another, one towing a load of late-cut hay, others moving items of farm machinery she couldn't name. But Helga wasn't the kind to be satisfied with ignorance, she made a mental picture of each contraption that clattered in front of the car so that she could ask Jethro for an explanation. With the window open by her side she breathed deeply as if she couldn't get enough of the cocktail of country smells. In the boot she had a plum tart she'd made herself yesterday under the watchful eye of Mrs Strang, the housekeeper. Ahead of her stretched hours of pure magic.

A herd of cows came into view at the curve in the lane, about thirty of them being shifted from one grazing area to another, prodded and coaxed by a young lad who clearly didn't have the upper hand. If I have to be held up, she mused silently, then where better than this? I've got all day ahead of me, just think, a whole day. When did we start to know each other, *really* know each other, Jethro and me? No time ago, that's the honest answer. For years we've met, lived in the same house part of the time. I never thought he noticed me at all. He didn't notice anyone except *her*. What is it people say when a person ends a romance and starts to look at someone new? On the rebound? Yes, that's it. But I'm not someone on the rebound for Jethro. We *know* each other; we don't have secrets. No, that's not true. The thing that's been at the front of my mind from the time Grand brought me to England is *my* secret. Jethro would have been shocked, embarrassed more likely, if he'd known. I wasn't at Owls' Roost many days before I was moved to Mother's beastly relatives, but always I remembered him. I expect everyone has to have a dream. That poor lad with the cows is probably dreaming of the day when he can march them along the road, obedient to his command! Just look at that one blocking his path and turning right round to stare at him. Helga chuckled as she watched the bovine disobedience; anxious as she was to reach Perivale Cottage, the slowness of the rural scene was all part of the wonder of the day. She let her thoughts drift back to where they'd been when the procession in front had come to a halt. Fourteen – can you fall in love at that age? I believed I had, but I didn't really know him. Even after I came to live with Sally, when he was home on leave he would never have talked to me then like he has since *she's* dropped out of his life. I wonder whether when Sally went to see him he told her about him and me being friends. I wish I could believe in praying. But I don't, not any more. Is that how everyone feels when their prayers haven't been answered? I used to pray so hard for my parents – and no one listened and helped them – I know it's no good asking that same God to make Jethro love me. So I'll try and be content with the friendship we have. Does he miss her? Of course he does: he was living with her, he was in love with her. Yet it's almost as if he has found a new freedom. Oh look, that funny cow has got tired of teasing the poor lad; it's pushing its way to the front of the line. Good – we're off!

Ten minutes later she parked Eliot's car by the side of Jethro's van and went in search of him, finding him in the chicken run. At the sight of her, his eager smile gave no hint that, just as hers had, his thoughts were carrying him back. Mum's poor plain Hun; gosh, but doesn't it show how being in the right place, doing the right thing, can change a person. She's not half bad looking. Or is that just because I like what I see? Something about her that makes you look twice, something sort of distinguished. But how can a girl of her age be distinguished? Not that Helga's ever been an ordinary girl. Right from when he'd first met her – and what a queer egg he'd thought her – she had had dignity that defied sympathy. In those days it must have been something she clung to as a cover for her loneliness. Looking back he felt a momentary shame that he'd done nothing to help her. Still, she'd fought and won her own battle and helping run the music school was clearly right for her.

'You've come just in time. I was collecting eggs to take to the village shop. We'll both go in, shall we? I've kept enough eggs back for us; I thought we could have omelettes. And tomatoes. Complete self-sufficiency.' They shared a beam of pride.

'Lovely, and pretty soon, Jethro, there will be mushrooms too. I've brought two big buckets of kitchen scraps to cook up for Josephine.' Josephine being the sow whose ultimate purpose was to provide a supply of pork and ham – and brawn too if the book Helga had studied was to be believed. 'Have you got the wood you needed for repairing the shed, Jethro? Can we get on with it today?'

'Yep.' One word, just casual slang, but it contained all his optimism for the outcome of the job. If to her the day ahead seemed cloudless, so it did to him. Capable Helga made a good 'builder's mate'; she wasn't averse to fetching and carrying at his command, even though she was as capable with a saw or hammer

289

as he was himself. 'Reckon we'll get the roofing on this afternoon. It'll be twice as quick with four hands.'

Just for a second, and before she could close her mind to it, she saw an image of beautiful Zena, the sort of girl every man must surely dream of loving; that same second was all it took to make her aware of her own tall, angular body, the strong features of her large-boned face, the capable hands and the feet that needed an unfashionably large size in shoes. It took all her not inconsiderable willpower to keep the smile on her face as she went with him to finish collecting the eggs.

Listening to the sound of Tessa's car growing fainter as Nick left her, Sally closed her eyes and held her face towards the sun. The warmth was like a caress. Later she would face the reality of his suggestion and of her own decision; but first, while her vision was clear, she had two letters to write.

In her ground-floor cramped accommodation, she took her writing pad, pushed her jars of make-up to one end of the tiny dressing table, and sat on the cane chair. In her clear, bold hand she wrote the first letter. Reason had told her she ought to accept that offer of promotion, yet now she knew exactly what had held her back and what she had to write. That done, she started letter number two, writing in her bold clear hand, then addressing the envelope: Mr E.G. Hall, Bastin and Hall, Solicitors . . . she would drop it in the post box in the village as she drove past. Over these last days she had longed for a blinding pointer towards her future, something of the vision that had come to Jethro, something to show her a way through the mist that had isolated her. She hadn't let herself acknowledge that what Nick was suggesting was what she had been yearning for; she had been frightened to let herself imagine the life they would have together . . . like it used to be, Nick had believed . . . but nothing was ever as it used to be: everything we do leaves a mark, a scar on our memory. Then, almost as she'd pictured them living again at Owls' Roost, had come something so vivid, so breathtakingly clear that she could feel the pounding of her heart.

'I'm right, Sal.' Nick's face had been so close. 'You still love me; we'll pick up the pieces. We've been fools, both of us. Tess too. Loneliness stops you seeing straight. And I was lonely: what man wouldn't be when his wife always put him second? Tell me you're glad I came, Sal.'

In that moment of clarity such wild joy had engulfed her! Holding her head back from him she looked at him very straight. 'Yes, Nick, I'm glad you came. You've shown me what I have to do.' It was as if talking to him had enabled her to pull a strand in the tangle of her emotions, unknotting the confusion.

With automatic care she changed her blouse, restored her make-up, brushed her sleek hair then packed an overnight bag. After her midweek two-day 'weekend' her next duty wasn't until the evening bulletins the following day. By half past seven she could be turning into the gates of the Szpiegman School. Even thinking the name softened the corners of her mouth. Was it only Simon she was being drawn to or was it something rooted in years of her adolescence? No one can go back, but this wasn't going back, it was going forward, the gentle pace of life's stream suddenly flowing fast as if pulled towards a weir and the onward rush downstream towards the wide ocean. Shakespeare's famous words echoed, 'If music be the food of love, play on, give me excess of it that the appetite might sicken and so die.' Oh but it wouldn't, it couldn't, it was rooted deep in her psyche. Was that why she had fallen in love with the handsome curly-haired violinist when she'd been no more than ten years old? Probably. But it wasn't that alone that made her love the man he'd become. Rather it was as if through all those years a part of her had been dormant, waiting for love that was complete and fulfilling. 'My dear friend Sally', and so she was, so she always would be. That and so much more. Something of him would always belong to his beloved Estelle – just as something of her would to Nick, to their shared parenthood, to a routine that might so easily have drifted on unchallenged. But it hadn't; when they'd run into turbulent waters, their craft had rocked and floundered. So ran her thoughts as she stopped in the village to post her letter then, her foot hard on the accelerator like a homing pigeon, she set out for Higworth House.

Eliot's welcome never varied. Helga wasn't expected home until late, so there were just the three of them for the evening meal.

'She and Jethro spend a lot of time together,' he said. 'A good couple, eh?'

'Dad, you're an incorrigible matchmaker. It was wonderful seeing him last week. I was frightened that he'd be upset by what

291

Nick and I had done. But he's his own person. Whatever it was that drove him away from what he and Zena had planned, then for him at any rate it's turned out right. He is *himself*.'

'Matchmaker I may be, but mark my words, Sally, if Jethro has found what he was looking for in life, then Helga is part of it.'

'Women have more vision,' Simon said, watching Sally closely. 'Think how near I came to teaching unmusical boys.'

'Vision, you say.' Sally looked from one to the other. 'That brings me to my reason for coming.'

'Reason? Since when have you needed a reason?' Eliot looked at her affectionately but she didn't notice. Her gaze was firmly on Simon.

'I had a visitor this afternoon. When I got back from house-hunting – dreadful places – Nick was waiting. Vision, that's what you said, Simon. He wanted me to write to the solicitor, to stop the divorce. He wanted us to make a new start.' Immediately she'd said the words she realised her thoughtlessness. For her it had seemed sensible to put the sequence of events in chronological order, starting with Nick's attempt to persuade her and finishing with the contents of the letter she'd sent to the solicitor. But one look at Simon threw her tale off course. 'Simon ...?'

'Go on. A new start ...?'

Eliot looked from one to the other.

'So you're going back to him?' he prompted.

'I didn't say that, Dad. We were talking about vision, about a new start. It was being with Nick that made me see. That's why I'm so thankful he came. I want to keep memories that are good, but for Nick and me it's over.' Then with a sudden smile and speaking this time just to Simon, 'Perhaps pride makes me glad he decided there was still wear in last year's model. The choice was mine.'

Reaching along the table Simon took her hand in his.

'Choice?'

'For me there is none.' Her fingers curled around his. 'Choice comes when there are two ways and one isn't sure. For me there is only one. Why did it take Nick's visit to make me see it?'

'You mean ...?' Eliot was frightened to rush to the wrong conclusion, but surely this looked like his dearest hope coming true.